Bended Loyalty

Kat Caldwell

Ladwell Publishing

Book Cover by MiblArt

Edited by Emma of Emmasedit.com

First edition ebook published 2024

Also by Kat

Historical Romance:
Aurora's Dilemma
Stepping Across the Desert
Across the English Channel

Contemporary New Adult Romance:
Coffee Stains

Mythological Christian Fiction:
An Audience with the King

Contemporary Fiction:
Bended Dream
Bended Loyalty
Bended Love

To my husband and daughters, first and foremost.
And to all those who feel like their dreams don't come easy.

BENDED LOYALTY

Chapter 1

THE VENUE'S CEILING WAS as black as a starless night sky when The Seethers took to the stage.

It was like most of the places they played, yet different. Tristen knew he would remember this music hall as the one that sealed their success. Where the scrimping and saving and playing for two people in the crowd finally made it all worth it. He and his brother had fought hard, and they had won.

This night was their trophy. The Seethers were on their way.

Tristen strummed the guitar strings as hundreds of people moved their bodies to the rhythm. Heads swayed or bopped. Fingers were thrown in the air in rock-and-roll signs, and all around, cell phone screens were lit up. Tristen couldn't see their faces, but he loved each person in the crowd. Gratitude for the moment filled him until he thought he might burst. This was it. This was what success felt like. He and Talon had crawled out of the heart of small-town Kentucky, opioid crisis's ground zero, to this place. Stage right at the House of Blues in Pittsburg, Pennsylvania.

All they'd needed was one band to recognize their talent and their drive. Sure, most of the crowd had come to see Art of Rendering, but that was what made opening for them so important. As they waited for the headliner, the concert-goers were listening to The Seethers. And it looked as though they were becoming fans.

Tonight would change his life forever.

Tristen approached Talon, his twin brother and their lead singer, as the music dipped into the chorus. Talon turned to him so everyone could see the mirrored faces of the twin brothers. The Pelton Vikings, they had once been called. What differentiated them now were the small details: Talon with his hair short, Tristen's long; Talon with his clean-shaven face and Tristen with his short blond beard. At the musical bridge, Talon threw himself to his knees and laughed into the microphone. Tristen stepped back into the shadows, fingers flying across the strings of his guitar.

The stage lights dipped and dived as they started the next song. Tristen felt famous, like he was Jimmy Page or Eddie Van Halen. The drums continued their beat, leading into Tristen's guitar solo at the beginning of their most popular song. He was nothing compared to the talent of Keith Richards or Jimi Hendrix, but it was his sixty seconds of spotlight, and he soaked up every second.

"Yeah!" Talon yelled, his voice muted without a mic nearby.

Tristen bent down over the stage, making direct eye contact with a woman with a wide smile who screamed in excitement at him noticing her. Like a rock star with groupies. His solo ended. He leaned into their other guitarist, Randall, as the woman's squeals merged with the music. The rhythm beat through Tristen's chest, becoming one with his heartbeat.

Talon hit the mic on cue, his deep voice purring into it. He brushed aside his blond fringe, a move that made the girls in front go wild. Off-stage to the right, Talon's wife stood dressed in black as usual, her typical scowl replaced by a smile. She didn't seem to mind the women screaming after her husband.

A few feet away from her stood Meegan, Tristen's girlfriend. She blew him a kiss and shimmied her body, sending a wave of pride and desire through him. He didn't need swarms of women after him. Not when he had Meegan. She was beautiful, a mixture of a Kardashian and Grace Kelly. Rich, ambitious, classy, and always supportive of him becoming more. She was the one who'd convinced him to quit his other side jobs to dedicate his time to the band.

And it had paid off. They were here tonight because of her.

He would spend his life making sure she knew how awesome she was, how thankful he was to her. Because of her, he didn't have to continue with the construction jobs, or random bartending gigs, or odd maintenance jobs. He loved that they were becoming professional musicians together. Life was good, and it could only get better.

Talon roared into the microphone. Micah joined him. He only had a couple of lines as backup singer, but his low growl added the perfect contrast in the song.

Don't say aloud what you're thinking about.

Baby, this is the life we got. Here and now.

Let's get out of this town, run, and follow the crowd. Or jump ship.

Together, we'll make it.

The drums beat, the guitar strings vibrated, and everyone in the crowd seemed to rise and fall, over and over, for two minutes and thirty-four seconds, until together, The Seethers hit the last note and the lights snapped off as though their music had caused an electrical surge.

Tristen was panting from excitement and nervousness. Randall clapped him on the back with his own yelp of energy. He grinned into the dark. Nobody moved.

The band, minus their drummer, stayed still under the shroud of darkness. The crowd finished clapping and started moving into restless curiosity. A shiver of excitement ran up Tristen's spine. Fooling the crowd was almost as thrilling as playing for them. Having watched Jake for the last five concerts, Tristen was beginning to understand the importance of showmanship when putting on a concert: the sleight of hand, the art of illusion and surprise. Jake was a natural showman and came up with ideas easily. Manipulating crowds into looking one direction, only to surprise them in the other, was his art form. It enhanced the concert experience and set Art of Rendering apart. They had fans who followed them from show to show just to see what would be different.

Tristen wanted fans like that. The ones who bought the T-shirts and defended the group no matter what. Live shows were expensive, but they were also the most profitable. The top pop stars and bands set up tours with one-hundred-dred-and-eight-plus shows. There was that much demand for them.

Tristen breathed out quietly, trying to steady his thoughts. His hands were sweating and his throat was dry, but he didn't dare move.

It all still felt surreal. When Talon had shown up at practice claiming he'd run into Art of Rendering at a party and that they wanted to meet with the band, it had sounded like Talon's imagination had gone off the deep end. But then it had happened. They'd all met together, jammed for an evening, and then Jake, the lead guitarist, had asked The Seethers to open for them in six cities. Obviously, they had said yes. For the first five concerts, they'd played their last song, waited a beat, and exited the stage. But not tonight. Tonight, Jake had put together a surprise.

Murmurs flitted through the crowd until a spotlight glared stage left and the drummer for AOR walked on to manic cheers. He lifted his sticks in the air, flashing a grin at the fans. Still in the shadows, Tristen bent down slowly for a swig of water from his bottle as the rest of Art of Rendering crept on stage.

Every hum in the crowd vanished. The air stilled. Tristen stood cautiously and got himself ready. Fingers poised, he joined the crowd's growing anticipation as the seconds dragged on. "Always wait a little longer than the crowd expects," Jake had told him just the other day.

Suddenly, a chord strummed through the speakers, wobbling through the air. The crowd squealed and shouted with glee.

AOR's lead guitarist hit the chord again, then another. And another. The stage was still in black, and no one else had moved. Tristen could barely see the shapes of the other band members.

Murmurs of excitement rose as a spotlight swooped across the stage, falling on the guitarist, illuminating his long dreadlocks. The crowd erupted, covering Tristen and Randall's entrance into the song. Their mics weren't up as high as Pascal's, but that didn't bother Tristen. All that mattered was this opportunity to play with AOR.

The rhythm quickened. Tristen's fingers fumbled, and for a split second, he froze. He waited, nodding to the beat, but the longer he waited, the more lost he became. Randall appeared in front of him, counting for him.

Then his fingers pounced, the notes connecting to Tristen's brain, and his fingers found their familiar rhythm. Pride replaced his anxiety as their fingers flew together. Randall grinned, his head bobbing up and down. Tristen nodded back.

The lights swooshed over them, then flashed to the center where Talon and Jake were facing off. Their voices cracked through the speakers, a mashup between a new song from both bands.

"And come tomorrow, I'll be all you have."

"Don't you know it's a crime…"

For four and a half minutes they sang, plucked the strings, and beat the drums. And the crowd went wild. Though the crowd's attention was mostly on Talon and Jake, every musician on stage played with a camaraderie that Tristen wished would permeate every corner of his life.

He closed his eyes and reveled in the sound of singing and cheering. This was winning. Though most eyes were focused on the singers, the cheers were for all of them.

"Hello, Pittsburgh!" Jake yelled over the crowd.

A backdrop lowered mid-stage, leaving The Seethers in the shadows. Now unseen by the crowd, they yanked the wires out from their guitars before fist-bumping.

"That was so awesome," Micah said, joining Tristen as he walked off stage.

Tristen gave high fives to the offstage sound and light technicians who wanted to congratulate them. Sweat dripped from his head, chest, and arms. They had given their all, and it had turned out to be the best set they'd ever played. And at the biggest venue they'd ever played. He almost couldn't believe it. The Seethers were finally taking off.

Lights blasted back on stage, revealing Art of Rendering plus Talon. Without a moment's hesitation, the guitars started in, then the drums, and Talon jumped in. Everything was perfectly timed.

A few feet away, Sandra still watched her husband. Her long brown hair bopped softly against her shoulders, her eyes, outlined in black, focused directly on Talon. By contrast, Meegan jumped up and down, dancing and singing as she always did. Tristen shoved his guitar in its case and ran over to her, picking her up and twirling her around.

"You were amazing," she sang out, covering his face in kisses. He caught her lips with his, careful not to get sweat on her dress, as she had warned him before the concert. His best girl was with him in the best moment of his life. "You're gonna be famous, and I'm gonna be famous, and we'll be famous together."

Her screams vibrated his eardrums, but nothing was going to ruin his mood.

At the end of the song, the crowd erupted in cheers and applause. Tristen and Meegan clapped and hollered for them. Talon singing with Art of Rendering was going to move them up the charts. Many of the fans in the crowd would become their fans. The mashup was recorded and ready to go out to all the music apps. Offers from other bands for tours would flow in. Maybe even offers from agents. And managers.

Micah and Randall caught his eye. Both jerked their chins backward. Micah had a baby and wife to get home to; their deal had been to pack everything directly after the concert. The rest of them would drive the van back to Cincinnati the next day.

"Gotta go, babe." Tristen kissed her again. "I'll see you in the back."

"I'm gonna stay and watch," Meegan said, flashing him her perfect smile before turning back to the stage.

He would have liked to watch the rest of the concert, but instead he followed Micah and Randall to their green room while Adam, their bassist, sauntered slowly behind. A deal was a deal, and he couldn't risk Micah getting mad. Not when they were on the cusp of being as famous as Art of Rendering. AOR were full-time musicians with money pouring in from Asia and all the Americas.

Maybe it wasn't over. Maybe AOR would invite The Seethers to join them on a tour of Asia. He'd always wanted to walk streets with noodle vendors and see the ultra-modern cities. Or maybe it would be AOR's upcoming Mexico tour. Even going south of the border would be an adventure.

"Let's get packed so we can see the last song," Randall said when Tristen entered the green room.

Because of Adam's organizational obsession, it never took them as long to pack up as other bands did. Anything not used during the concert or needed after the concert was already sitting in a neat, rectangular pile in their truck. Within forty minutes everything was zipped up and showers had been had.

"See you all at Pete's," Micah yelled over his shoulder as he headed out.

"Yeah, bye," Randall and Tristen called back.

Tristen clapped Adam on the back. "I'm going to head back-stage to catch the rest of the show. See you later?"

Adam waved his phone with a nod as Randall joined Tristen at the door.

Talon's voice drifted through the darkness as they climbed the stairs to backstage. AOR was on the finale. The ballad was the perfect way of convincing the fans the show was over—before going into a four-song old-school compilation of the songs that had made AOR famous. The fans ate it up every time. In fact, they expected it, and Art of Rendering was happy to give it to them. Lights from cell phones lifted into the air, swaying back and forth as the guitar riffs combined with the slower drums. Then the compilation began, and the energy turned manic as the crowd screamed along to the lyrics they knew so well. Tristen bobbed his head unconsciously to the rhythm again, marveling at the talent Jake had for putting together a concert.

The lights went out; Tristen felt the urge to join the wild roars of the crowd to garner an encore. Randall raised his eyebrows and smiled at the thundering waves of noise that crashed onto the stage. Tristen almost felt bad for the crowd. Art of Rendering never gave an encore. Jake said it was best to keep the fans wanting more.

Tristen stood up straight, ready to greet his brother, but no one walked off stage. Randall glanced over at him, shrugging. They both looked back at the exits. No one appeared.

Softer lights came on that didn't move or sweep across the stage. Tristen cringed. The lighting crew had done such an excellent job all concert, only to make the rookie mistake of showing Art of Rendering still on stage. But then, the band should have been off already.

"What the hell are they doing?" Randall murmured to Tristen, still focused on the stage.

"No idea. Maybe they're going to thank Talon," Tristen suggested as Jake grabbed a mic, waving at the crowd to quiet down. "It'd be great if he mentioned us again. Get the crowd to remember they want to buy our songs."

Randall nodded, grinning.

"Hello, everyone!" Jake shouted, his mic getting louder as he spoke. "How about our latest singer here, Talon Levisay from The Seethers!"

Tristen jabbed Randall in the ribs as they joined the crowd in clapping for Talon, who was walking out of the shadows. Jake thumped him on the back, presenting him again to the crowd.

"Yes! He did an outstanding job," Jake said, booming voice calming the fans. "We love you, Pittsburgh. We want you to be the first to be told."

Jake paused. He turned to Talon, who nodded in agreement.

Randall looked as startled as Tristen felt. Even with all the surrounding noise, the sound of his own heartbeat filled his ears.

"We wish Paul all the best in his recovery. His battle with cancer is going to be long and hard, though, and he won't be able to continue with the band. He wants to spend time with his family, his kids, and take care of himself. He's made the decision to return to Cincinnati to get the care and rest that he needs."

Jake paused for the crowd to clap and shout their support of Paul, the lead singer for Art of Rendering.

"We know you're going to love our recent addition," he went on, clapping Talon on the back again. "He isn't a replacement. No one can replace Paul. But he is going to help us finish this tour we've been promising you all!" The crowd cheered again, but this time Jake kept going. "This guy is his own legend. Everyone, please welcome Talon Levisay to AOR!"

Chapter 2

Tristen froze. There'd been a mistake.

"Phoenix, here we come!" Jake shouted as the lights went out for the last time.

Phoenix. Art of Rendering had tour dates after this. And The Seethers weren't invited. The only show The Seethers had scheduled was at Pete's, at a local Cincinnati venue, in December.

Tristen turned to find Randall inches from his face, cold blue eyes boring into him.

"What the hell?" Randall said under his breath. "What does that mean, Tris?"

Phoenix. New lead singer. Talon. "I don't know."

"That's a wrap!" someone yelled, and all backstage workers shifted into action.

Tristen looked around, trying to find Talon in the milling group of backstage workers. There had to be an explanation. Jake must have had it wrong. Or Tristen had understood wrong.

"What the hell does it mean?" Randall repeated. "Is Talon leaving our band?"

"I said I don't know."

Randall put a hand up to try and stop Tristen as he pushed past. "What're you going to do?"

"Find Talon!" Tristen shouted without stopping, Randall's footsteps and muttering right behind him.

Talon would be in the green room, Tristen was sure of it. He and Randall swerved quickly through the milling backstage hands, mic stands almost impaling him twice. They kept moving, despite the calls of irritation at their speed. Down the stairs and to the right. The acrid smell of mildew and sweat assaulted his nose, a smell he had barely registered before.

"What the hell is going on?"

Tristen whirled around. Micah stood in the hallway, his jaw set and his arms crossed. Micah was always fierce-looking with his wide, burly shoulders and full beard, but when he was angry, he became the third most intimidating man Tristen knew.

"I thought you left?"

"I was about to. Thought I'd see the last song from the perspective of a fan. I think I was the only one not clapping when Jake announced Talon was their new singer."

"I heard it from backstage," Tristen said. Shadows crept into his thinking, blurring his memory. Had Talon told him? Had he hinted at it? "I'm heading to the green room to get an explanation from Talon."

He opened the door, but only Adam was there. Randall and Micah marched in behind Tristen.

"So, Talon's left the band? When were you planning on telling us?" Micah demanded once the door closed.

Tristen felt himself buckle inwardly at the weight of not knowing. He went over the days before the concert, but he couldn't remember any sign from Talon.

"I'm just as surprised as you," he admitted. "Talon told me he was singing with them today because Paul was too sick."

"Wait, they don't want us to go with them to Phoenix?" Randall asked.

Tristen looked up out of his own whirling thoughts. "AOR didn't ask us to join past Pittsburg. We always knew that. They have some local band starting for them when they go to Phoenix."

"So that's it? We're done?" Adam asked. He threw his hat against the wall, then sank into a chair.

"Well, that's what we had planned," Tristen said, licking his lips to keep his voice from cracking. "We were offered these six concerts. And it helped us. You've seen the album sales. We've made more in the last few weeks than ever before."

"And yet we've barely made a profit, Tristen." Adam was always eager to point out they weren't making enough money.

"Yeah, and now Talon's jumped ship!" Randall was shouting, pointing at the door that remained shut. "Which means we're actually done."

Footsteps sounded in the hall. Tristen glanced at the door, expecting Talon to come through it, but when it cracked open, a shock of long black hair fell through as Meegan peeked in.

"Meegan, did you see Talon? Where is he?" Tristen asked. He was trying not to panic.

"I came here to see you guys. I thought he'd be here." Meegan's eyes were wide, sweat shining on her face.

Adam shook his head. "Man, this is so disappointing. I thought him singing tonight was going to help us out. Instead, it just helped him."

"I think it helped you out," Meegan said, pushing her way into the middle of them. "That crowd was crazy for you guys. And someone said we sold all the merchandise."

"See?" Tristen said, but Adam shook his head.

"At least we aren't losing money," Randall said.

"You guys don't get it, do you?" Adam asked, rolling his eyes. "It doesn't matter if we don't lose money. Breaking even isn't gonna cut it. We all pitched in five hundred dollars for this tour and that merchandise. If we don't make any money, we don't have any money to put together another tour. And this was only six cities!" Adam finished his speech at a roar.

No one said a word.

"Well, I'm glad I didn't quit my job," Micah said, picking up his bags. "I'll see you guys around. My cousin's here."

"You can't leave." Tristen's voice revealed the panic building inside him. "I mean, you're not leaving for good, are you? We have to figure this out. This is not the end of The Seethers."

"Exactly," Meegan said, her voice louder than necessary. Her face was rose pink. "You guys can't give up. Let's say Talon leaves—so what? You still have a band."

No one moved as she glared at each of them.

"Talon is the front man," Adam pointed out, his enormous arms crossed over his barrel chest. "It isn't just about keeping the band."

"Tristen." Meegan turned to him, her eyes reflecting his desperation. "Lots of bands go through transition. Don't give up. What about Nirvana? The rest of them became the Foo Fighters, right?"

Tristen glanced around. The others were unreadable. "Meegan's right. We're still a band. Don't we continue on? Isn't that what AOR is doing without Paul?"

"They stole our lead singer," Micah said flatly. "And we don't exactly have the clout *AOR* has to find another one. No one's pounding down our doors to sing with us."

"You ain't Dave Grohl, Tristen," Adam said.

Tristen swallowed, trying to not be offended.

"Exactly," Micah said.

"I'm not Dave Grohl, but we can still fix this," Tristen said, knowing he sounded desperate. "I look just like him. Besides, with or without Talon, we have another show at home soon, remember?"

The pause from the guys didn't give him any confidence. Neither did Randall, hiding a snicker.

"Sorry, man, but I'm out." Adam didn't look sorry; he looked very serious.

"Adam, please." His throat was dry, and the air seemed to lack oxygen. He clenched his fists to keep from hitting something, to keep himself calm. The room felt closed and pressurized. Breathing into the bottom of his lungs, Tristen let the air out slowly. "Guys, come on. We've been building this band for what, three years now? We can't just stop playing because of a setback. We'll find another singer."

Fear had taken control of his voice, but he didn't even try to temper it. Pleading was not beneath him.

"I got bills to pay, Tristen," Adam said. "And a woman who expects me to marry her and let her have kids someday. I can't do that if I don't have a consistent job. A job I can rely on. I ain't got time to play around anymore, man. I'm almost thirty. This was our chance, and it's gone. We had a good run. Let it go."

"You don't actually believe that, do you?"

They stood motionless, all avoiding eye contact. Tristen tried to swallow, but the muscles in his throat constricted the effort. He tried not to think about the thousands of dollars on his credit cards. Most of it for the band.

"Listen," he said, trying to find the inspiring words that would come next. He looked between his band members, their angry eyes staring at him.

"What?" Adam demanded.

Tristen scrambled. "We have to play Pete's in a couple weeks. We have a contract. Let's give ourselves time to cool down, okay? Then we'll see how we feel after the next show."

If he could get them back on stage together, he could convince them to fight for the band. They'd remember how much they each loved being on stage, and cooler heads would prevail.

Randall looked around at all of them, nodding toward Tristen. "He's right. We owe Pete's a last show. We'll show up and give a statement there. Adam, you can commit to that night, right?"

Adam looked at Tristen, who met his eyes. He gave a curt nod and marched out the door. "I'll talk to you all later."

Micah threw his hands up in the air before following Adam. "Fine. See you at Pete's."

They would need to come in for practice, but Tristen bit his tongue. No need to talk about that now.

Meegan, Randall, and Tristen stood in the silence, unable to stop watching the door.

"I don't think he's coming," Meegan finally said, peeling out of their circle to grab a bottle of water. "I say we go out and find food."

"What about you?" Randall asked Tristen. "What do you want to do?"

Tristen shrugged. "Get drunk and find Talon."

"And what? Fight him?" Meegan asked, coming over to him. She wrapped her fingers around the back of his neck, massaging his stiff muscles. Tristen kissed her, grateful she seemed to understand him.

"Nah. He'd punch him too hard," Randall said, winking. "Come on. Let's finish loading this stuff and go out. I need some whiskey."

Chapter 3

Tristen pulled his car up to the curb of his childhood home, a tiny WWII home in Pelton, Kentucky. The house was a perfect rectangle with three small rooms, one bathroom, and one linen closet. There was no entryway, just a straight walk into the living room. True to Kentucky style, the house boasted a small porch, reached by climbing six steps. These were ostensibly the reason he'd gone to the hardware store and was now armed with the material to fix the two wobbly ones.

The real reason was that he had needed a break from his mother, Ivy. Tristen looked at the house from the driver's seat and sighed. They were celebrating Ivy's birthday, which meant Talon was coming.

He'd arrived early because the truth was, he had nothing to do in Cincinnati, and he was driving himself crazy walking circles in his girlfriend's townhouse. Ever since Talon had left the band and gone touring America with AOR, Tristen hadn't heard from his brother. The only project he'd had to keep him busy during the last month was recording Meegan's album. Now it was done, he was on his own. Like a bum. Still, spending the entire afternoon with Ivy asking him why he never came to visit her anymore and why he hadn't brought Meegan to her birthday was making him wish he'd stayed home.

He laughed at the thought of bringing Meegan to Pelton with her diamond earrings, thousand-dollar shoes and diet of only organic food. Ivy would spend the time constantly making comments, while Meegan would slowly get angrier and angrier.

It was just easier to keep the two away from each other. They were too different to ever get along.

Tristen finally killed the engine, took a deep breath, and called Randall. He'd sent him multiple texts over the last week, none of which Randall had answered.

The call went straight to voicemail. Tristen tapped the call button again, putting it on speaker as he crawled out of his rusty Ford. This time it rang, but Tristen knew Randall wouldn't pick up until the fourth or fifth ring. In the meantime, he jerked open the passenger side.

"Hello?" Randall answered. His voice sounded far from the microphone. Another voice mumbled through the sound waves, telling him to ignore the call.

Tristen balanced the phone on his shoulder while he picked up the grocery-store bouquet of flowers in his elbow. He had to get something for his mother that was tangible. Otherwise she'd be angry. Once the flowers were safe, he grabbed the brown paper bag full of wood filler, a box of nails, and sanding paper. The three planks of wood would have to wait.

"It's me." He looked up and down the street for a sign of Talon, but the sidewalks were empty. He expanded his lungs to shake off his nerves at seeing his brother for the first time since the concert in Philly. The texts he'd sent to Talon had also gone unanswered, perhaps because Art of Rendering had gone to Mexico for a quick tour, but since social media said nothing about Talon being permanent, Tristen hoped that meant Talon was coming back to The Seethers. Especially since he'd tried to convince the guys Talon hadn't abandoned them. That probably he was just a temporary fill-in, regardless of what Jake had said on stage.

"I know, Tristen. There's something called caller ID."

"Right. Well, I heard from Pete's. They fixed the leak and want to know if we're okay to play on the twenty-ninth."

Randall sighed. "Yeah, man, I guess. It kinda sucks that they left us hanging for a month."

"But we signed a contract, so—"

"I know, Tristen. We signed a contract. I don't want to be those guys who don't follow through."

Tristen set the brown paper bag down on the porch steps and tried not to panic at Randall's strange tone. "Good. Good. I talked to Adam and Micah and they said they'd be there, too." Randall replied with a neutral grunt. "How'd the other night go? When you filled in for that other band."

Randall was a master guitar player in Tristen's eyes. He could play anywhere. When he'd posted to social media about playing with some band named Los Dos, Tristen couldn't help worrying.

A red, shiny Camaro sat at the curb where the Buglis used to live. Whoever had bought the tiny house had clearly spent most of their money on the car. The houses around this neighborhood were old, but not the kind of old that the do-it-yourself-shows renovated. These were tiny, one-bathroom houses contractors were pulling down when they could to build modern ones.

"It was fun, actually. Yeah."

"You are coming to Pete's, though, right?"

Randall didn't respond at first. "What's your brother up to? You talk to him?"

"He's back. We're celebrating our mom's birthday tonight." Tristen looked down the empty street. Talon should drive up any minute. He wasn't usually late.

"Did you talk to him about the band? What's his plan?" Randall pressed, doubt creeping into his voice. "I've seen AOR's social media. They look happy to have him."

"I've been watching too, and they haven't put out an official notice he's permanent," Tristen said. "You'll see, we'll be back together by Pete's, and everything will be fine. Don't worry."

Randall grunted. "No one ever says anything about him being temporary, either. Before we hang up—I can't show up to practice between December twenty-third and the twenty-seventh."

"But the concert is on the twenty-ninth."

"I know."

The silence was like a challenge, but Tristen refused to bite.

"I got my kids those days. There's no way I'm getting a baby-sitter and missing time with them."

Tristen held back a sigh. "I guess we'll be fine. Maybe we could practice on the twenty-eighth," he said, adjusting the brown bag in his arms. "Randall?"

"Yeah. Okay. Let's let the guys know. We can work through a show order on our group chat. Tell Talon he's an ass for me," Randall said. "Tell him he has to try out again, and that I'm not sure he's good enough to play with us."

"Ha, ha," Tristen said, ambling up the porch steps. Harassment for leaving was to be expected, but he hoped the guys wouldn't take it too far. Talon had never taken hazing very well. "Later."

"Yep. Talk later."

Randall hung up, allowing Tristen to drop his sleeping arm. He needed to replace the cordless headphones he'd lost on the road that fall, but until he had some money in the bank, he was stuck holding his phone while talking.

He left the bag for the repairs on the steps and took the porch steps two at a time. He let himself inside expecting Ivy and Bobbi, his aunt, to be sitting on the couch watching Entertainment Tonight.

Instead, Talon stood in the middle of the living room drinking a beer and watching a football game.

Tristen almost dropped his flowers in surprise. "Talon. I didn't know you were here yet. Where's your car?"

"Sandra and I were right on time," Talon said. "As usual. You're the one who's late." Tristen's same blue eyes narrowed in his mirror image at him, even as Talon's lips curled up into a smile. "And of course you've seen my car. It's that one."

Tristen followed his brother's finger to the window and on to the red car out front. "The Camaro's yours?"

Talon shrugged. "It was time for a new ride. Here, have a beer."

"There he is. And he brought flowers! Those for me?" Ivy shouted from the doorway between the galley kitchen and the living room.

Without warning, a beer can flew at Tristen. He sacrificed the flowers, dropping them to grab the can and avoid an explosion. "Damn, Talon, what the hell?"

"Nice catch. Maybe don't open it for a minute," Talon said, laughing.

"My flowers," Ivy mourned, her voice high-pitched, her bottom lip protruding. She came into the living room with two beers in her hands, handing one off to Tristen as she bent to pick up the flowers. "Take this one, and don't open that one inside. These are so pretty, Tris. Thank you."

She clinked her beer can against his and winked at her younger-by-two-minutes son before returning her attention to Talon. "He's so tan, isn't he, Tris? While you and I get whiter by the winter day, he's out getting tan."

Tristen looked his brother up and down. Now that he was looking closer, Talon looked like a bronzed statue.

"That's what happens when you're in the desert," Talon said.

Tristen wondered if he was too old to mock his brother while rolling his eyes. Their sister, Aimee, used to do it all the time while they were growing up. It might have been her most annoying habit, besides taking forever in their one bathroom.

Tristen downed his beer, swallowing his jealousy with the tasteless light alcohol. Talon had got an opportunity anyone in The Seethers would have died to have. While Tristen had been doing nothing, Talon had been touring. He shook his head and put down the empty can. There was no point in dwelling on it.

"Ivy! You got a phone call," Sandra yelled from the kitchen.

Ivy jerked into motion. "Coming!"

Tristen sank onto the couch next to his brother as she rushed into the galley kitchen. Talon didn't seem to notice. His favorite team losing was taking all of his attention.

"You're here on the twenty-eighth, right? For practice? Randall can't come from the twenty-third to the twenty-seventh, so I think we should try to practice on the twenty-eighth," Tristen said.

Talon kept watching.

"Talon. Hello."

"You're talking to me?" Talon's eyes focused on Tristen.

"Who else?" Tristen was starting to question his brother's sanity.

"Thought you were on the phone. What practice are you talking about?"

"We committed to a show on the twenty-ninth in Cincinnati."

Confusion flitted across Talon's face, crinkling his forehead. "Nah, Tris. Sandra and I are going back for her to see her parents in Bulgaria. The whole time she was finishing her degree, she didn't get to visit them. This year we can finally afford flight tickets. Man, having a normal paycheck is so nice. I mean, it's not tons of money. We still have to pay back Sandra's school loans and stuff, but it's a relief, you know?"

The words pulled Tristen into a black hole. The world wobbled for a second, like it had when he'd fainted at age fourteen after running in July. "What?"

Talon looked at him, his eyebrows raised. "I said Sandra and I are going back to Bulgaria. We can't be at your concert."

"My concert. You're saying this is my concert?"

"Fine, The Seethers'. Sorry." Talon looked over his shoulder to find an out. Or someone to rescue him from talking to Tristen.

"I don't know why you wouldn't come. We signed the contract months ago." Tristen tried to sound relaxed through his gritted teeth.

"The Seethers signed the contract," Talon said. Slowly, like Tristen was an idiot. "I'm with Art of Rendering now."

"Permanently?" Tristen realized he was breathing shallowly and took a deep breath to steady himself.

His own twin wouldn't abandon him like a piece of trash. Like he meant nothing.

Talon finally sighed. "Did you think I was coming back?"

The words hit like bullets. Talon's tone made Tristen feel stupid. He couldn't speak, so he said nothing. His embarrassment that he had thought better of his brother than he deserved slowly boiled into anger.

"The position with Art of Rendering is permanent. I'm with them now. You have The Seethers. It's a win-win."

Again, there was no suitable response. Tristen was proud to be part of The Seethers, but obviously, Art of Rendering was more popular and had greater success. And, of course, AOR had bi-weekly paychecks and agents and tours booked out. Tristen would be glad to be part of them, too. But showing Talon the comparison would make him sound jealous. Which, yes, he was. But mostly because Talon was just walking away and leaving him with the group of lesser value.

Tristen swallowed all his thoughts back until the only emotion he recognized was a sizzle of anger.

"You could have told us. It would have been nice to know so we could practice differently." Tristen took a swig of beer to calm his nerves.

"I thought it was pretty obvious," Talon said.

His tone was starting to grate on Tristen's nerves. Talon had always been the more popular, more athletic brother. The one people naturally wanted to be friends with. He was more personable, so people told him stuff. When they were kids, Talon always knew the latest gossip. He was the first to know when their sister's dad, Luke, had got out of jail, and had always made Tristen feel like an idiot for being the last to find out.

"When, exactly, was it obvious?" Tristen asked. His jaw hurt from clenching so hard.

"Uh, when I got the job with AOR."

"Oh, you mean it was obvious because you didn't bother to tell your band members or answer any calls or texts to explain yourself?"

Talon rolled his eyes. He shook his beer to find it was empty and eyed the kitchen enviously.

"You had a *guaranteed paycheck*," Tristen said, mimicking his brother. He could remember them acting the same way for every other argument all their lives.

"I had one from the construction job, but that wasn't what I was talking about. Although I would have taken that and still left the band."

"But why? We were already farther than last year. Things were moving. We had the six-city tour with Art of Rendering. Things were happening."

Talon stood. The energy surrounding him buzzed like he was just as angry as Tristen. Like he had a reason to be frustrated. Tristen's hands curled at his sides, but he kept the rest of his body still as he watched Talon, who found the corner of the ceiling more interesting than looking his brother in the eyes.

"You know, Tristen, that's the problem. You wait around for things to happen, and that isn't how life works." He shook his head and clicked his tongue.

You're the loser twin, got that? Tristen stiffened at the memory of the words. "I worked my ass off to get The Seethers where they are now."

Talon pulled back, a smile tugging at the corner of his mouth. If they hadn't been standing in Ivy's living room, Tristen would have punched that smile off his face.

"You never told me you were thinking of leaving. You just abandoned us and then didn't have the guts to come face us afterwards."

"Abandoned?" Sandra stood next to Talon suddenly. Her cat-like prowl always kept everyone oblivious to her entrance until she was already there. "He didn't abandon you, Tristen. He found a job that better fits him. They offered, and he accepted. Now you can have full control of The Seethers. There's no reason to be upset."

She sounded like a teacher reprimanding him.

"I'm not upset," Tristen snapped, too quickly. He needed to slow down before he exploded. "But it *was* abandonment. You never bothered to come back and explain anything to us. You never answered my calls or Randall's. You just ghosted us."

Talon winced. Or cringed. Tristen wasn't sure. "I'm sorry you feel like that. I thought making a clean break was best. Maybe

I should have called… but I don't know, I was busy. You don't know what it's like to jump into a band that's been together for years. I had to learn all their songs and how they interact. It was a lot. And I had to learn everything while being on tour."

Tristen said nothing. He had no sympathy for his brother and wasn't about to fake some to help him feel better.

Seeing he wasn't going to get a response, Talon continued. "Maybe if I was gonna be in town, I could do the show. As a goodbye. I'm sure the fans would prefer that, actually. But Sandra and I are leaving in two days."

Tristen counted to three to keep himself from punching his brother. The living room was too small, and Sandra was standing too close by.

He looked at his sister-in-law, who was still glaring at him as though he was the one who had done something wrong. Clearly, she wanted Talon to move on. She had always had a problem with The Seethers. Or maybe it was with him; Tristen wasn't sure.

"Okay, I'm back. Tell me about the tour." Ivy appeared, beaming between the three of them.

"I think we should turn the focus on the birthday girl," Sandra said, shooting Tristen a look. Ivy didn't miss it.

"Why?" She glared at as well, standing in lecture mode. "What did you do?"

Tristen threw up his arms. "I didn't do anything."

"He's mad I can't do the show on the twenty-ninth."

"Tristen! Why would he do your show? He's with another band now. You should be proud of him. He's always been the go-getter of you two."

Tristen pointed at Talon, the heat in his belly rising to his chest. "He left us hanging, scrambling to get things figured out without a frontman."

Sandra crossed her arms, her eyebrows raised. "Why don't you become the frontman? It's what you've always wanted, isn't it? It's why you went out to do solo gigs a year ago, to see if you could break off on your own." Hands on her hips, she scowled at him. "I think you were trying to do exactly what you accuse

Talon of doing. The problem is, he got there first. But you should look at the bright side. The Seethers is now yours. Do with it as you wish."

Tristen had three pairs of eyes on him and was caught off guard by the fact that Sandra knew about his playing solo in dive bars. He took another drink, pausing at the lip of the can to suck in air. "No. I never wanted to be the lead singer."

Even he could tell he didn't sound convincing.

"But now you can be." Sandra smiled. Her eyes, which always looked like they were plotting another person's demise, took on an even stranger glint. "Sometimes you have to cut the cord. It's not like you two have a contract that can keep Talon tied to you."

"I didn't think I'd need a contract with my brother," Tristen muttered.

"Come on, Tristen, get over it. You'll be a terrific frontman. It's time you do your own thing, you know? Not always lean on Talon. I know you can do it," Ivy said, pulling a joint from her pocket and placing it between her lips.

"What?" Tristen stared at Ivy. The words struck him as something she'd said before. And offensive. "Of course I can do it without Talon. That isn't the point."

"Then what's the point?" Sandra's wide eyes bored into his.

"Remember how you used to play and sing while we sat on the porch?" Ivy asked, changing the subject.

Tristen shook his head and chose not to reply. She spoke like it was a treasured childhood memory, but it had only happened about four times. At least two of those times, Ivy had passed out in the rocking chair from too much drink. Aimee had ended up singing the rest of the porch concert with him.

"Ivy, don't smoke that in here," Talon said, taking the joint away from her.

"It's my house, Talon. Don't tell me you've gotten uppity since you joined Art of Rendering."

"No," Talon said, glancing back at Sandra. She pressed her lips together and nodded. "But Sandra's pregnant."

Ivy squealed, tossing her joint to Tristen as though it was on fire. "You're pregnant? Do you know what it is?"

Tristen raised his eyebrows. He couldn't believe how stupid his brother was. As though he had any knowledge of how to be a father. All they'd had growing up was four of Ivy's boyfriends and Owen, the man who'd come forward when they were thirteen, claiming to be their father. None of them had been what Tristen would consider role models.

Ivy elbowed him in the ribs.

"What?"

Ivy hissed through her teeth. "Aren't you going to say congratulations?"

"Yeah, sure. Congrats, Talon."

"Ignore him," Ivy said. "Sandra, are you ready to be a mom? It's an amazing thing."

Tristen snorted, covering the noise with a cough.

"It's happening whether we're ready or not," Talon said, pulling Sandra closer. She gave him a rare public kiss before sauntering back to the kitchen with Ivy.

"We should get dinner going. Bobbi should be here with the cake soon. I saw her pulling into her driveway just now." Talon looked at Tristen, the air between them thick and awkward. Tristen stared back, wishing he had a slew of insults that would make sense to throw at his brother.

"What's wrong, Tristen?" Talon's voice was strangely calm and light.

"You want to know?" Tristen asked. He swallowed past the lump in his throat.

"Yeah, I do."

"You should have just told us. You should have said something."

"Weird," Talon said, his smile cold. "I seem to remember a time when you could have said something, too."

"What are you talking about?"

Talon folded his arms across his chest and glared. "Come on, man. You could have told me about you playing in those dives alone, but you didn't."

"Are you serious? That was when you had just gotten married and we were struggling to put together a second album. The other guys were picking up extra work and you were busy with Sandra. We were all trying to make a living, and I was trying out some new music on people in bars. What's the problem with that? I wasn't looking to leave The Seethers."

"Sure," Talon said, looking away. "Like you said, we're all just trying to make a living." He paused. "I think if they had approached you, you would've taken it. Just like you did years ago when I was supposed to win that fight. You saw an opportunity, and you took it."

Tristen opened his mouth to protest, but Talon put up a hand to stop him.

"It's whatever, Tris. I don't blame you. Which means you shouldn't blame me. I had the opportunity, and I took it. I'm a husband and going to be a father. You'd do the same in my shoes."

Chapter 4

"Hello, boys. Happy birthday, Ivy." Bobbi's large frame filled the front doorway. She grinned at them. Tristen noticed her hair had gone almost completely gray, though she couldn't be more than fifty-five. It gave her a certain distinguished look.

"Bobbi!" Talon shouted. A bit over the top, in Tristen's opinion; there was no need to shout.

Bobbi wrinkled her brow, probably thinking the same, but she accepted the bear hug Talon gave her with a hearty grunt. When he pulled away the cake box wobbled, almost falling to the ground. Tristen smirked as Talon lunged to grab it, hitting his forehead against the couch in the process.

"You couldn't help your brother?" Ivy snapped at him, rushing to check on her cake. It was still in one piece. Tristen shrugged, not bothering to explain how little he cared to help his brother with anything at the moment. "Did he tell you, Bobbi?"

Tristen gave Bobbi their more conventional side hug. She was his one and only blood relative, and though they didn't always see eye-to-eye, she was like a second mother to him. Looking back on his childhood, he was grateful for her. Especially that she'd lived just across the street his entire life. There were times she was the lifeline he needed, especially when things with Ivy got bad.

"Tell me what?" Bobbi looked between all of them.

"I need to start the grill," Tristen said to no one as Talon told Bobbi his news.

Sandra barely looked up from her phone when Tristen grabbed a beer and the lighter and headed outside for some fresh air. His anger had settled into a simmer. If Talon didn't want to play with them at the show on the twenty-ninth, then fine. Screw him.

And having a kid? Well, good luck with that. Fred, Darren, Javon and Luke had all passed through their house at some point. Luke, Aimee's dad, had stuck around the longest. He had also stepped into the role of stepdad the most, though Javon had been Tristen's favorite. He'd shown up for a few months while Luke was in jail and, in Tristen's opinion, had been the nicest. He'd taken them for ice cream, let them drive his Camaro on side streets with him, and had taught them how to grill.

Even with those four men around, Tristen had always considered himself the product of a single mother who'd got knocked up at seventeen. And she was certainly no example of how to parent correctly.

With the gas tank twisted open, it took one flick of the match to light the flame on the grill out back. The evening was cold and he'd left his coat inside, but he refused to go back in. He needed a minute. It would have been nice to have the boxing bag still hanging from the magnolia tree out front, so he could punch out his frustration.

The alternative was to talk to Meegan.

"Hello?"

"Meegan." Tristen thought for a second he might cry—which would be the icing on the cake for that evening. Like hell he was going to cry! He was just stressed. Rolling back his shoulders, he sniffed, glancing into the dark yard to assure himself that Luke's ghost wasn't there glaring at him.

I didn't give you my last name for you to cry. Levisay men didn't cry. The ground could give way to a hole six feet deep, but Levisay men didn't cry.

"What's wrong, babe? Party a bust?"

Tristen laughed dryly. "Typical party at the Levisay house. Might steal some of my mom's weed."

"Must be pretty bad for you to revert to that."

She was right. He hadn't smoked in years. He used to love the way it gave him an escape, but the last few times he'd only thought of Aimee, his sister, and how it might have been his fault she had died.

"What's really wrong?" He heard a blowing sound and realized she was probably painting her nails. She painted them when she was bored, then would go to get them done at the salon.

"Nothing."

"You wouldn't call me if everything was fine."

Tristen sighed. He rolled his neck in a circle, the vertebrae cracking. "Talon and Sandra showed up."

"Weren't you expecting them?" Meegan sounded delighted. "How are they?"

"Same. Talon's an asshole, and Sandra is always scowling."

"I like Sandra. She's so funny."

Meegan and Sandra barely interacted with each other. "Sandra is funny? But she's always so serious."

"Exactly. It's so funny how serious she is. How is she?"

"Pregnant."

He'd expected Meegan to be surprised, but he hadn't anticipated the squealing. "How exciting! Maybe we should have a baby. Our baby would be way cuter."

"There's no way you want a baby now. You just finished recording your first album. And it's going to be a hit, remember?"

Tristen wasn't sure he'd be a father ever in his life and since Meegan was only twenty-four and on the verge of her own career, he wasn't about to agree to a baby with her. He wasn't even sure how he was going to pay his bills in the next few months.

"I wasn't being serious, Tristen. And besides, that was fast. If I was them, I would have waited a bit."

"What do you mean?"

"I mean, they were separated for like six months this last year. They almost got divorced. I'm surprised they just went right away for the baby."

Tristen nodded as he arranged the patties on the grill. "I mean, I'm glad they got back together. I think Talon really loves Sandra. But they probably shouldn't have a baby ever."

"Ever?" Meegan no longer sounded sympathetic. "Why do you care one way or another?"

"I don't," he snapped. The silence on the other end was palpable. "I just think it's stupid. They're too young." He blew on the flame, though it didn't need it. He was the one who needed extra oxygen. "And he knows nothing about raising a kid. And he'll be on the road all the time."

"I can tell you don't care." Meegan laughed, but it was more sympathetic than he deserved. "If you're going to be crabby, let's change the subject. I gave Daddy my album for Christmas as a surprise. I know most of the tracks aren't completely finished, but he still loved it."

"Of course he did. You're a beautiful woman and an exceptional singer." Her album was good. He was afraid it might be too good—that she might shoot to the top and leave him behind. Which was why he needed The Seethers to work. Maybe he could write a new song to get them excited and back in the game.

"Thank you, baby. I love you. Anyway, that's not all." Meegan paused. "He's getting me an agent."

Jealousy hit him straight in the gut, but he ignored it. "That's great, Meegan." He wondered what could have happened if they'd gotten an agent for The Seethers. At any rate, he wasn't going to bring up that dumpster fire now. Talon leaving and the band being in trouble would ruin her good news.

"He got me Clay Hirson. Can you believe it? I gotta get moving on the album. I need it faster than I thought."

"It's done. I just need to tweak them a bit."

"You keep saying that." Tristen knew that hesitant tone of hers by now. "Daddy says we should be careful about how much business and pleasure we mix."

"Why?"

"He's an entrepreneur who's successfully sold several companies. I think he knows what he's saying."

Tristen chose not to respond.

Meegan continued. "You can still be my sound guy. He just thinks I should find a producer that Clay has experience with."

The back door creaked open then slammed shut. Tristen looked up to find Ivy coming out with a tray of burgers and brats.

"I got dinner," she sang.

"I gotta go, babe."

Meegan gave him a loud air kiss before hanging up.

"That the girlfriend you don't want to bring around?" Ivy asked.

Tristen took his time tossing the burgers and brats onto the sizzling grill. The fire heated his face, thawing out his nose and cheeks a bit. "I don't refuse to bring her. There just hasn't been a time that we coincide."

"What about Christmas?"

He should have seen that question coming. "What about it?"

Ivy's eyes searched his as though he had some sort of secret hidden in them. "Are you coming to visit?"

"If you want. Meegan's family always goes to New York, so she won't be around. And I'm doing the sound for some giant church on the east side on Christmas Eve. I could—"

"No worries. I'll hang out with Owen. I'm fine with that."

"Owen? Seriously?"

Ivy crossed her arms. "Yes. He and I go way back."

"Haven't you two tried to be together four or five times?"

"Only twice. First when he got me pregnant with you two. And then again when Luke left."

"When Luke went to jail?"

Ivy shrugged. "What's your problem, Tristen?"

There was no reason to hash it out now. It was her birthday. "Nothing. Date who you want."

Even in the dark, he could tell her eyes were narrowing, letting him know he had hurt her feelings. It wasn't true, though. Ivy was the kind of woman who shot back when someone offended her. But she didn't say anything.

The screen door opened and shut again as Talon sauntered down the porch steps, his shoulders bunched up to his ears. "Did you say Owen? I saw him today. He said you and he were back together."

Tristen tapped the burgers into place, enjoying the warmth on his face and chest before pulling the grill top down. Owen might be their biological father, but as far as Tristen knew, he was also the town mini-mafia king who, rumor had it, ran the boxing gym as a cover for several illicit enterprises. Tristen personally believed it. He was one of the boxers Owen had used to gain notoriety. He and Talon, the Pelton Vikings. It had been Luke's idea, but Owen was the one who ran with it.

"Is Daddy finally taking his rightful place?" Talon teased. He sounded slightly drunk.

Tristen glared at his brother, though Talon probably couldn't see him.

"Stop it," Ivy said, laughing. "Tristen, don't squish the hamburgers."

"I'm not squishing anything." He was cold, but he didn't want to admit it. And he wanted to be alone.

"And I'm sure you boys have had your nights of fun. You just never got pregnant." Talon opened his mouth, but Ivy stopped him with a shake of her head. "No, I don't want to hear details. But the truth is, Tristen, you could show some respect for Owen."

"Yeah, show respect to Daddy," Talon said.

"Shut up, Talon."

Talon sniffed. "I don't know why you're mad. I keep in touch with him. Don't want to miss out on that inheritance from all his 'business.'" Talon used air quotes to make his point.

Ivy laughed again.

"Want another beer, Tris?" Talon asked. "I'll get you one. It's freezing out here. Don't talk about anything important while I'm gone."

"We wouldn't dare."

The words hung in the air a moment before Talon stalked away.

"You gotta get over it," Ivy murmured once he was gone. "Staying mad about things only hurts you."

"I'm not mad about anything, Ivy," Tristen said, pulling the grill back open so she had to step away.

"Okay. I was just trying—"

"Let's just enjoy your birthday, okay?" Tristen snapped. Flipping the burgers onto the tray, he followed her inside.

Chapter 5

Christmas Eve morning was bright and bitterly cold, but temperature didn't matter to a runner. The minute the alarm sounded, Tristen had yanked on his running clothes, gloves, and hat and hit the pavement. It was a habit he'd begun at thirteen and couldn't shake.

Running had started out, if he was honest with himself, as way to prove himself to Fred, whom Ivy had dated for a year or so. Until Luke had got out of jail, Fred was the fittest monster of a man Tristen had ever seen. He ran every day and expected the twins to sign up for a sport every quarter. That was easy for Talon, who willingly did so, but Tristen had to be dragged to most of their sports activities, especially after he discovered playing the guitar. From Fred, Tristen had learned that what counted was proving to the outside world that you could do something. And you did so by competing.

Besides, boys played sports. "Are you a girl, Tristen?" Fred would ask him. Sneer, more like.

The playlist he'd creatively named 'Running' upped its beat. One mile in. Warm-up was over. His feet hit the pavement harder, faster as the river came into view—his favorite part of Cincinnati.

Back in Pelton, the loop he'd created for himself on his very first run had included the truck stop at the edge of town, because he knew from the mile markers that it was exactly three miles from his house. Little had he realized that first run that three miles there and three miles back would give him the worst leg cramps for days afterward. Hiding his sore muscles would have been impossible, had his mother been the kind to pay any attention to her kids.

When he could finally run again, four days later, he'd run into Fred just as the side ache and cramping calves forced him to a walk. It was just before six in the morning, and Tristen was in the Highlands Park neighborhood, where houses started at three-hundred thousand or above. He and Talon had mowed lawns there to earn cash since they were eleven; Crystal Allen, the prettiest girl in school and a pageant competitor, had a house there. And right next to it was Fred's black pickup truck, rusty and dirty, with dozens of two-by-fours sticking out of the back. Tristen froze in shock when Fred rounded the back of the truck, lifting his fingers away from pinching the ache in his sides. Fred stopped too, and for a moment they looked at each other with nothing to say. Then Fred's lips spread into a smile. Thankfully, it wasn't the kind he got when the switch came out.

"That's my boy," he had said, tossing his toothpick to the curb. "Your mama know you're out here running?"

"No, sir. Didn't want to wake her up."

"Why didn't you wake up that good-for-nothin' brother of yours? Tristen could use a run or two."

Tristen's body had turned from warm to cold. No one ever could tell them apart, but Fred had been living in the house for weeks at that point.

Fred raised an eyebrow. Even in a decent mood, he didn't like not being answered. Tristen swallowed hard, scrambling to come up with an answer for him.

"Yes, sir," he'd drawled. "I could. Ask him, I mean. Maybe he'll come with me."

"Good boy. You know, that brother of yours won't be able to get on in life without you. You'll have to cut him loose some day, course, but for now, you try to get him on the straight and narrow, you hear?"

"Yes, sir. Tristen'll be alright."

"We'll see." Fred tousled Tristen's sweaty hair, the touch surprising Tristen so much he almost jumped out of the way. "Go on now, before your mama wakes up. I gotta get this job done. Tell Ivy I won't be back till dinner."

"Yes, sir." Tristen foolishly waited a beat, wondering if he might hug him. When he'd realized he was standing alone like an idiot, he pushed his feet into motion, running well past the point where Fred could still see him.

He hadn't been sad when Fred left Ivy just three weeks later.

The playlist stopped abruptly, and a ringtone burst through the headphones.

"Yeah?"

"Merry Christmas." Ivy sounded tipsy already, and it wasn't even eight in the morning. "You coming to see me today? I have a present for you."

"I told you," Tristen panted. He wasn't going to stop just because Ivy had called. "I have a gig tonight. I'm working the sound for a church."

"Beware," Ivy teased. "They'll probably pay you and then ask you for a tithe."

She laughed hard at her own joke, though thankfully she moved her head away from the mic first.

"I'll watch out," Tristen told her, unwilling to play the 'how much do we hate church' game. They had already paid him, and he'd used the money to pay down some of his credit card debt from going on tour with AOR and make a contribution towards his student loans.

The summer Ivy was away for three weeks after swallowing half a bottle of sleeping pills, Bobbi had placed Tristen and Talon into something called Vacation Bible School. He'd never seen Ivy angrier than when she found out, but at eight years old Tristen had enjoyed it. They had food and games and movies in the large gym. He was happy there until the day a kid told him Ivy was condemned to hell for all eternity for trying to commit suicide.

"She's a dirty sinner," the kid had said, his mouth curled up as though eating something rotten.

"And your mom's a dirty whore," had been Tristen's comeback and reason for getting kicked out. Apparently, certain words weren't allowed at Vacation Bible School.

Bobbi had been pissed. She'd washed his mouth out with soap and made him babysit her two-year-old grandson for the rest of the summer.

"You coming to Christmas dinner?" Ivy asked, as though she hadn't heard him say he was busy.

Tristen bit his tongue to keep from saying something that would escalate the situation. "I'm not coming today."

"I didn't mean today. I meant tomorrow. Geez, don't get your panties in a bunch."

"Right. Yeah, I could get there tomorrow. Dinner, just you and me?"

"Meegan's out of town, right?" Ivy asked, but didn't give him any time to respond. "And anyway, I got stuff to do this morning and afternoon. And tonight I'll be with Owen. When you do bring her around, I promise I won't smoke joints in front of her if you don't want me to. Course, Sandra is cool. She gets me. But I realize that it's asking too much to assume I'll get two cool daughters-in-law."

Growing up, Tristen had learned it was better to focus on things said at the beginning of Ivy's rants. It usually threw her off guard and got her talking about something completely different. "What stuff do you have?"

"What?" The sound of inhaling something deeply, perhaps a joint or her vape, followed. "Oh, that. Nothing much. Going to go to Lexington. But whatever. It's nothing."

"All right then," Tristen said. His watch vibrated. Six miles in. This was the flying high moment, when his legs no longer protested and his breathing became regular. Unless he was trying to talk, of course. "I'll see you tomorrow."

"You talk to your brother lately?" Ivy asked, clearly unwilling to leave the conversation. "Since he got to Bulgaria?"

"No. I don't think my phone can reach Europe. Saw his social media, though. They have a ton of snow there."

Ivy sighed heavily into the phone. "I kinda hoped he would call for Christmas, you know?"

"Look, we'll try to figure out a way to call him tomorrow, okay?" Tristen said, desperate to get off the phone and focus on his run. He had to be at the church by noon. "I'll see you tomorrow. Merry Christmas, Ivy."

She echoed it back to him as he hit the red button, but instead of the music playing, his phone rang again.

"Damn it, Ivy." But it wasn't Ivy. It was Meegan on video.

"Merry Christmas from New York," she yelled into the screen. Behind her was the giant Christmas tree at Rockefeller Square. "Are you running? On Christmas Eve morning? Geez, Tris, that's going a little far, isn't it?"

"Merry Christmas," came a shout from off screen.

"Daddy and Mom say Merry Christmas," Meegan said. "You're bouncing all over the screen. Can't you walk while you talk to me?"

"Sure, babe," Tristen said through gritted teeth, slowing his pace to a fast walk. He checked his watch, but swallowed his sigh. If Meegan spoke fast, he could get back to running and finish the ten miles, but if his heart rate slowed too much he might be out of luck. "Merry Christmas. I miss you."

"I miss you, too. We should just get married so you have to come on these trips with me." Tristen was grateful she didn't wait for an answer. "Oh, guess what? Daddy knows this guy who owns a jazz bar in SoHo. Well, he used to own it, so we went back to see if he still did. It turns out his son owns it now. But anyway, he invited me to do a show there on December twenty-ninth and thirtieth. Like a pre-New-Year's-Eve thing. Isn't that cool?"

"Very cool, Meegan," Tristen said, trying to keep the camera still as he walked faster. "I wish I could go, but I have the concert with The Seethers."

"Look at us. Two musicians trying to make it," she said. "I better go. Don't go to that job without a shower."

"Obviously. Why would I do that?"

"I don't know." Meegan pouted into the camera. "Did you get me a pretty present? I can't wait to open it when I get home."

"You're going to love it," Tristen lied. He had no present yet. Sales started in two days. "Are you staying there through New Year's Eve, then?"

"What a good idea," Meegan said. "We could shop the sales. I'm going to talk to my parents."

"I gotta go, Meegan."

"Sure. Merry Christmas. Daddy, I have an idea!"

Tristen hit the red button for the second time and slipped back into a jog. With or without a steady heart rate, he was determined to finish his run. He needed it more than coffee.

Tristen wrapped audio wires around his arm as one of the departing lighting volunteers wished him a Merry Christmas. A few others, already bundled in their coats, shuffled past without noticing him. Not that it mattered.

"You about ready?" called Paul, the one who held all the keys to the building.

"Yeah, just about," Tristen told him. "I'll need two trips to the car."

"Throw me your keys, and I'll drive it up to the door."

Tristen pulled his keys out, along with his phone. The screen lit up with several missed calls and messages, mostly Merry Christmas texts. Talon had sent a generic group text to everyone he knew with a photo of him and Sandra in the snow. Sandra was even smiling. Another text was from Meegan confirming she wouldn't be home until New Year's Eve.

Another week alone. The bed was getting lonely without her, but it was better this way. He could do these odd jobs, then focus on Pete's. Once the guys were back at it, they had a lot of work ahead of them. It would be best if Meegan was occupied for that.

"Here you are," Paul said. He handed Tristen a small Bible with an envelope sticking out.

"I don't need—I mean, I already have a Bible," Tristen stuttered. He snapped his mouth shut and kept it shut when he couldn't think of a different way to say 'No thanks.'

Paul chuckled. "Can never have too many Bibles. Besides, you might want your Christmas bonus. We thought it was only right, since you're here after everyone else has already left."

"You're here," Tristen pointed out.

"I'm paid to be here, and I'm going home now. Merry Christmas."

"Thanks," Tristen said, waving the envelope. "I appreciate it."

To keep some semblance of pride, he waited until he was in his car to open the envelope, expecting fifty dollars but hoping for at least a hundred. Two crisp one-hundred-dollar bills slipped out.

"Nice," he muttered, turning the key and dialing on his phone at the same time. "Hey, man, you still running that poker game tonight?"

If he could win a few rounds, he could get Meegan a present that she deserved. The kind she got from her dad.

"Course. Buy-in starts at one-fifty."

"Count me in."

Chapter 6

"Merry Christmas, Bobbi."

"Yeah, yeah. I'm not calling 'bout that."

Tristen's head pounded in protest as he rolled over in bed. The poker game had gone well, doubling his bonus, but it had run late. He'd drunk more than a few whiskeys and hadn't had enough time to sleep it off.

"What are you calling about so early, Bobbi?"

"You better watch your tone with me, kid. You aren't too old to put over my knee with the switch."

Tristen would have laughed, but he knew it would annoy her and she'd hang up on him. Of course, he was too old and far too heavy for her to put over her knees. He'd been too big since he was sixteen, but that didn't stop her from threatening it.

"You still there?" Bobbi demanded.

"Yes, Bobbi. Waiting for you to tell me why you're calling. Is Ivy sick?"

"Well, she ain't dead, at least."

"Okay," Tristen drawled. Bobbi and Ivy fought and loved each other like sisters. When Tristen and Talon were ten, they'd acted as messengers between the two women because they refused to address each other directly—for an entire year. When the year was over, neither woman could remember what the fight had been about. "What is going on, Bobbi? You two get into a fight?"

Silence answered him. Bobbi didn't take kindly to snark, and his question had been mostly snark. He was a grown man, yet her silence made him feel like the switch was coming for his backside at any moment.

"Well, well, Mr. Tristen has gotten a bit big for his britches, hasn't he?" Bobbi said eventually. She sighed heavily, or blew out her cigarette smoke. "For your information, young man, I'm calling because your fool mother was working for some bike delivery place, taking lazy people a Christmas Eve snack."

"You mean Ryder? That company that delivers food to you?"

Another sigh into the phone. "I don't know what it's called. All I know is, my fool cousin got hit by a car while on a bike. I don't think she even knows how to ride a bike."

Tristen almost dropped the phone. "She got hit by a car? I thought you said she was fine!"

"I never said she was fine!" Bobbi practically yelled. Tristen had to turn the volume down a couple notches. "I said she ain't dead. Guess she wasn't moving, and the car was just trying to park, so it wasn't going fast, but she broke her leg. Damn fool."

Tristen sighed with relief. Just a broken leg. "Wait, why was she working for Ryder?"

"Extra cash, I guess. Anyway, you know your mama. She's gonna expect the works from you today. You coming over?"

"Yeah," Tristen said, groaning as he pulled himself into a sitting position.

"What's wrong with you?"

"Nothing. Just waking up. Had a rough night."

Bobbi snorted. Tristen was grateful she chose not to comment.

"Guess I should figure out Christmas dinner or something?"

"Dunno. I'm headin' to my daughter's house. You're on your own with Ivy. I just thought I'd warn you."

"Well, thanks for that."

"Sure thing. Have a Merry Christmas. Hope to see you around again soon if I don't see you today."

"I'll come around," Tristen said, though he had no intention of doing so. He didn't see the point in telling that to Bobbi.

After a shower and a quick stop for gas, he was on the road armed with a hot coffee and two painkillers. Without the usual traffic on the roads, he made it to Ivy's house in less than an hour and a half.

"Ivy?" he hollered from the bottom of the front porch steps. No answer.

He stepped over the nails and hammer left from her birthday and the project he'd planned to finish but couldn't because Talon decided they had to listen to his tales of the tour instead. The front door was locked. He didn't remember it ever being locked his entire childhood.

"Ivy?" Tristen knocked again, wishing he could see through the bay window into the living room. Trying to see inside, he almost fell over Ivy's rocking chair, which she claimed she had used when they were babies. He didn't believe her, but he liked the idea of the stories. Behind the rocking chair were three pots full of dirt, one with the dried-up remnants of a poinsettia plant. Tristen lifted it from the saucer to find an old key.

"Ivy?" This time he whispered in case she was asleep. The house was dark, with all the curtains pulled. He pulled the door closed behind him and crept into the galley kitchen.

"Tristen?"

"Shit, Ivy." He gripped the edge of the doorway, unable to hide how much she had startled him—which, of course, made her laugh. "I told you I'd come to see you."

"Look what happened," she said, lugging her booted leg across the floor. "Can you believe this? Apparently my bones are brittle, so I gotta start taking calcium too. Otherwise this could happen to the other one."

"How'd it break?" Tristen asked, opening the fridge to see what the options were for Christmas dinner. When she didn't answer, he closed the door and turned.

"I didn't say it was broken." Ivy looked at him, rolling a joint between her fingers. She could roll a joint with her eyes closed.

"Bobbi told me."

"You knew I broke my leg and didn't come to see me?" she said, her eyes narrowing as the lighter lit up her face. "You let me sit all alone, bored out of my mind, in that hospital?"

"Bobbi told me this morning, Ivy. I came right when I hung up on her."

"Oh, sure. But you could have called me on the phone. Like, you aren't even worried about me or how I'm getting along in the house or if I'm in pain?"

"I figured you would manage your pain just fine. And look, you are. Managing it just fine."

Ivy blew smoke rings in his direction.

"Cut it out, Ivy. I came right away. How are you doing?"

"It hurts a little, but I'm okay."

"What were you doing? Bobbi says you were on a bike. Working for Ryder."

Ivy pretended to be captivated by the Christmas tree lights blinking on and off.

"Ivy?"

"Yeah?"

"What were you doing when you broke your leg?"

"Car hit me while I was on a bike."

"Why the hell were you riding a bike?"

Ivy finally looked at him. "You think I can sue?"

Tristen sat down next to her on the couch. Talking to his mom sometimes was like talking to a little kid. But showing frustration with her never advanced the conversation, either. He picked up her booted foot and placed a pillow underneath it, forcing her to lie down.

"Pretty sure you need to get that swelling down. Didn't they say anything about that? Did they recommend you take an anti-inflammatory?"

"Yeah, they gave me stuff. It's over there. I wasn't sure if I should take it." Her eyes met his, and he glimpsed a glimmer of the woman she could have been, that deeper understanding of should and shouldn't, before her eyes closed again. "I wouldn't mind a painkiller."

Tristen picked up the bag and checked the contents. "Stupid doctors. Who did you see?"

"Emergency room. Duh. In Lexington…" Her words drifted off until he could barely hear them, but he didn't need her to repeat herself.

"They didn't look into your charts or anything?"

Ivy shrugged. "Guess not."

"You didn't take this, did you?"

"No," she said quietly. "Just been relying on my gummies. I thought maybe it was an opioid. Didn't want to disappoint you. Didn't want to relapse."

Her eyes were closing slowly. She must have smoked and taken gummies. The combination always used to knock her out for at least an hour. Her own special sleeping cocktail, she called it.

Tristen pulled out his phone and called Ivy's doctor, but all he got was the answering machine. "Of course, it's Christmas." He'd have to call tomorrow. In the meantime, he went outside and threw the medication into his glove compartment. Ivy had been strong the night before, but there was no telling whether she would stay strong.

A stiff wind snapped through the magnolia tree's branches as though saluting him. He didn't salute back. Maybe he wasn't an opioid addict like Ivy was, but he wasn't innocent. He and Talon had fooled around with different stuff, especially when Luke was in jail. However, they'd been too focused on sports and boxing to get into anything too heavy. Aimee… she didn't have boxing. She had chorus and theater. And no one thought those kids were doing anything. No one saw it coming.

It should have been obvious, but they weren't looking for it. Not until late one night when Aimee called, high, her voice garbled, the address she gave incomplete. By the time he and Luke found it, she was gone.

Tristen scrubbed his face with his palms. Those weren't thoughts for Christmas Day. Or any other day.

He shook the worst of his memories away and focused on the present. What they needed was food. And he doubted Ivy had much of anything in her kitchen. She wasn't the type to regularly grocery shop. He walked to the mailbox; the metal door hung down, unable to close from all the junk mail. Perhaps there'd be a coupon for Hank's, the local dive joint, for burgers. Or maybe Ivy would prefer to go out. In that case, he could use the money he'd won at poker to take her out in style.

He sifted through glossy papers, grocery store ads, realtor ads persuading Ivy to sell her house, and flyers for her to switch internet providers. Tristen sorted them, looking for anything important. Since Ivy tended to ignore bills until the last minute, he and Talon had convinced her a few years back to set up most everything on automatic bank draft, but the occasional something slipped through. Like parking tickets. Or ambulance bills.

Urgent. Do Not Throw Away.

First one and then two of them—looking very real and unlike junk mail. Tristen ripped them open.

One was a medical bill about to go to collections, and the other was a credit card bill she hadn't paid in months for over five thousand dollars. Tristen flipped the medical bill over. It was too soon for the weekend emergency visit, and he couldn't remember anything big happening that would create a two-thousand-dollar bill. Of course, there was no information that could help him sort anything out.

But the bills did explain why she had taken a job with Ryder. Which she now couldn't fulfil because her leg was broken.

Tristen looked up towards the bay window where Ivy was sleeping on the couch, just beyond the glass. This was not how he wanted to spend Christmas, but it was better to find out now than later. He would have to call Talon and see if Ivy could borrow some money. And instead of splurging on a crazy Christmas dinner out, he could head to Hank's for hamburgers and milkshakes and give the rest of his winnings from poker toward her bills. It wouldn't make much of a dent, but the money was free money, basically. He could have lost it.

One problem, though—Meegan expected a gift for Christmas, so he couldn't give Ivy more than three hundred. Or maybe two fifty after he bought dinner and filled his tank again.

He slapped his thigh with the bills and got in his car. It was the only plan he could think of. Maybe there would be another poker game soon. He'd just have to hope that his luck continued.

Tristen didn't bring out the two envelopes until after they had eaten their hamburgers and almost finished their shakes. Ivy had been so happy when he came home with the food.

"I haven't eaten there in years. I wonder if it's still as good," she'd exclaimed when she saw him come in with the greasy paper bags. All throughout their childhood, she had claimed she didn't eat out to save her figure. He'd later found out it was because they were poor.

"I found these in the mail, Ivy," Tristen said, placing the bills on the table in front of her. "Wanna tell me what's going on?"

The mood cooled instantly. Ivy sat back in her chair, exchanging her milkshake for her stash of weed and rolling papers, never taking her eyes off the bills.

"It's a crime to open someone else's mail," she said, her lips barely moving. The house was so still he heard her anyway.

"You gonna press charges, Ivy?"

She licked her rolling paper and cinched the joint closed, then took out her lighter and inhaled.

"Come on. We gotta figure this out. Why did you let it get this bad? And what is this medical bill?"

"That's from my appendicitis."

"From two years ago?" Tristen leaned back in his chair, gathering a memory from years before. "Wait a minute. Talon and I gave you money for that."

"Other things came up," Ivy said. "The money you gave me was great, and I appreciated it. And I did put some of the money toward the bill."

"What else did you do with it?"

"There was this great opportunity to invest. You know, lots of states, besides Kentucky because this state is stuck in the dark ages, have loosened regulations about weed. No, stop." Ivy waved the joint near his face when it was clear Tristen wanted to interrupt. "Just 'cause you don't like it doesn't mean that the rest of America doesn't like it. People are buying the products all kinds of ways. It's a booming industry."

Tristen breathed in through his nose to keep his heartbeat regular. When she paused long enough, he allowed himself to ask another question, even though he already expected the answer. "What kind of investment was it, Ivy?"

"Don't talk to me with that tone of voice, like you're clenching your teeth. It was an investment in a weed farm, and everything was going fine until—"

"In Kentucky?"

"Hell, no. In Virginia." Ivy shook her head. "As I was saying, everything was going fine until the county redrew their lines, and suddenly, they weren't gonna allow a farm unless we all paid a ton more money."

"Did you ever get any money back on the investment?"

"How? That's not how these thing work. The farm went under. Besides, I had to convince two people to invest under me. I had already gotten Rick from the factory. He was super excited. And his friend Marc was about to come on board when I got news that everything had shut down."

"But they sold the land, right? So you should have gotten some of your money back." Smoke rings hit him square in the face, but he refused to flinch. "Ivy."

"No, okay? Everyone had to get paid back first, and I was one of the last people to get in, so of course I didn't get any money back. Plus, Rick was real mad and he's my shift manager, so to keep the peace, I paid him back his thousand out of my own paycheck."

"How much did you put in?"

"Five thousand."

Tristen knew he couldn't lose his cool. Fred used to scream, and Luke used to throw punches into the wall, but Tristen wasn't like them and never wanted to be. Still, he wished he had some outlet to release his anger.

"Okay, so you lost five thousand." He breathed out slowly, trying to absorb the news.

"Well, six thousand, 'cause I paid back Rick. And then, you know, life happens. Like the internet went up, and food prices, and I paid a little each month, but then it just got to be too much. And the car engine had trouble, and I needed new tires." Tears started streaming down her cheeks. He knew they were real because she tried to wipe them away without drawing attention to them. When she brought on her fake tears, she wanted everyone to notice them.

"Okay, okay. Listen, we gotta get this taken care of. You need to call the medical billing place, this number here, tomorrow. You hear me? Tomorrow. And ask them what is the minimum that they'd take to get this paid in full. I have a few hundred stashed I can give for this credit card bill, okay? But we gotta figure something out."

"That's why I was working for Ryder."

"Ivy, come on," Tristen said, but immediately changed course. "You can't work for them anymore, so we'll have to figure something else out. Okay? What about work? Have you told them that your foot is broken?"

"I'm gonna have that medical bill too, now," Ivy said with a groan.

"Okay. Here, I got an idea. You're gonna have to consolidate this, okay? You'll just have to call some debt place tomorrow and do whatever they say."

Ivy crushed her joint out in the ashtray. Her eyes were red-rimmed, and her usually pretty face was hollow and strained. "I'll call, I guess. Just give me the number."

"I'll have to find it. But we'll figure it out, okay? I have to work tomorrow and the next day at this place called the Blue Canyon, but I'll come back afterward and help you."

"You singing? I'd love to come hear you."

"No," Tristen said, jumping up from the seat to throw away the melting sludges that had been milkshakes. "I'm doing some repair work around the bar. They need some new cabinets hung and a new sound system put in. Pays well enough, and I need cash 'cause I quit my job to take on The Seethers full-time. And we aren't exactly raking it in at the moment."

Ivy grabbed his hand and gave him a weak smile. "It'll take off. Look at Talon. He's doing so well. Your turn will be soon."

Tristen waited a beat before pulling his hand away. He was twenty-five going on twenty-six. He hoped his turn was next.

Chapter 7

The day of the concert at Pete's, Tristen woke up as usual to go for a run but found his body protesting every movement. He managed to make it to the bathroom and look in the mirror. A black eye stared back at him.

Memories from the night before started trickling into his brain when he saw the bruises around his ribs.

He'd gone to a poker game earlier in the evening. He was two hundred in the hole when the guy across the table, who'd spent the night chewing on a giant cigar, suddenly accused Tristen of cheating. Tristen refuted the claims, taking off his shirt to show he had no way to hide any cards.

That was when the first punch was thrown. He didn't know who hit him, just that it made him angry, and he immediately responded in kind. It was nice to find out he was still good at it, knocking the guy to his right out with two punches and putting the cigar-guy against a wall within a few minutes. Years had passed since he was in the ring, but it could have been yesterday, the way his mind and body had responded.

He couldn't help grinning at himself in the mirror. He hadn't known it, but he'd needed the win last night. Winning against the three guys who came after him was almost as good as winning money. Almost. More than the black eye, the problem last night was that the fight had put an end to the game, so he was two hundred poorer today instead of richer.

The day passed slowly as he worked to fix the sound at Blue Canyon. He wore a hat to hide the black eye and kept his groaning to himself each time he had to twist or bend down. That, too, was muscle memory. He'd had to hide his boxing during his last years of high school as well.

"Done yet?" Andre asked as Tristen gathered the cords and pushed them through a black tube to hold them together.

"Yeah, finally done." The job had been much more complicated than Andre had told him it would be, but his work in construction and odd jobs had helped Tristen figure it out.

"Pay you through the app or in cash?"

Tristen preferred cash. He still had to buy a present for Meegan, but he also had to send money for his and Ivy's bills.

"App is fine," he said. He would be less tempted to play poker with it if it was digital.

He called Ivy on his way to Pete's. The last time they'd talked, she'd told him what the consolidation company had said. "Pay off the smaller bills first. Which means the medical bill."

"Hey, Ivy, just checking in," Tristen said when she answered. He gave Andre a quiet wave goodbye and shuffled through the door.

"Tristen," she squealed.

"You sound happy."

"Why wouldn't I be happy? Your brother called."

That was unexpected. "That's nice. How's his vacation in Europe?" He tried to think of a way to ask if she had told Talon about the bills. After all, he should help out as well.

"He sounded happy. But then, I would be too if I was skiing in Italy."

"Italy? Damn." He had seen the posts earlier on Talon's social media, but didn't want to admit it in case Ivy read too much into it. He wasn't stalking his brother. He didn't actually care what Talon and Sandra were doing. The feed had simply pushed the pictures in his face. And he wasn't jealous of Talon seeing the world. Four countries in the last few months… It would be his turn someday. His turn had to come. "Did you tell him about—"

"That's what I wanted to tell you. Talon sent me the thousand to pay off the medical bill. The old one."

"So it's paid off?" Tristen began the short drive to Pete's.

"Yep." Ivy sounded proud of herself. Tristen was relieved and slightly vindicated. He had messaged Talon, but never received an answer from his brother.

"That's great, Ivy."

"It's a relief, is what it is."

"Did you hear more from the consolidation company?"

"Not yet. I'm gathering all my papers and stuff and emailing them to the person helping me. What's all that noise?"

"I just pulled up to Pete's. We're getting ready to play." Tristen pulled his car into a spot in the back alleyway. He didn't realize his mistake until it was too late.

"You said you weren't performing," Ivy said.

"I didn't think of it when you asked last week." Tristen cringed, but couldn't think of a better excuse.

"Whatever. I'll talk to you later, Tristen. Break a leg."

Ivy hung up, and Tristen stared at the phone for a second. Usually, Ivy sounded angry about him leaving her out. This time she had sounded almost sad. He was considering calling her back when the alley door opened.

"Tris? You're late," Randall called from the door.

"Sorry." Tristen hated that Randall was the one who got to point it out to him.

"Adam says he wants to get this over with." Randall kept the metal door open, holding his hands up when Tristen turned his frustrated glare on him. "His words, not mine. We got maybe thirty minutes. Those Va Voom girls are almost done."

The crowd erupted into cheers. Tristen tried to relax as they headed in, but a nervous energy clung to his throat. He hadn't been nervous going on stage since the first few times he and Talon had started their twin show at The Patriot Bar seven years before. He took a careful breath and tried to calm down. The twin show was how they'd discovered Talon was a better frontman.

"Nervous?" Randall asked as they entered their green room. Micah and Adam were already there, drinking beer.

"What? For Pete's? No way," Tristen said, rolling his shoulders back. "They like us here. I mean, Willis wouldn't invite us back if he didn't like us, or if his clientele didn't."

"Sure," Randall said. There was little conviction in his voice, but Tristen ignored it. The Seethers had made it this far—far enough to tour with Art of Rendering, even.

"Let's get some video for social media." The thrill of being back on stage shot through him. "Did we bring the camera stand?"

"Should be in there," Adam said, pointing to a bag in the corner.

"All right, would you check? We gotta get back into the game, you know?"

No one responded. Micah sat stretching and warming up his joint muscles.

"Where'd Randall go?" Tristen asked.

"I'm right here," he said from behind him, drinking a bottle of water.

"Come on, guys. We get to play for the crowd again."

Micah jumped up and down, then twisted left and right. "Tristen's right. Pete's has always been good to us, right? And we enjoy playing, all of us, right?"

"Sure, man. We like playing our instruments," Randall drawled.

He was such an asshole sometimes.

"I know we're still mad at my brother, but let's do this right—"

"Tristen, okay," Micah said. "We'll do this right. The people out there deserve a clean set tonight. But Karine Melanie offered me a job come next year. And I took it."

Tristen stopped looking for the camera stand. Adam and Randall surrounded Micah to thump him on the back, but the lump in Tristen's throat made it difficult for him to speak. He grabbed a bottle of water and drank it all in one go to give himself some time. Karine Melanie was probably as big as Art of Rendering. Maybe more.

"Congrats, Micah," he finally said. "When do you start?"

"Already started, actually. Our first concert is in Madison, Wisconsin, in a week. Then Chicago, then here in Cincinnati."

He listed off more cities, but the room was suddenly too hot for Tristen to pay attention.

"I think that's our cue." He grabbed his guitar and left, going over his set-up checklist in his head. *Check the wires, do a sound check on the small stage, find some water.* The Va Voom girls were gone already, giving him some space to be alone. And he needed a moment.

Pete's was small, but the stage was raised two feet off the bar floor, which made it one of Tristen's favorites. The intimacy of playing and singing so close to the customers gave him an energy he didn't get anywhere else so far.

And now, he might never be back.

If he couldn't replace Micah, and fast, The Seethers were done. Tristen glanced back down the hall. It was empty. For a moment, he wondered if they would abandon him. Just not appear on stage at all. Ghost him, like Talon had.

But the door to the green room opened, and Randall walked through with his guitar in hand. Tristen pushed his thoughts aside and started the sound check. They could find a new drummer, no problem. Drummers were a dime a dozen. And Randall and Adam would stay.

"Check, check."

The words echoed out into Pete's as Randall adjusted his mic. Tristen took a deep breath and nodded to him. He had been so nervous during Christmas that Randall would announce he was quitting that he had almost forgotten Micah and Adam. In the end, it was Micah who tossed the accelerant on the flame.

The soundcheck on the drums startled him out of his thoughts. They had a concert to give. Maybe they could relaunch under a different name. Tristen set up his phone to capture as much of the show as he could, his confidence higher. Tonight was going to be a good night. He was sure of it.

"Don't be down, man." Adam snaked an arm around Tristen's shoulders and pulled him into a side hug, finishing it as he always did with a punch to the shoulder that was too strong to be called friendly.

"Let's play some music," he shouted, receiving a tepid response from Randall and Micah.

About fifty people drank beer on the small main floor, with more filling the top balcony bar. It wasn't an AOR turnout, but it wasn't the worst they'd ever played. Tristen rolled his shoulders back and reminded himself he was supposed to play the same for one person as he would play for a thousand. The same energy, the same dedication.

"Hello, everyone getting drunk at Pete's," Adam said, his deep voice resonating across the room. "How's everyone doing tonight?"

A handful of people clapped.

"We're The Seethers, and we're going to play some songs for you. If that's okay." This time, Adam didn't wait for an answer. He hit the chord for 'Get On, Get Out' on his bass. It wasn't the first song on the list they had discussed, but Tristen swallowed his annoyance. The rhythm was catchy enough to wake people up. Adam hit the first two lines of the song, then shouted, "One, two, three, four."

Micah picked up the beat; Randall came in. Suddenly they were professional, putting the performance above their own feelings. Tristen focused on the task.

Before they reached the middle of the song, the people at the back were pushing their way forward. Tristen hit the mic and joined Adam at the bridge, a change they had made in the recent weeks. It sounded perfect. One reason he loved Pete's was because the lights weren't so glaring that he couldn't see the people. Dozens were dancing or swaying, encouraging them.

The song ended, and Adam signaled for them to keep going. Tristen bit back his annoyance at him taking over; it wasn't like it was his band. Still, the important thing was that they kept playing. The crowd moved to the middle of the venue to dance as they played.

It wasn't until after the fourth song that someone in the crowd shouted Talon's name. Tristen peered out into the dim club. In the back right corner, a group of young men in the back were laughing.

"What did you say?" Adam asked into the mic.

Randall continued to play the intro of 'It All Comes to This' in the background, but Adam stopped. Tristen followed suit.

"You suck without Talon," the guy shouted, clear as day. His boys laughed loudly.

"Things change, man," Adam shouted back. "If you don't like the way we play, you can spend the money on an Art of Rendering concert ticket."

Tristen strummed his guitar to drown out the idiots who intended to ruin the night. Randall joined in, and eventually so did Adam, but he was clearly seething. And once Adam was angry, he couldn't let it go. He strummed a little faster, forcing the rest of them to keep up.

It was Tristen's song to sing, but he missed the intro, and they had to go round again. He scanned the crowd. No one noticed except for the handful who had been ready to sing on the right cue.

He was sure the guy in the crowd yelled out, "Loser!"

After a deep breath, he belted into the mic at the right moment and made it through the entire song, blood pumping through his veins with every beat of the drums and strum of the guitar. He had found the rhythm, and he was flying. As the song came to an end, Randall stepped closer.

"Keep going," he mouthed.

Tristen's mind went blank, but that didn't stop Randall from going straight into the song.

Adam blared out his bass, glaring at Randall, who shrugged at the crowd. A nervous snicker moved through them.

"Okay, everyone, we're going to play a new song for you tonight." Off mic, Adam turned to Tristen, who still felt frozen. "You take the lead."

"Me?" Tristen asked, but Adam was right. He'd written the song. Adam didn't bother to answer before going to Micah, who was playing the old version of the song. They had tweaked it at the last practice to accommodate Tristen's voice, which Micah wouldn't know because he didn't bother to come.

"Let's go," Tristen shouted before stepping up to the mic. Adam hit his bass, standing just close enough to Randall to appear as though he was threatening him—but whatever fight was coming at the end of the night, Tristen would worry about later.

"Keep sayin' all you're sayin',
The words just fly by and you know
I'm findin' that all your lyin'
makes me want to just beeeeeeeeeee"– Tristen strained his vocal cords to hit the notes.

"Better than you. A better man than you."

Back at the chorus, Tristen tried to lower his octave to keep his voice from straining again, but it resulted in his voice cracking. The movement in the crowd slowly came to a stop. That would have been bad enough, but a water bottle sailed out of the audience and struck him in the face. It was mostly empty, thankfully. He'd been hit harder the night before, but the surprise was enough to stop him from singing.

Randall's fingers slipped off the guitar strings as he erupted into laughter. Half the crowd followed. Tristen swallowed. He wanted to rub his face, but he also wanted to pretend it hadn't happened.

Micah lifted his hands in the air in surrender; a voice announced over the speakers that throwing objects would be met with the highest penalty. As though to make a point, a security guard grabbed a guy's arm and escorted him out.

"All right, everyone," said Micah. "We aren't going to let that incident keep us from enjoying some music."

Someone in the crowd whistled.

"You call that music?" another man from the corner countered.

Tristen's fingers tripped over the strings. He looked at Micah, who nodded curtly before starting the beat to their most popular song. One of their first.

Assuming he would be the one to take Talon's place, Tristen started in. But Adam did, too. The song wasn't bad as a duet, and if they hadn't already struggled up to that point, perhaps they could have kept going and found a new sound. Tristen would think about that for days afterward, wondering why he hadn't just calmed down. But Adam wasn't supposed to be singing, and yet there he was, taking over again. So Tristen sang louder—which wasn't a good idea for his range—while trying to get Adam's attention. When he messed up a note, Adam turned to him and gave him a signal to let up and hit the harmony, but Tristen ignored it. He could see the guys in the corner laughing together.

His anger getting the better of him, Tristen pulled the mic from the stand and tried to engage the crowd, but they simply looked at him like he was a clown. He tripped up on the words. Adam looked at him, his left eyebrow raised—the look Fred used to give Tristen when he was angry, or Javon when he was annoyed. Tristen tried to move on, but he hit the wrong note again, this time on the wrong beat.

Adam stopped singing. Panicked that no lyrics were going out, Tristen scrambled to pick them up again, only to realize that Adam stopped singing because it was the musical bridge. Randall's solo. Randall stopped playing and waited, his hands crossed over his guitar.

Tristen turned to look at him. The last thing he saw was Randall's fist coming right at his nose.

Tristen fell back into the mic stand, the feet of the stand poking straight into his back. Randall walked away, and the crowd jeered. The lights went dead.

Chapter 8

A SLIVER OF SUNLIGHT landed across Tristen's forehead, burning a line across his skin.

Lifting his hand was like lifting a weight in a black hole. He grimaced. Falling forever would be better than the torture he was in now, his head against something rock hard, his back contorted to the right. When he had first woken up, the position seemed comfortable. Now he thought he'd never be able to straighten out again. His bones creaked with the effort of getting up, but his throat was too dry to moan.

"Damn drinking."

His throat was on fire, the words barely coming out. Everything hurt as he moved, especially his head.

Slowly, his brain cells connected long enough to shoot pain through his tingling hand. Tristen lowered it, wincing at the jumbled messages firing through his neurons—pain, numbness, tingling, heaviness. The night before came back in fits and phases, and he had to concentrate on placing them in the correct sequence in his head.

Mac, a guy involved in underground boxing whom Tristen had worked with five years before, when he'd first moved to Cincinnati, had called him two days earlier proposing an entertainment fight.

"I'll pay you five hundred, straight cash," Mac had said.

Tristen had no desire to be fighting again, but he needed money. After the disaster at Pete's two weeks before, The Seethers had broken apart with Adam telling everyone to never contact him again. When Mac called, Tristen had jumped at the chance to do something, punch someone and pretend it was Adam's or Randall's face.

He'd expected it to be easy, since he'd fought in the ring for Luke and Owen from the time he was sixteen until he left home at nineteen. The other guy was okay, but he made a rookie mistake in the third round, dropping his hand from his face. And Tristen was ready for it.

Pain blooming in his forehead reminded him of how much he'd drunk afterward. His stomach echoed the discomfort. If he had stopped when he'd won the boxing match, he would have been okay. Instead, he'd stayed to celebrate, basking in the shouts of congratulations and the pouring of expensive whiskey. Tristen pulled out the roll of bills that proved he had won the match and smiled.

The kid raised to always lose, whether called by his own name or by his brother's, had won.

On the bedroom chair, his pants from the night before boasted a large smear of blood. He needed to vomit. Or drink water. Maybe pee.

Tristen gripped the edge of the hard surface he was lying on and sat up. The world darkened for a moment before coming back into focus. The tingling in his arm finally ceased as a flood of warmth lit up his nerves.

Despite feeling physically sick, Tristen couldn't help being proud of himself. He had to; no one else would. He couldn't tell Meegan he had been fighting, and he wasn't talking to his brother. Not after Talon shared a video of Pete's on his social media with a laughing emoji. He'd deleted it afterwards, but not before Tristen saw it.

The room tilted again, stopping when he closed his eyes. Straightening his spine brought bile bubbling up. After some slow breathing, he could open his eyes again. His head rolled like a bowling ball, barely able to stay on his neck straight. The insides of his stomach lurched and flopped, but he couldn't help laughing when he saw that his bed the night before was the dining table in Meegan's townhouse. Shooting pain from one temple to the other stopped his laughter dead.

Tristen trudged upstairs to the bathroom. If he was correct, they were due to have lunch with Meegan's dad that day. Or maybe dinner. Hopefully dinner.

To his right, the sliding doors that led to the bedroom were cracked open. Tristen peered in. A soft snort escaped from a large heap of blankets piled on top of the bed. Meegan must be somewhere underneath them.

Tristen turned slowly. Perhaps a cold shower would make him feel better.

In the bathroom, he dared to look at his face. To his relief, he only had minor bruising. Anything more, and he wouldn't be able to explain it to Meegan or her dad later. He leaned into the mirror and touched a delicate spot on his cheek where a bruise was blossoming under the blond stubble. He could feel his opponent's fist against his face even now. He had gotten in a few good punches Tristen shouldn't have allowed. He checked closer. A few days of not shaving should hide it, and if he put some ice on it soon, it might not become much at all. There was a burn on his right bicep from running into the ropes, but despite everything, he looked better than he felt.

The head-throbbing continued as he slowly peeled off his clothes, but now he could differentiate between the hangover and the left hooks he'd received against his temple—the ones that lost him the second round.

Under his ribs, a large circle was already black, with speckles of red busted blood vessels circling out like a firecracker. He poked at himself to assess the damage, then took a deep breath. All clear. No broken ribs. He'd had several before.

Tristen rolled his shoulders back, admiring the muscle tone. He was back to the fitness level of when he and Talon had been boxing together. A level that didn't come easy to him but had been helped by the stress of Talon leaving and the band dissolving. Instead of sitting around Meegan's house worrying about what to do, he'd been hitting the gym almost every day.

The exercise had done nothing for his career, but he was pleased with the physical effects.

He wondered what Talon's fitness level was. He surely couldn't work out much with all the touring Art of Rendering did. Without thinking, Tristen picked up the phone and opened his social media. It never took long to find a post from AOR. Apparently the apps thought he wanted updates on them at all times. Probably because he couldn't help checking what they were doing. Thankfully, with over a million followers, he doubted they knew he was one of them.

In the latest post, Talon was sitting with Jake at a bar table, clinking large mugs of beer. The caption read: *Nothing better than playing at home.* They were in Cincinnati again, or at least in the vicinity.

Tristen sighed and forced himself to click the phone off. It didn't matter where his brother was or what he was doing. He needed to focus on himself and his own future.

He rubbed his face vigorously with open palms as his stomach lurched, possibly at the idea of seeing Talon again, or maybe because of his current disreputable state.

"Don't vomit, don't vomit," he murmured as sweat beaded on his forehead. He willed his body to cooperate, but it refused to obey.

"Tristen?" Meegan called as his dinner and drinks from the night before came out. Being punched in the stomach several times didn't help.

He grunted.

"Not feeling well?" she asked from outside the bathroom.

"Better now," he called back, wiping sweat from his brow and relieved to find his body cooling down. "I'm gonna take a shower."

Meegan's arm slipped through the crack in the door, swinging a bottle of green water through the opening. "Take this. It'll help you feel better."

"You can come in." Tristen took the plastic bottle from her. Tiny green pieces floated in it, though it didn't smell bad. Like water with a hint of apple. He sipped it slowly. It didn't taste like much, either.

"I'll stay out here," Meegan said. Her back was turned to him. She grabbed a thick lock of hair and combed through it with her long fingers. "Kinda stinks in there. You going to be okay for dinner with Daddy tonight?"

Tristen sighed with relief. "It's dinner? Thank God, I thought it might be lunch. I'll be fine."

"Good. He says he wants to talk to us."

Tristen's stomach knotted.

"I'm looking forward to it," he said. He had a feeling he was the one Simon really wanted to talk to; Meegan could do no wrong in her dad's eyes. "I'm going to head into a cold shower. I'll see you in a minute."

He saw Meegan shudder through the cracked door then disappear. Tristen closed the door and prepped himself for the cold, his mind swirling.

Meegan's dad, Simon, was polite with him but not very warm, perhaps because it was easy to assume that Tristen was mooching off Meegan. That would change. Hopefully soon. He had helped record Meegan's next album, which was going to be a hit, so he should earn some royalties from it. He was thinking of maybe finding more singers or musicians to record, since he had the know-how, maybe take a break from stage. After Pete's, he had no desire to sing in front of people again. Of course, he needed to find a studio he could work from and figure out how much to charge. Which all seemed like it would take forever.

In the immediate future, he could sell off the instruments and equipment that The Seethers no longer needed. And, if he was desperate, he could find a temporary construction job. At least he didn't have as much rent to pay, since Simon owned the building Meegan lived in. His living with Meegan probably didn't help his relationship with her father, but Tristen couldn't afford to change that.

Though he was sure he loved Meegan, her lifestyle was expensive. Simon treated her like a princess, so Meegan's expectations from Tristen were high. He'd never seen a woman need so many luxury items or high-end dinners. But he also admired that she didn't change for him. He preferred a girlfriend with high expectations over one who wouldn't fit where he was eventually going. Because at some point, he would be on top, far from where he was now.

The cold water landed like daggers in his back. Tristen turned off the shower.

If all else failed, maybe he could find a few more fights. Poker was all luck, but boxing wasn't. Not for him. He knew what he was doing. When the guys had bet on his opponent the night before because he was wide-shouldered, weighed two hundred and forty pounds and could bench press three hundred, Tristen had let them. He'd seen enough skinny or small guys win in the boxing ring. By the time he was eighteen, he'd fought in one hundred matches and seen countless more.

It was that knowledge that had won him the money last night.

"Thanks, man," he muttered to Luke's ghost. No one had seen Luke since he skipped out on Ivy six years before. Tristen imagined him dead; he'd had an affinity for working in the darker, seedier areas of life.

Family was another reason Meegan's dad didn't like him. Meegan could trace her mother's Lebanese roots back generations. Simon could trace his family tree back to some prince or duke or something in England. Tristen had met Ivy's dad twice in his life, had never met his other grandparents, and generally thought of himself as someone without a family tree. And certainly without roots.

He finished the green water, pleased to find his stomach still settled and his head throbbing less.

"What did you do last night?" Meegan asked, tiptoeing into the bathroom.

"Went to watch that poker game," Tristen said, marveling at how much better he felt. And how easily he could lie to her. "What I told you I was going to do."

"Aw, baby," she said, examining his face. "Is that a bruise on your cheek?"

Tristen touched it self-consciously. "Yeah, it was stupid. I ran into a corner last night."

"Poor Tristen," she purred. Her full lips pushed out, giving her a sexy, sympathetic look. She slipped her hands around his waist. He flinched without thinking. "What happened?"

"Nothing—your hands are cold. How was your night? You guys went out for karaoke?"

"I have to say, you're kinda sexy with that bruise," Meegan said, ignoring his question. She gave him a long kiss, her hands running up and down his sides. "Hey, sexy man, are you too hungover for—"

"Definitely not."

"Perfect, then we have a date for it after my voice lessons. No, after yoga. Wanna join me in yoga?"

Tristen groaned at her laugh. She tapped his nose.

"No, I don't want to join you in yoga."

"Have any job interviews today?"

The question caught him off-guard. She sounded light-hearted, but there was an underlying seriousness that was hard to miss.

"No. Not today."

"You gonna look for a drummer?" Meegan's eyes were wide, as though to appear innocent.

"No."

"So, you've decided that the band is done but you don't have a plan for the next thing?"

"I didn't decide anything, Meegan. The boys quit. Adam took his stuff and left yesterday. I haven't heard from Randall, and I don't plan on calling him."

"You're giving up."

The statement irritated him. "I'm looking at my options."

Meegan wrapped her manicured fingers around his neck and pulled him against her lips. At first he resisted, but she didn't deserve his annoyance. He wanted a relationship where they could talk about their struggles. He didn't want to be the silent guy that admitted nothing.

She moved back slightly. "I'm sure you have lots of options, babe. You did an excellent job recording my album, even if Daddy is making me find another producer to make sure it's perfect. But you could find more amateur people, you know? To build up your resume. I think you did a great job."

Tristen opened his mouth to argue but decided against it. Instead, he stepped away. Thankfully, Meegan let go easily. "I was thinking about that, but I wouldn't know how to start. This is Cincinnati, not Nashville. Not every Tom, Dick, and Harry wants to be a star."

Meegan laughed. His Kentucky accent had popped out at the old saying Bobbi used frequently. "Seriously, babe. You're such a boomer. But anyway" —she held her hand up against his protest— "I happen to know that Emily knows a guy who wants to be recorded. And will pay money for it." Her nails were silver; when she'd left for New York, they had been yellow.

"I don't have a studio or a setup."

"Got it figured out." Something about the way she smiled made Tristen's stomach drop a little. "Clay has a friend who's looking for a sound guy. It's for a charity concert. Her name's Watsu. She's a smalltime agent and producer, but Clay says she's going places. And if Clay says so, it's gotta be true." Tristen struggled to keep his face neutral. Even without meeting Clay, he didn't like him. "Anyway, Watsu needs someone like you. Plus, for every client you bring into her producing agency you earn a commission on top of your pay. Sounds perfect, right?"

He wasn't sure that was the right word. "I don't know."

Meegan dropped her smile. "Listen, Tristen. I'm trying to help you ahead of time. Daddy isn't happy you don't have a job. And he knows about this offer. He's gonna ask you about it tonight. I'm sure of it. If you say no to this, you better have something else to tell him about."

Tristen yanked his sweatshirt over his head.

"Watsu wants to meet with you. Clay said she'd be willing to see you tomorrow."

He pretended to be busy pulling up his socks so he wouldn't have to answer right away.

"Okay? Tristen?"

"Yeah," he said, kissing her quickly on the cheek before heading to the bedroom. "Okay, Meegan. Okay. Get me the info, and I'll see about meeting her."

Meegan folded her arms, pushing her breasts up. "You mean you'll go see her?"

They stared each other down for a minute, but he was out of options. "Yes. I'll meet with her."

"Perfect." Her voice perked up. She'd gotten her way. "Where are you going now?"

"I'm going to get some breakfast," he said. "And I think I'll go for a walk. I'm not feeling too great."

"I'll see you after yoga, right?" Meegan called as she started the shower. "You gotta be feeling okay by the time we have dinner with Daddy. And don't forget we have Emily's birthday party tomorrow night."

As usual, dinner with Simon was at an opulent restaurant Tristen had never heard of. Meegan had made him go out and buy a dinner jacket when he got home from grabbing breakfast, since he had forgotten his last one at a party a few months back. She had been too busy to go with him but made sure to call him over video to check what he was buying. After negotiating as much as he dared, Tristen had swiped his credit card for a five-hundred-dollar Ralph Lauren jacket that he hoped to return the minute Meegan wasn't paying attention.

They walked through crisp white tablecloths and waiters standing at the ready to pour the wine. Meegan marched in front as Tristen trailed close behind. She was always so confident in fancy restaurants; cool and collected, like nothing impressed her. Like she belonged there. Unlike Tristen, who couldn't help looking right and left, drinking everything in like a dog sniffing out a new park.

He eyed the food and resisted adjusting his tie as the hostess guided him and Meegan to a table where Simon sat all alone. A bad sign already. Meegan's mother kept Simon from saying things he might regret. Her absence caused a thin layer of sweat break out on Tristen's skin.

"Hi, Daddy," Meegan said, slipping into the chair the waiter held out for her. Tristen took his own seat without assistance as Simon greeted his daughter with a kiss on the cheek.

"Nice to see you again, Simon," he said, leaning forward. He had once read that leaning forward showed a person you were interested and engaged.

Simon looked at him with raised eyebrows and grunted a greeting. "I think we're ready," he said to the waiter. Tristen grabbed the menu. Nothing was less than fifty dollars, including the appetizers. "We'll take three steaks, the Brussel sprouts, a basket of bread, two whiskeys and a Cosmopolitan."

Tristen exchanged glances with Meegan, who gave the slightest shake of her head. As though he would have said anything.

"There's something we need to talk about before our steaks come," Simon announced. "I don't like holding on to any issues. It gives me indigestion."

"Yes, sir." Tristen wasn't sure what else would be appropriate to say.

"First, I want to say that you did a pretty good job working on Meegan's album. I have to say I was impressed, especially when she told me that you all didn't have the right equipment to do it like the real singers do it."

Tristen looked at Meegan, but she was focused on Simon. It wasn't true that they didn't have good equipment. They had used the same stuff The Seethers had used for their second album.

"I appreciate that, sir. I'm glad you like her album."

Simon held up his hands. Tristen closed his mouth. "You did a good job, but now it's time to hand over the reins to Clay and let him take it where he can. He's the one who can make Meegan into the star she deserves to become."

Tristen swallowed and nodded his head.

"Which means, what with your band breaking up and no longer working on Meegan's album, that you're out of a job. Now, this might sound harsh, but I'm sure you'll understand when you become a father. Especially if you have a daughter." Simon paused to take Meegan's hand and kiss it. "I know you're sleeping at the townhouse that I purchased for my daughter as an investment, and as a house if she wanted—but as long as you're unemployed, I want you to move out. Out of respect for me and for my daughter."

Even with the dinner jacket on, Tristen felt cold. He swallowed hard at the words, trying to come up with a response.

The waiter appeared again and set the drinks in front of them, but he was afraid to take his, afraid Simon might judge him in some way. Instead, he sipped his water and wondered if his face showed his embarrassment.

"Daddy," Meegan said after testing her Cosmo, "I think that's unfair. Clay actually got him an interview with a woman he knows. They're going to set up the sound for Seraphina's charity concert, and—"

"That's great, Meegan, but it sounds temporary. I want Tristen to have a full-time job before we talk again about him living in the townhouse."

Meegan protested again, managing only a "but" before Simon shook his head and turned to Tristen. "What do you have to say? Anything?"

"I understand," Tristen said, though he didn't like it. "It's your place. I'll be out by tomorrow."

"I'll give you two days," Simon said. He leaned back, looking pleased with himself. Tristen wasn't sure if he was happy to be finished with the conversation or happy Tristen hadn't protested.

The answer didn't matter. Tristen would still have to move out. And he wasn't sure where he was going to go.

"Your steaks, sir," the waiter said, bringing Simon's plate. Two other waiters stood back half a minute before placing more in front of Meegan and then Tristen.

Despite the meat looking like the juiciest steak he'd seen in years, Tristen had no appetite. He would have rather gotten up and gone home. But when Meegan picked up her knife and fork and turned the conversation to Simon's latest business moves, he followed suit. He'd be on his own soon. He might as well not let the free dinner go to waste.

Chapter 9

"HELLO, TRISTEN. IT'S NICE to meet you. I'm excited to have you on the team for the charity concert." Watsu extended her hands to grip his.

Despite her petite frame, she had commanded attention from the moment she entered the room. She wore black pants, a black shirt, and a black leather jacket that crinkled as she moved her arms. Her black hair was piled on her head in a thick, loose bun, and her dark eyes were lined with thick black eyeliner. The only color on her was her red lipstick.

Wearing the same pants and jacket as he had worn at the dinner the night before, he probably looked like he was interviewing at a bank.

Adjusting his shoulders, he focused on the moment. Thinking about the evening with Meegan's dad would raise his stress levels. He'd figure that bombshell out later. "Nice to meet you. I appreciate you interviewing me—"

Watsu waved her hand to quiet him. "You came recommended by Clay. You already have the job. Let's just get started on the timeline and what we need to get done."

"I heard you have access to a recording studio as well?" Tristen said.

"That's right. If you have people you want to produce, we can work something out. Steve and I do. He's my other employee. Do you think he'll want a full package?"

"Who?"

Watsu crossed her arms. Hired or not, Tristen started to sweat. "The client you want to record. I work to get clients on the charts, and usually, Steve records them. We could bring you on as a freelancer for this guy, or I can sell you hours at the studio."

"I'll have to ask him," Tristen said. At the moment, all he knew was that Emily knew a guy. He hoped it was real, otherwise he was going to look like a loser to Watsu. "You can give me the information on what you offer, and then he can decide."

"Of course," Watsu said. "Here comes Steve. You'll work as his assistant, since you don't yet have experience working in a live event."

Steve was a middle-aged bald man with a warm smile. Tristen grimaced a hello as they shook. Had he known he wasn't taking the lead on the sound, he wouldn't have come.

Except that wasn't true. Simon and Meegan had given him no choice.

"Hi," Steve said. "I follow your brother. Art of Rendering has improved so much since he joined."

"Thanks." Tristen couldn't care less if his brother's band was better, worse, or defunct.

"Let's get started," Watsu said, handing out a thick packet of papers to them before launching into the details about the concert, their schedule and the items each of them were responsible for.

"Hold up. This says February thirteenth. The concert's in a month?"

Watsu's eyes narrowed. "Yes."

"That seems soon."

"It is, Tristen. I was hired just two weeks ago because the other backstage systems manager backed out. I hoped to get you in here last week, but I had work to do with a top client." Steve rolled his eyes and Watsu gave him a look, but there didn't seem to be bad blood between them. More like siblings. "Is there a problem with the timeline?"

"No, sorry," Tristen said, looking between Steve and Watsu. Neither gave a sign they were going to elaborate. "Not at all. Just wanted to be sure."

Watsu continued without stopping for another hour, reaffirming what Tristen already knew: that office work didn't suit him. Or working in a group. Or work with another boss. He checked his watch, trying to stop his leg from bouncing.

"Need something?" Watsu asked.

"What? Sorry. I need to use the restroom."

"Let's take a break before we finish. Anyone want a coffee? I'll make a run."

Tristen shook his head and practically ran to the restroom. He didn't need to use the facilities. He just needed to get away.

"Hey, babe. How's it going?" Meegan asked when she finally answered on the fifth ring.

"Not great. Reminds me of why I'd rather work for myself," Tristen said. "I don't think I'm going to take the job."

There was a pause before Meegan spoke. "Tristen, you have to. You told Daddy you were taking it. I'll look bad if you quit now."

"Why would you look bad if I don't take this job?"

"I recommended you to Clay. And I promised Daddy. Besides, I don't want a loser boyfriend who doesn't do anything all day. You need a job."

The words ignited a memory from a past. How many times had a teacher or neighbor or someone in town told him in not so many words that he was a loser? Just because of who his mom was, how poor they were, or any other number of things. Even some of Ivy's boyfriends had made sure he and Talon knew they were losers before they bailed on her and them.

"I didn't know you thought I was a loser."

"I don't," Meegan said, her voice dropping to almost a whisper. "But Daddy was serious last night."

Tristen grimaced. His head was starting to pound. "Yeah. Speaking of your dad, did you get him to change his mind?"

"No," Meegan whispered. There were voices suddenly around her, demanding who she was talking to. "He won't budge. That's why you need to keep this job."

Tristen swallowed his panic. "Okay. Where are you? Who's with you?"

"Clay's with me. We're working on getting me momentum on social media. I'm telling you, Tris, he's the best agent ever. I bet if you had him for The Seethers, Talon never would have left."

Tristen didn't know how to answer that. He doubted they could have afforded a guy like Clay. "What are you two doing?"

Meegan was laughing. Maybe at something Clay was saying. "He's going to prep me for my interview on the Dinner with Daniella podcast in two days."

"That's cool. Where are you doing that interview? Online?"

"No way. Professional podcasts interview in person. I'm going to Chicago tomorrow afternoon. The day after Emily's party, can you believe it? At least I have that green drink now. Or maybe I should cut down on drinking. You know, Jennifer Lopez doesn't drink. I could lose a few pounds if I stopped."

"Yeah, maybe. Just don't expect me to stop," Tristen said, trying to sound teasing. He checked to see if Watsu was back with the coffees yet. The hallway was still clear. "How long will you be in Chicago?"

"Just long enough to do that interview and then another night to sing karaoke with Seraphina. We're gonna act like it's a chance encounter, but she already knows, don't worry. But it'll be so funny on social media. Great idea, isn't it? I can't believe Clay knows Seraphina. It's so exciting I can hardly contain myself."

Meegan sounded the opposite to how Tristen felt. His headache was getting stronger. "You're going to sing karaoke with Seraphina?"

"Like a setup, isn't that funny? Clay, how long will we be in Chicago? Two nights? Tristen, we'll be gone three days and two nights. Will you miss me?"

"Of course I will," Tristen told her. "But listen, what if I go with you? I could be your security or something. Keep you safe."

"From what?" Meegan asked, the excitement in her tone fading.

"You know, keep the drooling fans away. You're pretty, Meegan. There will be plenty of guys who will want to hook up with you."

"And I'm sure I'll be able to say no."

"I'm just saying I know how tours are. And they can get lonely and overwhelming."

"I'm sure I can handle myself. I know how tours are, too, Tristen. Remember? I was with you on the last two spots on your last tour."

"And it was fun, wasn't it? We could have that same fun again."

"No, Tristen. You aren't coming. I have to do this alone. Besides, Daddy would be furious, and you'd mess up that job."

"I could get another."

"No," Meegan said, firmly.

"Why do you care so much about this job, Meegan?"

"Because it's Seraphina's charity concert, and Clay is about two seconds from convincing her I should be one of her singers for her Be My Valentine Charity Concert." Meegan was hissing by the end, finishing with the kind of sigh mothers who encounter epic messes give. "Someone she had backed out."

So there *was* a strategy behind it. Somehow, that made him feel better. At least it wasn't just about having a loser boyfriend.

"Okay," Tristen drawled. "Fine. I'll do the job."

"Thank you, Tristen." Simon had obviously taught her well in the area of negotiation. "Go tell Watsu you're taking this job. And then I'll see you at the Feyton Hotel later."

"Why?"

"Cause it's Emily's birthday, remember? That guy who wants to work with you will be there."

"Right. I forgot."

"Looks like Clay needs me. See you later tonight, babe."

Steve popped his head around the corner. "You ready? Watsu wants to finish up the last details with us."

"Yeah, sure."

Tristen knew he probably looked ready to punch a wall, but Steve was nice enough not to comment on it. He trudged back to the meeting room and sat down, staring straight ahead. At least they were going out tonight. He'd have a few drinks, dance with his girl, and perhaps get his first client. And all that would help him get back in Simon's good graces. There was still the issue of where he was going to live, but he couldn't think about that now.

"Here, got you a coffee," Watsu said. "We don't have much more to go over."

"Thanks." His voice croaked, but he didn't repeat himself. Watsu didn't miss a beat.

She laid out the concert expectations—Seraphina's expectations, really. He tried to pay attention to the passwords and equipment they would use. And then she finally got to the performers.

"As you probably know, this is Seraphina's Be my Valentine Charity concert. As she's becoming a bigger star than before, she told me there will be two other big-name people," Watsu said. Tristen rolled his eyes, then pretended something was in his right eye before Watsu could get suspicious. Meegan wasn't a big name, but okay. "Hopefully we'll get their songs within the week. Before the big part of the show, Seraphina always has the local high school band perform. This time it'll be a drum corps and a middle school jazz choir."

"Great," Steve drawled.

Watsu let out a quick burst of laughter before clearing her throat. "That's enough, Steve. We had a terrible time recording a high school choir last year," she told Tristen. "Anyway, on the last page, I have the dates that I'll need you at the venue and the dates we need the final music edited and uploaded. Of course, that part depends on everyone getting us their music. Questions?"

"Nope. All sounds good," Tristen said.

"All right then. Thank you, boys. I'll see you both in a couple of days," Watsu said.

Steve winked with a click of his tongue. "See you then."

"Oh, Tristen. When you find out more about the person who wants to record, call me. I'll go over what my commission payout is and what I can offer them as an agent."

Tristen pulled out his phone, saluting in response. It buzzed in his hands as he watched Watsu walk away. He hoped it was Meegan calling to apologize.

"Hello?"

"Tristen Levisay?" growled a male voice. A somewhat familiar male voice.

"Who is this?"

"This is Owen, kid." Owen paused, though it was unnecessary. "Your old boxing coach. Your dad, though maybe that's too much to call myself."

"Yeah, might be," Tristen said, scratching his chin. He wished he had the guts to hang up and block the number.

He hadn't heard from Owen since he had left Pelton at nineteen, leaving everything behind him. Even when things had got rough and he'd needed some quick cash, he'd never gone back. Instead, he groped through the seedy streets of Cincinnati, a different beast than the seediness of Pelton. There were some things he'd done he wasn't super proud of. Sometimes boxing. Sometimes dealing or playing poker. And sometimes dating women on vacation who were willing to pay for some dinners or hand over presents for a fun night. Even that was better than going back to Pelton as a failure.

"Hey, Owen. Nice to hear from you." Another lie. Tristen swallowed back his shame.

Owen snorted a laugh. "Yeah, yeah. I wanted to call you, Tristen, 'cause I heard you're back in the boxing ring."

"What?" Tristen almost choked on the coffee he hadn't even asked for. "No, I'm not."

"Yeah, you are, kid. You boxed a couple nights ago. And what's real interesting is that you won."

"It wasn't a real match—"

"That's nice, kid. Like I said, I wanted to tell you—warn you, really. Mac, the guy you supposedly play poker with? The one who challenged you to fight? He's washed up. Got himself in trouble with the money. How much does he owe you?"

"Hey, yo."

Tristen turned around. A young man with long black hair waved at him from down the street.

"You know Mac?" Tristen said into the phone. His feet were tingling. Owen, his supposed father, had always had that effect on him. Ever since a kid in third grade told him Owen was a mafia king. The guy was double their height then and had at least two hundred pounds on them. In Tristen's head, Owen had never changed from that image.

"You Talon Levisay? The singer for Art of Rendering?" the black-haired man asked.

Tristen turned away to ignore him, but the guy started snapping photos, edging in closer to Tristen to get a selfie.

"Who's that?" Owen asked.

"No one." To the guy, Tristen hissed, "I'm not Talon."

Owen whistled. "'Course I know Mac, kid. I know everyone around. I know what they're running and who's playing. Don't get involved with him. For your own sake."

The man on the street moved closer, clearly annoyed Tristen was ignoring him. "Okay, I get it. You don't want to be called out. Can I get a picture with you?" he interrupted again.

"No. Get out," Tristen said through clenched teeth.

"You're full of it, man. You look exactly like him. See? You look like twins."

"That's because we are twins," Tristen snapped.

"Oh, shit. You're his twin? For real?" The guy glanced at his phone, contemplating the picture he'd just taken before shrugging. He grinned at Tristen and nodded, his long hair bobbing slightly with the movement. "Bet my friends'll still think it's Talon!" he yelled as Tristen moved away.

"You done with whatever that is?" Owen asked. It was the same tone he'd had every time Tristen heard him speaking to Luke. The kind he'd had when he came by their house and demanded to know where Luke's stash was after the cops arrested him.

Owen had taken it away before the cops showed up with a search warrant, probably saving Ivy from jail, too. "Here's the deal, kid. Whatever money Mac had coming to ya isn't gonna come."

"He doesn't owe me any money, Owen. I don't box for him." Which was true. It had been a one-off thing. He had thought about asking for more, but now he wasn't sure, which made him furious with himself.

There was murmuring on the other line before Owen answered. "All right, kid. Glad to know you didn't get entangled with a guy like that."

Tristen opened his mouth but closed it again.

"I wanted to invite you to fight with me. I could use your comeback to fill the places up, you know?"

"Not interested." He instantly regretted his fast mouth. Some cash would be nice. Maybe fighting for Owen wouldn't be so bad.

"You sure?"

Tristen didn't like Owen's tone. He gritted his teeth to keep himself calm. "I gotta go, Owen. I have work to do."

"I pay two thousand per fight, plus commission when I'm feeling generous."

There was a whistling noise in his ear. It took a moment before Tristen realized he was the one making the sound. He stopped immediately, but Owen had obviously heard him.

Owen chuckled, the wheezing in his chest giving an evil undertone to the laugh. "I need a guy Saturday."

He didn't give Tristen time to answer before the line went dead.

Tristen tried to relax, but his mind was racing. He could make money as soon as Saturday if he just said yes.

Chapter 10

Tristen straightened his tie for the twentieth time as the hotel elevator ascended. Every muscle in his body was tense. A night that should have been full of fun and partying was turning into torture before it started. He still needed to be out of the townhouse in less than two days. Simon hadn't let up on it, even threatening to put cameras in to make sure. Meegan laughed about that last part, saying her dad wasn't being serious. But Tristen wasn't so sure.

"Stop it," Meegan told him.

"What?"

"I'll send you home if you don't stop fidgeting. Come on."

The elevator doors opened. Meegan grabbed his hand and led him into a restaurant reception with a crystal chandelier dripping toward the floor and a hostess that smiled coolly.

"We're here for Emily's birthday dinner," Meegan said.

"Right this way," the woman said. She glided before them through the opulent space. White tablecloths, heavy silverware, and what looked like real crystal glasses.

Double doors opened into a private space decorated with hundreds of rose-gold balloons interlaced with giant bouquets of flowers. The small group of people already gathered turned as Tristen and Meegan approached.

"Meegan, Tristen!" Emily's squeal broke the gentle murmur of conversation.

Meegan ran in her stilettos to hug her friend. "Happy birthday."

"Thank you for coming," Emily said. She turned to give Tristen two air kisses.

Tristen smiled at the idiotic statement. Meegan and Emily's friendship wouldn't withstand one of them not showing up at the other's party, yet they always made statements as though they expected nothing from one another.

"Happy birthday, Emily," he said, handing her their present. Meegan had picked it out at a store he had never heard of.

"The minute you get famous and dump this man, I'm scooping him up," Emily said, swatting playfully at Tristen. When she squeezed his bicep, though, he wondered if she might be serious. "Guess who's here, already charming me?"

A man looking like a movie star from the 1950s stepped forward. Tristen rolled his shoulders back and stuck out his hand. The guy was too handsome to make any other man in the place feel easy.

"I'm Tristen."

"Clay," Meegan exclaimed at the same time. "I'm so glad you could come. Tristen, this is my agent, Clay Hirson."

Clay had perfect white teeth, a solid, square jaw that even Superman would have been jealous of, and a slim physique. Tristen disliked him on sight.

Emily laughed, throwing her shiny blonde hair back. "The same reaction I had, Tristen. You better watch it, or this handsome fellow will take your girl."

Clay grinned but didn't seem embarrassed by the attention. Tristen grabbed a glass of beer from the tray of a passing server.

"Nice to meet you as well, Tristen. Meegan, I have some news for you." Clay's voice was deep and, Tristen had to admit, sexy.

"What is it?" Emily asked. Her dress shimmered in the light as she bounced. Meegan grabbed her friend's hand and looked ready to explode. Tristen wished she wasn't so overly hopeful. Breaking into the music business was difficult. Meegan had the naïve belief she'd become Taylor Swift immediately.

If he had learned anything, it was that the music industry was hard and unforgiving. A person could spend years working towards something only to have it ripped out from underneath them, leaving them with nothing.

"I got you…" Clay said, enunciating each word slowly. Tristen finished his beer to keep from rolling his eyes.

"Come on, come on," Meegan squealed. Tristen tried to catch her eye, but she kept hers on Clay.

"Into Music on Air."

Their squealing filled the room. Once again, everyone looked at them. Meegan and Emily danced around each other while Clay watched, grinning from ear to ear.

Tristen knew he was expected to smile, but he couldn't believe what he was hearing. Meegan hadn't even released her album, and Clay was already getting her into places The Seethers had only dreamed of going. He jerked his hand forward, crashing into a server with several drinks on a silver tray.

"I'm so sorry," he mumbled.

"Tristen, isn't this great?" Meegan yelled, turning to him. Her face was so bright, so hopeful, so excited. He forced himself to smile.

"I'm so proud of you, Meegan," he said, raising his glass in salute to Clay. "That is really amazing. Is she going to sing at MOA?"

He intended to bring some reality into Meegan's world; obviously, she was going to network and not perform. But Clay nodded, his smile spreading wider.

"Are you serious? I'm going to sing?"

"Of course. You're my most talented client. I got you a five-song set and a duet with Seraphina. She likes your chemistry. And she said it would be a good practice run before you perform at her charity concert."

The screaming ensued again. This time Clay looked over Emily and Meegan's heads straight at Tristen. There was no malice in his eyes, but something in Tristen's gut twisted when he looked into them.

"Let's go tell Michelle!" Emily said. "Clay, you have to come. Otherwise she'll be so jealous that she won't believe us."

Tristen went directly to the bar. They had arrived early, but now the space was filling up fast.

"Can I get you something to drink, sir?"

Before Tristen could answer the balding server, a voice spoke up near him. "This guy looks like he drinks whiskey."

Tristen turned to find a man in blue-tinted glasses smiling at him, his glass of beer raised in a salute.

"I'll take a whiskey," Tristen told the bartender before returning his attention to the stranger. The man had stepped back, lowered his glasses and was looking Tristen up and down.

"Man, you are chiseled. What do you do? Lift those giant weights at the gym? Probably not drink beer all day long next to the pool, yes?" The man smiled, giving Tristen a view of his perfect teeth.

"I don't have a pool."

"Ah, man. You're missing out, man. It's the best place with the best view." The man made a gesture with his hands near his chest. "So many itsy-bitsy, teeny-weeny bikinis. You know?"

Tristen couldn't help laughing. "I'm Tristen."

"I know who you are. I'm Lin. Emily's friend. Well, Emily and I met a few weeks ago in Singapore. Her father and my father do business."

"You from Singapore?"

"Yeah, yeah. Singapore. I'm touring the States. I speak English because we all learn to speak English in Singapore. I know I speak it well."

Tristen raised an eyebrow as Lin let out a high-pitched giggle.

"Better to get it out of the way. All Americans ask me the same thing. Especially here in Cincinnati. They are so surprised someone from Singapore might want to see their city."

"I guess we don't see anything special about it."

Lin smiled. "My family has business here."

Tristen wasn't sure what to say. He looked around for Meegan and a polite way out of the conversation.

"That your woman? She's hot." Lin lowered his glasses all the way to look at Meegan. "She's the singer, right? Emily's friend?

Which would make you the producer, and just the guy I want to talk to."

"Oh? What about?" No reason to make Lin think he was desperate.

Lin stepped back with his arms wide. Then he opened his mouth and sang.

His velvet-smooth voice stopped everyone else in the room, silence descending so they could listen. Even the servers paused before remembering they had a job to do. Tristen shut his mouth, salivating at the prospect of producing an album with this man. The easy-listening-contemporary-crossover music genre wasn't his style of music, but he knew their sales numbers. Commission on the next Josh Groban would elevate his resume. Maybe even make sure Meegan didn't start making more money than him.

Lin finished, taking a bow at the burst of applause that followed his last note.

"Thank you, thank you," he said, nodding to everyone. But he turned his attention to Tristen. "What do you think? Can you record me?"

"Isn't he great?" Emily asked, running up on her heels with Meegan at her side.

"Very."

"Thank you, but I know I can sing," Lin said. "The question is, can you help me record it? I need a record produced before my cousin's wedding. At least one song at the top of the charts, so the bastard will stop being so smug. Smart plan, right? Emily here said you can help me."

Tristen tried not to laugh. Lin looked serious for the first time all evening. "Excellent plan. I can't guarantee you'll be at the top of the charts—"

"He recorded me, and now I'm singing at Music on Air," Meegan put in, clinking her martini against Lin's beer.

"That was all her," Tristen said. "Her talent is what's getting her to MOA."

"Tristen, don't," Meegan said, her voice low. "Stop being so humble. Besides, you're going to need something to do while I'm on tour."

Tristen nearly choked. Meegan narrowed her eyes as he coughed and sputtered, offering him a tiny cocktail napkin to clean the whiskey spewed on his own lapels. "Tour? Already? How are you going to do a tour and MOA *and* the concert?"

Meegan's eyes rolled to the back of her head as though his statement was the most idiotic thing she'd ever heard. "It's just a mini tour. To get momentum."

"Right."

"I don't want to sing to ten people at Music on Air." Meegan shrugged her thin shoulders. She pulled her black mane over one shoulder and ran her long red fingernails through the thick strands. "That'd be so embarrassing. I want a crowd, and Clay says he's going to get me one."

"Right. Of course. I want you to have a crowd too, babe." He had played for small groups, and he could attest to the fact that it was slightly embarrassing.

She sighed, placing her palms against his chest and kissing him lightly on the lips. "We'll talk about it later. I'm going to party with my best girl. You coming?"

Tristen put his arms out. "Lead the way, babe. Let's go party. Lin, we'll talk soon."

Lin lifted his hand in a distracted wave, his attention already directed at a woman nearby.

"Let's go, let's go," DJ AtoZ yelled to the crowd on the roof. "It's Emily Watson's birthday, and it's time to sing!"

Tristen's temples throbbed to the beat of the pulsing lights.

"Let's all sing Happy Birthday," Meegan shouted from next to the DJ. Tristen hadn't seen her in the last hour; she'd spent her time dancing with her friends. "One, two, three! Happy birthday to you…"

The crowd joined Meegan, swelling toward the front as they belted out the simple words. Tristen shrank back, away from the dance floor.

"These girls are so silly."

Lin. Tristen found him to his left. His black, shiny hair flopped back and forth as he shook his head, chuckling.

"That Emily. If she wasn't Paul's daughter, I would take her to bed. I bet she's dynamite, hey? And your Meegan." Lin let out a low whistle. "I bet she's hot, too. Where did you meet her?"

"We met when I was playing a club in Chicago almost two years ago. Then we ran into each other at a coffee shop in Cincinnati six months ago and hit it off," Tristen said. He led Lin to a small area with chairs and couches. It was far enough away that you could almost hear each other talk. He flagged down the bartender for two gin and tonics.

"The pink gin," Lin said, clicking his tongue. "Okay, so let's talk business."

"Now?"

"Why not? I want to record this week," Lin said, rubbing his hands together. They were small and slim and very smooth, as though he'd never done anything hard in his life. "I have twenty songs."

Tristen choked. "Twenty?"

"My voice teacher and I chose the twenty best," Lin said. "Well, we chose thirty. But we only have the rights to record twenty, you know?"

"I'll need to see the paperwork on those twenty."

Lin waved his hand. "Sure, sure. No problem. So, twenty. I started recording while I was in LA, but it got expensive, and the guy producing and mixing overdosed and went to a rehab clinic. I don't want to wait for him, so I'm coming to you."

"How many do you have finished?"

"Okay, okay. We recorded eleven. But I don't know if he finished them. You will have to see. Then he recorded the music for another five, I think, but I have not recorded them. And I need a hit before April. In Singapore, not here. Much easier in Singapore. But I need it to eclipse my cousin's wedding." Lin paused. Pulling his mirrored sunglasses down to the bridge of his nose, he continued. "Don't judge me. My cousin is an ass and is always getting the family's attention. So, maybe I take a little away. He'll see what it's like down here with the little people."

Tristen looked around at the so-called 'little people' with raised eyebrows. Lin burst out laughing. "Just kidding. Just kidding. I am not little people. But I still want a hit song. So, you ready to record?"

"Eleven plus five, huh? And you have four without the music ready to go?"

Their gin and tonics arrived, pristine ice floating in a pool of fizzy pink. Tristen had never tasted pink gin before and would never have ordered it, but it did look inviting.

"Hey, hey. Cheers, yeah?"

Tristen tapped his drink to Lin's, who grinned and wiggled his eyebrows under his glasses.

"Maybe you should record two albums. We could put together ten of the best songs you have now and make that a success, and then come out with another album less than a year later. So you spread the success long-term instead of becoming a one-hit-wonder."

"I need a full concert by next summer. I plan to go on tour."

Lin's self-assurance was somewhat intimidating. Tristen wished he could be so sure of something in his life.

"If each song is about three and a half minutes long, then with ten songs, you're already at forty-five minutes. And that doesn't include talking in between and such. Are you thinking of giving a concert for your cousin's wedding?"

Lin laughed, his shiny hair falling into his face. "No way. That guy's a bastard, I told you before. I don't have a concert lined up. That will be something I do a year from now, and then a tour. I'm too busy the rest of this year with the wedding, etcetera. So, I will get a hit song in Singapore and milk that, you know? Like, 'oh, my, I'm so surprised,'" Lin said, covering his cheeks with his hands. "And then I can play humble. Everyone will be like, 'this young man came out of nowhere and took home the prize,' and they will clap and cheer. And my cousin will be so mad."

"Sounds exactly right," Tristen said. He couldn't help laughing with Lin. "But what prize are you talking about?"

Lin whistled at a group of girls passing by before answering. "So many hot girls in America, Tristen. It's so hard to choose." He slapped his own cheeks, then grinned. "Who cares what prize? You get what I'm saying, no? My song will hit the charts; the public will love me, then I will go on tour. My family is well-known in Singapore. They will want me to be famous."

"Right," Tristen said. Lin's family issues reminded him of his own. He was going to be homeless soon. Which meant—he would think of that later.

Lin made a purring sound that caught Tristen's attention. He whistled at a woman in a tight, sparkly dress that left one shoulder bare who was making her way towards them. "I'll be back to talk business with you in a few minutes, Tristen."

Lin grinned at the woman, but she looked past him to Tristen. "Thought you were going to call me back?"

"I'm sorry?" Tristen scrutinized the woman, with her thick blonde hair that fell in waves over her shoulders. Her makeup was thick and dark around her lashes, but not enough to cover the irritation in her eyes. "I think you have the wrong guy."

"Do you really, Talon? You think I have the wrong guy? Your stupid beard doesn't change your look that much."

Tristen could feel Lin grinning at him, enjoying himself as he sipped his drink. "Talon's my brother."

"This is Tristen," Lin said before bursting into laughter, almost spilling gin all over the woman's blouse. Tristen wasn't sure if she believed Lin or not, but she tiptoed backwards before marching away.

"Who was that?" Meegan demanded. She glared between Tristen and Lin, the pulsing blue and purple lights giving her a Halloween-like glow.

"She thought I was Talon," Tristen said.

"Sure." Meegan's eyes darted between him and Lin. Lin shrugged.

"Let's go dance," Tristen said. "Lin and I can talk later."

Meegan glared at him but let him take her hand and lead her to the dance floor. She'd get over her irritation if he just paid attention to her.

Once on the floor, he twirled her around then brought her close, their hips slamming against each other.

"My, my, Tristen Levisay," Meegan said, giggling. "Is that your phone vibrating, or are you happy to see me?"

Tristen rolled his eyes but laughed with her as he pulled out his phone. "I should take this. It's my mom."

Meegan stopped dancing but didn't say anything before walking away. Probably to join Emily.

"Hey, Ivy."

"Just calling you back." She sounded tired and possibly nervous. Or high. He was grateful for the excuse to leave the dance floor and head over to a quieter area. "Sounds like you're at a party."

"I am," Tristen said, finally finding some quiet in the elevator. "Going to go down a floor. It's too loud upstairs."

"That's okay. We can talk tomorrow."

Tristen wanted this part to be over. Just ask her already, so he could start getting over his embarrassment. "I just wanted to tell you…" He paused again. He couldn't do it. "I'm coming out to Pelton. In two days. To check on you."

He could hear her sucking on her vape before she answered. "I'd like that, Tristen. But you don't ever have to ask to stop by. *Mi casa es su casa.*"

He hoped she meant that in the literal sense. "Okay. I'll see you the day after tomorrow."

Before he could make it back to the party, a notification lit up his screen. It was a selfie of his brother hanging out with Jack Brommwell, Kurt Vanguard and Valerie Ting, all at some social media influencer music event.

Chapter 11

On Monday morning, a buzzing noise interrupted Tristen's sleep, jolting him awake. He'd been dreaming about watching Meegan singing on stage. At one point in the dream, he was hooting and clapping for Meegan, and in the next, he was shrinking in size with every note that she sang. And no one noticed. No matter how much he tried to yell, no one seemed to hear him. The last vision of the dream was of a stagehand's shoe falling down on him, ready to squish him.

"What a night," Tristen mumbled. He rubbed his head, which was already aching. The image of the shoe coming down on him wouldn't disappear.

Next to him, the bed was empty. Meegan had left the evening before for Chicago, and he had spent the night by himself sipping whiskey and strumming his guitar with zero results. Willing himself to write a song hadn't worked.

Bunching his pillow into a ball didn't help to bring sleep back. It wasn't even six-thirty in the morning, but he was wide awake. From somewhere amid the wrinkles of the comforter, the buzzing noise sounded again.

"Geez, why are you so hard to get a hold of?"

"Meegan. Sorry. My phone was buried. Why're you up so early?"

Meegan sighed. He could imagine she wasn't thrilled. It was an hour earlier in Chicago, and she wasn't a morning person. "For some stupid reason, I have a photo shoot at seven. Gotta get ready before it. Why does the fashion industry wake up so freaking early?"

Tristen laughed softly as he made his way to the kitchen to get coffee. He could go for a run before heading to Pelton. Putting off his most embarrassing moment as an adult would be ideal. But then, so would getting it over with.

"You still there?"

"Yeah, sorry. Just distracted. Sorry you have to be up so early. But I'm betting you look pretty." Her sigh was sexy even through the phone. "What's the photo shoot for?"

"A magazine I've never heard of. Plus, Clay wants extra pictures that we can use on my social media and stuff. I don't know. I'm too grumpy to care right now."

"The life of a star is hard, babe." Meegan groaned, and he chuckled. "How do you feel about that interview today?"

"Oh, that's right. The interview. Yeah, I feel good about it. They just want a casual conversation. And then the karaoke stunt with Seraphina tonight. And tomorrow Clay is trying to get me a gig in some club. What?" A deep voice rumbled in the background, tensing Tristen's back. He hated the idea of Clay being with Meegan in the late and early hours of the day. The intimate hours of the day. "I guess some rich kid's birthday. I don't know. Clay is trying to create momentum, he says, before Music on Air."

Clay seemed to talk a lot about momentum.

"Right. Well, I hope you don't get attacked, since you declined my offer of being your security guard."

Meegan's soft laughter didn't help his already deflated ego. Maybe her opinion would change if she saw him boxing.

"I don't need a security guard, babe. I need a fur coat. It's so cold. I don't know how people survive the winters here."

"Well, I could come and be your coat. I'll wrap my arms around you as you walk, which will act as both safety and warmth."

"Because that wouldn't be difficult to walk in," Meegan said. "Oh, I gotta go."

"Call me later." Tristen pulled out his favorite mug from the cabinet as Meegan said goodbye. "Wait! Send me pics."

Meegan sent a kiss as her response and hung up. Off to her exciting day.

Tristen took a sip of coffee. It was a perfect day for a run, cold but sunny, but for the first time in many years, he didn't want to run. He wanted to curl up and go back to sleep.

Receiving several texts at once from Watsu about the music files he needed to finish in three days was almost enough to actually send him to bed. He stared at the phone as another text came in, this time from Owen.

Wanna take the fight? Two thousand is fair. Plus, I'll give you a percentage of the bets after I pay my guys.

The man hadn't changed one bit. Always in the middle of everyone else's business. When Tristen and Talon were boxing, Owen had decided what they ate for lunch, what classes they took, and who they dated. He'd also had a monopoly on their social life. The one time Tristen had dared to complain about it, Luke shoved him against the wall and told him to show some respect.

"That man you think is so nosy can't protect you if he don't know what you're up to. What you eat matters. Where you go and what you do matters. Who you date could land you in jail in this business. You don't know nothing, so keep your mouth shut."

It was the first time Tristen realized that boxing at underground matches could be dangerous. And that maybe he wasn't happy Luke was out of jail.

He looked back at the message, wanting to ignore Owen, but he couldn't.

No. Not trained enough.

He looked at the text, then erased the last three words. Insulting Owen wouldn't help the situation.

He added: *Headed to Ivy's later.*

His run could wait. He wanted to get to Pelton and talk to Ivy about moving in before Owen decided to crash the party.

The house was dark when he walked in, even though it was almost nine in the morning.

"Ivy? You awake?" Tristen called as he pulled the spare key out of the lock.

No one answered.

Tristen dropped his two duffel bags and computer in his old bedroom before knocking on Ivy's door. "Ivy?"

He pushed the door open to find it empty. Tristen walked in, pulled up the blinds and looked around, the room bringing mostly bad memories. Ivy in bed after Luke was arrested. Ivy crying after Aimee overdosed. Ivy refusing to go to work until Tristen literally pulled her off the bed, her butt hitting the carpet hard.

He looked around, a neat stack of envelopes on her nights stand catching his attention. The top one had ominous words in black on the front.

FINAL WARNING. DO NOT THROW AWAY.

The world zoomed in and out within seconds. Tristen pulled out the envelope and found another with the same warning. And another. And another.

His pulse beat faster. He'd seen these same words several times over the course of his childhood on bills. Sometimes he'd find them in the trash; other times they'd be spread across the dining room table. After Luke went to jail for attempting to sell drugs, Ivy had been too devastated to even get to work for almost a month.

When the bills with the warning words in bold had started coming in, she'd finally gone back to the factory. But Tristen remembered Bobbi coming to their house a lot during those days, and demanding Ivy sit down and pay attention. Owen came over a couple of times as well.

Tristen slammed the drawer shut and took the envelopes to the dining room table.

The first was a credit card bill. $4,261.87. His heart slowed. That was what he had found before. And she was taking care of it.

Tristen sank onto the bed with a sigh of relief. He picked up the rest of the pile and thumbed through the next five. They were all from the same bank, and all had URGENT or FINAL NOTICE or DO NOT THROW AWAY printed on the outside.

With a deep breath in, Tristen ripped one open.

The payment on your balloon mortgage is due in four weeks.

"Balloon loan?" His heart skipped a beat as he stared at the number. **$45,672.**

The front door opened with a bang. Tristen jumped off the bed and quickly put the letters back into their stacks.

"Tristen! Are you here?" Ivy called out. Before he could do more than spin around, she was at her bedroom door. "What the hell do you think you're doing?"

Her question triggered his built-up anger. Maybe he didn't have a right to be snooping, but she'd lied. She had told him the marijuana farm debt and medical debt was all she had. He tried to stay calm, but still the words came out louder than he wanted them to. "What am I doing? What the hell are *you* doing? What is this? How do you owe this much?"

Ivy shrugged. Tristen couldn't believe it.

"Why aren't you paying your bills?" he demanded, ignoring his panic. "You have a decent job, Ivy. What happened?"

"I do," Ivy said, pulling a joint from her pocket. "Do you?"

Tristen closed his mouth. It was just like her to be ready with a retort to turn the discussion around. He marched out of her room, not trusting himself with the anger he felt boiling over inside. Ivy's footsteps followed him as he left, but he didn't turn around until she spoke again.

"What's that?"

Tristen's stomach dropped. She was pointing at his bags on top of his old bed. "It's mine."

"Yours?" She inhaled her joint and leaned against the wall. "You planning on staying the night?"

Tristen's throat was so dry he wasn't sure he could speak properly. He did his best, his voice croaking at first. "I need to stay more than tonight."

Ivy raised her eyebrows. "Did you fight with the girlfriend?"

"No," he said quickly, scrambling to find an excuse that wouldn't make him look like a loser. But there was no other explanation than the truth. "She lives in a townhouse her dad owns. He doesn't want me there unless I can pay him rent."

"And you can't?"

Tristen remembered to breathe. "No."

Ivy smirked as she finished off her joint. "You can't pay rent, but you come here and try to lecture me about my money problems?"

"At least I'm not about to lose a house, Ivy."

Something like hurt swept through her eyes before she shuttered them again. "I don't need you coming here acting all high and mighty. Sounds to me like you're in your own pickle and came here to figure yourself out."

"I don't owe forty-five thousand dollars!"

"You got some nerve, Tristen Levisay." Ivy pointed at him, so close that her nail would poke his chin if he relaxed. "Let me ask you a question. What would you do if I said you couldn't stay here?"

She had him in a corner.

"I'd figure it out," he said, but she laughed.

"You're as stubborn as me," she said. "Oh, lord, Tristen. Let's just admit we got a problem." She limped to the couch and sank down as though she hadn't slept in years. "I gotta say, I feel better having this burden shared."

He almost snorted, but something about the look on her face stopped him. She'd been right; he didn't have any room to judge her. But it was still difficult to admit it.

"Can you tell me why?" he asked. "Why do you have a balloon loan out? And why didn't you pay for it?"

Ivy shook her head. "So many, many reasons. I took it out when Luke left after kicking you out. Randall and I got back together for a bit. He wanted to start that mechanic shop, remember? You were gone and Talon was off doing his thing and I was lonely. Besides, Randall is a nice guy."

Tristen said nothing. What was there to say? He hadn't bothered to visit Ivy for two years after Luke kicked him out.

Ivy sighed into the silence. Her body slumped into the couch pillows. "Well, there was an opportunity. And you know I've always wanted to quit the factory. I don't care if it's a mechanic or a flower shop or what. Just get me out of that factory."

Tristen didn't blame her. But he didn't like where this was going.

"So you took out a loan for him?"

"For us," Ivy said, emphasizing each word. "For us. He was gonna stay."

She fell quiet, and for a moment Tristen thought she might be asleep.

"I took out the loan. And then the place didn't work. And Randall took off. And I forgot about it. It seemed so far off. Until it wasn't."

"And now?"

Ivy sighed. "And now, I don't know."

Tristen leaned forward from his chair. "Owen called me."

Ivy's eyes rose from the spot on the floor she was staring at. "What did he want?"

"He wants me to box."

"Will you do it?" she asked, struggling to sit up.

"If I do, I don't know if it'll be enough. I don't know what he's willing to add to all this. Did you call Talon?"

"We talked, but I didn't tell him about the balloon loan. I just…" She paused. "I can't. When I asked him for money, he gave me a thousand and said it was all he had."

Tristen didn't believe it, but he didn't say so.

"If we don't pay this," Ivy said quietly, "we're both homeless."

"We'll figure it out," he said, though he wasn't sure how.

"It's my home," she said, tears filling her eyes. "It's the only home I've ever known." Her eyes were starting to droop, her head lolling to the side.

Tristen spread a blanket over her, kissed her forehead, and headed out the door. He needed to see Owen.

Chapter 12

TRISTEN SHIFTED INTO GEAR and set out to Top Gym, the place he'd spent the majority of his time as a teenager. Ivy was terrible with her finances, but so was he. Despite her not being the greatest mother, she was still the woman who'd given him life. She was his family, and he couldn't leave her in the dust. He didn't have it in him.

Maybe it was guilt that forced him to always try to save his mother. He was the one who'd gotten Aimee on marijuana, after all. And everyone always said it was a gateway drug. Didn't matter that opioids exchanged hands like candy in this part of the US. Tristen rammed his fingers through his hair with a sigh. Despite everything Ivy had done wrong, despite her own dark relationship with drugs, both illicit and legal, he couldn't leave her homeless. Wasn't that the golden rule, or whatever? Doing what he hoped she would do if he were ever in this much trouble?

Besides, while his childhood hadn't been stellar, Ivy didn't even talk about hers. What he knew from Bobbi was filled with alcohol and abuse. And a first pregnancy at fifteen that no one talked about.

Tristen slammed his right palm into the steering wheel. This sticking by his mother thing was going to cost him, even if it didn't make him homeless too. He doubted Simon would find sympathy for that.

He could call Talon to see if he had the money. It wouldn't hurt to ask. But Ivy had said she'd already spoken to him.

As if reading his mind, Tristen's phone rang. For a split second, he wondered if it was Talon with his twin sense, but it was Watsu.

"I'm not missing a meeting, am I?" Tristen asked. "I thought we weren't meeting until tomorrow."

"No. Did you think you were missing a meeting?"

The streets of Pelton, untouched by the last few years, passed by his car window. The only difference from when he'd been growing up were the nail salons and the coffee shop where the abandoned train station was. "I'm just making sure."

"That guy Lin called this morning. Looks like he wants to go all in with the full package. We'll have to work out payment for you."

At least something was going right. "That's great news. He approached me first, though, so I want executive producer on his album."

"We'll talk about it together. Can you meet today? He's coming in with his lawyer to sign the papers."

"I'm in Pelton. Had a bit of a family emergency. But I'll come back. I'd appreciate it if you waited for me."

Watsu laughed her short, clipped laugh. "Don't worry. He didn't want to come in until late afternoon. You have time to get here."

"What time are you thinking? Pelton is over an hour outside of Cincinnati."

"I can hold him off until five or five-thirty. Come by my studio office by then."

The day was already stressful, and it wasn't even noon.

The humidity and smell hit Tristen the moment he walked through the door. Everything in the place assaulted him with memories. The jump ropes along the front wall where he would spend ten, fifteen, sometimes twenty minutes at a time, trying to keep his mind blank so the time would go faster. Across from the jump ropes were the small punching bags where he'd punched and hit until he dreamed about doing it. And along the back wall stood the same lifting machines and free weights. Tristen shook the memories away, but they stubbornly clung to him.

A man left the locker room, the door swinging out wide enough to show the large white scales lined up just inside. Tristen slowed. For the first few months, he'd got a weekly lecture about not having enough muscle. Underground boxing wasn't held to the same restrictions as professional boxing, of course, but there was a code to pit men against another within the same weight rank. Honor was still important amongst those who lived in the underworld.

The tricks to add or lose weight in a day soon became his obsession; leaving the weigh-in marked in the correct weight category was the main goal. By seventeen, he and Talon became the top prize-winners for Owen in the underground circles. He had needed fresh blood to get back in the game, and Tristen and Talon provided that for him. Which moved Luke up the ladder in Owen's business. Boxing might have been the only thing that kept them together after Aimee overdosed and Ivy went off to rehab again.

Not that they were particularly skilled at the sport; it was more Owen's ingenious way of using them being identical twins to his advantage. While working for Owen, they were expected to shave and comb their hair exactly the same. Everything depended on no one being able to tell the difference between them, though many would claim to.

The scheme was that Talon was the winner twin and Tristen was the loser. Each match, Owen decided which of them would fight depending on how the betting was going. If winning would earn him more, then he'd put Talon in. It was the same for Tristen, except that his job was to lose. Their names won and lost the same amount until Talon complained it wasn't fair. To soothe Talon's ego, Owen let him win two more matches under his own name to move him higher in the ranking. Tristen tried to argue that losing on purpose was almost harder than winning, that he could beat some guys he had to lose against, but Talon and Luke laughed him off his soapbox. From that moment on he became known as the loser twin even to the audience, forced more and more frequently by Luke to lose under his own name. Until the night he decided he'd had enough.

Back then Owen's gym had already been worn down, but ten years later, it was like stepping into a boxing film from the eighties. Everything was in desperate need of renovation. The edges of the ring were worn, frayed and uneven. The weight machines were greasy. The ropes hanging from the small punching bags were glossy and black, with most of the bags fraying at the seams.

"Well, well. It's Tristen come to see me."

Owen stood at what constituted a front desk. It was an L-shaped glass counter that held sweatshirts, t-shirts, shorts and water bottles, all with the Top Gym logo on them.

"Hi, Owen."

"You saw your mama?"

"Yes."

"So you know?"

Tristen held back a sigh. "Yes."

"Upstairs."

Owen didn't wait for him to respond. He turned around and stalked up the black metal stairs to his office that overlooked the entire gym floor. Tristen followed.

For Tristen, Owen's gym had been a haven. He wasn't allowed to tell anyone that Owen was his dad, but he knew. He and Talon had found birth certificates in a box in the basement. Most nights after he came, he couldn't imagine a place he'd rather be. Almost every day, he'd ended up back at the gym. Owen's office was the place the outside world couldn't touch him. Where kids couldn't make fun of him for where he lived, or his tattered clothes, or who his mother was and why she showed up at the games drunk.

There were also times the gym had felt like a prison, especially when Luke was watching him, reminding him he wasn't as fast as he should be. Luke had no problem reminding Tristen that he wasn't good at anything else, and he was barely good enough for boxing.

"Your mama's in a mess of trouble," Owen said when the door to his office closed behind them.

"I saw."

Owen tossed him a paper that looked like a bank statement. "You annoyed that she's in debt?"

"It's not great," Tristen said grabbing the paper mid-air. "What's this?"

"Something that says Tristen Levisay is about twenty thousand in debt and counting. I looked you up."

Tristen's blood turned cold for a second. No way was he was that much in debt.

Owen watched him, his small eyes never looking away. "You don't think it's that much? Take a look."

Tristen obeyed. The numbers focused in and out, then stayed steady. The paper was correct. It was a full financial report, down to the cent. Twenty thousand dollars and eighty-one cents.

"Do you want to say anything about this?" Owen asked. "Sure, some of this is student loan debt. Course, the dumbest part about that is you didn't even finish the degree. The other dumb decision you made lately was quitting your day job."

Owen was right. Quitting his job had been the dumbest decision ever, but everyone said it took money to make money. And sometimes taking a risk is necessary. So he'd taken the risk. He just hadn't expected Talon to take another risk that would leave the band in shambles.

"How'd you get this?" Tristen was so shocked by the amount that he'd forgotten to be angry for a moment. But the anger came rushing in once he asked the question. "It's illegal for you to get this."

Owen laughed. "Of everything I've done in life, Tristen, this is nothing. I know a guy. I know lots of guys. Which is why I know a lot of information. Which is how I run my business. I needed collateral on a fighter I wanted."

The twinkle in Owen's eyes told Tristen he always got what he wanted. "So you thought you could coerce me into fighting?"

"I'm not coercing you to do anything," Owen said, throwing his hands up. "I'm offering you an opportunity. Ivy came to me for help, but I don't have the cash. With these fights, though, I think you could generate enough cash for her to keep her house. Maybe, if you win, you could even pay off some of your own debt, too. I mean, this?" He waved the paper. "This is only going to get worse. By the way, does your girlfriend know about this?"

Tristen closed his eyes to calm himself.

"You know, I wouldn't have looked into this, except that another job landed in my lap."

"What do you mean?"

Owen yanked on a drawer and pulled out a folder. From the sheets of paper inside, he pulled out one and pushed it towards Tristen. "Like I said, gathering information is one of my businesses, and people come to me when they want to find stuff out. Like who the guy is that's dating his daughter, and if he's trying to take his daughter's money."

The paper drew him towards it like a bad car crash. He couldn't help it. All the words Owen was saying pointed to Simon, but he had to be sure. Because it couldn't be that somehow Simon knew his dad and had asked him to check up on Tristen.

Unfortunately, the invoice showed Simon's name. And Tristen's.

"Did you show him this?" Tristen waved the document.

Owen's face softened, disarming Tristen for a second. He recovered and put his guard back up. If he'd learned anything from childhood, it was to stay alert.

When Owen's smile returned, it seemed sadder. Probably disappointed in Tristen's terrible finance management. "No, I sent him a different report."

"Thanks," Tristen said. He looked back at the document. "I'm working on this."

"You can work on it faster if you say yes. Plus, your mama wouldn't get kicked out of her house. If I can earn some quick cash using you, I can help her pay the house off."

"I'm here, aren't I?" His throat hardly let the words squeeze through. "You sure we can fix this for her? I can win enough?"

"I'm sure. And not just refinance, but pay it off, so she owns the house free and clear. And once I clear my fees, you could make more than two thousand a fight. If you win, maybe more."

Owen telling the straight truth was disarming.

"Good, but there's one catch. I fight, *I* pay off the house. You don't get to come out the hero if I'm the one taking the hits."

Owen squinted at him. "Yep, you're gonna take some hits with that flab."

Tristen snorted.

"I'm just busting your balls, kid. You look pretty good. And with the skill you already have, I think we can get this thing done. Course, you'll have to let Mac know you ain't fighting for him anymore."

"Cut the crap, Owen." Tristen was getting more comfortable. Settling into who he had been in a past life. "I'm sure you know it was just one time I fought with Mac."

"Technically two, right?" Owen grinned.

Tristen shook his head, but he was also impressed with how much Owen always knew. "How are things with the cops and such? You got them under control?"

"Getting arrested is no big deal. They never keep the fighters," Owen said.

"I don't want to get arrested at all."

Owen chuckled. "Simon wouldn't like it, would he? I can promise you this: if they raid us, I'll get you out right away."

"I don't want the record. I won't agree to this if there's a risk of getting arrested. I saw what jail did to Luke."

"Luke went to jail for trying to move drugs, kid." Owen shook his head when Tristen didn't budge. "There's always a risk. Besides, a record fits perfectly with the bad-boy rock-and-roll style!" Owen stood and thumped Tristen hard on the back. It was as close to a hug as he ever got.

"I don't want that look. I want to help Ivy not become homeless."

Tristen kept his gaze on Owen. Neither flinched.

"Alright. Don't worry, kid. If you get arrested, there'll be no record."

"You said two fights?"

Owen straightened up, leaning forward on his elbows over the desk. "Nice try. I said three fights. Can't make that kind of dough in two. Course, that's just paying for your mama's house. For your own debt we'll work out a few more."

Tristen held his gaze. Regardless of what he ended up getting paid for the fights, he knew the sums involved in these underground matches were phenomenal. If Owen thought he could get the debt paid in three fights, he could.

Owen grinned. "I promise," he said, spreading his hands as though to say they were clean. Tristen knew better, but he'd say no to the others. He could figure out his personal debts on his own. "That's all I need. I got some profitable fights coming up, and Phil, the guy I was thinking of getting in the ring, hurt his foot. You'd be doing me a favor as much as your mama. And me owing you a favor is a nice little trinket to have in your back pocket, right?"

"This Saturday?" Tristen asked. Anxiety pulsed through him at the proximity of the date. Five days away.

"Actually, first one's moved to Friday. It's an hour from here in the ho-dunk town of Whiteing. Next one's in Chattanooga. The last one's outside Cincinnati on Sunday, the twenty-sixth."

Tristen visualized the calendar. That would be two days before the concert. Which wasn't ideal.

"But you want me to win?" he asked. "Or lose?"

Owen leaned forward. "We're bringing back one of the Pelton Vikings. Let them figure out which one you are. I want you to fight. But you haven't trained professionally in years. While you're strong, I don't have a ton of confidence you'll beat out some of the guys out there these days. But winning means a bigger paycheck."

A shiver of greed rippled through Tristen.

"Look, let's finalize that you'll do these three fights, yeah?"

The negatives of accepting were multiple: the physical impact of fighting three fights in two weeks. The pain. The weight of losing, and the weight of winning. The possibility of getting arrested, despite Owen's assurances he wouldn't. Hiding it from Meegan.

But it would keep him busy while she was on her mini tour and at Music on Air…. And it was just three fights.

It wasn't like he was crossing a line he hadn't before. And, if all went well, Ivy would own her house free and clear.

Tristen stuck out his hand. Owen shook it with a grin.

"Let's go meet your trainer."

Chapter 13

"WHERE ARE YOU?" MEEGAN asked. Tristen could hear muffled conversation and glasses clinking near her phone.

"I'm waiting for Watsu. We have a meeting with Lin, that guy who wants me to record him." Tristen tried to stretch out his back. After boxing with Jared for almost two hours the day before, then driving to and from Cincinnati just to go over paperwork with Watsu and Lin, his body was as stiff as a ninety-year-old man's.

"That's great, babe. I told you sticking to that job was worth it."

Tristen unclenched his teeth. "Yeah. You were right. Except the drive from my mom's is brutal when there's traffic."

"You're staying at your mom's? Why don't you get your own apartment near me?"

Tristen bit back a retort. The driving was starting to take a toll on his energy, and he had to remind himself that Meegan didn't know about his own financial problems—something he would prefer to keep under wraps. "She broke her leg, remember? Thought I should be there to help her."

"Oh, that's nice of you." Meegan seemed surprised. Or maybe she knew he was lying. Tristen didn't want to find out. "By the way, did you see my Instagram lately? It's blowing up. Same with all my social media. I'm telling you, Tris. You gotta get on the video vibe. It's great for us musicians. People can see you and ask you stuff, they can listen to your music. Just last night

Clay recorded me doing some vocals, and I've already gotten thousands of likes."

Tristen grunted as he pulled up to the studio for the second time in two days. He hated social media and had always resisted getting on it. Meegan claimed it was simple, but for him it always felt complicated. There were times he would post in spurts, but then he'd forget for weeks at a time. None of the guys in The Seethers were good about it, despite everyone saying it would be better for them to be on it.

"Do you see it?" Meegan asked. She was expecting him to pull up her account.

Tristen fumbled with his phone. "Just a second. I'm trying to find the app. I haven't gotten on that one in a while." Except to follow Talon around digitally, but Tristen had been busy lately, and with an old phone the app had gone to the cloud after a few days of being left unopened.

"Tristen, seriously, you have to start being better at business and marketing. It's an expectation these days for us. All the top names are on social media. And if you don't like it, you can pay someone to do it for you."

She kept talking about marketing and posting, but Tristen wasn't listening. He was looking at a post with Meegan in it. Not her latest video, but a post she was tagged in. Someone had snapped a picture of her and Clay on the streets of Chicago. In the picture, Clay was brushing a stray lock of Meegan's hair away. They looked like a couple; Clay was almost cupping her cheek as he gazed at her. Meegan at least was looking away, but the caption read Tristen's own thoughts.

Rising music star @IAmMeegan out in the Windy City with what looks like her boyfriend.

"Are you listening?"

Tristen focused back on his girlfriend's voice, which sounded irritated. "Sorry, was getting distracted. Someone with the name Music-All-Day posted a picture of you."

"Did they?" The irritation in Meegan's voice was replaced by a squeal of joy. "That's an online music magazine. What did they say?"

"Well, they think Clay is your boyfriend. I can't blame them. This picture makes the two of you look pretty tight."

"Oh, stop. Clay is dating someone else, Tristen," Meegan snapped. Her voice changed again to happiness. "That is a good picture of me! And I don't know what you're talking about. My hair had just whipped me in the face, and Clay was helping me."

"Okay." Tristen wasn't sure he believed her, but he had no other proof.

"Yeah, okay. Cause it's the truth."

"Fine, Meegan. I just don't like that other people think you're dating. This was why I wanted to go with you."

"I can take care of myself, Tristen. This is going to be really difficult if you can't trust me with Clay, of all people."

"What's that supposed to mean? Clay's a good-looking guy. Successful."

Meegan sighed heavily into the phone. "I don't want to argue with you. But I also don't appreciate you accusing me of cheating."

"I didn't accuse you of anything." He knew he should calm down and give Meegan the default answers that she was right and he was wrong. He had no proof. It was just jealousy, but he was too tired to keep his tone neutral. "But maybe this would work better if pictures like that don't get taken in the first place. Anyway, I have to get to work. The job you want me to have so badly."

Meegan took so long to answer that Tristen thought she had hung up. "I gotta go, too. Clay is motioning to me. I'll talk to you later."

She hung up the phone as Watsu pulled into the parking lot.

"Bad day?" Watsu asked as Tristen met her at the back door.

"Little bit. Why?"

"You look a bit worn around the edges," she said, stepping back to evaluate him. "Like you haven't slept or something."

"Everything's fine. Don't worry about me."

"Glad to hear it," she said as they headed to the front door of the studio. "Lin should be here soon. Shall we go meet him?"

She held the door open, waiting for him to move through it. Tristen obeyed.

"Hello, my two expert producers. Are you ready to make me famous?" Lin shouted, chuckling when Watsu jumped. "You're like a rabbit—hoppy, hoppy. I'm going to make it a point to scare you more often. You're very cute when you're scared."

"Morning, Lin," Watsu said. She adjusted her jacket, though it fit perfectly. "You just startled me a little, that's all."

"Oh, that's not all, my angel in black," Lin said, wiggling his eyebrows. "You're looking beautiful this morning. Tristen, doesn't she look beautiful?"

Tristen looked back at Watsu and shrugged. "She always looks good."

"Oh, look out. What if your girlfriend hears you say that?"

"Mr. Lin," yelled a voice from the recording room. "I have your salts."

Lin rubbed his hands together. "Gotta get this angelic voice warm," he said, pointing a finger-gun Watsu's way with a wink. His staccato laugh penetrated the air. Tristen and Watsu followed him at a distance. "You go talk with my lawyer. That ugly guy over there in the suit."

"I have to finish some paperwork, and you need to sign the contract. Lin already signed it all and said he needed to get a recording." Watsu shoved a contract under his nose. "Bring that to my office once it's signed. I'll be finishing things up with the lawyer. I need to check the rights on three of the songs he wants to record," she said as she walked away, her stilettos clicking down the hard linoleum floor.

Steve stuck his head out of the studio door with a smile. "Hey, you coming in? Lin says he wants you in here. He won't record without you. He's a funny little guy."

"I'm coming, though I'm not sure he'd like to be called little," Tristen said. "Can I ask you—I signed the papers yesterday, but I didn't really read them. What is the contract here for me and Lin?"

Steve smirked and shook his head. "Always read the fine print, man. But basically, Watsu owes you a commission on procuring the client, and you'll be the executive producer, which I think are Lin's conditions. He must be bringing her a lot of money, 'cause I've never heard of Watsu giving exclusive producer rights to anyone."

"Cool," Tristen said. The thought of earning more money almost made him salivate. The sooner he could prove himself to Meegan, the better.

"Come on. Lin's ready. I'm going to grab a coffee while you take over."

"Right," Tristen said, stepping behind the soundboard. The different buttons and sliders that had been so intimidating before The Seethers had recorded their own albums were now familiar, though he still had things to learn. The stress he had placed on his muscles was showing up in simple movements, like sitting and reaching for things. And he had a fight in seventy-two hours.

Steve stepped back in with a paper cup of coffee. "What the hell is that guy doing?"

Through the glass, Lin was gargling with what Tristen assumed was salt water.

"Leave him alone. He's my ticket back into the game." Tristen rubbed his palms together, then worked on the metrics he wanted-ed.

"Yeah? No plans to get back on stage?" Steve asked, setting up his end. He hit a button to speak to the other side of the glass. Tristen made a mental note about the button's location. "Lin, could you speak into the mic?"

"Sure thing, boss." The answer came back muted. Steve adjusted settings and buttons until the studio mic connected.

"Sometimes this equipment takes a while to get warmed up," he explained. "I mean, it's not the latest, you know?"

No studio could keep up with every new piece of equipment, but it was good enough. Tristen flipped his own mic on into the studio. "All right, Lin. Time to warm up. Let's start with 'Fine Line.'"

"You betcha," Lin said, clicking another finger gun through the window.

The warm-up went well, so they started to record, running 'Fine Line' seven times before Tristen made Lin take a break.

"Just five minutes." He had received a text from his friend and mentor Elijah. *Call me when you can.* "I'll be right back," he told Steve, leaving the booth before Steve could agree or protest.

Outside, he stepped into a dark corner.

"Hey, man. It's been a while."

"Too long, man. We need to talk more often because clearly, your life is busier than I thought it was." Elijah's deep, Barry White laugh followed.

Tristen always thought Elijah had missed his calling as a voice actor, but Elijah disagreed. He was from the Lowcountry and had worked hard to be a lawyer ever since his uncle was sentenced to jail for twenty years for a rape he didn't commit. Elijah's uncle was one of the so-called lucky ones; his case was revised after he'd spent seven years of his life in jail. The judge had released him and wiped his record, but he was never the same. His marriage was over, his kids were estranged, and he'd struggled with addiction for the rest of his short life. Elijah swore his uncle never would have died so young if the state had done a better job at finding the real perpetrator.

"Yeah, there are a couple of things. First, did you get the pictures I sent?"

"Yeah, I saw the photos. They're all of a balloon loan coming due."

Tristen licked his lips. "What's your verdict?"

"That Ivy's in trouble if she doesn't pay the loan off."

Bile bubbled in Tristen's stomach. He had held on to a glimmer of hope Elijah would find a solution. He was a lawyer for bigwigs, after all. He probably got people out of things like this all the time.

"Did she try to refinance?"

"She claims she did, but I found out later she waited till she was past the deadline. And I doubt she was easy to work with when she went into the bank. You know, nothing is ever her fault." Tristen swallowed. Visions of Ivy shouting at managers, customer service reps, and cashiers throughout the years bombarded his brain.

"Got it."

Tristen pressed his palms into his eyes until he saw stars. "I was hoping you'd have another solution."

"On a different subject, I saw Meegan's song on the charts. That's pretty cool, Tris."

"It is. She's excited." But that wasn't what he wanted to talk about. "Is there anything you can think of, Elijah? I need to make some fast cash myself. Pay things off that I got stuck with."

"Do you? Well, as a lawyer and your friend, I'm not gonna mention what you're really asking out loud. First, because I don't recommend it, and second, 'cause I don't think you'll earn enough before the date without killing yourself," Elijah said.

Tristen looked at his fists. "I promise not to die. I just want—I don't know what I want."

"I'll come get you if you land in jail." Elijah's deep laugh made Tristen smile despite the ominous words.

"Thanks. That strangely reassures me."

One year into living on his own in Cincinnati, Tristen had taken on a few boxing matches at a seedy underground club. That time it hadn't been for money. He was bartending in the evenings at the Walcott and making good money, but he'd lived alone until then and felt like he was going crazy not having any real friends. One night at the Walcott, Elijah had recognized Tristen by the shiner he wore on his left eye as the guy he'd watched box the night before. A lawyer attending an illegal boxing match had made Tristen suspicious at first, but despite his prestigious degrees, Elijah was from Lowcountry first. He liked gold cufflinks as much as he liked a boxing match.

Elijah's tone was grim. "That's what I'm here for. We'll talk soon, Tristen."

Watsu came out of her office and marched towards him.

"Thanks, Elijah."

"Break's over," Watsu said. "Lin said he wanted to get through three songs today. We're on the clock."

"Sure thing. I was just headed back in."

Watsu gave him a stiff nod and marched away as Tristen headed back into the studio.

The three songs took up the full two hours Lin had booked and the rest of the energy Tristen had. By the time Steve yelled for everyone to wrap, Tristen wanted to crawl into his bed.

"That was outstanding," Lin shouted, his voice cracking at the last words. His voice teacher handed him a thermos, then said something that kept him quiet. Instead, he wiggled his eyebrows at them in thanks.

"That's me," Steve said. "I'll be heading out."

"Me too. See you all later," Tristen said. Watsu looked up, but barely waved before turning her attention to a woman with two large men in black who had walked in.

"Annie!" Watsu exclaimed, kissing the woman on both cheeks as Tristen dipped out.

Inside his car, he took a moment to gather some energy before driving home. His phone buzzed, lighting up with Meegan's face.

"What the hell, Tristen Levisay. I told you nothing was happening between me and Clay."

"And I believe you, Meegan."

"Then why'd you send some crazy woman to accuse me of cheating on you?"

"What?"

"This woman marched up to me today and accused me first of taking you from her, and then when she saw Clay, she accused me of keeping him while cheating on you."

"I don't know what you're talking about, Meegan." Tristen looked around the dark parking lot, though no one was around.

"Tristen?" Clay was on the phone. Tristen closed his eyes to keep his temper in check.

"Put Meegan back on, Clay," he said through gritted teeth.

"Listen, man. I understand this isn't your fault. But I gotta ask, did you ever have a crazy fan? Did you date a fan before Meegan? This woman had photos of you with her in compromising positions and everything. She kept trying to get Meegan to look. It was pretty traumatizing for Meegan."

Tristen rolled his eyes, but kept his voice even. "Meegan and I have been dating for two years, and I never cheated on her with any crazy fan. You know you can whip up some photos with photoshop or AI pretty easily, right?"

"I don't know, man," Clay said. "We didn't get a good look at the pictures, but they seemed real."

Tristen again held back a sigh. "My offer to come be part of her security still stands."

"No." Meegan wasn't on the phone, but he could still hear her.

It was just as well she said no, because at that moment, he didn't want to do anything for her. It was unfair of her to accuse him of something so stupid. He started the car and pulled out of the studio driveway, tires squealing. He had to get his frustration out somehow. He'd rather it be on the car than saying something he'd would later regret to Meegan.

"Let me talk to Meegan, Clay."

Shuffling sounds added to Tristen's frustration as he zoomed around a car which had slowed down far too early for the right turn ahead.

"What?"

"Babe, I understand you're mad, but this isn't on me. I didn't send anyone, and I certainly didn't cheat on you."

"Fine. I believe you."

She was angry. He understood that. But he also understood he had no real right to express his frustration with her comments.

"I'll see you soon, right? I miss you." Telling her the truth helped release some of his anger. He missed seeing her. He missed kissing her. He missed hearing all of her thoughts and opinions.

"I miss you, too. Maybe that's why I feel a bit crazy," Meegan breathed into the phone. "I'm sorry."

"It's forgotten," Tristen said, remembering when it was too late that she hated that phrase. "I'm headed back to my mom's. Had a recording with Lin today and a chat with Elijah. Unfortunately, he couldn't come up with a way for me to make money faster."

"What do you need money fast for?"

Tristen hit the steering wheel. He couldn't believe he'd messed up that quickly.

"Ivy, actually," he said, scrambling to come up with a partial truth. "She has a balloon loan that's coming due. We're trying to figure out how to get it refinanced or paid off. It's for about forty thousand."

"Are you serious?" Meegan didn't sound like she was considering helping. "What the hell did she take out a balloon loan for?"

Tristen sighed. "I don't know. I'm guessing her credit score wasn't great, and it was the only option they gave her."

"Tristen, do not loan her the money."

The comment was so quick and fierce that it surprised Tristen at first. He laughed awkwardly, not knowing what else to do. "Um, I don't have that kind of money."

Meegan was quiet, except for muttering to someone on her side of the phone. "And don't ask my dad for it."

"I wasn't going to ask you for the money," he said slowly. That wasn't a lie. He'd decided he wouldn't. Which was different.

"Good. First thing Daddy ever taught me was to not mix money-lending with friends and lovers."

"Right. But I wasn't asking, anyway."

"If she loses her house, we'll be there for her. To encourage her, I mean."

Tristen tried to digest what Meegan was saying.

"Yes. Absolutely," he said, turning the engine on the car. "I gotta go. I'm beat."

"Me too. Gotta get to my massage before this dinner party. Clay made me an appointment after that awful woman attacked me."

"Wait, she physically attacked you?"

"Well, no. But whatever. It was stressful."

Tristen relaxed his grip.

"I'll call you tomorrow," Meegan said. "I love you."

"Yeah. Love you," Tristen said, wondering what might happen to that love if Meegan found out about him living with his mom. Or the gambling he'd been doing. Or that he was going to fight illegal boxing matches.

He didn't want to think about it. She would have to stay in the dark.

Chapter 14

Friday morning, the day of the first boxing match, arrived faster than Tristen wanted it to. When he got up, he could hardly look at himself in the mirror. An unease had settled over him. He wasn't sure if it was the fact that he was back to boxing or back at Ivy's, but he couldn't stop thinking about a Greek tragedy they'd gone to see in high school where the guy looked back to see if his girl was still following him, condemning them both to repeat the same story over and over again.

Orpheus? Maybe. He wasn't sure. He and Talon had put aside Greek mythology to study boxing back in high school. And anyway, it wasn't exactly that, since he was actually worse off than he had been then. He was in debt, with a girlfriend who probably wouldn't be with him if she knew what he was up to.

Tristen shook his head. Thinking about Greek mythology or Meegan wasn't going to help him tonight.

"Where you off to?" he asked when Ivy finally left the bathroom after her shower.

"I got a thing," she said. "Bobbi is picking me up. What are you up to?"

"Finishing up some work, and then my trainer Jared is picking me up."

"For a fight? Already?" Ivy looked concerned as her eyes lingered over Tristen. "You ready enough?"

"I'm ready, Ivy."

She hesitated, which she rarely did, but she didn't say anything before Bobbi pulled up and honked the horn.

"Seriously, that cousin of mine could learn to have some patience. Don't get too hurt tonight," Ivy said. She started walking out the door before turning abruptly and kissing Tristen on the cheek. "Bye."

"Bye, Ivy." He watched her go, wondering if he should tell her that he wasn't going to a Gladiator show or anything, but he decided to let it pass. Even when they were kids she would sometimes get into these strange moods.

He spent the last few hours resting his muscles and editing the music for the concert. By seven in the evening, he and Jared were in the makeshift prep area, the hum of the crowd seeping in under the door.

Every underground boxing match Owen was a part of took place in abandoned factories, sheds, or barns. It was amazing how many there were in middle America.

"Here," Jared said, handing him a small white pill. "Take it."

"I don't want drugs."

"Yeah, well, you're going to need a little. It's just one of those Ritalin pills, or whatever they're called. It helps with concentration and not feeling the pain. At least, at the moment. You'll feel the pain tomorrow."

Tristen took the pill, cradling it in his palm for a minute. To take or not take it? He'd done so several times in life, never knowing what it was. This one, a small, off-white pill with no markings, could be Tylenol, or it could be MDMA.

Jared watched him, his mouth set in a hard line and his arms crossed over his chest. There was no use resisting. Luke had worked in Jared's place when Talon and Tristen were kids, and Tristen was sure no one had ever said no to him. Not when he could deadlift almost four hundred pounds when he wasn't drunk or high. Luke had claimed he never took steroids, and while he sold all sorts of drugs, he'd always said he only ever smoked weed.

There had been a few times when Luke had shoved a pill in his face when he was a teenager, and Tristen was expected to take it with no questions asked. He'd always claimed it was an anti-inflammatory.

Tristen pushed the pill into his mouth and swallowed.

Luke hadn't been out of jail long when he'd pulled into the high school parking lot just as Tristen, Talon, and a few of their friends were taking some pills a guy had grabbed from his house. It took months to live down the way Luke grabbed them by their ears and threw them into the back of the car. When the high kicked in, Luke made them scrub the garage clean.

"You wanna end up like my dead cousin?" he had asked them. "You're fourteen. You're too dumb to make choices like that."

He could yell or make them clean the garage all he wanted; they lived in rural Kentucky during the opioid crisis. Pills and marijuana were everywhere. While Luke was in jail, Talon and Tristen started smoking weed. Tristen made extra money learning to cook it into brownies and cakes. Around fifteen, they moved on to harder things, getting high on ecstasy one night, another with cocaine. Whatever they could get their hands on and afford. But in the end, they had sports and boxing to rein them in, keeping them too busy to spend every weekend being stupid.

For Tristen, it was the day Aimee overdosed that everything changed. He'd started only getting bad highs, filled with hallucinations or physical pain. Being high seemed like a betrayal to Aimee somehow. By the time he was twenty, he had no appetite for anything.

To erase the memories of Aimee lying on the floor of the motel she'd died in, like a doll discarded by its owner, Tristen jumped off the bench. Tingling started in his toes and ran up his legs. He crashed into the wall as a short, dizzy spell came over him.

"I'll be back. Get ready." Jared looked him over, then left.

Tristen got dressed quickly. All he needed was the shiny shorts with Owen's logo on them and the sweatshirt over his chest to keep him warm until the fight. Staying warm would help him not shiver, which someone could mistake for him trembling in fear. Not shivering at all was better.

He checked his phone out of habit. There weren't any more tags of Meegan in compromising positions with Clay. Instead, there were several selfies at a party. Then her new nails. Then her taking pictures of herself in the mirror. Tristen switched apps and checked on Talon, who also had several selfies but at least one picture of Sandra's baby bump.

The door swung open, noise blaring into the small room. Tristen tossed his phone aside as though caught being naughty.

Owen sauntered over, grinning, followed by Jared and a bald man with broad shoulders and a slight limp. "There's my fighter. That Talon you're looking at?"

Tristen dropped his fingers from rubbing his temples and nodded.

"He seems happy."

Tristen shrugged. Owen's presence reminded him why he was there, and his nerves were starting to take over.

"You ready for the fight?" Owen asked, his eyes shifting to Tristen's backpack.

"Absolutely." Tristen stood up and jumped in place to warm up.

"Good. I need your head to be in the ring, not on your brother. Although, if you're still mad at him, maybe you can use that. Pretend it's his face you're punching."

"Funny, Owen. We gonna fight or not?" Tristen watched the older man, noticing the tic in his right eye. But Owen didn't grimace or leer. Instead, he grinned.

"I wasn't sure you would show up."

"Why?" Tristen stopped bouncing. "I've never been the guy who says he'll show up and then not show. You're mixing me with Talon."

Owen chuckled. "Will you listen to this kid?"

"Three fights, Owen. I'm here. It's the first one. Let's go."

Owen made a signal for Tristen to sit down. "Chill. Ain't time to go out yet. You're always trying to get things over with. You gotta learn to enjoy the moment, kid."

"Well, he used to be the loser twin, so I'm not surprised he'd want to get another loss out of his way," the bald man said.

Tristen looked him dead in the eyes, but there was no use adding any threat to the glare. Owen chuckled again.

"Yeah, he lost more." His small eyes bored into Tristen as his lips parted into a smile that showed teeth. "But he knows how to win, too."

"This guy? Thought his specialty was losing."

Tristen forced himself to grin at the meathead.

"That was the past. Tonight, he's gonna win," Owen said, clasping him soundly on the shoulder. "At the very least, you're gonna give it your all."

"You said it didn't matter if I won or lost."

"No, kid, I didn't. I said nothing like that." Owen pulled out a cigar from his pocket. "Business is fickle, so most of the time, I don't know what I need from you until we begin. Right now, I'm going to need you to go five rounds without getting your ass kicked."

"Five? What the hell, Owen? I'm hardly trained for five rounds," Tristen exclaimed. Fear started trickling into his veins. Five rounds. That was a long time in the ring. Especially if he was losing, which he probably would be. The match during the poker game, the only match he'd boxed in over four years, had lasted two rounds. After thinking about it, he was convinced the fight Mac had set up was rigged to get him to consider boxing again. Like gambling, a small taste of victory could have a boxer coming back over and over.

"Jared doesn't think I'm ready for that."

Jared looked up from his phone. "You know what you're doing. Just go with your instinct."

Owen turned back to Tristen and shrugged. "You look fine to me."

"But five rounds?"

"Well," Owen said, puffing on the cigar. He looked at the bald guy. "I'm not gonna lie. It's gonna be hard for you to stay upright. But it's the least you need to do. Stay upright for five rounds. Got it? No KOs on your ass."

"Fine. But why not three?"

"You ain't an amateur, and we do whatever we want around here. That guy's trainer wanted seven. We settled on five. Got it?"

"Got it." Tristen lifted his chin. There was no way to tell if Owen was lying or not. For all Tristen knew, Owen had wanted five rounds from the beginning just to humiliate him.

"Prep 'em," Owen said, pointing at Tristen between the eyes. "He comes out in fifteen minutes."

He and his guy left, the closing door sealing off the noise from the crowd. Tristen didn't bother to look. He stood and jumped to warm his muscles, then pounded his gloves together. Energy soared through his body like fire.

"Think that stuff's kicking in," he told Jared. "I feel like I'm jumping out of my skin."

"It was a low dose, man." Jared shook his head. "Come on. They called your name."

He pulled Tristen up by the arm and marched him to the door. The noise hit his ears like a sledgehammer. Walking from the quiet locker room into the roaring auditorium was like stepping into a time warp.

He was victorious, he told himself. A superhero who couldn't lose. He would win the fight. Win the girl. Tristen eyed the blonde in a string bikini who pranced around the ring, careful to stay out of his way. Maybe he'd win that girl.

The thought made him laugh. A loud, gloriously full laugh he reveled in before turning on the crowd with a growl. It was nice to be someone else. To be the Pelton Viking.

The lights in the ring were dim, with a spotlight rolling through the crowd until it stopped on him, blinding him. His instincts kicked in immediately, like riding a bike. The trick was to keep his eyes open, following Jared blind until his sight adjusted. Squinting or wincing was a dead giveaway for a novice and could make people run to change their bets. It was the first lesson he'd learned as a kid. At his first fight, he'd squinted, and Owen had lost a lot of money. As punishment, Tristen had to go against a veteran boxer in Owen's group the next day at the gym.

Tristen jiggled his jaw. It still popped ten years later. That had been the moment he and Talon had been separated into 'winner' and 'loser'.

He cracked his neck, stretching it from side to side as his vision adjusted. Blood rushed at full velocity through his veins, bringing with it a shiver of energy. It was time to show them who he was. Tristen hollered at the men shouting next to him. They yelled back. He growled at the men to his left. They cheered and shouted. Pounding one gloved hand against the other, Tristen roared at the ceiling, invincibility coursing through his veins. He was Rocky. He was Mohammed Ali. He was Sugar Ray Leonard.

Anyone but Tristin Levisay.

Five rounds. Shit. *Five rounds.* He cracked his neck side to side again and did what he should never do; he looked at the faces. The bleachers, chairs, and floor area were full of mostly men, yelling and pumping their fists in the air. A few laughed. One of them, Tristen was sure, smirked.

Jared elbowed him in the ribs. He had slowed down, a sign of fear or trepidation. Tristen shook his head until his eyeballs hurt, then focused straight ahead. A small group of women dressed in pink bikinis huddled near the stage, their brightly painted lips smiling at the crowd and waving shyly whenever a man rushed up for a selfie.

In the ring stood a man in shiny blue shorts, tattoos all over his chest. His hair was buzzed down both sides of his head. Minus a braid or two, he looked like a tanned Viking himself. Tristen sat in his seat and tried to calm his breathing. He felt pudgy next to the other guy's rippling abs.

"Okay, that's Rat. He's a cheater, but you can get the better of him," Jared was saying in his ear. His demeanor was almost friendly, which Tristen appreciated. "Take water." Tristen opened his mouth to plastic-flavored lukewarm water. "There ya go. Mouth guard. Into the middle. Try not to get knocked out the first round."

Tristen walked forward, his chin raised, looking down his cheekbones at Rat. The referee, with shoulders twice as wide as the average man, went over the rules, but Tristen didn't pay attention. He looked at Rat's face, then at Owen, then the clock, then the paint job on the walls of the warehouse, which looked like it had been a school gym at some point, then at the referee.

An intense desire to punch someone was building in him. He thought of Clay's hand on Meegan. He thought of Ivy losing her house. He thought of Talon leaving and the rest of the guys abandoning The Seethers.

This was his time. It was a gift to get his frustration and anger out. He glanced at Rat, who hadn't moved. A smile spread across his face, revealing four silver teeth.

Tristen felt himself smile in return. But instead of fear, excitement pumped through him. He couldn't wait to pound his glove into Rat's face. His arms tingled with the effort of holding back.

Whatever Jared had given him, Tristen was going to ask for it again in the next fight.

"Shake," growled the ref.

Rat grabbed Tristen's hand in a vise grip. Tristen kept his limp. His brain moved at a million thoughts per minute. Rat was a veteran and considered him already beaten, since Tristen was less experienced. Rat might also be thinking Tristen would be an easy knockout. And there was no reason to change that expectation. If Rat expected an easy fight, Tristen could use that to his advantage.

The whistle blew, shaking him into the present.

The first punch landed on his chin, but he bounced away quickly. The impact was soft. Tristen landed a right hook, but his subsequent jab only hit air, throwing his body into space.

He needed to survive the first rounds without getting too hurt. And without using too much energy.

Relax, Tristen. Float the arms. Release the fingers. Once you hit, you can tense a bit. Right here, hold your arms from the middle of your back.

Luke's and Owen's voices streamed together into his consciousness. All the advice he'd been given from fourteen to nineteen.

The whistle blew suddenly, the two fighters separating instinctively to their corners.

"Not too bad," Jared said as he squirted water into Tristen's mouth and onto his face. "Let me see that. Got a cut on the eyebrow."

Tristen didn't feel anything. Jared could have been cutting his eye out, and he wouldn't know. All he felt was his heart pumping and the need to punch Rat hard in the face.

"Let's go. Second round."

Tristen charged forward. For a few seconds, he had Rat against the ropes, their roles from the previous round now reversed. After one blow, he thought Rat might have blacked out, but he reopened his eyes with his silver-toothed smile still menacingly intact.

The whistle blew to jeers and yells. Jared massaged Tristen's arms and shoulders, whispering advice in his ears that Tristen couldn't interpret over the crowd.

"Hit him in the jaw!" were the only words that got through to his brain. Everything was slightly fuzzy, and if Tristen focused for too long on one thought, his stomach threatened to revolt.

It makes me feel sick all the time, Tristen. I can't help it.

Tristen jerked to the right and left, trying to find Aimee, but she wasn't there.

A solid smack in his jaw orientated him back to the fight. Aimee wasn't there. And he wasn't fourteen.

"Get him!" roared Owen. He sounded inches from Tristen's ears. Rat bounced back, his face intent behind the gloves as Tristen straightened.

There was a glimmer of confusion in his opponent's eyes. The perfect time to charge. Tristen leaned into the animal desire in him to pummel something, to crush a living thing until it no longer existed. He threw a hook, then a jab. Then another and another. His left arm flew out, then his right.

Tristen held his fingers loose and freed the trained instinct within them until a strong hand pushed him roughly into his corner.

"That's enough!"

He looked around at the crowd. Men were throwing up their hands, jeering, or shouting. Jared pushed him into the chair and shoved cotton up his two nostrils.

"Damn it! Tristen!"

"Yeah?" A switch turned on, highlighting the fatigue in his body for a minute. "What?"

"Open." Tristen obeyed. Jared poured water into his mouth. "Just two rounds left."

Tristen jerked his chin up. "Two? Already?"

"Yeah, man," Jared chuckled, his hands on Tristen's shoulders, his mouth near his ears. This time, Tristen could hear every word. "And you aren't doing too bad. Get back out there."

The tone, maybe. Or perhaps the words. Something about it filled Tristen with momentum.

Crush 'em.

Luke used to say it all the time. Referring to the duffel bag at first, and then opponents.

Crush 'em, Talon. Show your brother how to defeat his opponent.

Tristen's left fist flew out too fast. Instead of hitting Rat, it flew through the air. A crack filled his ears as pain exploded in his eye.

The ring morphed into a black tunnel; the sound swept itself away into a vacuum, and Tristen saw and felt nothing.

Tristen touched under his right eye with the pads of his fingers, watching the skin lighten slightly, then return to the angry purplish red. He'd been awake since early that morning, battling nausea and pain. Exhaustion didn't even begin to explain what his body felt, but sleep was elusive. The two-star motel bed didn't help, nor the disinfectant smell the pillows had. That smell was the culprit for his first vomiting session. He was sure of it.

He remembered arriving at the motel with Jared. A small man with round eyeglasses had insisted on looking Tristen over right away. Jared had smirked from the corner as Tristen stood naked in the middle of the room, his feet sinking into the brown, crunchy carpet while the man made sure no bones were broken.

"Possible concussion, but nothing too serious. Ice and anti-in-flammatories. And stop boxing."

Jared patted the little man heavily on the shoulders. The doctor's entire body, if he actually was a doctor, quivered from the fake affection. Tristen, too exhausted to argue about anything, had taken the round, brown pills shoved into his mouth and gone to bed.

His body sank heavily into the mattress, and he immediately found a perfect position for himself. When Jared and the small man left, Tristen couldn't gather enough strength to wave good-bye. Just before he fell asleep, he wondered if the door was locked.

He'd woken up after two in the afternoon with an ache in his side and head. When the desire to vomit overrode his pain, he'd crawled across the crusty carpet to the bathroom, making it to the toilet just in time. After emptying his stomach, he'd filled the sink with cold water and stuck his face in it until some of the pain was numbed. With his stomach somewhat calm, he opened one of the bottles of water Jared had left, wincing when his lip split again. The red droplets dissolved into the water one by one. There was an ointment near the bed from the small doctor, but walking there wasn't worth the effort. It was easier to stay at the mirror inspecting himself.

Beside the black eye, a bruise on his jawline, and his split and swollen lips, his face wasn't as bad as he'd worried it would be. Nothing like the time his nose had been broken, or when he'd gotten two black eyes and a bloody ear. Tristen checked his hands, then arms and torso and legs, surprised to find he seemed fine. Just sore muscles from the tension and some bruises along his shoulders and ribs. Nothing he couldn't handle.

Yet his head ached like the devil. He eyed the bed, then pushed himself slowly towards the shower.

"How's my fighter doing this morning?" Owen asked over the phone.

"Fine. My head is aching, and my lip split again, but the doctor said I don't have any broken bones."

"You took the pills Jared left you?"

"No," Tristen drawled. He didn't know what they were, but he pulled them from his bag, popped two into his mouth, and swallowed.

"Take 'em. Aspirin can do miracles." Owen chuckled. Tristen eyed the pills warily. "Listen, I need you to come to the gym this week. I think we can get you in shape to win the next one."

Tristen groaned. The way his body was behaving, he couldn't imagine fighting again. "When is the next fight?"

"Next Saturday. Unless I got something special come up during the week."

"I'm not sure I can do that," Tristen said, panting through a stab of pain in his side. He'd known before today that fighting included training, but now everything seemed to be colliding. And Lin was a priority. "I have a job, Owen."

"Well, Tristen, you committed to these fights. I expect you to do your best, and damn, boy, you looked pretty good out there last night. Probably could've won if you'd been fully ready. And if not for that bad move at the end. And against Rat, damn! You pretending not to know what you were doing the first two rounds was genius. And then you came out like a tornado. Wish I had a video to show you. Anyway, come by the gym today—"

"And if I don't?" Tristen asked, silencing his groans as he sat down.

"I'd be real disappointed to hear you're not a man of your word. We made a deal."

"You could just give Ivy the money."

"Can't give her the money if I don't make the money. I ain't got that kind of cash hanging around. Do you?"

Tristen took in a deep breath slowly, pushing through the pain in his bruised ribs to get oxygen down to the bottom of his lungs before answering. "No. I don't have that kind of money."

There was a pause. Tristen looked at the phone. It was still connected. "Owen."

"Thought you'd have something to say about me seeing Ivy."

"None of my business," Tristen said, though the idea of them together turned his stomach. "I kinda thought she was still hung up on Luke."

Owen chuckled again. "Yeah, well, she's over him now. It's a shame. He stole Ivy from me a long time ago."

Tristen turned the television on to drown out the questions and emotions in his head.

"Anyway, you won me a lot of money last night, Tristen. Everyone was excited to bet on or against you. I want you to try your best to win me more money next fight."

"If I do, will you release me from the third?"

"Nice try. But be happy. You can start paying off that credit card debt. Or pay your girlfriend rent so you can get out of Ivy's house. You got some money in your bank account now."

Every cell in his body seemed to slide downward. Tristen checked his bank app. Sure enough, three thousand dollars had arrived that morning. He could pay his phone bill, fill up his car, buy the Bluetooth headphones he'd taken back so Meegan didn't find out.

Suddenly, the amount didn't seem like enough.

"When do you want me at Top Gym?"

"That's a good boy. Be there tonight by seven. And on Wednesday. Next fight is Friday."

"Fine." Tristen hung up.

The man that looked back at him from the dark phone glass needed to lie down. Watsu was sending him email after email, asking if he was going to edit the songs in the cloud and if he would come in the next day. Watsu didn't seem like a woman who would take no for an answer, but he wasn't sure he could survive all day at the studio. Before heading back to bed, he told her he would edit the songs from Pelton and have them ready when he went in on Monday.

Then he crawled back under the covers with every intention of passing out for several hours.

A message from Jared pinged. *Don't hang up on Owen again.*

Tristen threw the phone onto the bed. It was no use trying to go back to sleep.

Chapter 15

On Monday, Tristen arrived at Watsu's building ready to work with Lin again. Despite the physical discomfort of working on the concert stuff at his old desk, he thought it would be best to heal hidden from the world. Even though Ivy interrupted him about every forty minutes, he had somehow managed to finish the sound work for Watsu.

"Hey—whoa. Did you get punched in the eye?" Watsu asked, choking on her sip of water when she saw him in the break room. "Were you in a fight?"

Tristen forced himself to smile, glad he'd concocted a story to tell already. "Went back to my old boxing gym and got in the ring with some guys."

"And they decided to beat you up for that hair, right?"

"Maybe."

Watsu cuffed him playfully on the arm. Tristen's laughter died with a hiss.

"Sorry, does it hurt?" she asked, her finger pointing as though she might try to touch him.

"Only if you touch it," he said, moving away from the offending finger. The movement shot pain through his body, but he couldn't pinpoint the exact spot. Watsu frowned at his groan.

"I've got some muscle rub. You want some?"

Tristen winced. "I'm not sure it will do anything, but okay. I'll try it. When's Lin going to be here?"

Watsu took a moment to look over her notes. "You have about twenty minutes before he arrives."

"Okay."

"Oh, and I sent you an email with the information about the concert so far. They called for a sound check tomorrow, along with the lighting people. I think Seraphina will be there. You get the songs stitched together, the intros and transitions and all that?"

"Did everything you asked me," Tristen said, dragging his finger through the herbal goo Watsu handed him.

"And the one for their dinner?"

"Yep. That's done. It's two and a half hours at the end."

"Perfect." Watsu eyed him as he rubbed a small amount of her salve on his neck.

"This is great," he admitted. The muscles in his neck were already releasing their tension under the cooling effect.

"Has Meegan seen you yet?" Watsu asked as Tristen dropped to the ground. She grabbed a bag of ice from the fridge-freezer they used for the different waters singers might demand, tossing it near his head as he carefully arranged his body on the floor.

"No." Tristen rested his face against the ice. "She's having fun. Don't want to worry her."

"I'd be more worried about her realizing her boyfriend is the kind of man who thinks he can box."

Laughing still put pressure on his ribs, though the pain was less than on Saturday and Sunday. When he thought about fighting again in five days, Tristen wanted to run away.

His vibrating phone pulled him out of his thoughts. "Hello?" He closed his eyes and nestled up against the bag of ice again. The cold helped to ground him.

"Tristen!" Ivy yelled.

"What's wrong?" he asked, keeping his voice calm. Ivy fed off chaos. Being anything but calm when she was stressed usually escalated whatever situation she found herself in.

"They're threatening to drop me from my health insurance. They can't do this. Here, talk to the nurse."

"Ivy, wait," Tristen said, but it was too late. For a moment, he heard only muffled commotion. Then a female voice greeted him.

"Mr. Levisay? This is Nurse Francis." His body suddenly felt cold. "Ivy is a little upset."

"Not a little. I'm a lot upset." Ivy wasn't on the phone but was yelling loud enough for probably everyone in the clinic to hear her. Tristen certainly could. "Give me the damn papers. There. Signed. You have my permission to speak to my son. Stupid protocols."

"What has her upset?" Tristen asked, sliding his gaze over to Watsu, who seemed suddenly very interested in the paper she was holding.

"Ivy's been given her second warning. One more, and she could be kicked out as one of our patients."

"Warning? For what?"

"In line with our policy, we gave her a drug test today."

"What policy?"

"Anyone who comes in showing symptoms of being on a substance receives a drug test. We can't administer medication if we think it might interfere with something the patient has already taken."

Tristen waited.

"Right, so Ivy resisted, but finally agreed. In the sample, we detected traces of marijuana."

Tristen waited for more explanation. Nurse Francis stopped speaking as though to allow the weight of what she'd just said to sink in.

"Okay. Um, what is the protocol for that?" He couldn't help emphasizing protocol. A door slammed in the hallway, the sound echoing in his chest. Ivy was in the wrong. That truth could cycle in his head all day, but it wouldn't take away the brittle urgency that always came when something or someone depended on him.

Nurse Francis sighed, as though gathering energy to explain something complicated to a five-year-old. Tristen set down the pen he had been tapping nervously against the soundboard and took a deep breath.

"Sir, your mother has to adhere to the rules. One of which is that she won't take any other narcotic."

"Marijuana is a narcotic?" The urgency swelled, rippling anxiety through his middle. If he hadn't already been stressed, if he had slept better, maybe he could have controlled himself. "At least she had the sense not to take the pain pills the ER doc prescribed her. Or would you prefer she take them?"

"Marijuana is an illegal substance, Mr. Levisay. Whether or not you agree with the law, the medical community doesn't recognize it as a viable treatment for pain. And as a former addict, your mother must adhere to the rules that Doctor Robert puts into place for her own health and safety. We also have to report this drug test to her place of work."

"You're interested in getting my mom fired from her job?"

"Not personally, no. But there are rules, and she knows them."

"Is that right?" Tristen drawled. "What about the rules for the medical community when they were handing out opioids left and right? Were there any laws? Because that ridiculous fine the pharmaceutical companies paid the governments wouldn't even put a dent in the damage they caused to people like Ivy and my sister. The medical community gave painkillers to my mother in the first place and got her addicted to them, Nurse Francis. It was professionals who gave her opioids to deal with chronic back pain from working in the factory when they should have sent her to physical therapy. And while the state of Kentucky does not recognize marijuana, many states do. As someone who has seen the damage that opioids and the other various drugs you all in the medical community have seen fit to give out cause the people I love, I would prefer she smoke the damn marijuana before getting back onto the opioids that have taken so many lives. The ER doc who prescribed her painkillers should *lose his license!*"

By his last words, Tristen realized he was yelling. He pressed his palms into his thighs to stop them from shaking, clenching his jaw. "Hello?"

No answer. He checked the screen. The call was still going.

"Mr. Levisay. This is Doctor Robert, your mother's doctor. How are you, sir?"

Horrible. Especially now that he'd just gotten his mother kicked out of the medical co-op.

"Hello," Tristen managed to say. He knew he would have to apologize. They might not keep Ivy as a patient, otherwise. But he couldn't seem to find the right words.

"I hear you're frustrated, Mr. Levisay," Doctor Robert continued. "I can understand that. But I deal with many patients like Ivy, and I have strict protocols. While I understand your point about marijuana versus opioids, I hope you understand I can't have my patients coming in with illegal substances in their systems. Since I can't regulate illegal substances, I can't monitor their use while your mother is also getting treatment from me. Do you understand?"

"Yes." Tristen swallowed, humiliated by his own behavior. Angry at the situation brought on by the medical community, but ashamed for yelling at Dr. Roberts, who was a calm, kind man with graying hair who tried to serve his patients well. Sweat rolled out of his pores and drenched his clean shirt despite the air conditioning running.

He could rant about the system, but what was done in the past was already over. Nothing could change that.

"Good to know. We need her to test clean the next time she comes in, or we won't prescribe more pain medication. And we might have to kick her out of the co-op. Because of my malpractice insurance, I can't have patients taking illegal substances. I'm sure you understand that."

"Understood. I'll make sure she's clean when she comes in."

"I appreciate it."

A shadow fell on him as he hung up and slowly stood to his feet. It was Watsu. "Lin's here."

"Okay, start him listening to the last song. We need the harmony done. And we need him to choose the guitarist. He should understand. I talked him through it over the phone yesterday." Tristen took a deep breath and got up from the floor.

Lin walked past the studio window, waving excitedly at Tristen as he passed. Tristen lifted his hand to wave. He watched Watsu talk to Lin and his agent, Rocky. When she was done she gave him a thumbs-up to start the tracks for them to listen to.

"Something wrong?" Watsu asked when she got back.

"My mom didn't pass a drug test," Tristen said slowly. "The doctor says he'll have to throw her out of the co-op if she fails again."

"Geez," Watsu said, laughing. "Sorry, I didn't mean to laugh. It's hard to envision your mom. Mine goes to church about five times a week and doesn't believe in taking drugs unless dying. Even then, I'm not sure she would take them. She refused to be numbed for a cavity filling a few years ago. The dentist wouldn't fill her cavity without numbing the area, so they ended up in this sort of standoff. I ended up having to convince my mother that she had two choices: get the cavity taken care of on the dentist's terms, or have it rot out and cause more problems. She finally let him inject her, but she was mad at me for about a month."

Tristen snorted. "That's kinda crazy. My mom asks the dentist to give her that laughing gas stuff they give to kids just for the kicks."

Watsu's red lips parted in a smile. "Well, my mother grew up without a pair of shoes until she was almost a teenager. She met my dad when he was over there with the Navy. I think she was nineteen when they got married."

"So, our moms have poverty in common," Tristen said. "Mine wasn't even eighteen when she had us. Likes to tell everyone who will listen." He paused. Lin's sound was coming through tinny. He fiddled with the soundboard as Watsu hung back, watching. "I'm not sure she's ever been married, actually."

"We moved here from Vietnam when I was three. My mother swore she'd never go back, but I begged her to take me, so we finally went back together two years ago."

"I know how your mom feels," Tristen said. "Sometimes I wish I never had to go back to Pelton." Watsu laughed. "Anyway, Ivy didn't have much growing up either, but she was the lady who paid her friends for their pain meds after they got their wisdom teeth pulled. Anyway, let's move on." Bracing himself for Lin's commentary, he flipped the mic on. "Lin, give us your feedback. This one or this one?"

"Hello, Mr. Tristen! First one. Let's go, let's go. I have a hot date for dinner."

Tristen gave him a salute and sat down to concentrate. Watsu's phone rang, ending any further conversation, much to his relief. He was getting to the point of too much sharing with her.

Somehow, they got through the song choices and recorded Lin's harmony on two before the time was up.

"The next time we meet, we'll finish up the rest," Tristen said as they met in the sound room. He watched Rocky pour a yellow-tinted liquid from a thermos into a cup for Lin, who sipped it as though he were the queen, pinky pointed up.

"Yeah, yeah. I know already."

Watsu made a guttural noise in her throat. "Be nice to Tristen, Lin. He got beat up last night."

"I noticed. Makes you look like a real rough man. I'm a little jealous."

"I could beat you up," Tristen said dryly, but Lin just grinned wider.

Rocky made a signal that caught Lin's attention.

"Okay, okay. Gotta go. Big date with a lady." Lin held his hands out as though holding large breasts. "See you."

Tristen sighed when the door shut behind the two of them. He pulled out his ponytail and mussed his hair to give his head some relief, but it didn't help much.

"If everything goes like this, he'll have his album done in no time," Watsu said, clearly pleased with their work. "You're staying to do the editing, right?"

"Yep. I'll get it done. I'll work at home tomorrow and come back here on Wednesday."

"I won't be here, but Steve will. He has a client. And you're coming in for the concert meeting on Friday, correct?"

"Of course," Tristen drawled, sneaking a glance at his cell phone.

"I sent the details to your email two days ago."

"Right, I got it. I'll see you there," Tristen said, ignoring the itch to dig for the email. He hoped she didn't have an app that told her the date he read it.

Watsu clicked her tongue with a salute and sauntered out of the studio, the door closing behind her just as a message lit up his phone.

The text was from Micah and came with a video. Tristen knew he should just delete it and ignore it, but he couldn't help himself.

It was a video of their last concert.

He pressed play.

Nothing could have prepared him for how bad it was. He never would have imagined that was the experience The Seethers had given the crowd. Tristen looked around the empty hallway to make sure Watsu wasn't coming up behind him and pressed play again, the off-key screech smacking his ears once more. It wasn't the video quality that was so embarrassingly bad; it was their playing.

In the middle of Pete's stage, Micah looked ready to strangle someone. Tristen was singing off-key, his voice cracking twice. But what the video captured best was the jeering in the crowd—right until the bottle hit Tristen in the face. Then the jeering changed to laughter.

The video went black, small white letters asking if he wanted to replay it.

Tristen hit the delete button and took a breath before opening the door. The night air was chilly, drying the sweat from his body. For a moment, he stood in the semidarkness of the parking lot, willing himself to breathe and feel the cold. A strange vibrating sensation moved through his chest. The same feeling he used to get when Aimee was crying from her pain. The same feeling that had moved through him the days of Aimee's funeral.

But crying over this would be stupid. A waste of tears. He'd been at that concert. There was no reason watching a replay should affect him so much. Especially not to tears.

The Seethers were done. Over. No big deal. He'd figure something out and move on. He was figuring things out, damn it.

Chapter 16

Tristen pushed on the ignition button as a call came in from Meegan. Her voice burst loud and sweet through the speakers as he pulled out of the parking lot.

"Hey, babe," she shouted into the phone. Noise from what sounded like a party also came through. "Whatcha doing?"

Meegan had been drinking. Her voice gave it away. Tristen could see her in his mind, smiling and flirting with everyone around her. The light in the middle of a bleak party. At least, she always was for him.

"About to drive to—" Tristen choked before the words *Top Gym* could come out. He was meeting Jared to train, but Meegan didn't need to know that. "I'm headed to the gym. Been editing all day and I need to move. Where are you? Sounds like a good time, whatever it is."

The sound of her laugh reminded him how much he missed her. The ache had lessened with all the activity, but now he wished she was here. They could go out for a coffee, take a walk, find a new place to eat dinner.

From the noise on the other end of the phone, it didn't sound like she was missing him too much.

"I'm at a dinner-slash-art gallery thing. I guess one of the best ones in the area. I forget the name."

"Meegan, come meet these guys." Clay's voice was loud; Tristen envisioned him right next to her. His words sounded forced, but that was probably Tristen being paranoid. Meegan had called him, after all.

"Talking to Tristen. I'll be right there."

Tristen gripped the steering wheel while he listened to Meegan mumble something incoherent, then say "okay" five times before returning her attention to him. "OMG, Tristen. A woman wearing Oscar de la Renta just walked in. This place is insane. I thought I grew up with money, but these people are like the one percent of the one percent. My goal one day is to buy one of those. No, wait. My goal is to have Oscar give me one to wear."

"Why? Is it expensive?" Tristen asked. He hit the accelerator, swerving around a car, trying to turn left in the city traffic.

Meegan scoffed. "Oscar de la Renta isn't about the price. It's about prestige. About wearing him. This woman is wearing Oscar like it's no big deal. If no big deal cost eleven thousand dollars."

"Eleven thousand dollars? For a dress?"

"Oscar de la Renta!" Meegan whispered. She pronounced each word in staccato. It didn't help him understand any better.

In fact, the conversation was starting to bore him. He took a quiet breath, tried to calm his road rage against a driver slowly encroaching into the other lane ahead of him, and tried another subject. "Are you singing tonight?"

"Yes. I'm up for an after-dinner show. Just about forty minutes. It's a charity dinner or something. Man, t hese people have money. Wow. I think Big Mistress just walked in with Cupie."

Meegan was breathless. He'd never heard her so impressed before. Usually, he was the one looking at people in awe of their money.

"I don't know what that even means, Meegan."

"Sorry, babe. Just star-struck over here. How's your mom?"

"My mom? She's fine. You're coming home before Friday for the charity concert run-through, right?"

"We're going to try, but the weather isn't looking great. Seraphina knows, though, so it'll be fine. We'll just do a run-through the day of."

"Are you sure?" Tristen pulled into Top Gym with a sigh of relief. All the driving was killing his back.

"Of course. We already sang it together. Sorry, babe, but I gotta go. Clay is motioning to me. I'll either be home for the run-through or the next day, okay? All depends on the flight. What day would that be? Sunday?"

"Tomorrow's Thursday."

"Right. So tomorrow late or Friday early. Bye, babe!"

"Bye," he said, but she was already gone.

"What's up, jackass," Jared called from the door.

"Are you always this pleasant to work with?" Tristen asked.

"On the treadmill for thirty," Jared said, shrugging away the question.

The line of treadmills stood right at the front of the gym. Tristen frowned. He hated the treadmill—running was only fun outside—but Jared didn't look in a mood to argue. Tristen stripped off his shirt and got on the machine. "This where you usually work?"

"I work where Owen gives me work. For a few months, I was running this place until he could find a manager. That guy over there—Nate's his name. I prefer training people."

"Owen pay you enough for that to be your entire job?"

Jared stood with his arms crossed, his massive chest blocking almost the entire view behind him. He jerked his thumb upward. "Warm up at five point seven at least, pansy."

Tristen obeyed, his feet catching up with the treadmill mat over and over. Jared stood with his arms crossed, watching and listening to the high-pitched whirl of the machine. "You always ask personal questions of people?"

"I was just wondering what makes people work for Owen."

"He pays well."

"Makes sense," Tristen said, getting into the treadmill's rhythm.

"You're a better runner than I thought you'd be," Jared said when the clock finally ticked past fifteen minutes. Outside, he rarely considered time while running, but that was how boring treadmills were. "You race?"

"Nah," Tristen said between his inhales. "I run for the fun of it. Started when I was twelve, and my mom's boyfriend said I needed to lose weight."

"Luke said that?"

"Nah, not Luke. Another guy my mom was dating." Tristen paused before asking, "You knew Luke?"

"I knew him."

Five minutes left on the clock. Tristen glanced at Jared to get a feeling for how old he was but almost lost his balance.

"Steady," Jared drawled. "What're you trying to look at, anyway?"

"You," Tristen panted. "How old are you?"

"Twenty-eight. But no, you don't know me. I worked out in the oil fields when I was a pup. I was on the last oil job Luke did, I think. He talked about you all a lot. Had your pictures in his locker."

"What year?"

"Must've been four years ago or so. Out in Texas. When I almost got my hand cut off, I decided oil work wasn't for me. No matter how much it paid." Tristen turned the treadmill down to level five to look at a long, white scar that curled around Jared's wrist and up his forearm. "Took me a while to recover my strength from this. I can't get into the ring anymore, but I can train you jackasses to win. Well, most of you, anyway."

Tristen grunted and looked away.

"Push-ups. Give me fifty. And I can count while talking, so don't cheat."

"When did you see him last?"

"You mean Luke? Saw him for the last time after my accident. He was back in Pelton for a bit. Haven't seen him since."

Tristen completed the push-ups and stood up just as a fifty-pound medicine ball came towards his abdomen.

"Catch," Jared said, five seconds too late.

"Oof. What the hell, Jared?"

"Be ready. Don't miss it," was all Jared said.

Tristen wished he had. He hefted it back to Jared.

"You and Luke didn't talk much, did you?"

"Luke didn't believe in talking to kids. That's what he always said, though sometimes he was kidding." Tristen grunted as the ball came back hard.

"Use your core to absorb the weight coming at you. And stop showing me you're suffering. Poker face. Let's go. Twenty more."

"You like this job?" Tristen panted. He was tired of talking about Luke.

"It's not bad. Keeps me in shape. Besides this, I got some seasonal construction things going as well. What do you do? When you aren't fighting for Owen, I mean."

"I don't fight for Owen." The fifty pounds came back at an angle, throwing him off guard. He took a few deep breaths before he could throw it back. "This is a one-time deal."

"Three times."

"Whatever. I was in a band. Now I'm a sound guy, I guess, for a small production company. Freelance stuff. Not like it's permanent." Tristen stuttered out his explanation, mentally kicking himself for offering more information about himself than Jared deserved to know. Or probably cared to know.

"You could come work here. We need guys to train others."

"No. But thanks."

"Your dad's a good guy," Jared said, changing the subject. "Get to the heavy bags. Warm up your arms."

Tristen kept the medicine ball in his hands and took a long look at Jared. "Owen or Luke?" he finally asked.

"I'm talking about Owen. I didn't know you thought of Luke as your dad."

Tristen threw the medicine ball back hard, but Jared caught it easily. "I did back when Aimee was alive and Luke was around. He was around more than Owen."

"Man, my dad wasn't around a lot either. Came back a few years ago and wanted to fix things from before. He had heard I had a daughter and wanted to be part of our lives. Thirty around-the-worlds."

Tristen caught the ball, then started circling it around his head. First to the left, then to the right. He left the counting to Jared. "And? What did you do?"

"I finally let him start coming by. Don't regret it either." Jared looked around the gym and Tristen thought he was done talking, but Jared's focus came back to him. "Maybe both of them are more than you give them credit for."

Tristen hated being told stuff like that. Forgiveness is better and all that. Walking away from people who are incapable of treating you like a person is better. He dropped the ball, panting from the exertion. The best option was to let the conversation go and focus on his training. He needed to finish the fights and get back to figuring out his life.

He slammed his right fist into the heavy bag. Then his left. Then each again. And again. Jared didn't have any idea what he was talking about when he said Luke was a good guy.

He focused until all he saw was the black bag. His arms shot out automatically again and again, obeying the commands Jared called out. Hook, hook, uppercut, uppercut. Jab, jab, hook, hook. Over and over, until the punching bag became the magnolia tree in front of his childhood home. Jared's voice slowly turned into Luke's bark. "Jab, jab, hook. Again. Do it again. Push-ups, now." From one day to the next, Javon had moved out of their lives and Luke had moved back in. Ivy was ecstatic. Tristen remembered a feeling of dread of the unknown. Luke had come back looking like the Hulk with his muscular shoulders.

Tristen's arms flew out faster and faster, sweat flying into his eyes. He closed them, and the magnolia warped into the hospital bed. Aimee was sleeping, her leg bandaged, as Luke dozed, draped over the metal side bars.

"Enough. Take a break."

Tristen opened his eyes just in time to catch the water bottle coming at him. The cells in his body swayed from the sudden stop. Jared strapped on two sparring boards, the sound of one hitting the other popping.

"Let's go. Hit me."

Punch forward, straight forward, you see? But don't let your other arm down. Protect yourself always.

Left. Right. Left, left, right. He could see his and Talon's first boxing bag swinging against the magnolia tree. Thwack, thwack. They had stolen sand from the public parks to fill it with. Tristen assumed it was the mixture of mulch and pebbles that gave that first bag its unique sound when they punched it.

He watched his arms. Jab, jab, hook, hook. They were stronger than when he was fourteen. Bigger. They were the arms of a man, no longer those of a teenager afraid of the guy who had gotten out of jail. Hulking up at the gym seemed like the only thing Luke did for three years. He'd filled their tiny hallways and scared Tristen more than before.

"That's enough." Jared tossed him another bottle of water without warning.

Tristen caught it midair, the sudden change startling. He looked around and shook his head, sending sweat flying over the bag. He was the adult man again. There was no Luke.

"Nice job, Tristen, nice job."

Tristen grimaced as he drank the cold water. He had always wanted to hear those words from Luke. Or Owen. Javon was the only one who'd ever said it. Once. In response to how Tristen had washed his prized car.

"Thanks, Jared," he said, his voice coming out rough.

"That's it for today. See ya tomorrow at eight-thirty. I sent you the address."

Chapter 17

THE DAY OF THE run-through, Tristen woke up at sunrise with more energy than he'd had in several weeks. He no longer wanted to curl under the covers and hide from the world. Instead, he woke up before his alarm, went for a run, and then hopped in his car to Cincinnati before Ivy finished her first cup of coffee.

"For someone who lives here, I rarely see you," she complained when he said his goodbyes.

"I spent all day here yesterday," Tristen told her.

"But I was gone half the day, so it doesn't count."

Tristen told himself it was better that way. He had no plan to stay with her once he had some money. He didn't even plan to stay in Pelton. It would be better for Ivy if she didn't get used to him being around.

"Hey there," Watsu said as they both got out of their cars.

"Brought you a coffee," Tristen said, holding up the brown cardboard carrier. He hoped it wasn't too obvious he was trying to buy her favor. "By the way, do you know how long this run-through will be?"

"Why?" Watsu asked, eying him as she gently pulled out the coffee marked W. "You got somewhere you have to be?"

"No," Tristen said slowly. Steve was crawling out of a family-style van at the back of the parking lot. "Kind of. But later tonight. I need to be somewhere by seven-thirty."

Watsu looked at him over the rim of her sunglasses. "You know this is your job, right? And that it isn't some nine-to-five gig?"

"I do, yes. But I didn't think it would be over twelve hours. I'm just asking, Watsu."

"Asking what?" Steve asked, panting from his slow jog over.

"I got you a coffee. Latte with an extra shot."

"Nice," Steve said. "What are we asking?"

"How long this will go," Watsu said dryly. She gave Tristen a look of disgust before walking away. Clearly bringing her coffee hadn't been enough.

Steve looked at Tristen, who shrugged. "You know if this will go past six in the evening?"

"Nah," Steve said. "Shouldn't. These are professionals singing their own songs."

Tristen opened the back door to the theater, expecting the usual antique-store smell, but was pleasantly surprised by the smell of paint.

"They renovated," Steve said, looking around in awe. "That explains why they chose it. Last time I saw this place, it looked ready to fall over."

Watsu popped her head between them, startling Steve. "Meeting time."

"Right." Tristen held his arms out for her to lead the way. "We're ready for it."

On stage, a group of thirty people who seemed like the types to be more worried about their social media following than putting on a concert milled around. Tristen looked out from the stage, surprised to find several tables scattered about the floor instead of chairs.

"I like this new setup," Steve said, shrinking away as a girl taking selfies moved into his space. He surveyed the audience, then looked up at the ceiling. "We'll have to check for dead zones, although those sound panels will help. Looks like they thought of everything."

Tristen followed his gaze. "They look new, too. We're probably the first ones to check the mics, though."

"True." Steve turned to Watsu. "We gonna start this meeting, or can Tristen and I get to work?"

Tristen checked his watch, but Watsu glared at him, so he shook out his arm as though he meant to stretch.

She shook her head. "Don't know. I've talked to two different people so far. I've never been part of the sound in a live show, but this isn't at all what I thought it would be like. Oh, that woman is Melanie, I think."

A woman dressed in a navy pencil skirt and a silk top took the microphone.

"Hey, everyone. I'm Melanie, the event coordinator for Melodies Against Cancer, Seraphina's charity that gives to cancer research, and I want to welcome you here today," she announced. "We're very excited to move from a small charity dinner to a much larger music concert this year." Applause from the group interrupted her speech. Steve rolled his eyes. "Yes, thank you. We think it's going to be a lot of fun. This year Seraphina thought it'd be fun to bring in other singers and groups. We have a much bigger venue this year, which allows for a bigger crowd. I know you're wondering what that means, so they gave me permission to tell you. First up, we have an up-and-coming star, Meegan Ornay. Of course, Seraphina will sing four songs. Art of Rendering will go after her for three tracks. And to top off the night, we have the local Marshall High drum corps performing."

Excited murmurs rippled through the crowd of workers, but Tristen thought he'd heard wrong. "What did she say?" Watsu gave him the side-eye, but he ignored her and asked again. "Who did she say was playing after Meegan and Seraphina?"

Watsu rolled her eyes. "AOR," she hissed. "I already told you that."

Except that she hadn't. Or he hadn't listened. Tristen couldn't believe he had gotten roped into a job doing the sound for a concert his brother was going to perform at. As if life couldn't get worse.

Somehow he got through the positive affirmations Melanie recited next, breathing through his anger and trying to decide if he should quit. Just when he decided he would, he remembered Meegan. She'd be pissed if he quit now. And it could potentially hurt his reputation. And he wasn't sure if he would still get Lin as a client.

Melanie droned on about how to treat celebrities and influencers during and after the show as Tristen closed his eyes. He would have to stay. He knew that.

Watsu cleared her throat, jerking him back to the moment just as Melanie said something about a dinner.

"Dinner?" he whispered.

"That's the gala part. We have to set the playlist, which you should be done with, and make sure the sound works during that." She paused.

"I'm done with it. I sent it to the cloud yesterday."

Watsu nodded curtly. "Good. We also have to check the mics for the auction. Nothing too big."

Tristen nodded, still unable to pay attention.

"What's wrong?" he whispered to Steve, who was frowning into the large space.

"Nothing. Just checking where we might start our work. I'm thinking there, there, and there. And we'll bring in the panels from the truck to help insulate that corner over there. At least they used heavy curtains to portion off the stage. That'll help the sound."

"They're ending," Watsu hissed at them.

Tristen looked up as Seraphina marched up the steps to the stage. She was a woman who commanded attention. Not because of her beauty, though she was good-looking with her long, black hair, heavy eyelashes and wide smile, but more the way she inspired magnetic attraction a person couldn't help. And an automatic desire not to disappoint her. Jake, Art of Rendering's founder and lead guitarist, had the same thing, though in a smaller dose.

"Thank you all for your hard work," Seraphina said, flashing her famous smile and moving her gaze from left to right over the crowd. "Together, we're going to raise thousands of dollars for cancer research, a topic near and dear to my heart. Now, let's have a great run-through and a wonderful gala."

Watsu handed Tristen her clipboard, her eyes following Seraphina as she walked offstage. "I'll go see what mic they're putting on her," she said.

"I'll check on Steve at the sound booth," Tristen said, hopping off the stage.

The sound booth was in the back of the event space, with curtains on either side. Cameras were set up above the box to capture the sound check and, eventually, the concert. Inside the box, Steve was downing a large can of energy drink and rolling his eyes at whatever information was coming through his earphones.

He tossed him a headset. "Channel 3."

"Got it. How's everything looking?" Tristen surveyed the equipment. It looked thirty years old. "We're going to need to bring in our stuff."

"Already coming in."

Tristen followed Steve's nod to a corner of the theater, where two young men dressed in khakis and polos were dragging a box between them.

"This is the strangest operation I've ever worked in," Steve said, flipping switches that didn't seem connected to anything. "Half of them don't have any idea what they're doing."

"Bloody hell!" shouted a voice from the back.

Steve and Tristen exchanged glances.

"As long as I get paid," Steve muttered before pressing the side of his headphones. Tristen nodded.

A group of young women who didn't seem to have any responsibility erupted into clapping as Seraphina walked back on stage dressed in a sequined dress.

"She knows it isn't a dress rehearsal, right?" Steve said through the headphones, chuckling.

The answer on channel three was not amused. "Seraphina always dresses fabulously."

"Channel nine it is," he said, snickering at Tristen. They switched channels, then started Seraphina's music. Only half the speakers worked.

"Keep going," Tristen called out, rolling his finger. He plugged in his own computer, tapping his fingers to the rhythm of the music, as he waited for the screen to light up. With a few more taps and switches flipped, Seraphina's music filled the hall.

"Well, slather my backside and call me a biscuit," Seraphina said, her white teeth gleaming in a smile. "I wasn't sure you'd figure it out."

Her husky laugh reverberated through the speaker before it broke into a high-pitched squeak. Those in the room covered their ears before Steve flipped it off.

"I'm on it," Tristen said, already on his way to the offending speaker.

"What's going on?" yelled Melanie. Her words came out muted, with no power behind her mic. Watsu pointed to the headset, and Melanie quickly pulled the mic down to her mouth. "Are you unable to do your job?"

"You didn't give us time to ring out the wedges this morning," Tristen said. "Just give us a minute."

"Want me to go up on the stage?" Steve asked through the headset.

"I'll go up. I'm already down here." Tristen jumped onto the stage, following each cable and adjusting as he went. "Okay, I'm able to access everything now."

"What do you want to pop in for the tuning?" Steve asked.

"We should try one of Seraphina's again. Then one from AOR and Meegan to mark the differences."

"What of mine do you need?"

Tristen whipped around. Seraphina was watching him. One eyebrow lifted, her hands on her full hips.

"We need to tune the room. Make sure the frequencies your songs are on mix well with everything we've done. We wanted to play your songs to do that."

Seraphina brushed her hair back with her fingers. "You want me to sing or not?"

Tristen exchanged looks with Watsu.

"Yes, we want you to sing," Watsu said. "We could get your sound perfect that way."

Seraphina pinched her nose. "Honey, you don't have to suck up to me. I would have been fine if you said no."

Watsu's eyes widened for a brief second. Seraphina chuckled, waving about her ringed fingers.

"You ready then?" Tristen asked. Watsu was still frozen, seemingly speechless.

"You got it, babe." Seraphina winked.

When the music started again, Tristen took his tablet around the venue, fiddling with the EQ graph at each place. By the end of the song everything measured perfectly.

Steve laughed in Tristen's ear. "Get me the last bit in the left corner there, babe."

Tristen threw him a dirty look.

"Jake," Seraphina squealed. This time, the speakers held steady with no squeaking.

"I guess we know the speakers work," Tristen said, rubbing the vibrations out of his ear. On stage, Seraphina ran to embrace Jake from AOR. Tristen swallowed hard. Talon probably wasn't far behind.

"Tristen, we need you in the back." Watsu's voice sounded like a warning through the headset. He started backing toward the sound booth, but stopped short when he saw his twin standing with his arms crossed, watching the stage from the shadows.

Feeling overexposed in the large room, Tristen made his way to the soundboard, his eyes never leaving his brother. Talon stood still, his gaze on Jake and Seraphina. He didn't even smile until Jake finally turned, his arm thrown around Seraphina's shoulders, and introduced her to Talon. Seraphina and Talon shook hands before all three of them wandered off-stage, fine-tuning the sound for the concert clearly forgotten.

"You okay?" Watsu asked, eyeing him. "You look pale."

"I'm fine," Tristen said. Apart from his hands and feet tingling—but he had no intention of telling her about that.

"Is that your twin?"

"Just my doppelganger," Tristen said. Watsu didn't laugh.

"Hello? Anyone still out there?"

Tristen, Steve, and Watsu started at the sound. On stage stood Jake with his guitar and a stool.

"We're here," Steve called.

"Great, can we set up for acoustic? Seraphina said we were running sound checks."

"Uh, sure. No problem. Can you strum a bit? I have to find your mics."

Jake strummed Johnny Cash's 'I Walk the Line', then moved into another song. Something familiar, but not familiar enough to grasp. Tristen looked at Steve.

"Go adjust the mic, Tristen," he said.

Jake stood alone on stage now, but Tristen still hesitated. Meeting his brother as a sound guy was up there on the list of the most humiliating things to happen to him. He thought of fifth grade, when he'd had to write about an embarrassing moment in his life. If only he could warn his ten-year-old self that falling down in front of Mary Sue was nothing compared to this moment.

There was nothing he could do, though. Especially with the look Watsu was giving him. Tristen jogged down the aisle just as Talon strolled back on. He looked comfortable, owning the entire stage with his presence. And to think Talon hadn't ever wanted to be a musician. He'd thought it was a dumb idea. A dream that would never happen. At least, that was what he'd said when they were teenagers.

Tristen shook his head before hopping onto the stage. The irony wasn't even remotely amusing. Talon hesitated when he saw him, then saluted him with his water bottle as though he wasn't surprised at all.

Jake started strumming and whistling again as Tristen adjusted the mics. The notes of the song stirred distant memories, but he still couldn't put his finger on the song. The words floated just out of reach.

The guitar strings grew louder and louder, bringing with them memories of Pelton and of Aimee sitting in her bed, smiling at him as he sang to her.

Talon stepped up to the microphone. "Uh, hey, guys. This is a song dedicated to my sister, Aimee."

"*Hey, Aimee, please don't cry. The sky has enough tears. Hey, Aimee. I know you're scared. Give me your hand. I'll be right here.*"

Tristen jerked his head up and stared at his brother. Talon crooned into the microphone, but Tristen's mind saw something different: Aimee's face slick with sweat, the residue of the marijuana tea, and the final fade of pain from her face as she fell asleep to his singing.

His song. Not Talon's.

Chapter 18

"You okay?"

Tristen looked down to find Watsu staring at him, her forehead wrinkled with concern. The song and Talon faded from his attention as he focused back on Watsu and the job at hand.

"Yep. I'm fine." He pulled his shoulders back until her hand fell away and picked up the tablet.

"Steve's asking for the weak point." Watsu's gaze penetrated him.

Tristen held up the tablet, pretending he might get better reception, and strolled away. Hopefully Watsu would think he was just engrossed in his work.

"Steve? Yeah, sending you the data now," he said through the headset as Talon's last chord disappeared into the air.

"That was beautiful," Melanie exclaimed. Several people around the venue were sniffing and wiping their eyes, their gaze transfixed on Talon and Jake on stage. Tristen bit down on the pen in his mouth until he heard it crack.

"Thank you," Talon said into the mic. "That means a lot. Thank you."

Sometimes Tristen wished they were ten again so he could wrestle his brother to the floor. Or at least stick his tongue out at him. Or yell some obscenities. When no one was listening, of course. He stood waiting for Talon to say more, to give him credit. After all, Talon hadn't written a song in his entire life. In fact, music hadn't even been on Talon's radar until Aimee was gone.

But Talon turned away and started talking with Jake. Nothing about Tristen writing the song—both lyrics and music.

Everything was always so effortless for Talon. But, of course, Talon never allowed other people's feelings to come into his life equations.

Tristen walked back to the sound booth without saying a word. If he said something, Talon would laugh. Feelings. That wasn't something a Levisay had. Especially not about a song he'd written when he was fifteen.

"Would you guys mind playing again?" Steve asked, rolling his fingers in the air at Tristen. Tristen groaned silently, but made a U-turn before he reached the sound booth. "We need to make some notes."

"Sure," Talon said, immediately going into the song again.

The lyrics taunted Tristen as he tried to focus on the sound quality from the point of view of a listener. He marked numbers, flipped to the next screen, and measured decibels and EQ levels, all while memories of Aimee scrolled through his head.

He saw her sitting in the hospital bed in a gown with lions on it right after being diagnosed with juvenile rheumatoid arthritis. Then with her leg bandaged after the doctors replaced some of her bone with metal. Then there was the memory of her trying to walk as she cried in pain. And the memory of her trying to play like other kids, but the pain taking over so many times.

It was a long process that seemed to never end. And got worse when they found a tumor.

Tristen assumed the hospital and surgery would be the worst of it, but he'd been wrong. The worst was when Aimee was home all day in bed, too sick to rise and too sick to lie down without being nauseated. The doctors had said the medicine might make her dizzy, but Tristen hadn't known it would make her vomit until her body had nothing left to give. And even after her belly was empty, she was reduced to moaning in discomfort.

Ivy, hooked on sleeping aids for all the years he was a kid, rarely woke up, but Tristen did. Unable to sleep himself, he used to sneak into Aimee's room and rub her back, trying to soothe her into sleep. After a few days, exhausted and desperate, he made her marijuana tea. He never asked if he could and Aimee never told anyone, either, because it soothed her enough to sleep and sometimes eat. She only needed it for a few months, until the tumor was gone and she stopped taking the meds. He never knew she went back to the marijuana when she turned twelve. Not until she got caught smoking it outside the school. Then she told everyone that Tristen had gotten her addicted years before.

Besides the tea, Tristen had played guitar for her almost every day. It was mostly Dolly Parton, Pink and some Lady Gaga, though he managed to get in some Johnny Cash as well. He had learned on his own, plucking out the basic notes so he could at least sing to her.

But one night, an especially awful night when even the tea didn't help Aimee's pain, he strummed something different. Something that came up from deep within him.

About his baby sister's pain. And his helplessness. And the injustice of it all.

Once boxing took over his life, Tristen couldn't spend as much time with Aimee. She joined choir and band. She flat-ironed her hair and wore button-down shirts. No one thought she and her boyfriend were taking opioids. They were too busy with Talon and Tristen boxing.

"Tristen," Watsu barked through the headset, as though she'd called him several times without him answering. "Tell Talon to stop."

Tristen marched over to his brother. "Stop singing. We have to fix something."

The command was met with groans. The anger Tristen was trying so hard to keep in check threatened to bubble up, but he smashed it down. Just like Owen had taught him.

Talon's slow grin caught Tristen off guard. Before he understood what his brother was doing, Talon's arms wrapped around Tristen and squeezed hard. The hug awakened the sore muscles in his chest, but Tristen's throat was so tight the groans couldn't escape.

"I missed you, bro," Talon said a little too loudly. "How you been?"

"Good, man," Tristen said.

"I need you to move the speaker on the right," Steve said through the headset.

When Tristen walked over to the offending speaker, Talon followed. He even helped him move it.

"You boxing again?" he whispered.

Tristen rolled his eyes. He should have known his brother would notice his healing black eye. "Play the first song again. Watsu, be ready to let me know."

Thankfully, Steve only needed part of the song to declare the sound perfect.

"Okay, that's it. Anyone who's here for decoration and ambiance setup, you need to stay. Everyone else can go," Melanie called. "We'll see you all next Sunday for the real deal."

"What happened to a Friday evening run-through next week?" Tristen asked as he joined his group in the booth. Glancing over his shoulder, he was relieved to find Talon wasn't following him.

"Change of plans," Steve said. "Apparently, the celebrities all have lives outside of this concert."

"They're all going to Music on Air."

Steve snorted. "I wondered about that. Jealous, Watsu?"

"I'll be there next year," she told him with a coy smile.

Tristen sighed as he looked at the schedule. "So, this was all the run-through we get?"

Watsu nodded.

"Steve, is that normal?"

"They put on concerts all the time individually. They're pros."

A frazzled woman with a stack of papers interrupted them. "Here, I need you to sign these before you leave." She threw a document at each of them. "Get them back to me before you leave."

She left again before they could say anything.

"Just a contract that says we'll show up and if we don't, we'll pay a fine, all that," Watsu explained.

"Here, I signed it," Steve said. "I'm going to pack up. See you two later. Tristen, I'll call you and we'll go over the songs over the phone."

"Got it." Tristen saluted his coworker and signed his contract.

"Hey, Tristen! You guys in charge of the instruments?" Talon yelled out as Tristen reached the woman with the papers.

"Here." She grimaced as he shoved them toward her, placing them under the other papers. "What's up, Talon? You need me to take your instruments?" he asked.

"I do, thanks," Talon said, walking away. He looked back and seemed surprised to find Tristen gathering the instruments himself. "Dude, I meant your minion. I thought you were the one in charge."

"What do you mean? In charge of what?" Tristen challenged, standing up to face him.

Talon shrugged and looked away first. "I thought maybe you'd be doing more than grunt work."

"I do whatever my boss tells me to do." Tristen waved his hand towards the sound booth at Watsu.

Talon looked where Tristen was pointing. "Can you come to the back? We have some stuff we'd rather you take with you now. There are too many days between now and the concert to leave them here."

Tristen lifted his hand for Talon to lead the way, then followed, keeping his frustration in check.

"Over here. We have two guitars, one bass, and those bags over there. They have our names on them—not sure what they are, though. I could call Jake and ask."

"As long as they aren't drugs, it's fine," Tristen said.

Talon laughed. "Remember the Halloween spiders?"

"And the fake Christmas tree." It felt good to talk to Talon again. Almost good enough to forgive him stealing the song.

Talon shook his head. "Luke hid drugs in the weirdest places."

"They worked, though," Tristen admitted. "Cops searched our home twice and found nothing."

"Except for Ivy's weed that one time."

Tristen chuckled. "I forgot about that. She was lucky there was hardly anything left, 'cause I was giving it to Aimee."

They stood in awkward silence again. Tristen hated prolonged silences, so he broke it first.

"Did you talk to Ivy lately? She broke her leg."

Talon ran his fingers through his short hair, still not looking at Tristen. "I talked to her through messages. She told me she was doing fine. We were in Mexico on a tour, you know? Just got back a few days ago. I sent her some cash, though. She said she needed it for a new rehab class she wanted to take."

"Rehab class?" Tristen knew nothing about a rehab class. Talon didn't seem to know more either.

"Said she wanted to stop smoking weed before the baby comes." Talon's eyes took on a far-away look Tristen had never seen before. "Man, this life is something else."

"Sounds pretty nice. You get to travel and see places."

Talon shook his head. "Nah. I mean, yes, seeing places is cool. But sometimes we're in a place for maybe a day. Sandra came to Mexico. We had some time to see Mexico City and those Aztec pyramid things, but the rest of the tour was a blur. I couldn't even say what each town looked like."

"Still," Tristen pressed. "There are plenty of musicians who barely make a living."

Like me. The unspoken words hung on his tongue. Tristen hoped Talon hadn't thought the same thing.

"I was going to set up a grocery delivery service for Ivy, but she told me you had moved in with her, so I figured it wasn't necessary."

Tristen knew it was a question about his moving in more than anything.

"Yeah, I thought she could use some help." It was no use keeping the truth from his brother. Tristen wouldn't mind getting back to the way things had been years before, when they shared everything with each other. "Simon told Meegan I couldn't live in the townhouse if I couldn't pay rent. And since I can't pay market rate rent, I kinda had to move back to Pelton."

"That sucks. But I'm sure with this job you'll be back sooner than later. Come on, I'll help you load these up," Talon said. He looked ready to get away from the conversation. Or maybe get away from Tristen. "You got a truck in the back?"

"Yeah. Steve should have it in position by now," Tristen said.

But Watsu, not Steve, sat in the driver's seat, showing no intention of getting out.

"Pick up the other end," Tristen said.

"You getting something to eat later?"

"Maybe," Tristen said, dead-lifting one of the longer bags. He shoved it into the back of the van and checked his phone. "Damn." Four missed calls.

"What's wrong?"

"Meegan. I missed her calls."

Watsu slapped the side of the van to get their attention. "You two almost done?"

"Almost," Tristen yelled back. "Grab that end, Talon, then we'll go get the last few things."

"I thought about inviting Ivy to the concert," Talon said as they heaved the parts of a drum set into the van.

Tristen looked at him in surprise. He purposefully never invited her. Putting her in an environment of booze and possibly drugs seemed unfair to her—although this concert wasn't in a bar, or that typical rock-and-roll atmosphere. And yet he still hadn't thought to invite her. It was second nature to keep that part of his life separate.

"I thought she'd like it. She's never seen me on stage. But Claire wouldn't give me tickets, and in the end, it's not the right place for her."

"You think?"

Talon waved his hand toward the venue. "I mean, look at that place. It's too hoity-toity for Ivy."

Tristen sighed with relief.

Talon yelped as he set his load into the van. He shook out his hands, rubbing one finger in particular. "I gotta be more careful.

Almost took out a finger there. Did you notice I learned to play the guitar? You didn't say anything."

"Now that you mention it, yes. I was so busy it hadn't really registered," Tristen said.

He paused for a moment as Talon dramatically shook out his finger. Now was the perfect time to bring up the song. The only time. He'd get the words out before he could change his mind.

But before he could say anything, Talon spoke. "You wanna come out with us later?"

Tristen stopped rearranging the back of the van. "With who?"

"Me and the guys. I think Seraphina might come out." Talon shrugged.

Tristen rubbed his sweaty hands against his thighs and shook his head. "I'm going to head out. Gotta get somewhere."

Talon looked at him. "Going to a fight?"

Tristen stopped moving. "What?"

"You back fighting again?"

"What I'm doing is none of your business, Talon. But yeah, I'm trying to earn some money. For Ivy. One of us has to."

Talon snorted and crossed his arms against his chest. "You saying I don't do enough for our mom? Wow. Seriously. I sent her money. And I'll set up the grocery thing if you can't handle getting her food. If I had been here, I'd have jumped at the chance to box again. Anyway, it's not like you're even grateful about this job. I mean, I'm the one who told Clay about you."

The words hit Tristen in the gut. "Meegan told Clay about me."

Talon licked his lips and looked around, just like he used to in high school when he had a group of guys egging him on to fight someone. "When I heard The Seethers broke up, I felt bad for you. I called Clay and told him you did a good job with our album and Meegan's, and asked if he knew of anyone who could use your services."

Tristen refused to flinch. His insides were on fire. He wanted to tell Talon he didn't need his pity, but he forced his fists to open, relax. "Well, thanks. Meegan thinks she got me the job."

"Talon! Where you been?"

Tristen and Talon both turned to find Jake barreling down the hallway dressed in his usual black jeans, vintage T-shirt, and thin metal chain holding his wallet. "We were looking all over for you. Hey, Tristen. Nice to see you. Thought Talon ran off on me."

Jake chuckled, but given recent history, Tristen didn't find it funny.

"No worries, man," he said, wanting more than anything for his brother to leave. "We're done."

"See ya, Tris," Talon said, then turned and walked out with Jake, their conversation about upcoming practice floating through the hall.

Chapter 19

"You look like a caged lion," Jared said, looking up from his cell phone.

Tristen stopped mid-step and tried to stay still, but he had too much nervous energy. He went back to pacing, six steps forward and six steps back. It kept him warm in the shiny boxing shorts and kept his mind from driving him crazy.

"You nervous again? Your mouth getting dry? You gonna vomit?" Jared chuckled at his own joke.

"No," Tristen snapped. The buzzing sound from the crowd placing their bets and anxiously awaiting the start of the match suddenly hit his ears. He knew he was about to fight, yet his head was somewhere else. Being unfocused was a good way to lose. "I'm thinking of something else."

The tingling in his legs grew stronger. Each time he thought of Talon singing his song, he became angrier. His brother had no right to take it. But more than with Talon, he was angry at himself. He'd had a chance to confront his brother and he hadn't. As usual. He'd just let him take whatever he wanted. "It's getting cold in here."

"So warm up. It'll help get your head in the right space."

Tristen glared at Jared.

"Come on. High knees."

He complied. Three minutes of high knees. Then one hundred push-ups, finishing off with five one-minute sessions of jump rope. By the end, he was warmed up but no less angry.

"Lookin' good, man," Jared said as he wrapped Tristen's hands and put on his gloves. "They're gonna call you now. Let's go."

He flipped off the lights and opened the door. Shouting and jeering flooded the makeshift locker room.

"Here comes the Pelton Viking, Tristen Levisay!"

The announcement echoed off the walls of the abandoned warehouse as the crowd cheered, clapped, or booed. Tristen held up his right fist to the crowd, growling at the men nearest him. The two braids Jared's girlfriend had given him slapped against his cheeks each time he looked right or left.

The Pelton Viking. It was laughable. He couldn't even confront his own brother.

As usual, the fight was in an abandoned building. This one ran the length of at least two blocks. Outside, the brick was crumbling and stained black, with broken windows and graffiti covering the doors and walls. Inside there was a new makeshift building. It rose ten feet up, leaving the rest of the factory exposed. In the middle of the new walls was a boxing ring with wooden planks as bleachers set up around it.

Tristen focused on the center of the ring where the fight would happen, his voice already dry from screaming. His vision tunneled for a split second before coming back.

He swallowed hard and forced himself to concentrate. During the ride to the gym, he had almost asked Jared if he'd brought the pills. Something told Tristen they weren't going to be offered this time, and the idea made him listless. He knew Jared feared Owen more than he cared about Tristen's nerves, so he kept the request to himself. He wondered, though, if it was how Talon had won so many fights.

"Tristen!" Owen was shouting above the noise from his seat, motioning him over. "This guy is a beast," he yelled in Tristen's ear. "I don't want you to get too hurt. Play defensive to get him tired before you go in for the knockout."

"You think that's how to win?"

Owen dismissed him with a slap on the backside and no other answer.

The noise of the crowd dimmed. Tristen walked towards his corner before remembering he had to work the crowd. He ran at them, crashing into the ropes, then springing back before he ran at the other side. The waves of cheers vibrated through every cell in his chest and arms.

"Here comes the Night Beast! The man who hasn't lost a fight in six months!"

The declaration startled Tristen, though he tried to hide it by jumping higher. Jared signaled to him to sit, and Tristen obeyed, opening up space for the Night Beast to enter the ring and work the crowd as Tristen had.

The man was enormous. His broad, sculpted shoulders held up a large, neckless Goliath head.

"Look at me and stop right now," Jared yelled, pulling Tristen's chin until he looked at him.

"What?"

"You're showing your fear. The Night Beast is huge, but he has no actual skill. He's clumsy and relies completely on his strength. You can beat him."

Tristen wasn't sure if he believed Jared, but he knew that if he didn't get in the right headspace in two seconds, the fight was already over.

"Let's go!" Jared yelled. Tristen slipped the mouth guard into his mouth and stepped forward, banging his gloves together as he stood to listen to the fight rules.

"Greet." The ref's face stayed neutral, but Tristen knew what he was thinking. That Tristen was dead meat. That the Night Beast was about to mark his twentieth win. That the fight was going to be a short one.

"Head in the fight." Luke's voice screamed in his ear, whooshing in like a hurricane.

The Night Beast's glove missed him by a few centimeters. Tristen jumped back, shaking out his head and his thoughts. No more emotions. Head in the fight.

The Beast came at him again, but Jared was right. The guy's bulk made him slow. Tristen bounced, leaned, and swerved.

Then missed. He managed to move, but a jab to the Beast's chest did nothing. Not even a ripple. Tristen tried to bounce away, but this time, he was too slow.

The explosion of pain blocked out all sound and light, but Tristen knew enough to bounce backwards and duck. Didn't matter if he looked like a fool to the crowd. The lights came back to his vision in time to watch the Beast's fist just graze his braid, flinging it with such force that it whipped the back of Tristen's head.

Tristen ducked into a squat, then bounced back. Jab, jab, hook to the left, and an uppercut to the chin. The Beast's head whipped back, and the sound of the crowd roared in Tristen's ears as the whistle blew.

One round down. He had forgotten to ask how many he had to fight.

"What the hell is going on with you?" Jared asked as he rubbed down Tristen's arms. "Keep your damn arms up. He's seen how unfocused you are. Believe me, his trainer over there is giving him all the tips on how to get to you."

Tristen widened his eyes to focus on the ring across the way. Sure enough, a small man with a large, flat nose was whispering into the Night Beast's ear while staring directly at Tristen. The Beast stood suddenly, punching his gloves together, ready to get back into the fight. He waved at Tristen with a smile.

A shiver ran down Tristen's spine. Jared felt it and slapped it out of his back, jolting him out of the chair.

"Get in the ring and fight, Tristen Levisay. You can do better than this."

Tristen knew he couldn't. Still, he put his gloves up and bounced into the ring. He evaded a few jabs, but calculated wrong on the next one and caught the Beast's right glove in his neck.

"Get 'em, Tristen!"

Within six jabs, Tristen had the Beast against the ropes, but it didn't last long. For all his bulk, the Night Beast could duck well.

Tristen should have backed away, but he turned early and caught a glove right in the nose.

Blood shot out in front of him. He jabbed forward, his vision cloudy, but only hit air. Thankfully, the bell rang.

"You lose the next round, and it's over," Jared yelled. "What do I have to do to get your head in this fight?"

"I don't know, man," Tristen panted. "Something just isn't connecting. I don't know why."

Jared patted the side of Tristen's head, something Luke used to do. *"It's all in there, you know? In your head. You can't control your head, you can't control anything."*

But that was the problem with fighting. He wasn't in control.

"How 'bout you just try not to embarrass yourself, yeah?" Jared asked. "Go out there punching. Stop thinking and start hitting."

Right.

The whistle blew. Tristen did what he had to do; he rushed to the middle and started in hard. A jab, then a cross. More jabs. Left, right, left, but each time he hit the Beast's glove. He bobbed to the left and tried again, this time with hooks. He finally landed a hit, but it wasn't enough.

When Tristen pulled back to recenter himself, the Beast seemed to grow out from the middle of himself, doubling and tripling in size. It wasn't real, Tristen told himself, but his hesitation was too obvious. In came a hit from the side, and then directly to his face. Tristen tried to duck, but his head whipped to the left, a crackling sound accompanying it.

And the whistle blew.

"Damn it, Tristen!" Jared pushed him back into their corner chair as the referee lifted the Night Beast's arm into the air. Screaming rose, directed at him. He heard his name over and over again, but Tristen ignored all of it. He didn't care. They could all go to hell. If they lost money, shame on them for betting he would win. It was their own gambling problem that made them hope beyond rational hope the loser twin would finally win.

"That was a crap fight. Absolute crap. You could have done better."

Tristen focused on Jared massaging his muscles over the lecture. Because he didn't care. Could he have done better? Perhaps.

The roar of the crowd came in waves until Tristen found the melody hidden underneath. The beat of the drums from someone pounding the floor and the whistles from his haters rose into a song that was almost nice to listen to.

"Get up."

It was a command, maybe from Owen, but Tristen didn't heed it. He stayed in the chair and listened to the music.

Chapter 20

"Good fight," said the Night Beast. Tristen had expected a voice deeper than pure darkness, but it was slightly high-pitched.

"Thanks," he said, shaking the meaty hands that had beaten him. "You, too."

"You get that head in the fight, and you'll win," the Beast said, shaking his finger. "But then, I wonder if you even care to."

Tristen watched him leave, hoping Owen hadn't heard the comment. But, of course, he had.

"I thought the same thing," Owen said, folding his arms across his chest. "I wondered if you even cared to win."

"You should wonder if I can win," Tristen countered. "Am I able to win?"

"You can win. You won once when it counted," Owen said, pulling his fingers out of his armpits to point at Tristen.

"I technically won more than once."

"Oh, so now you're keeping score? No, no. I like that. I want you to keep score. You won more than once. But it was that big win that changed everything, wasn't it?"

"It was the big win that got me kicked out of the house."

"I thought that was you running your mouth," Owen said, grabbing Tristen's bag. He jerked his shoulders forward. "Jared's already gone. Come on, I'll take you back to Ivy's. I don't trust that asshole trainer not to call the cops on us."

"Thought you had the cops all tied up in a pretty bow," Tristen said, though he followed Owen out. Getting arrested didn't sound at all like what he wanted to do that night.

"I give a few a paycheck, but not in this county." Owen sighed as he held the metal door open for Tristen to pass. The night was dark. Not one light in the abandoned parking lot worked. Which, of course, was the point. "I'm getting too old for this, kid."

The admission was surprising. "Thought you enjoyed being the big guy in town. The one everyone fears."

Owen wheezed a laugh as he started the truck. "It gets to a point in a man's life when no one fears him. I didn't think of this when I was younger. Never thought of getting older. I was just driven by revenge and a sense of injustice."

"*You* were driven by injustice? The guy who sells drugs?"

"I never sold them, kid."

If Tristen hadn't grown up where he had, Owen's conviction might have convinced him. But he knew better. "What the hell you talking about? You're the king of drugs."

"Oh, yeah?" Owen asked. They merged onto the highway, the oncoming cars sharpening the dull ache in Tristen's head. "Is that what you heard?"

"That's what Luke used to say." Tristen pressed the warming ice pack harder against his eye, blocking the glare of the head-lights.

"Luke is an ass who doesn't know what he's talking about."

Sometimes, though they'd worked together, Luke and Owen would let their feelings about the other man be known to Tristen and Talon. He'd never understood how they worked together if they hated each other so much. He let it go.

"You know, Talon was right. I didn't believe him, but I'm thinking he was right."

"About what?" Tristen asked, exhaustion pulling his eyelids down.

"That you don't know anything. That you've never paid atten-tion."

"What exactly do I not know?" Tristen asked, tossing the ice pack onto the floor and leaning forward, headache be damned. "I know Luke moved drugs for you. Even stored some of your drugs around our house. And I heard you exchanged people for them."

"What the hell you talking about? I don't traffic in people." Owen's voice was calm, but Tristen's nerves were shaking.

"Miley and Tiffany ring a bell?" he demanded. It was the only proof he had, but it was the proof the rest of the town had used.

"Those girls were being raped by Mark, their daddy. I got them to Texas, where an aunt of mine took them in. Couldn't say nothin' to no one 'cause otherwise, Mark woulda found out."

Tristen faltered. "That's not what Luke said."

"I told you that Luke was an ass. He didn't know half the things he liked to think he knew."

"What about selling drugs?"

"I moved them. Made a lot of money. But I didn't sell them. Didn't want my town to go under 'cause of the drugs. But you said Luke stashed drugs at the house? That was when he was skimming off the top of what he was moving. Had a lot of problems like that. Things I didn't think of when I took the jobs. Soon enough, it cost me and him."

"It cost him jail time."

"He deserved it, Tristen." Owen seemed to be gripping the steering wheel. "He got caught in a sting operation selling drugs. Like an idiot. And he almost got you hurt. I'm just glad I found out about it, at least in time to get you out. But he deserved every bit of jail time he got. Stupid man, using you to sell his dope. He thought I wouldn't come after him. That things were settled between the two of us. Like hell. When I saw he was using you and Talon, I let the fool set his own damn trap. Even though I could see it from miles away, I didn't say a word."

"You could have stopped him from getting caught?" Tristen's voice echoed through the truck.

"Sit your ass back, and don't you talk to me like that again." Owen glared at Tristen until Tristen sat back. Not that he was obeying. He just wanted Owen to focus on the road. "Luke was a grown-ass man who made poor decisions and put you in danger."

"That was a crappy year, Owen," Tristen said through gritted teeth.

"It wasn't easy for you all, but Luke made his decision and suffered the consequences."

"He was trying to pay for Aimee's medical treatment."

"He didn't have to put you in harm's way, Tristen."

"Well, I'm sure getting Luke out of the way wasn't a hardship for you, but it was for us. Talon and I had to buy food half the time. Not having Luke's salary was rough."

Owen gave a gritty, exasperated sigh. "Ivy and Luke were broken up beforehand, if you would bother to recall."

What he recalled was him and Talon scrambling to find food, get Ivy out of bed and to work, and making sure Aimee was taken to her doctor appointments. But also, Owen was right. Luke had moved out. Tristen had been at his new place when the police trapped Luke in a sale.

"It made you into a man," Owen said, as though responding to Tristen's thoughts. "Never hurt a kid to grow up and contribute to the family."

"Ivy got bad that year."

"Even before that year. She started rehab just as Aimee went in for her surgery, remember? I made that happen, Tristen. She wanted to get off the opioids, and we worked something out together."

It was hard to piece everything together, but what Owen said made sense. He hadn't connected the timelines before, but now that he thought of it, they all lined up. But lined up or not, nothing took away from the terrible job all the adults in his life had done when he was a kid.

"You know, it seems like you're trying to convince me that you're a good guy. But I don't remember you ever bothering to be a dad while Luke was gone. Or ever, really," Tristen muttered. "Just like Ivy."

The words had just left his tongue when his body flew forward as the truck came to a screeching halt, several feet before the stop sign ahead.

"What the hell, Owen?!"

"What did you say?" Owen growled.

Tristen turned and faced him. "Did it hurt your feelings, Owen? Because that is the truth."

"You can say whatever you want about me. I deserve any comment about being a terrible father. I know that. But don't you dare imply that Ivy didn't do her best."

There was no need to imply. Ivy's best wasn't good enough for kids. And Tristen wasn't about to have Owen tell him otherwise.

"You just admitted that Ivy and Luke were split at the time. And I recall seeing you a few times in the very early mornings while Luke was in jail," he said. More than twice he'd woken up to find Owen sneaking out of the house.

"Whadda you saying?"

"Why didn't you give it a go? Why didn't you try? Why didn't you tell me then that you were my father?"

The truck became eerily quiet. He could tell Owen didn't want to talk about it, but Tristen couldn't let it go.

"I found out from Mrs. Kinder that Ivy and you were inseparable in high school. She's the one that pointed out you were my dad. It was great, you know, pulling weeds in her garden and being told who my father was. It was a real nice touch to a real shitty year."

"Your mama and I go way back," Owen finally said, easing the truck back into drive. His voice was softer and far away.

"I know." They were already in Pelton. Just a few more minutes and Tristen would be in bed.

"Well, okay." Owen didn't say anything again until he pulled up to the curb in front of Ivy's house. "Come to the gym tomorrow for some rehab. Sunday, too."

Tristen swallowed back his disappointment. There was no answer to his questions, apparently. "I have work."

Owen sighed, but Tristen couldn't tell if he was angry or tired. Without anything else to say, Tristen pushed open the truck door and stood in the night air, the icy wind soothing the sting in his face.

"Even if I wasn't what I should have been, I always looked out for you, kid."

Though he could barely see his face, Tristen met Owen's eyes. "It's just hard to believe it."

"Yep. I get that. But take this little thing we got going on. I was out of this underground business, more or less, I mean, but you needed something," Owen said. "When Talon told me he dropped the band for another one, I knew you would need something else."

"We're doing this for Ivy. I wouldn't be here if she wasn't going to lose her house."

"Everything happens for a reason, though, doesn't it? Your two needs aligned, and here we are."

"I wasn't looking for a chance to get back into the ring."

"No," Owen said with a deep inhalation. "But you had just lost your entire ecosystem, except for your pretty little lady. Then Simon hired me to look into you, and I saw you might need more help than I had thought. You took on all that debt, Tristen."

Tristen snorted, but had no comeback. The debt was all his. "Were you coming to find me before you found out about Ivy?"

Owen hesitated, then nodded. "You needed something going for you."

"And your conclusion was that I needed boxing?"

"Well, it's a fast way to pay all this stuff off, at least."

That wasn't something Tristen could deny. "That's true, I guess. It's a weird way to be a dad, Owen."

"I'm unconventional," Owen said, his teeth gleaming in the streetlight. "I'll see you tomorrow, yeah?"

Tristen hit the side of the truck lightly and stood back. "Night."

Chapter 21

TRISTEN STOOD IN THE middle of the parking lot at Watsu's studio Saturday night, trying to decide what to do. He'd spent all afternoon working on the dinner music compilation, a two-hour track that had taken him five hours in the studio.

Which might have earned him a night sleeping in his car. He wasn't sure he could stay awake for the drive back to Pelton.

Before he could decide, his phone rang, startling him out of his trance.

"Hello?"

"Tristen." Loud music almost drowned out Meegan's voice, and he was almost positive he heard Clay in the background.

"Meegan," Tristen said, his voice hitching. He cleared his throat. "Where are you?"

"You answered. I thought you were avoiding me. Just a second. I'm talking to my boyfriend."

Tristen closed his eyes and gritted his teeth at the image of a man hitting on his girlfriend. "Meegan?"

"Sorry, Tristen. Where was I?"

"I asked where you were," Tristen said with false patience.

"I'm home in Cincinnati. The flight finally took off after hours of delay. Didn't you listen to my voicemail?"

"You're in Cincinnati?"

"Of course." Meegan laughed again. She sounded like a dense movie star, snickering at everything everyone said. The sound irritated his nerves. "We're near the stadium at a bar. Aren't you going to come?"

"I'd rather hang out with you alone."

Meegan was clearly not listening to him. Her attention seemed to be on several people at once. Tristen waited for her to focus on him again.

"Sorry, babe. What were you saying?" Meegan shouted over the phone.

"I said, why don't you come here? I want to see you."

"I sent you a text with the address an hour ago," Meegan shouted. "Come out! They're having karaoke. You owe me."

The way he saw it, Meegan owed him. And the last thing he wanted to do was go out. But talking over the noise seemed like a waste of time. If he didn't go, she'd be annoyed. And all he would accomplish was getting drunk alone.

"Fine."

The noise and music faded as Meegan said something again, but it came through garbled.

"I'll see you soon." Meegan squealed into the phone, the noise piercing his eardrums.

"Meegan. That hurt my ears."

"Sorry… sent you… address. Come fast."

The line went dead as a message came with the address for Bullet Bar. Another was all exclamation points, followed by the news that she would be signing a contract with Seraphina for a song. Together.

Tristen got into his car, conflicted about Meegan's news. Which wasn't good. He was her boyfriend and should feel happy for her. He cringed when Seraphina's *Cloudless* came on the radio. It was hitting number nine in the countdown, according to the radio DJ. Tristen's mood darkened. Nine out of millions of songs out there. If he wrote and sang pop, he would have a music career. Songs about love and jealousy sold like hot cakes.

Except that he'd look ridiculous up on stage. An old-school rocker with a hint of folk from the Midwest competing within pop culture? Not a chance. He still wouldn't make it. There wasn't anything different enough about him. Just another man trying to write music.

The car passed Langston Street, where he'd lived for a bit after leaving home. A nice reminder of his streak of failure. Before that had come his failure in Lewisville, where he'd gone to college for a whole two semesters. Then there was the almost-success and definite failure with The Seethers.

Tristen sighed. A couple of blocks down the street he'd just passed was the warehouse where The Seethers had recorded their second album. The album did well for an indie band. Enough for them to think they would make it. They'd talked about making plans for a bigger tour after the small one with Art of Rendering.

He scoffed at his stupidity, his belief in things turning out all right for guys like him.

Of course, everything had changed after that tour. For Talon, it had changed for the better. While he was running around as a sound guy, scrambling to pick up any pieces that resembled a career. And Meegan. He couldn't forget Meegan, who wouldn't even let him be part of her success. Not after getting Clay. Didn't matter that he was the one who'd recorded the first album that had set the stage for her blossoming career.

Tristen pulled his car into the crowded parking lot and crawled out. The bar wasn't any less crowded.

"Tristen."

Despite the loud hum inside the bar, he swore he could hear his name. The bar was crowded, and there was a terrible screech coming from the front. Someone was trying to sing a Chloe Parker song and failing miserably. At least he wasn't the only failure in the crowd.

Suddenly warm, feminine-scented arms threw themselves around his neck. He stiffened, breathing in deeply before realizing who it was. Meegan. Her scent and nearness instantly calmed him, transporting him away from his thoughts of self-pity and into a place where he wanted to be better.

Now he was glad he'd come.

"Tristen." She pressed her lips to his.

His body warmed at her touch. He ran his hands over her thighs and up the sides of her chest.

"Let's go make out," he said in her ear. She giggled and pulled away, shaking her head with a teasing smile.

"Not now. Later. Come on. Everyone's over there. It's amateur night and I'm up soon." She pulled him behind her toward a large round table. "I'm glad we ran into AOR. Jake is funny. And kinda hot."

"What?" Tristen stuttered.

Talon stood at the table talking to Watsu and Clay. He saluted Tristen with his drink when they locked eyes.

"I'm going to need a drink."

"You can get one at the table. We bought some bottles."

Tristen pulled his hand away from Meegan's as she led him to the table. He would have turned around and left, except that everyone had already seen him. Even Talon. He wasn't going to give his twin the satisfaction of seeing him run away.

"Hey, man. You should check your phone more often," Talon said. He grinned. "What do you want? We ordered some bottles. Grab a cup."

"Yeah, thanks. Maybe whiskey."

"Number fifteen, get ready," said a woman from the small stage at the edge of the bar.

"That's us," Meegan cried, downing her drink. She yanked Talon's arm to follow her to the stage. He laughed, flashing his white teeth and glancing around at the women as he followed.

Tristen scanned the crowd, locking eyes with Jake, who immediately made his way over. He held out a filled cup to Tristen, leaving him no choice but to take it. "Here. Talon told me to make you a Jack and Coke."

Tristen took a sip, then turned to watch Meegan. Maybe if he seemed occupied in ogling her, no one else would talk to him. But Jake didn't get the memo. He stepped in closer and leaned toward Tristen.

"By the way," he said, too close to Tristen's ears. "I want to thank you for letting us use the song."

Tristen tore his eyes away from the stage. "The song?"

"The song you and Talon wrote. Thanks for signing off on it."

"When did I sign off on it?" Tristen asked. He narrowed his eyes at Jake as the man pulled something from the bag propped up on the table.

"Right here," Jake said. "I brought you the copy. Michelle was supposed to give you one. For your files."

Tristen slowly closed his mouth as he read the piece of paper he had signed. It wasn't a payment contract. It was a contract giving Art of Rendering the right to sing his song. Slowly, his mind pieced back together the moments at the venue. There had been a second when he'd noticed his paper was slightly different from Steve's, but he hadn't stopped to figure out why.

Anger burned in his chest. He felt cheated, and yet there was his signature.

"We also gotta talk about payment," Jake continued. "Talon was saying we could pay you through the bank account you used to have with The Seethers, since it's set up as a business account. Or would you prefer it to be your personal account?"

"Hello, everyone," Meegan said to the crowd, receiving a cheer as she introduced herself and Talon.

Tristen gulped his whiskey and Coke before answering. "The business account is fine. Talon should have the information. How much are you paying me?" He glanced at the paper. "This doesn't say."

"We consulted a lawyer, and he told us to offer you this. A one-time-use contract for two thousand."

Two thousand was better than nothing, but the anger still hadn't disappeared from his chest. Tristen sipped his drink. It was cold and strong. It'd be so easy to gulp it down. Along with another. And possibly another. "I like the way you changed it a bit. You guys give it a certain flare."

Jake smiled. "Art is done better together, you know?"

Tristen resisted the urge to roll his eyes. Or punch him in the face. If they had wanted to do something together, they could have called him before they stole his song.

Jake grinned, bopping his head as Meegan and Talon hammered up "Jolene" by Dolly Parton. "They're good. Maybe we should have Meegan sing a song with us on the album."

Tristen smiled half-heartedly, keeping his eyes on Meegan and Talon. His brother had always enjoyed being the center of attention. Usually, it was being the star of a sports team for Talon, more than on stage. When Aimee and Tristen used to sing together, Talon would usually make fun of them. It wasn't until after Aimee died that Tristen found out Talon had a better voice than him.

It was strange how life, so far, had turned out. When they were eighteen, Talon had wanted to stay behind in Pelton even after Luke kicked Tristen out. He had a construction job and was applying to become the football coach for the local high school team. After he interviewed twice and didn't get the job, which they assumed was due to who their parents were in the small town, Talon finally made his way to Cincinnati, where Tristen was living.

Back then Tristen was bartending and working odd jobs to get by. When Talon joined him, he had just started filling in live music on Thursday nights at a small bar in downtown. When Michael Burtz, an old jazz singer who drank at The Minuet where Tristen bartended, met Talon, he suggested they turn the Thursday night gig into a twin show. "Two handsome guys singing. Whew! The ladies will love it. I can't even imagine the tips you'll get."

It took some convincing to get Talon to join him, but Michael Burtz was right; the tips were good, and the ladies were even better. That first night, Talon had held a hundred dollars in tips in his hand. He'd needed no more convincing after that.

Tristen smiled at the memory.

They ran the twin gig for two years, living off the tips from performing and bartending as well as some construction jobs on the side. Just when they were getting bored, their friend Micah approached them about forming a band. Talon was game immediately and Tristen, with nothing else on the horizon, followed.

The idea of becoming a successful band promised a future of excitement and fun, a life far away from the struggle Tristen had watched his parents go through every year of their lives.

Or so he had thought.

How quickly everything could turn. Talon was a rock star. Even as he sang with Meegan, people shouted at him for his autograph. Tristen downed the rest of his drink, pushing the pitying thoughts inward with his whiskey.

Talon and Meegan bowed to a roaring crowd. Jake suddenly leaned in, his breath smelling of tobacco and alcohol, his voice roaring in Tristen's ear. "Why don't you get up there?"

Tristen snorted.

Jake blinked, then shook his head. "You're talented. I never thought you'd give music up."

His nerve left Tristen speechless. Jake sounded serious, almost genuine. "Can't keep going when you lose your singer."

Jake polished off his drink before he turned fully towards Tristen. "I was talking more about you giving up your music. That modern, folk stuff you do on your own. That's the music you should play. Like that song for Aimee. It's good. People who hear it always love it."

"Yeah. I guess." He didn't ask who loved it. He didn't want to find out they'd been playing it in other places. He wondered if Talon was using the other songs he used to write and had left behind.

He looked around for someone to save him, but Meegan wasn't bothering to take notice.

"I saw you play in a cafe in Lexington once. You were incredible. I felt a little jealous," Jake said. "Imagine my shock when I found you were part of The Seethers, a young band we hired to open for us."

"Huh," Tristen muttered, too low for Jake to hear. He'd never told anyone that he drove into Lexington to play alone sometimes. He'd been wondering how Talon had found out. It was during a temporary lull when Talon was getting married, but those had been good months. Alone in Lexington, he could test out new songs and mixes before showing the rest of the band.

Jake held up his drink. "I'm gonna get another drink. You want one?"

"Yeah, thanks."

Jake moved aside, leaving the space empty while Talon left Meegan alone on stage. Someone moved in close at the table, watching the show with him. "She's very beautiful."

Tristen's entire body startled at the voice. He turned to find a woman standing next to him. Lamia—he was sure it was her, the girl he'd fooled around with one time back when he and Talon were still playing the twin gig. She hadn't had the boobs then, and had bleached her hair blonde, but it was her.

"What are you doing here?"

Lamia pulled herself back with a sharp inhale, her mouth forming an open circle. She even flapped her hand over her chest, as though insulted, before exploding into giggles with her own performance.

Tristen lifted his cup in mock salute, which she grabbed out of his hands.

"Coke and whiskey? Are you in college or something?" she complained. "You used to drink vodka tonics."

Tristen swore under his breath. Vodka tonic was Talon's drink. "You got some nerve, Lamia. We were together for one weekend, what? Four years ago?"

"Try six months." Lamia crossed her arms, raising her ample chest higher as her left eyebrow popped up. "You were supposed to come see me weeks ago. There was something important going on." She tapped a long fingernail against her red lips. "That's right. You're going to be a father."

Tristen turned, glancing at her belly—which did seem a little more round—before meeting her eyes. She looked to be on the verge of punching him in the face. He lowered his tone to keep them both calm. "I'm sorry you've gotten yourself into trouble, Lamia, but we haven't been together since that night I got drunk in Lexington."

Lamia laughed. A loud, full cackle that drew the attention of several people around the table.

On stage, Meegan held the last notes of the song as long as she possibly could, well past the music set up in the karaoke machine. The crowd loved it.

"I thought I'd stay here and have a little chat with your girlfriend. We can solve where you were this summer."

"Fine with me. I was with Meegan and the band."

Lamia smiled, her mouth wide and open, but he could see her confidence falter slightly. Of course, there was another person in this world that looked a lot like him. And while he thought he and Talon had an unspoken rule about not using each other's names when it came to women, he wouldn't put it past his brother at this point. Tristen eyed the bar for his brother, but couldn't see him anywhere. Meegan, though, was marching straight towards him.

"Want me to leave?" Lamia asked.

"Nope. I want you to ask her about the summer."

"Hey," Meegan said, sliding up against Tristen's side. "What d'ya think of our mini concert? Oh, look, this bar allows stray cats in."

Her smile was cold as she assessed Lamia.

"Meegan, can you tell Lamia where I was this summer?"

"You were with me."

Lamia flipped her hair over her shoulder. "What every girlfriend who can't satisfy her man would say."

Meegan gave a small nod before smiling at Tristen. "True, except that we played this game where we marked every day that we spend all day and night together on the calendar, and there wasn't one day not marked off."

Tristen smiled. Marking the calendar had seemed like a stupid game at the time.

"You think you can treat me like this?" Lamia screamed, her face turning red. "After everything I've done for you? I'm done, Tristen. I'm done hiding and pretending for you. I'm going to make your life miserable. You owe me."

Her voice swelled with every syllable, hitting a crescendo at the last two words. Grabbing a nearby drink, she flung it in his face. Droplets of gin and tonic rolled into his eyes and, unfortunately, into his nose when he gasped in shock.

Before he could think of what to do, Talon was next to him. He tried to shove his brother aside, but he didn't flinch. "Get off of me."

Talon grabbed at the back of Tristen's neck, pulling him in close. "You look like shit. And it won't look great on a police report to have a boxer threatening a woman."

Tristen tried to pull away, but Talon's grip was strong. All those years of playing different ball sports. And, anyway, he had a point.

"Go back with the others. I'll escort the lady outside."

Talon turned until his body was between Lamia and Tristen. Lamia seemed to lose color from her face, but Tristen couldn't be sure. Talon swept her arm into his and started walking quickly to the door.

"Come on. Let's go back to the table," Meegan said. She pulled on Tristen's sleeve, but he kept watching Lamia look at Talon, like she couldn't believe what was happening. He had expected her to push him away. It was as though shock had replaced her fire.

"You go ahead. I drank too much. I'm going to the toilets."

Meegan walked away, muttering angrily to herself. If he hadn't been so wound up, maybe he'd go after her. Pay attention to her. Make sure she wasn't angry with him. But something was up with Talon, and Tristen needed to know what.

Perhaps it was twin intuition. Twin RSP was what Bobbi used to call it. Whatever it was, he wanted to know if Talon had cheated on Sandra or if Lamia was just crazy. One thing was certain; he hadn't slept with Lamia in years.

He stopped, causing the guy behind him to run directly into his back.

"Geez, man. What the hell?" The guy shook liquid off his sweater.

"Sorry about that," Tristen said, scanning the crowd. Talon was leading Lamia out the door already.

"Whatever," the guy muttered, but Tristen barely registered it. He pushed through the crowd, no longer caring about anything other than catching up to the other two.

At the front, Tristen pressed himself into a corner near a window. Cold air seeped through the cracks, sending shivers through him, but he had a semi-perfect view of Lamia standing on the sidewalk. Talon stepped back into view, his arm outstretched and head shaking.

Lamia said something, her finger pointing to the bar and then back at Talon. Talon wasn't intimidated. He chuckled and shrugged. Tristen could have sworn he said, "That was Talon." He couldn't be sure, but the way Lamia's eyebrow went up, it looked as though she didn't fully believe him.

Every cell in his body seemed to swell with anger. Whatever was going on with Talon, he didn't like it. He had a bad feeling it was going to involve him, and he didn't have time for that now. Between the song and now this woman showing up out of nowhere, Tristen wasn't sure where to focus his anger.

"Tristen?"

He turned. Meegan looked concerned and sad, and that was probably his fault. "Let's go home, yeah? Let's not get involved in whatever that is outside."

Tristen was tempted to say no. He wanted to punch his brother in the nose when he walked back into the bar, but the possibility of sleeping next to Meegan that night, feel her body and hear her soothing voice, won the day. He let his shoulders relax, took her hand, and followed her out of the bar.

Chapter 22

He woke up next to Meegan a few hours later, his head pounding. Not from the alcohol, but from dreaming all night of being in an overly crowded bar that was so loud he'd walked with his hands over his ears. Talon was there, and he kept pointing at him, saying, "That's Talon, my brother."

Tristen slipped out from under the satin sheets and tiptoed downstairs to the kitchen. Meegan had the best coffee machine, and he was looking forward to sipping a cup while looking out the back windows as he used to. With the deep aroma filling the kitchen, his thoughts moved back to the night before and Talon.

It wouldn't have been the first time either of them had used the other's name for something. During the driving exams, they'd gone in as each other. Tristen had taken the written test twice and Talon the driving test twice. During school they were constantly tricking their friends or teachers, usually in good fun. But when it came to girls, Tristen had never used his brother's name. In a small town like Pelton, he would have gotten found out. Plus, it seemed a bit creepy.

Of course, he hadn't been married and on a break from his marriage during the summer, but Talon had been. And his brother wasn't stupid. If he'd wanted to get back together with Sandra, which he had said over and over again during that five-month break, he might have thought using Tristen's name would be safer for a fling.

The Madagascan coffee hit his tongue. The dark, bold flavor took him back to when Emily had invited him and Meegan to her parents' estate for the first time. They had a house on the rolling Kentuckian hills that looked like it belonged in the English countryside, and on what they called the "veranda" Tristen had tasted Hawaiian coffee for the first time. He'd moved in with Meegan a few months later and felt like a kid at Christmas when he found all the different varieties of coffee she kept on hand.

"It's like wine," she had said. "Different foods require a different coffee."

The sound of slippers shuffling down the stairs brought him back to the moment.

"Good morning," he said, pulling Meegan close. He kissed her head of tangled hair. As beautiful as she was all made up, he never changed his opinion that she was the most beautiful in the morning. Raw and without a trace of makeup. Her hair was always wild, as though a tornado had spun through it, and he could see the tiny lines at the corner of her eyes when she smiled. This was the best moment with her.

"Morning." Meegan yawned and took the mug of coffee from Tristen's hands. "I was thinking how I wish you could come to Music On Air. Last night was so nice."

She winked at him. He couldn't help chuckling.

"Last night was nice," he said, emphasizing her word. "But you missed your chance to invite me. I can't abandon Steve now, as much as I probably would if you spent two minutes convincing me."

Meegan smiled over her mug of coffee. "Next year we'll both go, and we'll both be performing."

The chances of Tristen performing at Music On Air in one year's time were almost nonexistent. That truth broke the fog of the morning. He'd been in a trance, probably from the excellent coffee, but now everything stressful about his life popped up, like neon lights suddenly turning on.

"Well, I'll at least be there with you," he said. "I'll be your biggest fan, dancing and waving my arms like crazy."

Meegan's eyes narrowed briefly. "Are you seriously giving up music, Tristen? What are you going to do if you don't pursue music?"

"I'm looking into things. I like what I'm doing with Lin. I liked producing your album, too. Like you said, maybe it's something I could do."

"I liked my rock 'n roll boyfriend," Meegan said.

Tristen poured more coffee instead of answering. He'd liked being her rock 'n roll boyfriend.

"I think after this I'll find a few places to play again. Like before The Seethers. I miss playing in front of people."

"By yourself?"

"Probably. I don't have anyone else to play with. The guys from The Seethers all found other things."

Meegan sighed. "You should call one of them. Your folk music isn't going to get you anywhere. The people making money these days are pop singers, rappers, and the people crossing genres."

Tristen disagreed, but he didn't say so. Instead, he slid his hand across the table to hold hers just as she pulled her knees up to her chest and held the coffee close. Tristen struggled to hide his hurt, but Meegan didn't see it anyway. She was looking out the window.

"When do you leave?" he asked. The ticking of the clock was suddenly very loud.

"Clay is picking me up in an hour. We want to go over some strategy things before heading to the airport." She peered at Tristen, then looked at the clock. "Don't you have to record Lin today?"

"I have to leave in an hour, so I won't be in your way," he said, failing to keep his tone neutral.

Meegan exhaled. "Once you can show Daddy you have a paycheck, you can move in again and we'll get better."

"Better?"

Meegan waved her hand between them. "This. This awkwardness. It's because I'm a woman and more successful right now and you're having a hard time. And I get it," she continued when he opened his mouth to protest. "I get it, babe. You're a man who's always taken care of himself. I know. I don't blame you, really. But I can't change anything either. I can't slow my career down so you can catch up."

"I never asked you to slow down." Tristen moved to the sink as anger and hurt threatened to make him lose further control of his voice. He took in a deep breath. "I don't want you to slow down. I'm just trying to figure out my own stuff."

The seconds passing from the wall clock was the only sound for a minute.

"Okay. Fine. We can talk more about this when I get home." She kept her attention on him, though, so Tristen didn't move to head upstairs.

"What?"

"That woman last night. What did she really want? Was she hitting on you?"

"No."

"You two looked, I don't know, familiar with each other."

Tristen decided to go with the truth. "She's someone I had a few nights with about four years ago. She showed up a few times at the bar."

Meegan shook her head and laughed dismissively. "I can't blame you, really. She has all the goods a young man looks for."

"It was nothing, Meegan. We both have former"—he thought carefully—"people in our past."

"If she was in your past, why did she show up last night?"

Tristen hesitated, his dream coming back to mind. "I think Talon got involved with her."

"Talon?" Meegan sounded doubtful.

"Yes, Talon. I wouldn't put it past him. He stole my song."

"What?" Meegan stood up. "Seriously, Tristen. I'm trying to have a conversation with you, but whatever. I have to get dressed. I don't know what you're doing with that woman, but I don't like her. And if you're having an affair while I'm out building my career, I want you to just tell me now."

"I am not having an affair," Tristen said through gritted teeth. He kept the mutual accusation on the tip of his tongue. No use making this conversation worse.

Meegan walked to the sink and took a long look at him. Tristen resisted storming away, but he was pretty sure his anger showed on his face. "Tristen, I'll believe you," she said, cupping his cheek with her hand. "But do not make a fool of me."

Tristen pulled away from her touch and squared his focus on hers. "The only way this is going to work is if we trust each other. I trust you and you trust me."

"Exactly." Meegan inhaled deeply and closed her eyes. "I'm going to do some yoga and center myself before Clay comes over. We have a lot of work to do before we leave. Please be sure to take all your stuff so Daddy knows you aren't living here. I don't need that stress."

She gave him a quick kiss before heading to the basement to her yoga corner.

Tristen thought about following her and getting a more satisfactory answer instead of the feeling of defeat he was left with, but he didn't. Instead, he headed to the shower. His biggest opportunity to have a producer company was meeting with him in less than an hour.

Lin had the energy of a three-month-old puppy and more stories to share than a library. Tristen had never heard so many words spoken in so little time. There was no escape from him, either. The moment he finished singing a song, he appeared next to Tristen, ready with another story or to finish what he hadn't before. For two days Tristen experienced zero silence.

"Did you see this picture of your girl? I can't believe she's your girl. Wow, man, she's so hot. Watch out. That handsome agent will get her one day, you'll see."

"Look, it's a video of me skydiving. No, watch till the end. Ha! Isn't that funny? My face went right into that girl's boobs!"

The second day was supposed to take four hours, but at this rate, it would be at least double that.

"See here? You know her? She wants to marry me for my money. That's one I shouldn't have slept with. Well, her and her sister. They're crazy. Really, really crazy. They tried to kill me once. No, I'm serious! They pushed me off the yacht. They don't know that I can swim, though, even when I'm drunk. My father made me swim thirty minutes every morning. Discipline to keep me in line." Lin burst into giggles, and Tristen couldn't help joining him. He couldn't imagine what Lin had been like as a kid.

"All right. Last take. Your voice okay?"

Finishing his bottle of tepid lemon water ranked higher in importance than responding verbally. Lin's fingers gave strange gestures that Tristen interpreted to mean to wait. Steve, who had less patience for Lin, marched out of the room.

"What's with that guy?" Lin asked, before belching lemon air into Tristen's face.

"He's fine. Don't worry about him. We need another take, okay? And don't stop in the middle of the song. Even if you mess up, just keep going."

"Gotcha." Lin winked, still smiling.

Tristen didn't believe him. Despite all his crazy stories and being a party boy, Lin was a perfectionist with his singing. He pushed himself harder than anyone Tristen had worked with before.

Quiet descended for a moment as Lin left to enter the recording booth. For all his annoying faults, he was growing on Tristen.

"I'm ready," he said, giving Tristen the thumbs-up when the music started.

"That guy is unbelievable," Steve said, walking back into the sound booth. "Sorry, I needed a break. He's got my wife beat on talking."

"Ouch. Is that an insult to your wife or to Lin?"

Steve rubbed his balding head. "I don't even know anymore. My head feels too full to think properly. By the way, I gotta go in about fifteen. This has already taken more time than it should have."

"No worries, man. I'll finish up here."

Lin crescendoed into the part he kept messing up at. Steve and Tristen both held their breath and watched him through the plexiglass. The long notes were no problem; it was the beat of the staccato that normally gave him issues. Inside the sound booth, Lin closed his eyes, his fingers curling into fists as he hit the first, then second, third, fourth, the pause and then the fifth.

It wasn't until he didn't stop to groan or squeal in joy, but continued the song, that Tristen and Steve let out a collective breath. They didn't speak again until the song finished.

"That was great, Lin," Tristen said through the mic.

"I was just fooling you that last time," Lin replied, his usual laugh following. "Wait, I'll come in there."

"I'm out. See you at the venue Monday," Steve called out over his shoulder as he rushed out.

"Bye, Steve," Lin said. "Bye! Man, he must be deaf. He didn't even turn around."

"He's in a hurry," Tristen said, packing up his gear. He still had some editing to do, but he'd rather do it in Pelton.

"You going to Music on Air, man? I hear your woman is going."

"She is, but I'm not. Got work to do here." Tristen tapped the computer full of Lin's songs, but Lin didn't look impressed.

"That's no good, man. You shouldn't send her alone with that agent of hers. Musicians always sleep with their agents."

"Just because you slept with your agent doesn't mean she'll sleep with hers, Lin," Tristen drawled.

Lin giggled. "True, true. But seriously, Tristen, you saw those pictures. He wants her. I wouldn't trust that agent. He's too handsome. You're fit, but that guy is all glamour. And girls like glamour, you know? Well, girls like Meegan like glamour. Because she is all glamour. And you are not glamour."

"Thanks. I appreciate you telling me that."

With a click of his heels, Lin gave him a mocking salute. "I'll keep an eye on Meegan for you, yeah?"

"Sure, thanks, Lin. We'll talk soon. I'll let you know when these songs are ready."

"Soon, we will be number one in Singapore." Lin gave a hoot, then jogged out, his fist raised in the air.

Tristen took a deep breath and set to work. "Right. Number one."

Chapter 23

Tristen spent two days editing Lin's album and any other last-minute tracks Watsu sent him. With Ivy gone most of the time and little food in the house, he ran on mostly caffeine drinks and beef jerky. By five in the morning of the fight, he was ready for a change of scenery. Just like he used to as a kid, Tristen tiptoed out of the house in his socks, laced up his shoes outside, and headed out for a run.

Everything going on his life was creating an uncomfortable buzz under his skin. It wasn't just nerves over the fight or the chance of being arrested; it was that he couldn't stop thinking about the fight between him and Meegan, wondering if she was accusing him of what she was doing. He had no proof she was cheating, and he knew that thought process wasn't going to get him anywhere. Still, it was difficult to turn it off as his feet created their own rhythm against the pavement, lulling him into the easy-to-access thoughts. Meegan. Clay. Talon. Lamia. The betrayals and misunderstandings and lost chances. The utter failures on his part.

He thought about the concert and Lin and Watsu; whether he wanted to chase a working relationship with her if she asked him to stay. Or did he want to go out on his own? Both sounded scary in their own way.

He hit the replay on his music and picked up the pace, concentrating hard to keep his mind blank until he rounded off the country highway and entered Pelton. At the intersection that led to Ivy's house, he turned in and headed home.

It was only six-thirty, but Ivy was already sitting on the top stair of her porch, sipping a cup of coffee. The coffee he'd insisted on buying even though it cost almost fifteen dollars a pound. He'd been too spoiled by Meegan to drink the generic stuff Ivy always bought.

She didn't see him at first. He slowed; something about her caught his attention. She sat still, her lips moving slightly, mug in one hand and a pamphlet in the other. Unsure if she was in a sleepwalking trance or meditating, Tristen walked quietly up the walkway.

"Hey," she breathed as he got closer. "I didn't realize you were out this early."

"I couldn't sleep."

Ivy held up her coffee. "Me either. My foot was giving me some trouble, and the birds were so loud. I thought I might as well start my day. You want a cup of coffee?"

"Yeah, I'd like that," Tristen said, surprised to find he wasn't lying. Sitting with Ivy and a mug of coffee seemed like the best idea in the world at the moment.

"You take it black, right? If not, I can get some cream," Ivy said when she returned.

Tristen nodded eagerly and took the mug from his mother. "Black is good. Perfect, actually."

They stayed like that, both of them sitting on the steps, observing the quiet street.

"Nice morning, isn't it?" Ivy said. "I never used to take the time to enjoy the mornings. Always thought that was nonsense."

"You thought mornings were nonsense?" Tristen teased. The coffee was good. It warmed his sweating body as they sat together.

Ivy scoffed into her mug. "I thought taking the time to enjoy the moment was nonsense," she said. "I let so many days and hours go by, just hustling through. As though if I kept busy, then one day everything would magically get better."

Tristen narrowed his eyes, wondering how much he should argue with her. He'd never seen Ivy as a hustler. She'd held a few jobs during his lifetime, sure, but nothing that put her in the rat race.

"I'm sorry you got stuck with me as the one meant to raise you," she said, squinting up at him.

"What?" He was in no mood for some deep discussion. The coffee was helping, but he didn't have the energy for a talk about their family issues.

Ivy kept her gaze steady on him, smiling as though seeing something in her mind's eye. "I never should've had kids. Wasn't built for 'em."

Tristen adjusted his position to put his feet up against the railing. Now that he knew the conversation would not be a real one, he could get comfortable. "Good to know, Ivy. I mean, good for you to realize. But I guess we all knew that before."

Ivy choked on her coffee when she giggled. "I'm serious," she said when she could finally catch her breath. "I didn't think too much about it when I was young, you know? Whether I should or shouldn't have kids. I should've at least waited. Maybe I would have been better at it if I waited."

"Maybe, but whatever. We're here, and we don't regret being alive, you know?" he said, the words out before he could weigh them. He'd forgotten Aimee.

Ivy didn't yell or cry. Not like she had years before when he had forgotten to call on Aimee's death anniversary, something Ivy had decided she didn't want to celebrate the next year when he called. Instead, she nodded and wiped at the corners of her eyes.

"Well," she whispered. "Everything happens for a reason, right? Or so they say."

The words stirred up a force of anger within him he couldn't tamp down.

"What the hell kind of reason would it be for a young girl to overdose on some drugs her boyfriend gave her?" he asked, his voice low and vibrating. He closed his eyes, trying to catch his breath. The last thing he wanted was an argument.

Ivy didn't argue. She sighed heavily as she stood up and went back into the house. Tristen stayed outside, assuming she had left the conversation, but she came back a few minutes later with the coffeepot and a box of muesli cereal.

"It's all I got," she said, holding out the box of cereal. "And I don't even have any milk. It's just you and me, honey. Talon's off somewhere, and Aimee's dead."

Tristen sipped his cooling coffee and watched the magnolia leaves move with the wind.

"We weren't the only ones affected by the opioids, Tristen. Did you know Aimee's boyfriend, Patrick, died, too? Just a few months after Aimee."

"Not surprised," Tristen said. "Taking those drugs was stupid, and Aimee knew it. All she had to do was watch people struggle around her to get off them."

Although she had been young and sick when Ivy went into rehab. And she was dead when Ivy relapsed.

"We all know what's bad for us," Ivy said. "But we do them anyway to see if we can numb the pain. Or stop thinking about something. Or stop being afraid. Why else did you take stuff?"

Tristen shook his head. "I didn't take drugs all the time. She was involved in other things. Had a life ahead of her. She should have known better."

"We should all know better. But that's the problem, right? We can always see what another person should do, but not what we should do for ourselves. Even after getting off opioids, I couldn't stop marijuana. And when she died, well, you know. I couldn't put the bottle down. For a while, I was so scared of not having a buffer against real life. Like, if I was sober, I would feel everything. Turns out, feeling can be freeing, too."

"Getting philosophical today, aren't you?" he quipped. "But okay, I'll humor you. Sure, it's hard to change ourselves and easy to point out to others what they should change. Like Talon having a kid."

"What's wrong with Talon having a kid?" Ivy asked.

Tristen regretted he had said anything. "Nothing."

"I'm excited for a grandbaby, Tristen. Why aren't you happy for him?"

"I can be happy for him and still think it's a colossally terrible idea. I mean, you said it earlier—maybe if you had waited. Talon should wait. He can't have enough money to have a baby. Besides, he and I don't know how to be dads. I mean, look at our role models."

"I love your brother, Tristen. I love you both," she said. "And I did say maybe I should've waited to have kids, or maybe not have them, but I can't imagine my life without you three. Even Aimee. I mean, at the end, life don't have much meaning without kids, you know?"

"If you say so," Tristen said. "But I'd rather not mess a kid up. And if Talon can abandon his twin brother, I hate to imagine how much he could mess up his own kid."

Ivy sat back down on the step, her medical boot clacking hard against the rotting wooden railing. "Well, he's gonna try his best, and Sandra will do her best to keep your brother in line."

Tristen opened his mouth to make another snarky remark, but Ivy continued without giving enough pause.

"Your brother has always been one to do whatever he wants to do. Even when he was little, he was like that. Always making you tag along, of course. And getting you in trouble first, before even he did. But I still love him."

"Right," Tristen said. "Well, I might love him, but it's hard to like him sometimes."

Ivy nodded. "I get that."

"What do you mean?"

She shifted to lean toward him, forearms on her knees. "Tristen, you gotta let this thing with your brother go. It's like you internalized this idea that you can't do anything without him, and now you're just waiting around for him to come back. But he ain't coming back."

"Does it look like I'm waiting around?" Tristen asked, turning to face her. "I'm here fighting for Owen. So you don't lose your house, buy the way."

"And so you don't have to think about moving forward," Ivy shot back. The fact she wasn't yelling but speaking calmly threw him off balance. "You tend to not do anything without Talon, Tristen, but this time you have to."

"I moved away from Pelton without Talon."

"Luke threw you out, Tristen. You never would have left without Talon otherwise."

"But I left. So you can't say I don't do anything without him. It's just that we're a good team together."

"Did you make the band before or after Talon came?"

Tristen didn't want to hear any more. He stood up, setting the empty mug on the steps. "Because we sold ourselves on being twins. It's what got us the gigs."

"But you didn't bother doing anything before Talon got there. You dropped out of college," Ivy pointed out. "I was so proud of you for being in college. But you dropped out. You worked lame construction jobs, bumming around like Luke until Talon came."

"We're twins, Ivy. We were doing well. And The Seethers would have been successful if Talon hadn't left. If he thought about someone other than himself for once in his life, maybe we would be figuring this house thing out together."

Ivy smiled. "Like I told you, I love your brother, but when kindness was being dealt out, he somehow got passed over. I got a feelin' he's scared of something. He has a need for some money and fame."

"Don't we all?" Tristen muttered. "I'd certainly like to earn more. I wouldn't mind being famous."

"I can't blame him for putting Sandra and the baby above us."

Tristen tried to interrupt, but Ivy shook her head. He knew better than to provoke her. Last thing he needed was the neighbors seeing them have another knockdown, drag out again.

"I wish he was here, but you are. And I'm grateful for it. I hope when this is over that you'll stop looking for Talon to come back and set off on your own. I hope that you'll stop believing that damn lie Luke used to tell you and find out what you want in life."

Tristen stepped back, fighting the need to run. "I don't think of anything Luke used to tell me."

Ivy's eyes filled with so much pity he wanted to slap her. He took another step back to make sure he didn't.

"You seriously think I can't do anything without Talon?"

"I seriously believe you think you can't do anything without Talon," Ivy said.

Tristen didn't say anything.

A rumble down the street drew their attention. Owen's truck pulled up to the curb, and Owen hopped out.

"Morning!" he shouted, forgetting the sleeping neighbors. "Didn't expect you to be up, darling."

He kissed Ivy on the forehead. Tristen couldn't help but watch. He would never have imagined Owen being tender, but he had now seen it with his own eyes.

"Just having some coffee with my boy," Ivy said, patting the wood beside her. "Wanna sit and have some?"

"You aren't doing your thing today?" Owen asked, taking the mug of probably stone-cold coffee from Ivy and sipping it without making a face.

"What thing do you have?" Tristen asked.

Ivy looked only at Owen, acting as though Tristen had said nothing. "It's not till later."

"Then let's head out for some breakfast," Owen said. "Gotta get this boy some protein for his punches and carbs for his energy."

"Maybe extra carbs in case you get busted," Ivy said, rolling her eyes. "You don't have to be the fastest, Tris, just faster than a few of them."

Owen nudged her playfully, but she jumped away, her smile only for him. Tristen had to admit she looked happy, but it still grossed him out.

"You aren't expecting trouble, are you?" he asked Owen, partly to get him to stop staring at Ivy.

"Trouble? Never," Owen said with a smile.

Chapter 24

WHAT FELT LIKE A few minutes later, Tristen walked into the fight venue. Inside, two men and a hulk-like woman were setting up a transitory bar to one side. Leaning against it was his brother, a lazy smile on his face.

"Hey, brother." Talon's grin spread further across his face when he saw Tristen. The paper in his hand was limp in the air's humidity, but he waved it anyway. "I have my money on you. Well, some of my money on you."

"That's nice of you, bro," Tristen said, eyeing his brother. Talon grinned.

A meaty hand clamped down on Talon's shoulders, startling him. "You scared me, Owen." They gave each other a quick hug.

"Good to see you, Talon. But the only one who should be scared is the guy Tristen's fighting tonight. You ready for it?" Owen asked. He leaned his bulk against the bar, positioned just right to have a full view of the entrance.

"You mean for the fight against the guy who's twenty pounds heavier than me and who knocked his opponent unconscious last fight?"

Owen grinned. "It's going to be great, isn't it? Don't worry about the weight class. You have feet like a cat and nine lives, too. Remember when that one guy knocked you out of the ring when you were a kid? He was bigger than you, but you got back up."

"I remember that fight," Talon said, taking out a brown pharmaceutical bottle and popping two long white pills.

"Yeah," Tristen drawled. "I remember I ended up losing."

He didn't want to admit that his hands shook at the thought of going into the ring against The Alabamian. Jared had told him enough about his opponent to get his nerves twisted in knots. The Alabamian threw an average of six hundred punches every match and landed one third of them. He also hadn't lost one fight in the last two seasons down in the South.

Before leaving Ivy's, Tristen had taken a long nap to regain some energy. Unfortunately, he'd had a nightmare in which he got pummeled until he had no face. In his dream, he watched the gloved hands come at him time and time again, knowing he was going to die and wishing he could tell Meegan he loved her.

Tell Ivy that he forgave her.

Tell Talon he missed him.

Now, standing and looking at Talon, nothing was further from his mind.

"I won that night," Talon said, chuckling. "That was a great night. It was my tenth win in a row, remember, Tristen?"

"We went for beers afterward at Guy's bar, which turned into shots, and we were too hungover to fight the next day."

"Damn lucky, too, 'cause that fight got rounded up," Talon said, smiling at the memory.

Tristen remembered. They had been lucky, even if Owen made them clean the locker rooms for getting drunk. "I always thought maybe you called the police on them, Owen."

Owen laughed, a deep guffaw that sounded genuine. Instead of denying their accusation, he hit the bar and lifted his beer.

"To Tristen," he said.

Owen saluted with his drink before pouring its contents down his throat. Tristen and Talon did the same.

"I'm going to find Jared and get warmed up. I'm sure he has a whole regimen he wants me to do."

The arena was starting to fill up. Men milled around between the bleachers and bar area. At the front near the ring was a small VIP area where men and women dressed in more expensive outfits sat drinking glasses of wine and hard liquor, playing like they were in Vegas. Tristen remembered Meegan and her Oscar de la Renta comments. These women looked like their outfits cost eighty dollars, not eleven thousand. But that was the difference between the two of them.

"You're late," Jared said when Tristen entered the locker room. He held out two pills and a bottle of water. "Owen said you get to decide. I'm not to convince you one way or the other."

Tristen swallowed back his nerves and shook his head. "I don't want them tonight."

Jared laughed. "You sure? The Alabamian is huge. Some stimulation wouldn't hurt. You aren't in shape enough to win without these."

"You don't think so?"

"I don't need to think, man. I know." Jared put the pills away. "Don't know why Owen took this fight. You ain't gonna win. Not a chance. You're smaller; you're weak."

A nerve in Tristen's neck pinched. He ignored the discomfort and focused on the foe in front of him. "What is your problem?"

Jared shoved him away like a volleyball. "You fight like you don't care. Or worse, like you're scared. Scared of what would happen if you hit for real. When the rest of them go out there, they go for real. You go like you want to be someplace else."

"I do want to be somewhere else," Tristen spat back, stepping toward Jared again. This time, he didn't push him away but kept steady eye contact.

After a pause, Jared shook his head. "I believe you. And that's what's gonna make you lose tonight. Because you go out there wearing those words on your forehead, and The Alabamian is going to see it."

"That guy can't even read."

Jared cracked a smile. "Don't joke, man. You're gonna get hurt. You should forfeit."

Tristen jerked back. The locker room was quiet enough to know he'd heard correctly.

"I'm serious. Tell Owen to find another fight for you."

They stood between the naked pipes and abandoned metal table, Jared with his arms crossed and Tristen thinking as the buzz outside grew.

It was an idea. He could take the loss and tell Owen he'd fight a different one. They could make up him being sick, or use the forfeit to their advantage while he trained a bit longer. He knew he could win against some guys, just not The Alabamian.

Except that Owen would have to take a big loss. And his reputation would suffer. And then they wouldn't have the money for Ivy's house in time.

"No. I'm going to fight. Get my mom's house paid off and maybe some of my own bills. I'm gonna win. Or at least bet against myself."

Jared picked up the wrap from the metal table and started wrapping Tristen's left hand. "You going back to the band?"

"Maybe." He stretched out his fingers under the wrap. The lie didn't sit well with him. "Probably not. I'm in between things."

"My bad, man," Jared said, grabbing the other hand to wrap. "So you treat music like you treat boxing?"

"What do you mean?"

Jared looked at him, still wrapping his hand perfectly. "I mean, 'if it happens, it happens.' That's how you live life, isn't it? You're not that serious about anything, because you're semi looking for something better." Tristen yanked his hand away the moment Jared was done with it. Jared smirked as he tossed the rest of the wrap into his bag. "You box like a girl, you sing like a girl."

Despite his anger, the words also made him laugh. Probably from the nerves, but it reduced the tension that had been sitting on his chest for the past few hours. Unfortunately, the laughter was short-lived. Then the silence came back.

"What the hell does this have to do with girls?" Tristen finally asked.

Jared waved him forward to get the gloves on, and Tristen obeyed. He had said he wasn't going to forfeit.

"Shit, you're right. Girls would do a better job. I know my daughter would."

"Piss off, Jared," Tristen said, no longer laughing.

"I'm serious. She don't go into things just to lose. No, she doesn't. I taught her better than that. Whatever she goes into, she does her best. Boxing. School work. She doesn't quit like you do."

"Except you're the one who told me to forfeit, which is quitting. Do you do that with your daughter?"

"Warm up, Tristen," Jared said, a sudden edge to his voice.

Tristen did push-ups against his gloves, then high knees, then side lunges before Jared spoke again.

"Sherriff's out there. Owen invited him. Guy's a sleaze. Likes drugs and fights and women, all of which Owen has at the ready."

Tristen stopped mid squat. "Is there gonna be trouble?"

Jared paused, finished off the wrap and looked Tristen in the eyes. "Owen paid him off, but you forfeiting would get us out of here."

"Or arrested faster. If the Sherriff needs a win, he'd just raid us once the announcement was made."

Jared looked at the door as though he could see the crowd gathering, then back at Tristen. "But we could be gone before the announcement. We got phones, don't we?"

A cold shiver ran up Tristen's spine at the thought of getting arrested. He'd had nightmares about going to jail since he was a kid. Locked in a cell. Using the toilet where everyone could see and hear. Having to navigate the social hierarchy. No.

But the pot was so big tonight. Even if he lost against The Alabamian, they'd still make almost enough money to pay off Ivy's loan. He had told Owen to bet a little on him as the loser, too. Just in case.

"Speaking of phones," Jared said, signaling to Tristen's vibrating duffle bag.

Glad for the distraction as the noise outside grew, Tristen answered the phone without looking who was calling. "Meegan?"

"Tristen!" Lin's face filled the screen as he shouted. Behind him, blue and purple lights swung back and forth over what looked like a rave. "How are you, my friend? Do you hear the music? Listen, listen."

"Lin, I can talk to you later—" Tristen paused. Something about the music caught his ear. Then he started laughing.

"Do you hear it? You hear it, yes? That's me. I'm singing." The phone's image shook back and forth as Lin laughed hysterically. Tristen couldn't help smiling… until Lin's phone moved to the left. Meegan was there, dancing in her usual shimmy and shake with Clay right next to her, his hand gripping her lower hip. There were a few inches of air between Meegan's ass and Clay's hips, but not enough.

"Isn't that your girl?" Lin moved closer.

When Meegan saw Lin with the phone, she immediately smiled and waved. Then she suddenly jumped away from Clay and straightened up.

"Tristen," she shouted. "I didn't know Lin was talking to you. Did you hear his song? DJ Dash worked the chorus in."

"I heard it," Tristen said.

"What? I can't hear you. I'll call you later?" she asked.

From the side, Tristen could see Clay reaching out for Meegan's hand. He could also see her pushing it away while still smiling into the camera for him.

The camera screen became a blur as Lin moved it back to his face. "Talk to you later. I have to go dance with some ladies."

"That was interesting," Jared said when Tristen put his phone down. "That guy has crazy energy."

"He's my client. The guy you assume I don't take seriously."

Jared chuckled. "I said you don't take your music seriously. But what do I know? That didn't look like anything serious. Guess I'm in the wrong business."

"Not if you want your girl to not cheat on you," Tristen muttered.

The satin robe flew across the small space and hit him in the chest. Jared wasn't much for the royal treatment. "I saw that. Looked like she was trying to push that guy away."

"Did it? Or was it more like she was trying to hide something from me? That's her agent. The guy she's with constantly since her album came out."

A loud whistle sounded from outside. The buzz from the crowd lessened.

"It's time," Jared said.

The declaration startled Tristen, reminding him where he was and what he was doing. He couldn't afford to get distracted now. It was too late to forfeit.

Jared jabbed his fingers into Tristen's shoulder, pointing him painfully to the door. The announcer cried out his name as he appeared and he didn't respond, even when Jared jabbed him in the back ribs. The spotlight, weaker this time, found him and Tristen raised his face toward it. Looking straight at the light caused yellow blotches to appear, temporarily impeding vision. But that didn't matter. In his mind he saw Meegan grinding up against Clay.

Tristen growled in frustration, and the crowd grew louder.

"I want to see a fair fight. Clean punches. None of that MMA stuff. This is old-fashioned boxing. Got it?"

The Alabamian, inches taller than Tristan's five foot eleven and much more than twenty pounds over Tristen's weight, growled in response. Panic ran goosebumps up and down Tristen's skin. There was no use. No matter how hard he hit this guy, he was sure he wouldn't even scratch him, let alone beat him.

"He looks meaner than he is," Jared said, rubbing down his shoulders. "Watch for his right hook. He loves those. Just bounce. Get him off balance."

Tristen would have preferred to run, but the bell rang. First round was starting.

"Come on, Tristen!" At the side of the ring, Talon stood smiling.

From the left came the right hook Jared had told him about. Tristen bounced and ducked. A couple of jabs to his opponents were all he got in before he had to retreat.

"Get 'im!"

Tristen moved and jabbed, moved and hooked, but his defense was weak, and The Alabamian's fist hit him squarely in the jaw. Pain blossomed up to his eyes, but he pushed it away and bounced blindly. There was a whooshing sound. Tristen ducked, remembering the training he'd done blindfolded during high school.

"Where am I?" Owen would yell as Tristen threw jabs into the air.

Tristen ducked. His fists flew out. Jab, jab, uppercut, uppercut. His glove made contact with The Alabamian's face three times, but it wasn't enough. A large gloved hand shot out toward Tristen and clipped him on the head, sending him into the ropes.

"Get off! Get off the ropes!"

Tristen heard the screams, but his brain and limbs didn't connect. He saw the fist coming at his face and tried to duck, but The Alabamian had him cornered. Out came another fist, knocking his head to the left. Then in his belly. One, two, three. Tristen coughed and sputtered, grabbing The Alabamian by the head and pushing with all his might.

"You fight like a girl," someone screamed.

Tristen punched left, then right, knocking into his opponent's head several times before he got in another that rattled Tristen's teeth.

"End!"

Tristen stumbled to his seat, focusing on one spot while Jared whispered to him and stopped his cuts from bleeding.

"Come on, now, Tristen. You can do this. Give it back hard."

"Thought you said I'd never win," Tristen said, his voice just above a hoarse whisper.

"Well, you won't like this, but hell if I prefer The Alabamian to win. Get out there and beat him."

Tristen went back. For what seemed like seconds and yet years he was against the ropes, his head and face pummeled by The Alabamian. Between punches he opened his eyes, finding an opportunity to duck and clock him hard in the ear before he was back in the seat.

"Damn it, Tris! You aren't even trying!" Owen screamed at him from behind the ropes.

Talon looked bored.

Tristen turned away and tried to tunnel his concentration, but his eyes connected with a man who stood still in the midst of the crowd. A man with piercing eyes that he kept permanently narrowed, his lips set in a hard line. He wasn't cheering or booing. He wasn't hurling insults or heaping praise. He stood quietly, watching.

Just as he had eight years before. Another voice from the past drowned out the crowd. It was the fight between him and Talon, the last one they'd ever had, though no one expected that then. Donovan, one of Owen's guys who'd somehow made it from New York to Pelton Kentucky, had been Tristen's cornerman, since Luke had chosen to be Talon's.

"Let's go, kid," Donovan had said. "You almost have him."

"You want me to win?"

Donavan didn't answer.

Tristen looked to the opposite corner at his twin brother. His chest rose and fell, his eyes staring back. "I'm supposed to let him win."

He looked at Donovan and got his answer. Talon was making mistakes. It would be too obvious. This was his chance.

They both charged forward again. Tristen stepped slightly to the right, his right foot stumbling just a little to the left. The telltale smirk on Talon's lips told Tristen his twin had bought it.

The uppercut that Tristen thrust to Talon's chin sent him flailing. Tristen wasted nothing. Within seconds, his gloves beat against Talon. Left, right, left, right. Talon's glove shot forward, straight for Tristen's nose, but he put up his gloves and ducked.

If he had been going to lose, Tristen would take a pause. But not this time. His arm was tingling with the possibilities, and he wouldn't have stopped it even if he could. His glove connected with Talon's face.

Suddenly, Tristen's arm was raised in victory. Talon was on the ground.

Luke had been angry for a week before kicking him out of the house.

Tristen blinked as the memory cleared. In the stands, a group of women stood where he had seen Donovan. Tristen scanned the crowd, but only saw men engaged in the action in the ring.

Suddenly, Jared shoved him forward into the middle of the ring. A flame that hadn't been there before now burned inside him. He pounded his fists together, fanning the fire. His lungs burned with it until he was panting.

The crowd roared in his ears and he roared back, imagining flames rising out from his open mouth. The Alabamian sneered, but there was a seed of doubt in him, and Tristen was determined to capitalize on it. They had three more rounds to go, and he was going to go down fighting. If he was going to lose, everyone would know he'd lost trying to win.

Behind The Alabamian, the crowd egged them both on. Men and women yelled, laughed, and threw out their hands in rude gestures.

The whistle blew, vibrating into Tristen's chest, turning up his desire to win.

A glove hit him in the jaw, throwing his face toward the other side of the ring. All he could do was bounce, bounce, glide, and prowl until he regained stability. The Alabamian followed his movements, one glove slipping down. Immediately, Tristen's glove crashed against the man's enormous head, the impact vibrating up into his shoulder. For good measure he threw a left.

"Again!"

Whether it was real or in his head, Tristen followed the advice of the scream. Right, then left. Bounce away. The Alabamian got in a few punches, but he barely registered them. He was on the prowl. And the counter punches only felt like angel kisses.

The Alabamian's glove grazed his shoulder, throwing the large man off course. He was either exhausted or no longer focusing. Tristen could see it. He knew the feeling. This was the time to knock his opponent out.

But the whistle blew.

Chapter 25

"Last one, now. I can't believe you're still in this fight. The Alabamian looks real bad. You got this. Just one good hit, and he'll go down hard."

Tristen tried to absorb Jared's words, but it was difficult to focus on any of them.

Bad… one good hit… down.

He looked up to see his opponent struggling to sit upright. His head kept lolling forward, his body on the brink of shutting down to save itself. Just one good hit, and Tristen would win.

Win.

The round started with both slowly circling each other, their exhaustion palpable. It occurred to Tristen that The Alabamian had to be thinking the same thing: *one more hit.*

Gloves trembled and gave false starts. Eyes focused. The Alabamian's arm shot out. Tristen bounced on his toes and ducked. He breathed in, then came back at him, placing all the strength he could muster into a right hook. The Alabamian stumbled, but he didn't go down.

Over the jeers and screams of the crowd, one voice rose above them all in Tristen's head. *"That all you got?"*

The Alabamian's lips didn't move, but Tristen heard him. His left, then right, came at him in a flurry. Jab, jab, jab. Two out of the three missed him, but the last sent him backward. Tristen caught himself before heading straight into the ropes.

"Can't do anything right."

Jab, jab, cross, uppercut. The Alabamian's head whipped back. There was no time to cringe at the snapping sound, like muscle twisting over bone. Tristen barely had time to cover his face before several uppercuts came at him.

"I can't, I can't. That's all I hear you say."

Tristen stepped to the left. The punches stopped.

"You gonna cry? You gonna cry? You gonna cry?"

A loud cry, half moan and half roar, filled the ring. Tristen marched forward, the swelling in his eyes impeding his vision. The Alabamian saw him; Tristen knew he saw him, and yet he remained glued to the spot.

Tristen jabbed, then sent out a cross. The Alabamian's head rolled, and his arms dropped to his sides, but Tristen didn't take the chance. His right came up for an uppercut, then his left, then his right and left again. The Alabamian's eyes swelled into one in Tristen's vision. The surrounding sound tunneled away. Only the grunts of air pushing out of The Alabamian's lungs entered Tristen's ears. And one other voice.

"Your arms are barely moving. You call that a punch? My grandmother would laugh at that puny arm. Who the hell do you think you are?"

His right arm jabbed nothing but air. Tristen stepped back to watch The Alabamian's eyes roll in, and his body crumble like a statue taken out at the knees.

A powerful hand gripped Tristen's arm and yanked him away. The ref blew the whistle, then called out the countdown aloud.

"Ten, nine, eight."

The crowd quieted, some people biting their nails, some softly counting with the ref.

"Seven, six, five."

Tristen's heart sped up. No movement from the fallen Alabamian.

"Four, three, two, ONE!"

Jared's body slammed into his as the ref declared Tristen the winner. He could hardly move; someone raised his arm into the air to the loud cheers of the crowd. His thoughts were fuzzy, and his eyes felt three times their size, but Tristen was pretty sure he could see Talon smiling. And over on the other side stood Owen, yelling and pumping his fist into the air.

The heavy belt sat on his hips. Confetti and balloons fell from the ceiling. Owen yelled something, but the crowd drowned him out.

Tristen saw Talon jerk his head to the left, wide-eyed and nervous. The crowd became restless, then the murmuring started. Jared grabbed Tristen by the arm hard and yanked him out of the ring.

"Hey, what the hell?"

But Jared didn't listen. He kept pulling him forward by his arm, stubby fingernails digging into his flesh. Inside the locker room, silence descended.

"What's wrong Jared?"

"Gather your shit," Jared barked, pointing at the duffel bags. "Sirens. We've got to go now."

Talon burst into the room looking frantic and panicked. "I gotta get out of here. I can't stay here. I can't get arrested," he gabbled as he paced back and forth.

Tristen pushed aside all thoughts and sensations of pain, grabbed his things, and then grabbed Talon. "Jared's truck is out back. Get in it and let's go. Now. If you don't, you'll get caught." Jared threw Talon the keys, and he gathered the duffel bags around them. "Why are you still standing there? Let's go!"

Talon bolted from the room through the back door with Tristen and Jared directly behind. The night air was cool, the quiet only broken by squealing tires on the other side of the parking lot.

"Get in the truck!" Jared shouted. "Talon, unlock it."

Talon pointed the keys and the lights on the vehicle flashed, but when Tristen arrived at the passenger side, none of the doors were unlocked. Talon hopped in and started backing away, with Jared and Tristen yelling after him.

"Let us in!" screamed Tristen.

Talon stared at him while the sirens got closer, turning somewhere nearby. Realization filled his eyes, then he pressed down on the accelerator and sped off down the back road, forcing Tristen to jump back.

"He left." Tristen stood, stunned, next to a space where the car used to be.

"In my truck, the bastard." Jared dropped the duffel bags as a cop car squealed to a stop next to them.

Tristen thought about running. Jared's body jerked as though he would, but within seconds, the car doors whipped open.

"On the ground!" rang out from two voices.

He didn't need to turn around to know a gun was pointed in their direction. Jared dropped to his knees, then fell prostrate on the ground. Tristen followed, slower, to give his body some care. He hadn't checked yet to see if anything was broken. Halfway to prostrate, a boot hit his back, pushing him quickly down.

"You the fighter tonight?" the cop sneered, boot grinding him into the asphalt. Old anger rose within Tristen as he tried to move his face to one side so he could breathe air and not asphalt. Tiny rocks, or perhaps pieces of glass, cut into his cheeks as the cop pulled his arms together behind his back and cuffed them. "That should keep you still."

We'll be back, don't you worry. And we'll find what your dad is hiding. And if we don't, you'll be going to jail.

The words from long ago echoed in his head as though spoken by an audible voice. Fear shivered down his spine, mixing with anger. It was the first time he'd ever had the metal cuffs around his wrists. The hopelessness it filled him with was like a two-ton weight pushing him further into the ground.

"We'll be back for these two. Let 'em cool off a bit on the ground. There's more to arrest over there."

"Stupid morons. They could have gotten away," chuckled the other cop. He gave Tristen another shove on his back before following his partner. Tristen lifted his upper back to see one cop jogging away and another sauntering as though out for a night stroll.

Next to him on the asphalt, Jared swung to his side, brought his knees up to his chest, and rocked into a seated position, all the while mumbling choice words for the cops and for Talon. Tristen's body shivered involuntarily on the ground, the first aches of the fight peeking out from under the stress. Sitting up was too much effort.

"Get up."

"Don't want to."

"Get up so you don't pass out. Stay awake. This could take a while."

Tristen turned to his left side, but the pain crushed his lungs. Panting, he turned to the right without too much pain. From there, he imitated Jared in slow, jerking movements. "You been arrested before?"

Jared took his time to respond, watching the shadowy figures of the cops surrounding the abandoned factory with narrowed eyes. "Yeah," he said finally. "I told Owen to be careful with that sheriff. The minute the guy needs to fill a quota, I didn't doubt he'd be after us. Doesn't seem like the smartest guy."

"Huh." Tristen couldn't make a coherent phrase in his head. He stared into the darkness, willing the minutes to go by. Owen would come get them.

"You're in *jail?!*"

The conversation was going from bad to worse. By the time Tristen had been allowed to make a phone call, it was already two in the morning, Kentucky time. Only midnight in the mountains. Still, Meegan had told him she'd just fallen asleep because she had to get up early. She also sounded drunk.

"Look, Meegan, I'll explain later."

"You'll explain now. I mean, I'm already awake, so go ahead. Explain."

"They're only going to give me ten minutes."

"Oh, I didn't know that's how it went. You know why? Because I've never been arrested."

The cop standing guard just a few feet away shifted his belt, his gaze constantly on Tristen. They wanted him to admit he was the fighter, but he hadn't. He actually wasn't sure what he was supposed to do—Owen had never prepared him for it—but he assumed the less he admitted, the better. It wasn't making him any friends with the police.

"Listen, Meegan, I just need some help with bail. Is that Clay with you? At midnight?" Tristen asked, referring to the rumbling sound near the phone that sounded suspiciously like a man's voice.

"Don't get off topic, Tristen," Meegan snapped. "You're the one in jail. How much is bail?"

"Five thousand."

"Five thousand? And what then? Do I get the money back? I mean, we're talking half an Oscar de la Renta dress here."

"Not even." Tristen hoped she could hear the teasing in his voice, but he was afraid it only sounded tired and irritated. All the adrenaline was out of his body by now. "Meegan, I know this sounds bad."

"It's sounds worse than bad."

"Can you listen to me for a second? I got into trouble and I need your help. I'll pay you back, I promise. But I need to post bail and go home and sleep before—" Tristen stopped himself. He didn't need to tell her that he needed to get warm before his body started shivering uncontrollably. That would force him to explain what he'd been doing tonight, and he was still hoping to get out without admitting who he was.

"I need to get sleep as well."

Tristen inhaled slowly and tried again. "Meegan, please. I'll tell you everything when you get back."

"You got yourself into jail, you can get out. I send five thousand to the police station in ho-dunk Kentucky, Daddy is going to find out. And he cannot find out that I'm dating a felon."

"I'm not a felon, Meegan. I haven't even been charged with a felony."

"Whatever. I'm starting to think Daddy was right, that half the reason you're with me is for the money so you can screw up and still be safe. Well, that's going to change, Tristen. We'll keep separate accounts and—"

The phone line went dead.

The receiver weighed a hundred pounds as he placed it back in the cradle. He looked at the shiny handcuffs. If they weren't in front of him, he wouldn't believe it himself.

"Let's go. Back to cell block."

Tristen followed the cop slowly down the hall. When it came to the block he'd been in before, Tristen stood still as the door was unlocked, then slowly walked in.

"Everything check out?" Jared asked as the door to the holding cell slammed closed.

Tristen nodded, looking around. The cell was still dingy gray. And still smelled like urine. "Got some stitches," he said, pointing to his eyebrow. "No broken ribs. Just lots of bruises."

"Nurse hot, at least?"

"Old man," Tristen replied with a smirk. He sat down slowly on the metal bench and looked around. Guys loitered around the perimeter of the cell, some of them probably from the fight. No one felt like talking or looking anywhere but at the ground. "Who'd you call?"

"Owen," Jared said. "He didn't answer. You?"

"My girlfriend. She's pissed."

Jared laughed. The other guys in the block stared at him, one guy startled awake. All of them looked as though they'd never heard laughter before. "You really are green when it comes to this. You don't ever call the girl. She'll always be pissed."

"Yeah. Found that out the hard way. Where's The Alabamian?"

"Not here." They paused when they heard clanking down the hall. "A few posted bail already."

Jared uncrossed his arms and sat up straighter. His sigh was that of a man physically uncomfortable. "Owen used to be untouchable. I don't think he's had the cops raid his fights in years. I guess everyone's glory days come to an end."

"You think they're taking him down?"

Jared breathed in deeply and shook his head. "I don't know. What I know is I should find another job, but there ain't anything I could do. I got one record of assault and a few misdemeanors. If they charge me tonight, I'll go to jail for breaking my probation. Not that they care or follow up with me on any of it. My probation officer never calls."

"I've never been arrested," Tristen admitted, feeling like the words were a sign he lived a privileged life. "Almost was once when Luke sent me in his place to deliver drugs. I was twelve."

"What happened?"

"Owen found out and pulled me at the last minute. But it didn't matter, except that I didn't get involved. Cops showed up at my house later that day and found some of the stuff Luke had hidden there."

"He was moving stuff for Owen?" Jared asked. "That doesn't sound like Owen."

"That's what I always thought, but last week Owen told me otherwise. Anyway, bet you never thought that about Luke, since you held him in such high esteem."

Jared shrugged. "I never said that. I don't hold anyone in high esteem. People are complicated, Tristen. Luke never did anything to me to judge him as bad. But I also know being around stuff would be tempting. Just a few sales, and you could have yourself a little safety net, you know?"

"You sell stuff?" Tristen asked.

"Hell, no. Got a daughter to think about. Besides, Owen doesn't move that kind of stuff anymore. He got out the moment his debt to the cartel guy, Rudolfo, was paid in full."

Tristen stretched out, but quickly shifted his feet away from a puddle of spit on the floor. Perhaps it was the events of the last week, where he was, or the hits to his head last night, but suddenly he wasn't sure about anything. "You think he'll come get us out?"

"He'll send someone to post bail."

"Can't let his best trainer rot in jail, right?" Tristen attempted a smile.

Jared gave him a funny look. "No, man. I know he'll come because of you. You're his son."

The two of them didn't speak more for a long time.

Another guy's name was called. The metal hinges squeaked as he was led into freedom. The heavy silence that followed pulled Tristen's eyelids down, even though the cell was freezing cold.

"Stand up and stay awake," Jared said suddenly. "Did they check you for a concussion?"

Tristen stood up, his muscles protesting as they stretched. "Yeah. Said to stay awake and watch for sudden changes in pain or something. I can't remember." For a moment he was more awake, but then he heard snoring in the corner, and his shoulders started to slump forward. He knew if given the chance he'd fall asleep standing.

"How do *you* stay awake?" he asked. His tongue was heavy as he tried to pronounce the words. Jared smirked at his effort.

"Pleasure of your company," he said. "And training instead of fighting."

"That's probably the biggest secret," Tristen said, sitting back down with a heavy sigh. He watched the clock tick past six in the morning by pressing into the bruises that hurt the most.

A young cop came and unlocked the door. "Levisay and Hoovan. Your bail's posted."

Tristen looked up to find his twin standing just outside the cell door, looking serious. He grinned at Tristen when they locked eyes.

Jared stood at the call of his last name, but he didn't smile when he saw Talon. "Hey, look. It's the jackass."

"Want to get out of here or not?" Talon asked. He rolled his shoulders like he always did when he got defensive, his grin dropping away. "I posted bail for both of you."

Jared's shoulder smacked Talon's hard as he came out of the cell, pushing him backward. Talon narrowed his eyes but said nothing. The better of two decisions on his part. None of them spoke as they shuffled through the paperwork and gathered their belongings.

Outside the small police station, the sun was already breaking over the horizon. The hours inside the police station had passed like a vacuum, swallowing hours whole without warning.

"Breakfast?" Talon asked as they walked to his car.

"Where's my truck?" Jared demanded, turning on him.

"I'm taking you to it. It's fine."

Jared snorted but got into the car.

"Look, man, I was in the truck. What good would it have done for all of us to get arrested? Then who would have bailed you out?"

"How much do we owe you?" Tristen asked, but Talon shook his head.

"Nothing. Owen paid for it."

"Where is Owen?" Jared asked from the back seat.

Talon didn't answer as they pulled into a gravel parking lot. Jared's truck was parked in the far corner.

"You sure you don't want some breakfast?" Talon asked, turning to look at Jared, who didn't bother to look back.

"I'm going to take a shower and get to bed. See ya around."

Chapter 26

Talon turned to Tristen the moment they started driving. "What is that guy's problem? I got you out."

"I don't know, Talon," Tristen said, not bothering to cover his sarcasm. "Maybe he spent the night in jail after someone drove his truck away without him in it."

"I'll give him that, but seriously," Talon said, shaking his head. "It wouldn't have made sense for us all to get arrested."

Tristen was surprised his brother didn't understand human fundamentals, but he didn't have the energy to explain things to him. "Whatever you say, man. I'm too tired to fight."

"You shouldn't go to sleep yet."

"I've been up all night. I think I'm fine. Ivy home?"

"Yeah. She was hella mad when I got home," Talon said. "I hid at a hotel last night. Didn't want to go back to the house. Just in case."

"In case of what?"

Talon glanced at him. "You know. The cops and stuff."

Tristen didn't say how dumb his reasoning was. He just wanted to get back to a shower and bed.

"When I went back to her house this morning, she sent me to get you, which I would have done hours ago if I knew you were in jail. I went to hers this morning expecting to see you there."

Tristen sat up, pain shooting through his head. "What?"

Talon shifted in his seat, his eyes darting to Tristen and back to the windshield. He was nervous. Probably lying. Or at least not telling the whole truth, which Tristen assumed was that he'd probably guessed the cops had got them but had been too chicken to show up to post bail right away.

"I-I thought Owen would have gone. Ivy was mad cause he had called her to tell me to post bail. And since I didn't show up right away, you had to sit at the station a bit longer."

"A bit longer?" Tristen deadpanned. "What about your phone? Why didn't Ivy call you?"

Again, his brother shifted. Tristen closed his eyes to keep his anger in check.

"I turned it off. I didn't want the GPS on."

The morning sun was hitting him directly in the face, giving him the perfect excuse to keep his eyes shut. In his mind he told Talon he was an ass, but Tristen wasn't sure if the words made it out of his mouth coherently.

The sun was still shining on his face when he opened his eyes. He wasn't in Talon's car anymore, but in his childhood room, where he'd been sleeping for the past few weeks. The clock on the small desk next to his bed read two-thirty.

The muscles in his ribs protested as he turned onto his side, but it was the smell that wafted up from his clothes that got Tristen out of bed. He hadn't showered after the fight or the arrest, which meant he might have to burn everything touching his body just to get the odor out.

"Good morning," Talon called from the couch when Tristen exited the small shower.

His limbs were heavy, but somehow, he managed to follow his brother into the galley kitchen.

"I've been waiting for you to wake up. I got brunch stuff."

"I don't remember getting into the house," Tristen said once a sip of coffee was in his belly.

Talon laughed. "You acted like you were three sheets to the wind, but you managed to stumble in by yourself. Bobbi told me to let you sleep it off since you'd been awake all night. So, I left you alone. No getting around what Bobbi says, anyway. But now it's time to eat, 'cause I'm famished. All I had was a peanut butter sandwich while you were snoozing."

He pulled out peppers and onion, already chopped, from the fridge, along with a carton of eggs and a block of cheese that looked too expensive to add to an omelet. But if Talon wanted to apologize by making the most expensive eggs in the world, Tristen wasn't going to stop him.

With his energy draining again, he sank into a chair and drank his coffee quietly. Outside, the street was empty with a few eager birds making the only noise.

"Where's Ivy? With Owen?"

"She went somewhere with Bobbi. All secretive and stuff. Told me to mind my own business when I asked."

"Sounds like Ivy." Tristen refilled his mug and sat down again as Talon set two heaping plates on the table.

"*Bon appétit*, or whatever the French say."

"What do the Bulgarians say?"

Talon chewed slowly while he thought, but eventually shrugged. Tristen shoveled a large bite of eggs, pepper and cheese into his mouth, the salt and spice waking up his hunger.

"This is great. Thanks, Talon. I didn't realize how hungry I was."

"You never eat before a fight, so I figured you'd be starving."

"If you hadn't locked me out of the truck, we could have eaten sooner," Tristen said through a mouthful of cheese.

"I panicked, okay? Sometimes we gotta make decisions."

Tristen put up his hands, his plate empty but his stomach still craving more. "Want more toast? I'm gonna make me some more."

"Gotta watch my bread intake. I'm not training like you."

The conversation dropped off, replaced by the buzzing of the toaster.

"Damn. I can't believe I was in the ring last night."

Talon's eyes glittered as he looked up, food halfway to his mouth. "With The Alabamian, Tris. And you won."

The sensation of his arm being raised came back to him. He chuckled. He couldn't help it. "I can't believe I won against him. Did you know he's gone two years without a loss? And within seconds of the place being raided. Didn't even get the belt this time. Nothing. Just a run into the parking lot, where I ate asphalt."

Talon clinked his spoon against the coffee cup, looking out the window.

"How's Sandra and the baby doing?" Tristen realized he hadn't asked since he'd found out about the pregnancy. The butter and jam on crunchy toast would help him hide any reactions to the answer that he might have.

Talon shifted in his seat. "She's good. Real good. The baby is a girl; did Ivy tell you?"

"No, she didn't." The idea of a baby girl coming to the family triggered a memory. "I remember Ivy coming home with Aimee, even though we must have been, what, four or five?"

"I think we were over five, yeah. I remember, too."

"You excited to be a dad?"

Talon pushed his plate away and leaned towards Tristen as he managed to put half a piece of toast into his mouth. "I gotta tell you something about that woman that showed up on karaoke night."

"Lamia?" The butter melting on his tongue reminded him of a time they'd gone to a diner. He must have been eleven or so, and he'd been so hungry he ate the pats of butter when Bobbi wasn't looking. "What about her?"

"I slept with her last summer. A few times."

Across the street, Bobbi's old van pulled into her driveway.

"I figured as much. And you used my name."

"I didn't mean to. She came up to me one day when I was at a bar by myself and called me Tristen. She was drunk and I was depressed and it just seemed easy."

Tristen snorted. Easy was the way to describe Lamia for some things. "That's kinda low, man. I don't think we've ever screwed a girl using the other's name."

Talon's silence didn't convince Tristen it was the one and only time he'd done it.

"Problem is, it wasn't just one time. I mean, that woman is persistent. And, whatever, I was lonely with Sandra gone. She told me she wasn't coming back, so I told myself it was fine. But then she did come back, so I had to break it off with Lamia."

"What about the kid? Did you really get her pregnant?"

Outside, a car door slamming caught both of their attention. Ivy was standing next to the van, talking to Bobbi.

Tristen turned to Talon, waiting for an answer. His brother shrugged but wouldn't meet his eyes. "I don't know. She never said anything about a kid."

Tristen took in a slow breath. He didn't care whether Lamia was pregnant or had a kid or whatever. He just wanted her off his radar.

"You need to break it off with Lamia. Tell her the truth. And please don't screw anyone using my name again. That's nasty. And confusing."

Talon chuckled. "I appreciate you're not mad. I think I would be."

"I'm too tired to be mad. But please, figure it out. I don't need her telling Meegan we slept together last summer. Things are rough with Meegan as it is."

"Trouble with the princess?"

Tristen grunted at Talon's nickname for her. "Ivy's crossing the street."

"Listen, I'd appreciate it if you didn't tell Ivy about Lamia. I know you two are living here together and sometimes conversations can come up, but please don't. I can't trust Ivy not to ever tell Sandra. And I don't need Sandra knowing. We were broken up and on the verge of divorce, but obviously she'd get all worked up about it if she found out."

"That you slept with someone only a few weeks after she left? Someone you met at the bar. I can't imagine why."

Both of their phones dinged, cutting the conversation short.

"Owen's paying out."

"How much did you make?" Tristen was curious. If Talon had made a lot, it meant he'd bet on Tristen winning.

"Enough," was all Talon said.

Tristen checked his messages, forcing himself to keep a poker face. *Sending your two thousand. Gotta make some different transactions to get you the rest. You have Ivy's coming and then some winnings of your own. Only fair. Good job last night, kid.*

"My boys are home," Ivy cried out when she stepped into the house. "Both of them. Did you leave any eggs for me?"

"I'll make you some fresh ones," Talon said, jumping up. Ivy took his seat and sipped his coffee, the sound of eggs cracking making Tristen's stomach rumble again. "Tristen, did you seriously make Jake pay you royalties for that song of ours?"

Tristen's brain took a minute to switch from thinking about food. "What? What song?"

"The song we're singing at the concert. The one about Aimee."

"I didn't make anyone do anything," Tristen protested. "Jake offered. Said he did so because you talked to him."

"I complained to him about your attitude about it. I saw you getting all mad while we were singing at the run through. He probably thought you'd come after us or something, since you're back home and acting like you don't have any money."

The anger in Talon's voice surprised Tristen. Ivy looked between the two of them, unusually quiet.

"I don't know why you're so mad," Tristen said, putting his mug into the sink. He needed to lie down again if he was going to be okay for the concert tomorrow. "Jake offered to pay me royalties."

"It's not just your song, Tristen. Those royalties belong to The Seethers."

Tristen raised his eyebrows. The Seethers had never performed that song. Only he had, a few times when he was in Lexington.

They had thought about adding it as a hidden song on their second album, but eventually they'd decided against it. Of course, that was when Talon and Sandra were having so much trouble, so Talon probably didn't remember the discussions.

"It's not The Seethers' song, Talon. It's my song. I wrote it for Aimee."

"Whatever," Talon mumbled, sliding a plate of scrambled eggs towards Ivy. "It just makes me look bad, Tris. I brought the song to them and they liked it. I said it wasn't going to be a problem, but then you made it a problem. I don't understand why you had to do that."

"*Because it's mine!*"

Ivy jerked her head up at Tristen's shout.

"Tristen, calm down," she said. "No need to get mad."

Tristen threw her a glare. He didn't need her to become a mom suddenly.

Talon shook his head, clearly gritting his teeth. "You have a way of ruining everything."

"Excuse me? I ruin everything? You're the one that left The Seethers and ruined that."

Talon laughed, the sound unsettling. "You know what's funny? For the first talks with Jake, he thought I was you. He kept bringing up Lexington and seeing me play there, and I thought he was just getting confused with our twin shows. I straightened him out on the names and we signed the contract and everything, but it wasn't until a few weeks ago that I realized you had snuck away to play on your own in Lexington. Sandra was right, you always planned to go out on your own. And I just think it's funny that you care so much about me joining AOR when The Seethers breaking up literally gives you what you always wanted."

Tristen stared at his brother, trying to process what he had just said. He watched Talon pick up his keys, kiss Ivy on the head, and salute him. "See ya tomorrow, Tris. I gotta get out of here."

Ivy and Tristen looked at each other wordlessly as Talon's car engine revved and eventually faded down the street.

Chapter 27

"ALL RIGHT, DOORS ARE opening in ten minutes, everyone. Take your places."

Tristen rubbed the muscles in his neck as Melanie spoke. A hand with two brown pills in the palm darted under his chin.

"It's anti-inflammatories." Watsu looked at him, her hand still out. Tristen swallowed them down, grimacing a smile of thanks. "I don't know what's up with you. I just need you to stay alive."

"Looks worse than it is," Tristen told her. Watsu raised her eyebrows and looked him over before turning on her heel and marching away.

The lights dimmed at that same moment, and Seraphina took to the stage.

"Caffeine?" Steve offered.

Thick curtains surrounded the sound booth on two sides. Large, round tables set with fine china and crystal glasses stood between it and the stage. The enormous crystal chandeliers were lit, looking like ripe fruits hanging heavily from the ceiling. Just beyond the sound booth, the reception area was buzzing with the sound of milling people. Like at a red-carpet event, there were photographers and a backdrop with the night's top donor logos printed on it. From the sounds of the snapping camera, everyone was taking full advantage of it.

"You look pale," Steve said, knocking Tristen out of his thoughts.

"I'm tired. And sore."

"Probably not the best idea to challenge yourself to a boxing match two nights before this event."

"Probably not," Tristen admitted, hoping to move away from the topic.

Steve tapped his finger against the soundboard, sipping on his coffee, clearly with something on his mind.

"Tristen, if you're in trouble, you can tell me. I won't tell anyone, and if I can, I'll help you."

"I'm not in trouble, Steve. But thanks."

"Then what is it? What's going on?"

Tristen looked at him, ready to lie or deflect, but then he realized it didn't matter. It didn't matter if Steve knew.

"I competed in an underground boxing match for some money. And it got busted."

Steve snorted, tiny coffee particles flying out into the air. "Damn. Okay. Didn't expect that."

"Thought I got beat up by my drug dealers or something?"

"Seemed more rational. Underground boxing, is that real? I mean, are you fooling around with me?"

"It is," Tristen said, lowering his voice as guests dressed in silks and chiffons and black tuxes filtered in and found their seats. "I'm sure there are drugs there too, so you're not far off."

"Is that how you're getting through this? You on drugs?"

Tristen chuckled. "Just some pain relievers. I got some sleep in yesterday, and I'm used to feeling a bit beat up. I'll be okay, but thanks." He took a breath. "I appreciate that you care enough to ask."

"Gotcha," Steve said, patting him on the back. "Okay, it's about time to rock and roll. Put your headset on."

Tristen took a deep breath, willing his eyes to stay open. Everything was going fine. The sound hadn't echoed or shrieked. The mics worked, and the audience seemed to be enjoying themselves. But he was struggling. The room was warm, and he was getting desperate.

He pushed his finger into the sorest spot on his ribcage, which sent hot, blinding pain through his chest. Steve looked ready to run away from him.

"What're you doing?"

"Trying to stay awake."

"Okay." Steve laughed. "They have three songs, and then it's the Seraphina and Meegan duet to close out the show. Then it's dinner," he said to every person wearing a headphone.

Tristen knew his brother was on stage, but he kept himself busy watching the board. However, there wasn't much to check or do. Though the crowd was closer to their sixties, they whistled and cheered for Art of Rendering, who were smart enough to play two classic rock songs that everyone knew before pulling out Tristen's.

"This last song is dedicated to my sister," Talon said from the stage.

Steve gave a signal. Tristen stood up and slowly upped the volume of the background music as Talon started in on the vocals.

The room settled from singing classic rock to watching the stage as though mesmerized. By the bridge, half the room was swaying in their chairs while others were dabbing their eyes with their napkins.

"The power of songs, man," Steve muttered.

The music seemed to swell into Tristen as he stared. It was *his* song. He'd written the music and the lyrics, although Art of Rendering had tinkered with it. Still, they hadn't changed it enough to claim it for their own. Those were his words that were captivating the audience, making some of the women cry. And that made him proud, even though AOR didn't say anything about it being his song, which he guess he should have anticipated. People didn't announce who wrote every song, but still.

He hadn't yet worked through what to make of what Talon had said. He'd been too tired, and wasn't sure he would get anything but anger.

"Tristen?"

The lights went out; Steve had already moved into action. Tristen jumped forward and pressed the buttons he was supposed to for the last song. Last song, and the concert would be over. There was still the dinner, but at least it was mostly background music and making sure the mic worked for the speeches.

The lights burst on. Meegan and Seraphina were already on stage in matching sequined dresses, mashing two songs together. The best part of the show, regardless of Meegan's involvement in it, was about to happen, and Tristen couldn't wait.

"Ready?" he asked into channel three.

"Ready."

"Count down. And five, four, three, two, go."

From off stage, a drumbeat sounded. Followed by two more, then two more, until the entire college drum line was hitting the beat. Out they came, bouncing and pounding their drums, lining up on either side of the gala attendees, everyone watching them in delight.

Seraphina and Meegan kept singing, and the drums kept beating. Tristen couldn't help but be swept away by the music. The beat was deep and loud in his chest, vibrating faster and faster until Seraphina hit her highest note, and the drummers hit their drums all together one last time.

Everyone in the audience stood and cheered, rising to their feet to call for an encore.

"All right, ya'll," Seraphina said, smiling her wide, red-lipped smile. "We don't have an encore for you, but I appreciate you calling for one. We could ask the drumline if they'd give us another song, though, huh? What do you guys say?"

The drum line answered in a wave of drumsticks hitting the snares, as though they hadn't rehearsed for that very thing. Tristen rolled his eyes but couldn't help smiling. The drumline was his favorite, especially when they started weaving through the tables, the beat becoming so loud at one point he was sure his heart was beating in rhythm. Just when it almost became too much, they hit their drums one last time and marched off backstage.

The audience clapped and cheered, but no one called for another encore.

Tristen tossed off his headset and slid down the volume levels. They'd done it. The entire concert was done.

"Nice," Steve said, smacking Tristen's hand hard. "Great show, man. I enjoyed working with you."

"Same. It was more fun than I thought it would be."

"Go out and stretch a bit," Steve said. "Nothing is happening right now that I can't handle."

Tristen didn't have to be told twice. He grabbed his phone and sent Meegan the text he been waiting to send. *Can we meet?*

"Want anything while I'm up?" he asked.

Steve shook his head, his smile fading as Watsu marched up to them. Her mouth was set in a hard line, her forehead wrinkled at the middle.

"What's up? You didn't like the drumline?"

"Drumline was fine. Why?" she asked, her eyes narrowed and darting between Tristen and Steve. When they said nothing, she flung out two white envelopes. "Your payment. Steve, I know you still have to stay for the sound during dinner, but Tristen, I want to talk to you outside for a minute."

"I was just asking Steve—"

"Steve is fine. Come with me." She turned and walked away, clearly expecting him close behind her.

Without the lights and energy from the speakers, the air at the entrance of the theater was much cooler. Tristen breathed in, finally feeling awake.

"We need to talk." Watsu's speech was clipped and grim, her face pulled in toward the mouth as though she'd eaten something sour.

"What's up?" A sense of dread was already falling on him.

"I called Lin."

"What? Why? Is something wrong?"

"I thought there probably would be, but he said everything was going exactly as he wanted it to."

"And this made you upset?"

Watsu reared back at the comment. Like a copperhead ready to pounce. "I was surprised, since your work hasn't been at all what I expected."

"What do you mean? I've shown up when I was scheduled to be."

Watsu crossed her arms, her eyebrows snapping up. "It isn't about showing up on the hour that you're supposed to. This business requires exceeding expectations. I called Lin to see if you were doing that."

"You were spying on me."

"He's a big client for me. I need to make sure he's happy."

"A big client for you?"

Watsu's eyes narrowed further. "I pride myself on treating my clients well. Like they deserve."

"I came to you for a job interview, and in the process asked if you had access to a studio. That's when I brought Lin in and you got your cut. He isn't your client."

Watsu relaxed, but Tristen didn't. During his time with Meegan he'd learned quickly that a woman relaxing her shoulders might just be the moment she pounces. He stayed on guard as Watsu found her words.

"You're not really a team player, Tristen. You show up for the minimum."

"Okay." Watsu looked as though she wanted to continue, but Tristen wouldn't let her. It was his time to speak. "I don't understand what you wanted me to show up for. I did the edits you wanted me to do. I showed up for the run-throughs we had scheduled. I recorded Lin on his time. And if the concert went well and Lin is happy, why are you unhappy?"

Anger flashed in Watsu's eyes. She pulled out a paper and waved it in front of him.

"Lin doesn't want to work with me. He says he doesn't need my services. And I have to say that putting together a live event with you again is not something I would look forward to. I know you and Steve get along well, but your performance wasn't impressive. I think you'd be happier elsewhere. I won't be needing you for anything else. Here is your paycheck."

She slammed the envelope down on the bar and marched away. Tristen waited until she was a couple yards away before he ripped it open.

Inside the envelope was a check for five thousand dollars signed by Seraphina. Compared to the amount of time and energy the concert had taken, more fights would have been a better way to earn the same amount.

"Want a drink?"

Tristen hadn't noticed the bartender with the black earlobe stretchers standing at the end of the bar. Probably witnessing him getting fired. "Whiskey. Neat."

He downed the whiskey to the last drop and signaled for another pour. He was tempted to look for Talon but dropped the idea immediately. Sandra might be here, and he didn't know what to say to his brother anyway. Telling Sandra the truth and watching the hope of a future drain from Talon's face gave him a satisfying feeling for a second, but Tristen pushed the idea away with the rest of his whiskey.

Laughter came from the hall that led to the backstage area. Meegan's laugh. Answered by a man's low tone.

Tristen downed his whiskey, focusing on the burn down his throat and in his stomach as a warm body slid into the velvet chair next to him.

"Hello."

Tristen turned to find Seraphina smiling at him, her sequin dress shimmering under the chandelier light.

"Oh, you're not Talon."

"Nope. I'm Talon's brother."

"That's right. You're twins." She sat down gingerly on the barstool and smiled her signature wide smile at him. "Well, thank you so much for all your hard work. Give me a glass of champagne, will you?" She smiled at the bartender too. "Meegan, come on over here and let's celebrate."

"Hey, Tristen," Meegan said as she slipped easily onto a stool. "I got your text."

Seraphina pointed at him. "Isn't it crazy how similar they are?"

"They're twins," Meegan said after ordering her glass of wine. Her eyes slid to Tristen's hand, but she didn't reach out.

"Aren't you two dating?" Seraphina asked. "Or are you dating the brother, Talon? Now I'm getting all mixed up."

Tristen's eyes met Meegan's. They weren't hostile, but they were distant. Sad, even. He might have looked the same. "We're dating."

"Oh, my," Seraphina drawled. "Well, well." She looked Tristen up and down, and then back at Meegan. "Maybe I should let the two of you talk."

Meegan closed her lips around the wine glass and tilted it back. "I have to go say goodbye to a few people, then I'll meet you here, Tristen. We'll go home and talk."

Tristen stayed where he was. He couldn't say why, but he knew he would go home with her. And they would either make love, or they would break up. There was no other alternative.

Seraphina slid the champagne glass until the base touched his fingers. "*À la tienne?*"

"Not much to celebrate."

Seraphina shook her head. "No, baby.'" Her long eyelashes slowly folded in a wink. "New beginnings are always something to celebrate."

"If you say so," Tristen said.

"I say so," Seraphina confirmed. "Because I know so. You know how many new beginnings I had to make to get here? How old do you think I am, Tristen?"

He looked at her and shrugged. "Maybe twenty-eight?"

Seraphina laughed, her bosom shaking, her sequins shimmering. "I'm thirty-nine years old. And I just hit the charts last year. Last year, can you believe it? I've been singing since I was twelve, been writing music since I was sixteen. Even sold a few hits to other performers, but no one wanted to hear from me. You know what number album this is for me?"

"Second?"

"Seventh. I just about gave up hundreds of times, but something inside of me always screamed to keep going. I learned to look at a new beginning like a blessing. I've been part of bands that have come and gone. I've made solo albums and group albums. I've tried acting and producing and, well, everything," she said, signaling to the bartender to top her off. "Everyone thought I was too fat or too ugly or too loud or too much. No one wanted Seraphina until last year. And when they finally came to me, at first, I wanted to give them the big middle finger, you know? Cause where were they when I was nobody?"

Tristen nodded. "But you didn't."

"I didn't," Seraphina said, shaking her perfectly coiffed head, her black eyes shining. "It's just the business, you know? Today you're somebody and tomorrow you're nobody. Think about it. There are plenty of talented people out there who aren't gonna make it."

"That's crap, though," Tristen said. "I want to make it. I just don't know how."

"Work, baby," she said, lowering her lashes in another slow wink. "And never give up. I told myself I'm gonna savor this moment because tomorrow might bring a new beginning, and I'll just have to step into it. Just like you have to. You can go kicking and screaming, or you can stand up straight and walk in with curiosity."

Meegan stepped into the lobby again, her coat in her hand. Tristen slapped the bar gently with his palm. "Nice to meet you, Seraphina."

Seraphina chuckled. "*À la tienne* then, Tristen."

Chapter 28

THEY WOULD HAVE MADE love—if the lights had been turned off and Meegan hadn't seen the bruises on his ribs. She immediately connected them to the late phone call from jail.

"What is going on, Tristen?" She sank onto the edge of her bed, their urge to tangle up into it washed away. Tristen picked up his shirt and pulled it back over his head, marveling at how much it hurt suddenly. It hadn't hurt to take it off. When sex had been on the table. "Are you dealing drugs?"

"What?" He couldn't help laughing. "Why would I have bruises on my ribs if I was dealing drugs?"

"You were in jail."

"For illegal fighting."

"Like dog fights?" Meegan paled under her perfect makeup.

"No," Tristen said quickly. He sat down next to her and picked up her hand. "I was boxing. For money."

"For money?"

"My mom was going to lose her house, so Owen suggested I box again. Win some money."

"Again? And who's Owen?"

Tristen traced her knuckles with the pad of his finger. "I used to box in the underground during high school. With my brother. We were the Pelton Vikings."

Meegan slowly pulled her hand away from him and crossed the room. "Boxing? Illegally? I thought you were a musician."

Tristen reached out for her, but she kept her distance. "Listen, I'm done with it, I swear."

"Oh, you bet your ass you're done with it. Have you been doing this the whole time we've been dating?" She paced the bedroom to the windows and back.

"No, just the past few weeks," Tristen drawled. She was much angrier than he'd thought she'd be. "Owen, my biological dad, knew about some fights and managed to get me in. It was the only way I could make enough money to help my mom. All I have to do now is gather the money and figure out how to move it into her account. But then it's over. I'm done with boxing. And I know you're angry about me getting arrested, but I promise you it's the first time."

Meegan snapped her head around, dropping her nails from between her teeth. "I know you haven't been arrested before. Daddy wouldn't have let me date you if you had."

"Your dad looked into me?" Tristen asked. "Before last month?"

Meegan shrugged. "He's protective. I mean, he had his reasons to be suspicious about you and clearly, he was right. All this time he thought we wouldn't work because of your family background. You purposefully kept things from me. You lied to me."

The barrage of underhanded insults left Tristen dizzy. "I didn't lie to you. You just never wanted to listen. You were out having fun with Clay and didn't want to hear about my family problems."

"I don't even know who you are, Tristen," Meegan hissed. She waved her hands at his abdomen.

"You don't know who I am? I'm Tristen, the same guy you've always known. I had no money to give my mom. I had to do something. I'm not about to let my mom become homeless. You'd do the same."

"My parents know how to be responsible and not end up in that situation," Meegan yelled.

It would have felt better if she had slapped him in the face. He knew Ivy wasn't a perfect person and God only knew she wasn't a very good mom, but Meegan knew nothing about her. Meegan had no right to compare Ivy to her parents, who were probably worth millions.

His breath was coming quicker, his anger threatening to erupt out of him. But he closed his eyes and took a deep breath. "I had to save my mother's house," he said, his voice low. "Since you didn't want me around while you built your career, I agreed to three fights. The last one got raided."

"Excuse me for wanting to be successful, Tristen," Meegan answered him, her voice rising. "And to think I spent these last few weeks dreaming about us as the dream team of musicians. We would tour together or meet in the same city. Of course, that's when I thought I was dating a musician, not a boxer."

Anger soured his stomach, but he didn't want to unleash it. She had a right to be upset. "Meegan, listen. I had to help my mom. That's who I am. Things happen in my family, and I do my best to fix them. I can't walk away. Especially this time. I mean, I had nothing else to do."

"You could have worked on your own career, Tristen," Meegan snapped. "Face it, you needed to save her house for your own good."

That was not an accusation he'd been ready for. "What?"

"I know you're in debt. Daddy told me. But you didn't even have the decency to tell me the truth about why you moved to Pelton when I asked. I guess I should have seen that as a red flag."

The pounding at his temples was worsening. "Your dad told you I was in debt?"

"Yes," Meegan snapped. "And to think I defended you!"

Tristen unclenched his hand and closed his eyes to focus on breathing. "It's not normal of you to know that stuff and not tell me that you know."

"Stop, Tristen." Meegan waved her hands. "Stop. You don't get to tell me what is normal and allowed and what isn't. What else have you kept from me?"

"Nothing," he said, but she continued pacing as though he hadn't said a word.

After a few minutes of silence, she stopped in front of him, her hands on her hips, her jaw set. "I think we're going to have to go back to a trial phase. Where you have to prove yourself to me again."

"What do you mean, 'a trial phase?' And what the hell does 'again' mean, too?"

"The first six months of dating is the trial phase. Daddy taught me to do that. Don't you remember how I never spent the night and wouldn't let you spend the night? And I didn't introduce you to my parents until after six months either. It was the trial phase." His confusion must have shown on his face, because Meegan rolled her eyes and shook her head. "I'm basically an heiress, Tristen. There are things I have to do, to be careful of. There are men who just want to marry me or date me for what I'm going to inherit."

"I never asked you for your money."

"No," Meegan drawled, "but you also got pretty comfortable with me paying for a lot of things in the last few months. I didn't see it until Clay and Daddy pointed that out to me. I guess it's because I'm so in love with you."

Tristen sputtered his defense.

Meegan watched him, her black hair flowing over her shoulders. "I still love you. Which is why I'm willing to give you another trial phase. So I can learn to trust you again."

The image of Clay touching Meegan's hair, causing social media to speculate about their relationship, flared in his mind. "You need to learn that you can trust me? I'm not the one running around Chicago in a dress up to my crotch while my agent is brushing hair from my face. Or with my agent at all hours of the day, in my hotel room."

"Excuse me, Tristen. Are you daring to accuse me of something?" Meegan's body edged to the side. A sharpened knife ready to pierce him through. "You're the one who got arrested. For being with a prostitute, for all I know. Maybe that woman with the giant boobs you seemed so interested in."

Tristen hated how she could change topics so quickly. Just like Ivy. "What woman? And why the hell would you think I got caught with a prostitute?"

Meegan drew back; she threw up her arms. "I don't need this."

"You don't need what? Me to challenge your accusations? Why would you think I was with a prostitute? Are you talking about that woman, Lamia?" Her eyes shifted just enough to tell him she was. "Shit, Meegan, I told you the truth about her. Talon just admitted to me the other day that he was with her last summer, but I wasn't. You and I spent almost every day together."

Meegan yanked a pile of clothes from her decorative chair and started folding as though she had a vendetta against cotton-wool blend. "I have to fix my first album so it's ready to release while working on the second one. I just don't need this right now."

Tristen swallowed hard. He had recorded and mixed her first album and considered it done. As done as Lin's was. If Clay thought something was wrong with Meegan's album, it was possible there was something wrong with Lin's.

The dresser drawer slammed shut. "Do you even know how embarrassed I was when you called me about being arrested? Who gets arrested, Tristen?"

"Rappers?" He smiled. Meegan didn't. "I just wanted to pay the bail. I would have paid you back today." Meegan's laugh interrupted him and burned up the last of his patience. "I never would have dared ask you to leave your hunky agent and your precious Music On Air. I knew you wouldn't bother coming for me. You'd rather I rotted in there."

"Like you have any money to pay me back today, but whatever, make this about me being the bad guy." Meegan's finger wagged a centimeter from his nose. "*I* didn't do anything illegal this week, Tristen Levisay. I only worked towards my goals and dreams. You should be glad you're with a woman like me. But I deserve a man who's willing to let me be me, who's ready to pick me up when I'm down. This is the last time you're ever picked up by the police. And even still, Daddy isn't going to like it. You're going to have to prove yourself again."

Tristen backed away from her finger and her narrowed, flashing eyes. It occurred to him that in the past few weeks, ever since she'd started with Clay, she hadn't asked how he was doing back in Pelton. She hadn't asked him about Lin or anything else about his life besides him staying with Watsu and the concert. The rest of their conversations had been about her. Granted, he hadn't wanted to tell her about the boxing, but it was as though she'd thought he was just sitting around waiting to be let back into her bed.

"Do you understand?" Meegan demanded.

"I understand that what you want is a man waiting around for you, willing to do everything you say. Is that why you're with me? You see me as the poor boy who can't do better than you?"

Meegan looked surprised at the accusation, but not outraged.

"You don't understand something about me, Meegan. I grew up with nothing and have gone back to nothing, but I was never with you because I wanted your money. I thought you were beautiful and fun and, yes, I'm in awe of your life and how confident you are in every situation. But you mistook my awe of you for desperation. I'm not desperate. Maybe I gave the wrong impression. Or maybe I acted desperate for a while, back when The Seethers broke up and I didn't know what to do. But I was lost, Meegan, and you didn't even care."

"It isn't my job to help you find yourself, Tristen. I want to be with a man who knows who he is and where he's going."

Tristen picked up his coat and slung it over his shoulders. "I'm confident in the kind of man I am, Meegan. The kind who doesn't leave his mother to go homeless. Who will do what it takes for those he loves. And I'm good with being that."

Her only answer was a condescending snort and a crisp turn away from him.

A small part of him hoped she'd turn around and say something. When she didn't, Tristen walked to the door. "I wish you the best, Meegan. I'm sure I'll see you around on the scene."

Another drawer slamming answered him as he strode through the bedroom door and out towards the garage. By the time he'd grabbed the last two boxes of his packed stuff, Simon was cursing him out through the doorbell camera, but Tristen ignored it.

After all, the ending of one thing meant the beginning of another. Just like Seraphina had said.

Chapter 29

A NOISE OUTSIDE JOLTED Tristen awake, the sudden movement angering his sore muscles. Sunlight seeped in at the sides of his blackout blinds, ruining any chance of going back to sleep. Every muscle in his body creaked and protested as he slowly sat up and begrudgingly pulled up the blinds.

From his childhood window he could see a group of birds fluttering out from one tree branch to another. The winter hadn't been too cold to bring the birds out every morning. They chirped and squawked, flying from branch to branch from the very moment the sun rose. Each time they passed each other, they looked like they might crash, but they never did.

Tristen stared as the memories of the night before pressed down on him. He was jobless again. And now single.

"New beginnings are always something to celebrate," Seraphina had said.

New beginnings were becoming a pain in his ass.

He swung his legs out of bed, swallowing a groan, then trudged into the kitchen for coffee. Ivy's bedroom door was open, blinds up and empty. In the kitchen there was a strong pot of fresh coffee and a note saying she'd be back later.

The steam from his coffee gave him a semi-facial as he stared out the window. It wasn't that he was devastated about Meegan, but he wasn't impartial either.

His phone lit up with Lin's face and ringtone—the man himself singing "My Way".

"Lin. A little early for you, isn't it?"

Either Lin hadn't gone to bed yet, or he woke up at full speed. He chuckled heartily and launched energetically into a speech about leaving Watsu's company.

"I don't like the way she does things. She's so serious. All the time. She even yelled at me for scaring her again in the hallway." Lin clicked his tongue into the phone. "I don't like working with people who think they're above comedy, you know? I just want to make sure that you and I are on the same page."

Tristen took the opportunity of Lin taking a breath to ask, "What page should we be on?"

"That we are still working together. I fired Watsu but I didn't fire you. I still want you."

"You fired Watsu, and she fired me."

There was a strange, strangled sound on the other end of the phone. "Are you firing me?" Lin exclaimed. "I need you to finish the album. I'll pay you double."

"Lin, I'm not firing you. But if you want to pay me double, I won't say no."

"I'll do better than that. I'll give you royalties. Howard, write up a royalty contract for my producer, Tristen Levisay. Le-vi-say. It isn't hard." Sounds of a struggle between paper and pen carried over the sound waves as Lin grumbled something in a foreign language. "There. See? It's not hard. Okay, my man. You will get royalties."

Tristen sipped his coffee instead of sighing. Two million songs on the music apps, and most of them went unnoticed and never listened to. Royalties were almost worthless.

But royalties be damned. Tristen still had a paying client. His one hope of not being a complete and total loser. "Thanks, Lin."

"Okay, okay. So, we're good?"

"You and I are good, but I gotta find a studio where we can finish. We're gonna make you sound like Josh Groban."

Lin groaned. "I'm better than that guy. Why does everyone compare me to him?"

That opinion was subjective, but not worth arguing.

"Okay," Lin went on. "How many songs we have left?"

Tristen flipped his laptop open. "You have nine already fully finished. Just gotta mix the last two to make it eleven."

"You sure it's enough for an album?"

"Very sure, Lin."

"This will be done in time for the wedding?"

"Absolutely."

"And then we do the second album. I have a title already. It's going to be called *Lin Goes to Church*," Lin said, exploding in laughter.

"That's funny," Tristen said. Lin's laughter was contagious. "This first album is good. After some tweaks, I think we can release it."

His mind betrayed him by reminding him of Meegan's comment the night before about her album, and he struggled to put it away. He would do everything in his power to make sure Lin's was good. And besides, there was no evidence Meegan hadn't been exaggerating for the argument.

"I knew I could trust you. It's in your face. You just have that kind of face, you know? The ladies know. By the way, how is Meegan? Still hot? I also need to pay you. I can finish my payment to you instead of Watsu. Send your details to Howard. Howard! Text Tristen your number."

Tristen was no longer sure what question to answer first.

"I have to go back to Singapore, but you will be ready when I come back, yeah?"

"When will you be back?"

"Summer. I have to see my mom. She moved to Nashville. Crazy lady. She loves country music and the mountains now. Just a new phase. Anyway, two weeks for the album, okay? I need it up on the charts by the wedding. My big middle finger to my cousin," Lin said, his laughter darker this time.

"Two weeks," Tristen repeated. "When it's up, I'll send an invoice to you and not to Watsu. And I'll be ready by summer for you. You just let me know."

Relief flooded over him in cold waves as he hung up. With a sudden burst of energy, he grabbed the two boxes of stuff he had taken from Meegan's townhouse and headed out the back. Ivy wouldn't normally complain about boxes, but in her boot she was clumsier. The last thing he needed was for her to fall again. Finding his own place was at the top of his list whenever he got the funds from the fight in his bank account.

Voices drifted over the fence from the front. Tristen glanced through the boxes to find Ivy getting out of Bobbi's car across the street. That was the second time in so many days. At least they were getting along. It would be harder to leave Ivy alone in the house if she and Bobbi were having one of their stand-offs. And he had every intention of moving out as soon as possible.

The shed was packed full of old holiday ornaments, two lawn chairs, gardening tools he wasn't sure anyone ever used, and crutches. After playing a round of Tetris with everything, Tristen shoved his two boxes inside and shut the doors. Outside the shed, the crutches leaned forgotten against the wall.

"Morning."

Ivy was leaning against the front of the chain-link fence.

"Didn't expect you up so early. Didn't expect you to come home at all, honestly," she said as he locked the door.

"Where were you and Bobbi off to so early?"

Ivy's smile faltered. "Nothing. Had to help Bobbi with…" She looked behind her as though looking for Bobbi. "There was one of those garage sales at the big houses she likes to go to."

"Did you find anything?" Tristen asked. The crutches snagged on something in the yard as he dragged them behind him. He gripped them harder.

"No." Ivy's eyes narrowed in on the crutches. "What're you doing with those?"

"Thought you could use them." He held them out to her. They stopped at Ivy's hips. Aimee had taken after Luke, shooting up to five-foot-nine by the time she died, but she'd been small for an eight-year-old at the time of her surgeries. He didn't get more than a smile from Ivy. "We should give them away. No use holding on to them."

"How many years has it been?" Ivy's voice was soft. Her fingers fumbled when she took them from him. "Twelve?"

"Has to be about that," Tristen said, taking the crutches back. He set them against the black trash can, making a mental note to take them to the second-hand store sometime. Throwing an arm around Ivy's shoulders, he pulled her close. "Come on, let's go inside. I'm getting cold out here."

The sun reflected off Ivy's watery eyes as she looked up at him. "Talon told me he sang your song at the concert last night. Have you two talked about the other day?"

"No." The truth was, he had avoided his brother the night before and was almost certain Talon had avoided him. It helped that he and Meegan hadn't attended the afterparty. Maybe if they had gone, he would have taken his frustration out on Talon instead of Meegan. Although, given how she felt about him and the fighting and jail, it would have just put off the inevitable.

"Something wrong?" They made their way slowly up the stairs, Ivy hobbling in her boot. "You and Talon gotta figure out a way to get through this. You two fight more as adults than you did as kids."

"Did he tell you he brought the song to the band as though it was his? And when Jake paid me royalties for it, which is only fair, Talon got mad."

"That doesn't sound like Talon." Ivy plopped onto the couch with a sigh. "Get me a coffee, would you?"

"It sounds exactly how Talon has become," Tristen said, speaking louder from the kitchen. "Want some bourbon in it?"

Ivy chuckled. "It's only nine o'clock. No, I just want it with cream."

"Time never stopped you before," Tristen teased, handing over her milky coffee. "You know what else he told me?"

Discretion, his history with Ivy, and privacy told him to stop—screamed at him from the back of his head—but he couldn't. Nor did he want to. It felt good to get it off his chest. And maybe he wanted Ivy to know something about Talon she had been so far unwilling to see. "Jake thought Talon was me when they first started talking about him joining AOR."

The metal spoon stirring against the mug stopped. "I know. I was there when he said it." The stirring started again. "I can see why you're mad at him."

"Yeah, 'cause that was the tipping point," Tristen said. Ivy didn't respond, but she did set her spoon down and wait for him to go on. "Listen, there are great things about being a twin. We've had a lot of fun being so identical." Tristen started pacing the living room. Three steps forward, three steps back. "But maybe what I'm angry about is the way he's taking advantage of our situation. I don't mind if he pretends to be me for some things. Sometimes it's funny, you know? But sleeping with a woman under my name. And a woman *I* was with for a short time—using my name like that is shitty. I mean, it's not exactly the reason Meegan and I broke up, but it's one stressor in the mix."

"You and Meegan broke up?"

Tristen stopped pacing. "Last night. But that's not—"

"You're right. We'll talk about that later. Go on."

Tristen hesitated. Something was different, off.

"Go on," Ivy insisted.

"I don't even know what I'm mad about." He sighed, sinking onto the couch next to her. "After seeing him on stage last night, I can't deny that Talon's a good frontman. He's better than me, anyway. It pisses me off that he tried to pass off my song as ours, but AOR paid me for it, so what do I have to complain about?" Nothing, was the answer, but Ivy was good enough to keep quiet. "Besides, I don't think I want to work with a group. It's so much about running after people and coordinating schedules. I'd much rather just play music or whatever. Maybe do my own thing."

Ivy carefully slurped her coffee, her free hand gently massaging Tristen's head. If he let himself, he could fall asleep here. Somewhere in the depths of his memory he recalled lying on a bed and a gentle hand massaging his head, but he couldn't place if the hand belonged to Ivy or Bobbi. It seemed more like a Bobbi thing.

"Of all the things I was unprepared for with becoming a mom," Ivy murmured, "I think the difference between kids is the biggest. I mean, everyone expects twins to be the same. Which couldn't be further from the truth in your case."

"What do you mean?"

She smiled. "I'm a bad mother, I know that, but you're my baby and I also know you. My boy who would always make sure I remembered Aimee's medicine and Talon's sports games. You making sure everyone was okay, even if it meant trying to convince the police that Luke was covering for you."

"I was supposed to be the one selling it."

"It was still his stupidity and greed that got that meeting put together in the first place. He was the adult, Tristen." Her energy was picking up, but suddenly she seemed to let it go. "Luke doesn't matter. We're talking about you. I'm not surprised you would prefer to work alone. I think that's the right decision. Because otherwise you're making sure everyone else is okay."

"I was in The Seethers for myself too, Ivy."

The massaging stopped. "What have you done these last few weeks? Boxing to keep me in my house, and the concert to make sure that girlfriend of yours would take you back."

"That isn't true."

Ivy turned steely eyes on him. "Isn't it?"

Tristen chose coffee over answering.

"You tend to do what others want to do so that everyone is happy. That's what you did with Talon your whole life. You did what Talon wanted, so you guys would be together. Talon never chose to do what you liked. Bless his heart, but Talon rarely thinks of anyone but himself."

"Where is this analysis coming from? Are you dying?"

She chuckled, shifting her position on the couch. "I started going to therapy."

"You're joking."

"No, I'm not," Ivy said. "I'm going to therapy."

"What do you need therapy for now? All the hard stuff is down and behind you."

Her knuckles turned white against her coffee mug, and for a brief second Tristen thought she might throw it.

"It's been one shitty life, Tristen. I mean, except for some parts like you and Talon and Aimee. I joined to quit smoking weed and maybe stop feeling so chaotic. Like this whole balloon loan. I got myself in over my head and I can't figure out how. I thought maybe therapy would help me set my thoughts straight. Stop me from making dumb decisions. Because what would I do if I didn't have you or Owen? I mean, there's no real reason for you to do this for me. Or to give me any of the money. It was you in the ring getting punched and bruised over and over again, so why shouldn't you just say the money is yours and leave me to figure out where to go next? No one would blame you. They all know I'm a terrible mom."

"I *could* take the money and run," Tristen mused, pretending to take the idea seriously.

Ivy shoved him gently with her shoulder. "I'm so lucky to have you, Tristen. I hope you know how grateful I am."

The light shifted. Leaf shadows danced along the old, wooden floor and lumpy couch.

"Maybe therapy is doing something for you. You don't sound like the Ivy I know."

"It's helping me. Maybe you should give it a try."

"Nope. No, thank you. I don't need some shrink digging into my childhood."

"Okay," Ivy said, but she turned and looked straight at him. "I'm glad you're here."

Tristen shifted. Frank talk was not his comfort zone.

"I want us to get to know each other again, Tristen. Have a better relationship," she said, stumbling over her words. "That's not it exactly. I mean to say, I want to be a better mother to you," she said, rushing on before he could respond. "And if it's too late to be a better mother, maybe we could be friends? Or whatever people are when they're adults, but their mom had kids too young to act like an actual mother."

She waited for his answer, looking more like a young teenager than a woman in her mid-forties. Barely seventeen years separated them, which might be why he'd stopped treating her like an authority figure so long ago.

"We only have each other now, Tristen," she said, choking on the tears that welled in her eyes. "I mean, it's not like Talon is dead or anything, but he's gonna be busy with the band and the baby. He won't come around as much anymore."

"Come here," Tristen said, pulling her in for a hug. She was so tiny, all her force of nature completely gone. He felt her breath rattle through her chest as she tried not to give in to her tears, and was suddenly battling his own urge to cry. "Thanks for letting me come back home, Ivy."

Maybe being home wasn't too bad.

Chapter 30

THE DOORBELL INTERRUPTED THEIR mother-and-son moment, though Tristen was glad for the emotional reprieve.

"You expecting anyone?" he asked her.

She nodded. "Owen."

"Right, the man of the hour. Let's see if he got the charges dropped," Tristen muttered as he opened the door.

"A man could wither away waiting for you to come to the door," Owen drawled. He was leaning against the outer wall, looking very comfortable on Ivy's porch. "You get lost or something?"

"Why are you ringing the doorbell? Why don't you just come in?"

"Well, hello to you as well," Owen said, a grin plastered to his face.

"I tell him too, but he won't listen," Ivy complained from the couch. "Just like a man."

Tristen was glad she hadn't changed completely.

"You doing okay?" Owen asked as he followed Tristen into the kitchen. "A little birdie told me you broke up with the trust fund cutie."

The way information got back to Owen would have been fascinating if it was anyone else. The fact that it was him made it annoying. "How the hell do you find out these things?"

Owen twisted the toothpick in his mouth and grinned. "I'm always on the lookout for you boys."

"Like a stalker?"

"Like a father," Owen said without missing a beat. Tristen breathed in silently. He wasn't sure he was ready to give Owen that title yet. "Simon called to say he didn't need me anymore. He'll call when she gets another boyfriend."

Since the next one would be Clay, the man Simon had chosen as her agent, Owen most likely wouldn't get that call, but Tristen ignored that tidbit. A message popped up on his phone from Owen. *Bank. Money. Balloon payment.*

"You ready to go?" Owen asked aloud, putting away his phone.

"Right. Sure. I'm ready."

Ivy's eyes darted between the two of them. "I see. Now that we all get along, we're going to start having secrets. I'll tell you now that my therapist won't like the sound of that."

"No secrets, babe. Just some business," Owen said, helping her off the couch.

"I'm going to take a shower," she said with a sigh. She wacked Owen playfully on the shoulder and winked. "Wanna join me?"

Tristen moaned. "Gross. I'll leave, then, and do the business by myself."

"Your mama's barely in her mid-forties, Tristen," Ivy called back, shutting the bathroom door behind her.

The men got into Owen's car and started off down the road. "I forgot to tell you, Tristen. I got the charges dropped."

Relief filled him as they drove towards Top Gym. "Thank you. I was gonna ask, but didn't want to bug you."

"You wouldn't have been bugging me, kid, but anyway, there was no need. I made you a promise and was determined to keep it. Even if that sheriff was an asshole. But little did he know that the assistant city attorney is in my pocket."

Owen never ceased to surprise him, but the particulars of his business were a topic for another day. When Tristen had more energy to follow what was probably a long discussion. "Well, I'm out of a job, so if you have any fights coming up, I'm in."

Owen grunted as he took a sharp turn left on a yellow light. "I'm done with the fighting now, kid. There are some issues I need to iron out."

"You in trouble?" Tristen asked.

"No real trouble. Giving it up was part of the deal I struck with the city attorney. That I'd step away. They think if I'm gone maybe the fights will stop, which isn't true. These young guys are determined to keep going. There's a lot of money and they're greedy. Greedy and violent, which I want no part of. I found a second chance with Ivy and I'm not giving it up. Life is getting shorter, ya know?"

"Glad to hear you're sticking with Ivy." Tristen thought of Ivy's comments and, selfishly, himself. The last thing he needed on his plate was a breakup between his parents.

Owen sighed. "Long as she'll have me. I'm too old to throw this opportunity away."

"You gonna be okay?" Tristen asked. "Some guys don't do well in retirement."

Owen spread his hands over the stirring wheel as he pulled up behind the gym, where a man in a hoodie was waiting for them. "Yep, I'll be fine. It's just one part of my activities. Besides, I'm getting too old for that stuff. Things aren't how they used to be. That's Brody there. He's our first stop."

"Morning," Brody said as Owen and Tristen joined him outside. The air was icy, and Tristen hadn't brought anything but his coat. He stuffed his hands into his pockets to keep them from freezing.

"You did a good job the other night," Brody began, two gold teeth showing when he grinned at Tristen. "Had I known it would be Owen's last, I would have shown up."

"That's never a good idea," Owen said, chuckling. Brody grinned back. An obvious inside joke between them that Tristen didn't get.

"Your win made you almost three thousand, which we'll send over bit by bit to you in the next few weeks. We gotta be careful with this money, unless you wanna be reported to the IRS," Brody said. "But don't worry, we got you covered. Owen put you down as an employee of the gym when you started, so it'll look like an additional paycheck for a while."

Tristen looked at Owen in surprise. It was a clever move he wouldn't have thought of.

"For the moment you have some money. The biggest issue is the payment of the balloon loan, which is due in—"

"Two days, I know," Tristen said to encourage Brody to the point. He was tired, and his eyes were starting to throb.

Owen spoke next. "Here's the thing, kid, we got some of this money in a few digital currencies and stashed around different places."

"We also have cash," Brody interjected, holding out an envelope. "You can tell the bank that you gathered cash from different places and want to deposit it. It's less than ten thousand, so they don't have to notify the IRS, but they still might."

Tristen felt the blood drain from his body. "What?"

Brody chuckled. "Don't matter a bit. Just tell them that you gathered cash from friends and family 'cause she has to pay off a loan with Thomas Rhinehart and Sons."

"You sure this isn't gonna flag anything?"

"Can't say anything for sure, but in the end, regular people have these balloon payments to pay off and gotta do it somehow. I doubt the bank will pay much mind."

"Right." Tristen breathed out slowly. "Between what you gave her account the last few fights and this cash, what are we at?"

"A little over thirty-four thousand."

"And then I send over the stuff in my account," Tristen murmured, checking his app. "I only have three thousand."

"But you have another four in the Zym app and then another almost four in the Nver app. You just have to start the transaction. Might have to give two checks to Rhinehart and Sons."

Brody pressed on the Zym app and pointed to the login. Tristen followed his instructions for both apps, then dared to relax his shoulders when it claimed the transactions were in progress.

"My work here is done," Brody declared, throwing his hand towards Tristen to shake again. "It was nice working with you, Tristen. Owen, I'm sure we'll talk at some point."

Owen lit a thin cigar as they watched him saunter away in silence.

"Can you give me a ride to the bank?" Tristen asked. "I wanna get this over with."

He couldn't see Owen as they climbed into the car, but Tristen was sure he was smiling. Despite the circumstances of what had brought Owen and him together again, they had somehow found a way to a relationship. Tristen couldn't help chuckling.

"What're you laughing at?" Owen asked as they pulled out of the gym parking lot.

"I don't even know," Tristen said. "Maybe the absurdity of all this. Maybe I'm just tired."

"All what?"

Tristen waved his hand around the air as though it would suffice as an explanation. "Life, maybe. I mean, just a few weeks ago I came home for Ivy's birthday pissed off that Talon had left the band. All I wanted was for him to come back so we could focus on selling the album and maybe set up a few more concerts. I wanted everything to stay the same, and in the following weeks not only did nothing stay the same, but it all fell apart. Down the tubes." Tristen whistled, imitating something falling down a deep hole. "Just all went to hell."

"Life does that sometimes," Owen said. They pulled into the bank parking lot, but neither of them got out of the car. After a few minutes, Owen spoke again. "I know the circumstances weren't great, but I have enjoyed these last few weeks. Are you thinking of staying for a bit, or are you planning to go off and become a music sensation?"

The question hit him where it hurt the most, the pain coming out in a burst of laughter. "I have no clue," Tristen finally said. "I'm no music sensation, so that's probably out of the picture. I have to work on my one client's album. I guess I could get a place of my own by the time we finish with this thing for Ivy and the money finally comes in. But I don't know, Owen, honestly."

"Well, you got time to figure stuff out, but you should go back to music someday. You've got talent."

"You've never even heard me play," Tristen said.

"I saw you once in Lexington at that Irish bar. What was it called? Paddy's or something. I saw you in there."

Owen seemed earnest, honest. But it wasn't possible. Owen must have heard about him later on. "How would you have seen me in Lexington?"

"I'm everywhere, Tristen. I deal in the business of information. A few years back, I was in Lexington to meet a client. Happened to be near that Irish bar. It has an outside patio and all that. Nice place. You were up on the balcony level, crooning into the microphone like you were Johnny himself." Owen hit his knees and hummed a few bars of Tristen's song "One Day". Talon and Darren had made fun of it, calling it folk music.

"I played there maybe four or five times." He hesitated. "You thought I was good?"

"Real good," Owen said. There was a glint of triumph in his eyes. It made Tristen uneasy.

"Well, thanks for that. But playing at Paddy's won't get me the kind of money I need to live on my own."

"You could work for real at the gym. It could be a family business."

"I don't know," Tristen said slowly.

"I'm giving it to Ivy." That was an unexpected development. Owen glanced at Tristen, his smile weak. "More or less. I'll still be a partner, but she's gonna run it. I have a few other business things going on the side, and she had all these ideas about making it better. She wants to add a women's Pilates center in it."

"Seriously? The place smells like jock strap."

Owen chuckled. "I thought I'd give her a chance to do it. She's always wanted her own business. Back in high school she wanted to open a flower shop. Course, being an idiot, I shot that dream down. She was pissed."

"Pilates and flowers," Tristen said, amused by the idea of Ivy owning a gym. "You could rename it."

"No way. The name stays."

"Because it's such a good name?" Tristen asked dryly.

Owen ignored him. "What do you say about working there? I'll need—I mean, Ivy will need another boxing teacher, since Jared is going to take over managing. And I'm sure your mama would like to have you around. You could keep an eye on her while I'm gone."

"Where are you going?"

"I got some stuff to do," Owen said vaguely. "Down in Florida. Nothing illegal or anything."

"Sure. How long will you be gone?"

"Couple of months. I want the guys in the boxing world to believe me when I say I'm out, you know?"

Tristen opened the door and stepped out of the car. The idea of Owen needing to get out of town sent a chill down his spine. He didn't want anything to happen to him just as they were getting to know each other. Another strange turn of events over the last few weeks.

"So, whaddaya say? Will you help out over at the gym?" Owen asked. "Just for a few months, if you want."

Tristen yanked open the door to the bank and jerked his head towards the lobby. "Probably take you up on the offer. While I'm stuck in Pelton, anyway."

Owen broke into a wide grin. He slapped Tristen on the back. "It's gonna be great. Like a real television family."

"A sitcom," Tristen agreed. "But I'm only working until I find a way out of Pelton."

"Whatever you say," Owen said. "Come on. Get this thing done. Then we'll pick Ivy up and tell her the good news over lunch."

Instead of them both picking Ivy up for lunch, it turned out to be only Tristen.

"Where's Owen going?" she asked as Owen's truck disappeared down the road.

"He got a call and then said he needed to do something. So it's just you and me, and I'm taking us out to celebrate."

"Celebrate what?" Ivy asked.

Tristen held out a paper for her to look at. He had planned to give it to her over lunch, but he couldn't wait that long.

"It's paid? In full?"

Her surprise confused him. "Wasn't that the plan? When Owen told you he and I had a plan for your house, what did you think we were doing?"

"I thought you'd make a little money to make a payment. You know, grease them up so we could negotiate a payment plan."

"The loan is due in two days, Ivy."

"I know," she said, her voice getting tense, but he could still see the confusion in her eyes. "Owen said not to worry about it, so I thought he was asking for an extension or something. You paid this all off? With your boxing?"

Tristen nodded.

Tears began to stream down Ivy's face.

"Thank you," she whispered, her teeth gnawing at her bottom lip. "But I don't know how to repay you."

Tristen wrapped his arms around her and pulled her close. "You can repay me by being a good boss at the gym. Making me your favorite employee."

Ivy laughed, the sound muffled against his sweatshirt, which was left wet when she pulled away. "I promise. Now, let's go for lunch. I'm starving."

Chapter 31

"You look like you're still sleeping," Ivy called out from the front door of the gym as Tristen lumbered towards her, weighed down by duffel bags full of new boxing gloves. "Wake up and get in here."

"I could use a little help here, Ivy," Tristen called back. He wasn't surprised when she waved him off.

"I don't have a coat on." A typical excuse that Tristen couldn't help being amused by. A month had passed and he was still in Pelton, still in his old bedroom, though that would change in a few weeks when he started renting a room from Jared.

Jared stood at the bottom of the stairs inside the gym with his arms folded, as usual.

"Everyone's so helpful today," Tristen complained, making sure to groan as he set the duffel bags down.

"There's coffee made upstairs," Jared said. "Thought you'd be in sooner."

"Why? It's eight-thirty in the morning. I'm not even scheduled until noon, but Ivy texted me to bring these things in. Said you needed them stat."

Jared opened the bags and nodded in approval. "We have a new young teens class starting this afternoon. I wanted these gloves for them."

"So maybe a thanks would be appropriate?"

Jared stared at him, eyebrow cocked. "You need a thank you each time you do your job?"

Tristen snorted, knowing his soon-to-be-roommate was kidding.

Ivy waggled her way between the two men and looked up to make eye contact. "Are you two ready? We got some things to go over."

"Let me get some coffee first," Tristen said.

"And let me put these away," Jared said, the only thing that bought Tristen time to run to the coffee pot and back. Had it just been his excuse, Ivy would have barreled forward with their morning meeting.

Once they were ready, Ivy started marching them through the gym with the finalized blueprints for the renovation. The back left-hand corner would become a climbing wall, while they'd be closing off the right back corner for a Pilates studio. The boxing ring would move slightly to the left-hand side, and the reception desk would move close to the front door. It would be colder during the winter months, but controlling who came in and out would be easier.

Tristen had to admit her ideas were good.

"It looks good," Jared said. "Do we come within budget?"

"Almost, especially if we do the painting and a few other things on our own. And we just got the building permit yesterday," Ivy said.

"We can start in certain sections, rope them off while we're working," Tristen said, his finger sweeping across the back of the gym. "Maybe even close the place for one or two days to do a deep clean."

"Clean?" Jared asked.

"How else are we gonna get the girls to come do their Pilates? They don't wanna be reminded everyone here is sweating," Ivy pointed out. "I gotta go outside for a smoke."

Tristen checked his watch.

"I haven't had one all morning, Tristen," Ivy said before he could comment. "Don't start with me. I'm down to three a day."

"Getting some women in here wouldn't be bad," Jared said, always the one to change the subject if it looked like Tristen and Ivy were going to argue.

"Women aren't gonna want to hang out with the likes of this guy here," a voice said from behind them.

Talon stood looking like a rock star in mirror sunglasses, though he was indoors, ripped jeans, and a leather jacket. Money looked good on Tristen's brother. He looked younger, fitter and more confident. And Tristen was genuinely glad to see it.

"Hey, Talon, what're you doing here?" They hugged as they used to. Jared slipped away after a quiet greeting to Talon. "Where's Sandra and the baby bump?"

"She had to work. It's just me." Talon jerked his chin at Tristen. "You have a minute? I need to talk to you."

"Sure. I guess we could go upstairs to Ivy's office. Did you see her yet? She just went outside for a smoke."

"Still hasn't quit, huh?" Talon asked, shaking his head in disappointment. Or maybe disgust. Tristen wasn't sure.

"She's still trying. Says she's down to three a day, so you gotta give her props for that." Tristen led the way to what had once been Owen's office, holding the door open for his twin to walk through. Talon's low whistle echoed in the small space. The previously paneled walls had been painted cream, the cabinets painted black, and it now smelled of coconut.

"Damn," Talon said as they sank into the low leather seats in the corner. "Ivy really did a number on this place. Doesn't even look like where we'd get lectured back in the day, does it?"

Tristen thought the same every time he saw it. "How was Canada? I saw your pictures. It looked pretty cool."

"You mean pretty cold," Talon said, leaning casually into the couch. Every pose he made was a rockstar pose. Tristen was glad to note he wasn't jealous. "The tour was good, though a bit much on Sandra. She got tired a lot. I've never seen her fall asleep at five in the evening before." Talon laughed at whatever image was in his head. "Pregnancy does some weird stuff to your woman, man."

"When's the baby due?"

"August tenth." Talon smiled proudly. Tristen was glad he wasn't the one becoming a father, but he was also glad Talon seemed happy about it. Elated, even.

"I thought I'd see Owen while I was here. We left things a little tense," Talon said, his demeanor changing.

"He's still in Florida. Ivy gets updates more than me."

"I hated him for a long time when we started fighting," Talon admitted. "He felt like an intruder, even though he was our dad."

The comment surprised Tristen. "Yeah. I guess that's how I saw it, too. Like he was invading into our space. Putting his nose where it didn't belong."

"I saw the five of us as a family back then. With Luke." Talon sighed heavily. "I miss him. Luke, I mean. Even with the crazy life he gave us."

Tristen shrugged. "I think I gave up on him a long time ago. When he kicked me out, I thought he'd come by one day and say I could come back. But he never did."

"He had his own demons, Tristen."

Tristen shook his head slowly. "I know. And I can say that I honestly hold nothing against him anymore."

Talon leaned forward, his forearms on his knees. "Everything in the past few weeks has made me think about Sandra and the baby coming and what kind of dad I want to be."

"Really?" Tristen asked. He also leaned forward from where he sat at Ivy's desk.

"We're moving to Portugal."

"What?" A small part of him had expected the apology he'd never received from Talon, not this.

Talon laughed out loud.

"Wait, are you kidding?"

"No, I'm not kidding. I'm serious." Talon let his sunglasses slip down to his nose and grinned. "What d'ya think? Pretty cool, huh?"

"I don't know. I guess all I can think of is… why?" Tristen asked, still trying to recover from the surprise.

"After our trip to Serbia over Christmas I haven't been able to stop thinking about it. Everything is just so chill and cheap over in Europe. And life as a family is better chill, you know? Plus, Sandra would be closer to her parents."

It took a second to clear his throat. "Well, I'm happy for you, Talon."

Talon stretched his back over the chair, still smiling. "You gotta come visit someday."

"Right. Of course." This time jealousy hit Tristen, hard and cold, right in the middle of his chest. He looked out at the gym through the office window. Talon with AOR. Talon with a viable job. Talon living his dream life. Talon moving to Europe.

He turned to the window that opened to the gym below, his therapist's words circling in his head. *Remember where you were and how you felt just a few minutes ago.* He had felt content and proud of Ivy, and even proud of his brother. He couldn't allow himself to get jealous when his life was moving forward, just in a different direction.

Inhaling slowly, he returned to the conversation. "What about Art of Rendering?"

"That's the best part," Talon said eagerly. "Peter is from Germany, so he was on board to move right away. German taxes are too high, though, and it's cold, so we decided on Portugal. The whole band. We gotta get over there and settle and get paperwork down, but we have a lot of fans in Europe, you know?"

"That's awesome, Talon." The words came easily. Tristen was glad not to have to fake them or their sentiment.

"What're you going to do, Tristen? I heard around town that Meegan's album is out and doing well."

"I heard that, too," Tristen said. "But apparently she changed it enough to be able to take my name off as a producer."

Talon's smile faltered. "Seriously? That's kinda raw, man. I didn't take her for that kind of person."

"It's okay, honestly. I could probably sue her or pressure her, but it's not worth it. I still have Lin. His album came out in Asia two weeks ago and hit the charts right away. I think they were all surprised the guy could sing. That or Lin has marketing people that are unbelievable. He'll be coming back this summer to work on his second."

"You're a producer now." No sarcasm in Talon's tone. Tristen nodded. He liked the title. "Maybe you can produce our next album."

Tristen doubted Talon had the authority to offer that job, so he brushed it aside.

"Where are you living?" Talon asked.

"Now? With Ivy. We managed to pay off her house."

Tristen could tell Talon didn't remember anything about the house from the way his eyes squinted. "Oh, right. The house. Makes sense. I guess it's half yours now."

"What? No. It's Ivy's. I'm moving in with Jared in a few weeks, but honestly, living with her hasn't been that bad."

Talon's eyes narrowed again. "Seriously? You were the one who always promised you'd never come back here. And now you're saying it isn't that bad?"

He had said that. Many times. But things had changed. "Ivy and I have a new respect, I guess, for one another. We've been getting to know each other better and I'm learning, well, I guess to accept her for who she is. It helps that she's going to therapy."

He left out the part about him going too. He'd only had a few sessions covered by insurance, so he figured he wasn't really "going to therapy." Just a few sessions to get himself back on track.

Talon stood, his grin wobbling slightly. "I'm glad to hear that. Ivy always wanted you to come back. And now with Sandra and me going overseas, I'm glad to know you'll be nearby."

Tristen had no intention of sticking around Pelton for more than a few more months, but he didn't bother to say anything about that.

"Well, brother, time to get going. Just wanted to tell you about our move. And something about the other thing." Talon's voice lowered considerably. "About Lamia. I talked to her and made sure she knew the situation."

"And the kid?"

Talon shook his head. "That wasn't a real thing. Don't worry about it. You won't hear from her again."

"Huh." He didn't have any choice but to believe Talon.

Talon grinned again and pulled Tristen in for a hug. "I'm gonna miss you, man. You promise to come visit?"

"As soon as I can, Talon. As soon as I can."

A guy who looked vaguely familiar rang the bell above the gym door. He was tall, thin, with a sharp nose and black, shiny straight hair that almost hit his shoulders. The mirror image of Rob, a guy from high school.

"Damn, Rob! Nice to see you. I haven't seen you since we graduated," Tristen said, grateful for a reprieve from the mundane task of ordering shirts and shorts and printing up flyers. "What're you up to?"

Rob grinned from ear to ear as they shook hands. They had grown up playing football together. "Came in to see if it was true. Tristen Levisay, back in town. And taking over the boxing gym."

"It'll be more than that soon," Tristen said. "And I'm not taking over anything. My mom is the owner now. I'm just helping her out."

"I see," Rob said, looking around.

"You here to sign up for something?"

"Maybe. I'm looking to put my nephew on a boxing team. He's a bit small and gets teased a lot, you know?" Rob turned to show a small, skinny boy with a mop of brown hair sitting on a chair. "Adam, come here. Meet Tristen. He'll be your coach."

The kid looked up from under his hair. He didn't bother to move the strands aside. "Hi."

"Hi, Adam. Wanna learn how to box?"

The kid shrugged two bony shoulders. "Sure. I guess."

"Jared." Tristen turned to look for him, practically running into Jared as he marched forward. "This is Adam. He wants to join a boxing group."

"Rob," Jared said, not making a move to get Adam.

"Nice to see you, Jared."

Tristen looked between the two men, then down at Adam, who shrugged. "Is there a problem?"

Jared shrugged. "I don't have a problem with him, but Owen did."

"Owen had a problem with my dad," Rob explained. "They were something like enemies."

"Well, I don't have a problem with Rob, so since we're on the same page there, Jared, take the kid and show him around. Get him in the ring and see if he's willing to commit," Tristen said.

Jared glanced at the kid, then motioned for him to follow and walked away.

"Go on, Adam," Rob said. Adam grinned and ran to where Jared was holding up two boxing gloves, waiting.

"How you been, man?" Rob asked, punching Tristen lightly on the shoulders. His sleek black hair danced with the movement. Tristen remembered being jealous of Rob's hair, because Molly Tubberman thought it was hot. "I never expected you to come back."

"Me either, man, but life has a funny way of bringing you back to where you started."

"You're telling me. I came back to run the camp my dad used to own. I guess I own it now. It's this giant acreage that used to host different VBS weeks for the churches, plus other summer camps and school trips. Whatever. And I've had this vision to make it into a rock camp for kids."

"A rock church camp?"

"No, man. Like a regular camp, but about learning music. Rock and roll."

That got Tristen curious. Had there been something like that when he was a kid, he would have been pounding on the doors to get in. "What's it called?"

"Camp Soul," Rob said, grinning. He pulled out a card and handed it to Tristen. "Could use a guitar teacher. If you're into that sort of thing."

Tristen burst out laughing. He was tempted to say yes for experience's sake, but shook his head. "Teaching isn't my jam. We'll catch up soon, yeah?"

Rob nodded, looking over at his nephew, who was trying to copy a boxing bounce. Instead of staying in the imaginary small circle, the kid was wobbling all over the place. "He looks pretty good."

Tristen held back his laughter. Rob looked almost as proud as a father.

"Tristen! Something's wrong with the computer," Ivy shouted from the front desk as papers flew everywhere.

"I'll be right there, Ivy." Tristen jogged over to the merchandise desk, leaving Rob to watch Jared and his nephew. A simple click of the button, and the screen was back to where she'd had it before. "See? No big deal. You must have swiped off the page or something."

"I didn't swipe off of anything," Ivy complained. The bell ringing over the entrance stole her attention. "My T-shirts!"

A UPS deliveryman and a woman carrying a basket walked through the door.

Ivy ran to the deliveryman. "Can you bring them over here for me, please? Please? I recently got my cast off my foot and can't carry heavy things."

"She's got a way with people, don't she?" the man in brown muttered as he maneuvered through the gym to the stairs.

Tristen barely registered the guy's muttering. He was looking at the woman who had come in at the same time. Her hair was swept to one side, her face round with wide eyes. There was a simple beauty about her he couldn't seem to look away from.

"Hi," he said. "What can I do for you?"

The woman smiled and held up her basket. "I have a delivery for someone here."

"Scarlett!" A client named Cory ran over, sweat dripping down his forehead. The worry wrinkle on the woman's face relaxed at his shouting. Tristen waited to see if Cory, a loudmouth and slightly annoying client, would kiss her on the lips. And couldn't help smiling when he didn't.

"Got a ham and cheese?" Cory asked. "And kolaches? Yeah, I'll take two of those. Tristen, try her food. It's the best around."

Cory knew everyone and everything. Which made him particularly difficult to train, since everything Tristen taught him, Cory claimed he already knew.

"I've got a couple extra if you want to try them," Scarlett offered.

"What would you recommend?" Tristen asked, staring into her eyes.

"How about an empanada and a sausage kolache? Those are my best-sellers."

"Come on, I'll walk you out," Cory said, inching closer to Scarlett. A protective move if ever Tristen saw one.

Tristen retreated behind the merchandise counter and sank his teeth into a juicy, spicy pork empanada. It was the most delicious thing he'd eaten in a long time.

"Bye," she said, supposedly to everyone, but she looked at him longer than anyone else. Or maybe he was just hoping she had.

"Bye," Tristen called back. He kept his eyes on her until she looked at him. Scarlett's face flushed.

"You done staring?" Jared called out. "We're supposed to change out the new heavy bags."

Tristen grinned. "And start painting, remember?" He walked over to Jared. "New beginnings all round."

Epilogue

"How's everyone's Memorial Day weekend going?"

Tristen was getting used to the sound of his voice through a microphone again, having to engage the crowd instead of the luxury of going out and simply playing songs on his guitar or singing backup. Doing things on his own had its rewards, though the first few times he had sweated through his shirts from nerves. Now, almost five months into living in Pelton and three months of playing every other weekend, Tristen felt he was getting back to himself. Life was almost back to normal.

"Play another song, sexy boy!" The shout was followed by wolf whistles and giggling from a group of women in the back of the beer garden. Tristen smiled, which set off more whistles. It certainly helped his ego to have drunk women around again.

"I'll play you a song, young lady," he said, setting off more laughter and shouts. "In fact, why don't you come up here and we'll sing together? Should we go with Amy Winehouse or Lizzo?"

The women tried their best to get their loud friend up on the stage, but she refused. Beet red in the face, she finally shouted, "Sing Lizzo!" before disappearing behind her friends.

"You probably think I won't," Tristen said as he adjusted his guitar. "But I will. I will. I'm not just the local indie folk singer."

"Let's hear it then," Jared shouted. Bastard.

Singing Seraphina or Lizzo and even Britney Spears somehow scored him the most tips. It could be disheartening to think about, when his own songs didn't seem to excite the crowd as much as him imitating a woman, but Tristen tried not to take it personally. He started the track he had produced himself, his own guitar melody for his version of Lizzo's "Juice." Women of a certain age sang with him. Others started dancing. It was a beautiful evening in the beer garden, and everyone was having a good time. Tristen included.

"Thank you all," he said, raising his voice above the shouts and clapping. "Get more drinks and food, and in half an hour The Grievers are coming on to take you into the evening. Thank you all again!"

"Nice job," Jared said, handing Tristen a cold beer as Tristen pulled the wires on the mics. "I've never come to one of your shows before. You can actually sing."

"Thanks. I'll take that as a compliment."

Jared grinned, watching a group of women creep forward and drop a few bills into Tristen's tip jar. "I would have tipped you if you had dressed like Lizzo."

"Maybe next time." Tristen laughed and winked at the women. "I'll give it a thought. Can you help me bring my stuff to my car?"

Jared's forehead wrinkled as he looked at Tristen's meager supplies. There wasn't much, but between the pedalboard, his guitar, the tip jar, his binder, and the other things, it took him two trips at least. "You're such a teenage girl. I thought being friends with me had manned you up." Despite his salty attitude, he grabbed the pedalboard case to pack it up.

"You gotta get some new insults," Tristen told his friend as they dragged his stuff out the back of the beer garden.

Jared turned and challenged him with a stare-down.

Tristen closed the trunk and locked everything inside. "You called me a girl when we first met," he explained.

"No, I said you hit like a girl. Which is true."

"A girl wouldn't have brought down The Alabamian. Not even on steroids."

Jared grinned and clinked his beer bottle against Tristen's glass. "Fair enough. It was true. You're better now that you've been training with me. Come on—it isn't often your mom gives us both the night off. Let's go have ourselves a good night. I'm going to find myself a real woman." He looked Tristen up and down. "One prettier than you."

He sauntered away into the crowd that was getting louder by the minute.

"Hey, Ted, will you get me a beer?" Tristen yelled to the outdoor bartender. He didn't get paid to play at The Sandlot, but he did get beer for free. Almost as good.

Ted handed a cold beer over in a plastic cup just as a G-chord soundwave passed through the air. The Grievers were getting ready. Tristen maneuvered further in towards the stage to get a closer look. He loved seeing bands and players set up now, using it as inspiration for his own live playing. The band was probably in their forties, smiling as though they'd hit the jackpot and were excited to play for a small-town bar full of people ready to drink away their work week.

Tristen smiled into his beer. He felt the same way. For a while, he had lost that excitement with The Seethers. Instead of focusing on the experience and the music, he had been stressed out about the numbers. It felt good to rub his guitar-calloused fingers against the plastic cup. Despite still being in Pelton, his life was coming back together. And now that Owen was back—he'd shown up out of the blue at Ivy's last week—he was sure his time in the small town would soon be over. Until then, he was going to do his best to enjoy it.

The woman in the band stepped up to the microphone, a tambourine in hand. The guitar strings hit the speakers with a song from The Cranberries, a song that told the age of the band right off, but no one in the crowd seemed to mind. The woman closed her eyes, caressed the air around the microphone, and let out a wail that sounded almost identical to Dolores O'Riordan.

While everyone else let the music be part of the atmosphere or listened intently, Tristen watched the band members and tried to put his finger on what was bothering him. They looked content to play their music there, but Tristen had been just as happy to play every venue. To a certain point.

He threw back the rest of his beer and went in search of a table. "Mind if I set this here?"

Tristen turned to find a woman with round eyes, brown hair tipped with red, and a wide smile setting her purse on the tall table near him. It was Scarlett, the woman who had come into the gym way back in the beginning of February.

"Course," he stammered.

"Course you mind, or you don't?" she asked. Her eyes sparkled. "What're you drinking?"

"It was an IPA. It's good. Aren't you Cory's friend? The one who came into Top Gym a few months ago with the best empanada I've ever eaten?"

Her mouth burst into a wide smile, lighting up her face. Tristen was struck again by how pretty she was.

"I am. And I'm glad you liked the empanada." She glanced around the garden. "I'm Scarlett, by the way."

"I'm Tristen. My mom owns the gym." He could have slapped himself. He'd lost his touch.

"I see. Well, I better go in or I'll die of thirst," Scarlett said, flapping her arms as though about to jump into a pool.

Tristen couldn't help laughing. He watched as she turned towards the bar and braced herself to wiggle between the crowd. The black slacks that stopped just above her ankle weren't anything special, but they hugged her round hips in the right way, and the shirt that wrapped around her chest and tied at the waist emphasized a curvy figure and showed just enough cleavage to be tasteful.

Unfortunately for her, she was too nice in the crowd. More impatient people shoved ahead of her constantly. If they had drinks in their hands she moved away, possibly to avoid a spill, but in the meantime allowed more people ahead of her at the bar. She glanced back, and Tristen didn't bother to pretend he wasn't watching her.

"I think I'll wait," she said, joining him again at the table. "It's too crowded, and this shirt is new."

Her shirt had cost probably twenty dollars at Target or H&M. It was cute that she was worried about it anyway.

"What do you want?" he asked her.

She looked up from her phone, her eyes narrowed. "That wasn't a ruse to get you to buy me a drink."

"I didn't think that." He leaned into her as the music started. She smelled of the lotion from the mall that he and Talon used to buy Ivy for Christmas when they were teenagers. Something and cucumbers. "I'm taller and scarier. I'll get the drinks. What'll you have?"

Her lips were only a few inches from his, and when they opened, he had the crazy urge to kiss them, feel their fullness with his. He stepped away. Clearly, he needed to get his hormones under control.

"I'll have whatever you're having. It'll make it easier."

The entire time Tristen was at the bar, after shouldering his way there, he watched the woman. Except for the two minutes it took to tap his card for the payment. And in those two minutes, Jared had found her. There was only one thing to do: discredit him from the start.

"Hey, Jared." Tristen lifted his chin in the direction Jared had come. "Back so soon?"

Jared didn't miss a beat. "She's married. And her friends weren't anything to look at."

"Damn, Jared. You're harsh. They aren't too bad. I'm not sure what you're doing around this town if your standards are so high."

"Wait till that one smiles, Scarlett," Jared said, pointing his drink toward a woman with thin, blonde hair. The woman smiled to show tiny, stained teeth. "Addict."

"Maybe recovering," Scarlett said, nodding.

Tristen looked between the two of them. "Do you know each other?"

Jared and Scarlett looked at each other and laughed.

"I'm friends with the brother of one of Jared's friends. We all grew up around each other."

"And Scarlett's sister and I were in the same class." Jared looked at Tristen with a grin. The same one Talon used to get before doing something stupid. "Did you know this guy think you're pretty?" he asked Scarlett.

She looked at Tristen, startled, as he handed her a full plastic cup.

Jared slammed the table and walked away, chuckling, while Tristen started to sweat as though he were in front of a crowd of thousands.

He dared to glance at her. "You are," he said. "Pretty, I mean."

"Well, I rarely get told that," she said, her voice breathy. "Jared said you're a musician and that I missed your show."

"I am. And I guess you did. I'm just a local guy though. Nothing special."

"Oh? Jared said you were in a band."

"Not anymore. I work at Top Gym."

The woman was now singing a Janice Joplin song. She had talent.

Tristen looked at Scarlett, who looked up at him with wide, clear eyes. He hadn't eaten all day and he could feel the effects fuzzing his critical thinking. Her lips rounded around the beer bottle. He wondered what it would be like to press his mouth against hers.

"Hey, Scarlett. Sorry I'm late." This voice was attached to a petite woman with dark brown hair and wide-set eyes.

"No worries, Camilla," Scarlett said.

Tristen sipped his beer to cool his head.

"Who is this?" Camilla said. "Hello, you."

"This is Tristen. He works with Jared at that gym in Pelton. Tristen, this is Camilla, my friend."

"Nice to meet you."

"You, too, Tristen, but I'm taking my girl away now," Camilla said, before dragging Scarlett away.

Scarlett threw Tristen an apologetic look as they left, but it was probably for the best. If he was going to leave Pelton, he didn't need to start a relationship.

"I'm heading out," Jared said in his ear.

Tristen almost spilled his beer. "Shit, Jared. You scared me."

"I know. You were too busy watching Scarlett's ass."

Tristen waved him off and stayed as the bar started to empty out. He didn't want to go home yet. The music was good, and he was starting to feel somewhat at home. When the set came to an end just two songs later, he felt a loss he hadn't felt in a while. He was the one who had paid most attention to the band, but that was okay with him. Something within him was revived again.

"Great set," he called to the drummer.

"Thanks, man."

Tristen nodded, searching through the remaining patrons for Scarlett, but there was no sign of her.

His phone rang as he nursed his beer alone.

"Hello?"

"Nice to speak to you again, Tristen." The voice was breathy.

"Lamia?"

"That's sweet. You remember me."

"How'd you get my number?"

"It wasn't that hard, darling. We were lovers at one point not too long ago."

"Actually, you and I were together twice four years ago. You were with my brother not too long ago."

Lamia sighed into the phone. There was another sound, like a baby, near the phone.

"I thought you'd try to brush off your responsibility. I don't know what I saw in you, Tristen. I thought you were a better man than that."

"Listen, Lamia," Tristen started, but Lamia wouldn't let him finish.

"I called you, remember, Mr. Levisay. Do you hear that?" She paused, and the babbling sound got louder. "That's your son talking to you."

Tristen's blood turned cold. He couldn't believe it. Not only had Talon lied to his face about Lamia not having a kid, but he hadn't settled anything with her about who had slept with who. Obviously.

His anger starting to rise, he tried to stay calm. "No, Lamia. That's not my son. I wasn't with you last year. That was my brother, Talon, using my name."

"If that's how you want to play, Tristen, then that's how we'll play. Either way, the truth will come out, because I'm not about to let you walk away from your responsibility. I'll need money to raise this boy right."

She hung up before he could respond. He looked at his phone, dread washing over him. He might have been a bigger fool than he'd thought to trust his brother.

"You look like you need a whiskey," a waitress said as she passed by.

Tristen looked up. "That might be exactly what I need. And maybe a good lawyer. But I'm going to head home."

The waitress smiled, and for a moment he wondered if he had misinterpreted something. She lingered just a little longer, smiled just a little wider, but then she was on to the next table. Didn't matter, anyway. He needed to get home and talk to Ivy about this new revelation.

On his way out to the front of the bar, Tristen's phone pinged again. Tristen unlocked it. It was a picture of the baby: a wrinkled, tiny thing wrapped in a blue blanket.

He let out his breath slowly. He could prove that baby wasn't his if he had to, though it would involve Meegan. But at the same time, the baby being Talon's presented just as many problems.

There was no getting around talking to Ivy about this one. Especially since Lamia didn't seem to be giving up, despite Talon's assurances that "she wouldn't bother him again".

As if she could hear his thoughts, Lamia followed the picture up with a text.

Despite you changing your phone number and moving back to your little hometown, I found you. And I'm not going to let you get away with neglecting your son. You'll pay for leaving me alone with him. I'll see that you pay the maximum. And if you don't, I'll see you in court.

Did you enjoy Bended Loyalty? Leave a review on GooglePlay.
    What will happen with Lamia? Will Tristen get even with Talon? Get *Bended Love.*
    Want to read the story of how Tristen left Pelton the first time? Get *Bended Dream* for FREE!

Continue the story

Bended Love

Chapter 1

AT THE DING OF the kitchen timer, Scarlett pulled the oven door open and whisked out her second-to-last batch of scones. Pretending she was on a reality cooking show, she hurried to place the last batch inside the scorching oven, then ran to set the timer again. Imagining that someone like Gordon Ramsey was ready to pounce on any little thing she did wrong helped to keep her entertained as she prepped for the farmer's market.

The initial burned-alive feeling from the oven heat disappeared, leaving her to the most satisfying, or the most disappointing, part of her job: evaluating the product. This time it was satisfying. Another fifty seconds was exactly what the scones had needed. Baking was such a precise art that even such a short time could make a huge difference, depending on the day's humidity. Scarlett congratulated herself with a sip of flavored tonic water.

Having baked for six months in this kitchen, a pool house her only private customer let her use, Scarlett was beginning to perfect her system. Once the scones were in, she usually kneaded the sourdough once more before letting it rest. When the last batch of scones were done, she would up the oven temperature to heat the pizza stones, then quickly dump the sourdough on the hot stones, swipe them with a clean razor to allow them to blossom in the oven, and slip them in to bake. Then she cleaned the kitchen.

Through the kitchen window the pool's cool, sparkling water taunted her. It was only June, but Kentucky heat was already bearing down on them. And though the pool house had air conditioning, the electrical bill was the one thing Scarlett had to pay for in order to use the space, so she rarely turned it on lower than seventy-eight. Carole Barten, the property owner and the top realtor in the county, had given her permission to use the pool anytime, but Scarlett got the feeling she hadn't really meant it. After all, jumping into the pool while she was technically renting the space to create her business would look odd, to say the least. She and Carole weren't friends; they conducted business together, so Scarlett wanted to look professional. And splashing around during working hours was anything but.

Another timer beeped, reminding her she didn't have time to daydream about the pool. There was a farmer's market in the morning, and she had already been paid for the four dozen cookies Carole had ordered. Trying to keep up with her checklist, Scarlett grabbed the bread dough that had doubled in size and dumped it onto the counter. Just as she sprinkled the counter with flour to knead it one last time, her phone rang. Had it been anyone other than Carole, she wouldn't have answered.

"Scarlett, doll, how're you doing? Baking the cookies for me? That's wonderful." Carole spoke in the cadence Scarlett expected from east-coasters. When they'd first met, Scarlett assumed she had studied at Harvard or Brown. Carole had actually never been to college, but she'd been married to a man for two years from the Boston area. "Do remember I need a sheet of perfectly round cookies to place into the oven. Don't forget, like you did last weekend. I want the house I'm showing to smell like I'm baking. If there's no smell I might as well buy them from the store."

Scarlett pulled each sourdough boule across the smooth counter one last time before letting them rest. She glanced at her watch. "I have everything here for you and ready." It wasn't ready, though. She had forgotten to leave six cookies raw from Carole's order. Again. This was the third week in a row, so she'd have to make up a new batch before leaving.

"No broken cookies, right? I don't want any broken ones like last week."

The cookies had broken because Carole had dropped the box. Even admitted as much.

"There won't be any broken ones. I've made them very sturdy."

"Alright. Please leave them at the house on the counter. The cleaners should leave the sliding door open for you," Carole said.

"Okay." Scarlett left the boules and went to check her supplies, crossing her fingers she had brought enough vanilla, sugar, and chocolate chips. "I'll leave them there. Is there anything you need?"

"One more thing."

Scarlett bit back an expletive. In all her planning, she had forgotten to make up the brownie batter. Now she didn't have enough chocolate chips to make the brownies and leave Carole her raw cookie dough. She'd have to bake the brownies at home in her small apartment. With the crappy oven that sometimes over-heated.

"Have you seen Don around? My husband?"

The question made Scarlett pause. It sounded friendly, but also out of place.

"He hasn't come around the pool house," she said cautiously. "I haven't been up to the house yet. When I go up there, I can ask him to call you. If I see him."

"No, don't worry," Carole said quickly.

"Okay."

Carole started speaking to someone else, hanging up on Scarlett without bothering to say goodbye.

"You're the one who called me," Scarlett muttered. She dumped two cups of flour into a bowl she had recently washed and reached for the baking soda as a giant splash sounded in the pool outside.

Scarlett froze. Carole didn't have children, and she couldn't imagine her letting local kids use her property out of the kindness of her heart. The local smalltown kids had started daring each other to break into properties where the owners worked all day and never used the pool. Scarlett had heard about it on the radio news as she drove her nephew, Ben, to school. He was just finishing sixth grade, but even he knew all about it. It was becoming the thing to do when they got bored, apparently.

Fear froze her in place. Most likely they'd be teenagers. Perhaps bigger than her five feet five inches. She wondered if they would run scared at the sight of her or if they would confront her. Maybe she should ignore it, since this wasn't her place. But they might try to enter the pool house. And she needed to leave here in less than two hours.

Slowly, she moved around the small table to peek out through the window.

In the pool, a woman was wrapped around a rather hairy-shouldered man who was definitely not a high-schooler. Scarlett peered closer, trying to stay hidden behind the curtain. The man's hands pulled at the strings of the woman's bikini until the woman shrieked and laughed. She threw herself backwards into the water, her giant, perfectly round breasts exposed.

And also exposing Carole's husband. His salt-and-pepper hair, usually perfectly combed, was dripping water droplets and in full disarray. Once the woman came out of the water, Don yanked the dangling pieces of her bikini off, before gripping her breasts in his hands and kissing her hard on the mouth.

Scarlett couldn't believe her bad luck. This was not something she wanted to get involved in. Carole didn't seem like the type who would appreciate another woman knowing her husband was cheating. And there was no way to sneak past the lusty couple without being noticed. Plus, ever since she had refused Don's suggestion of exchanging the electrical bill for a romp each week, he had made it a point to complain about Scarlett's use of the pool house to Carole loud enough for Scarlett to hear. And if Carole wasn't around to complain to, Don would stand with his arms crossed and glare at her until she looked away.

Everything about this was awkward.

Suddenly Don's eyes moved towards the pool house, as though he could feel her watching. Scarlett stepped further into the shadows, but Don was already wrapping a towel around his waist and marching towards the pool house. He sauntered in as she started beating the butter and sugar.

"Hey there, Scarlett," he drawled. "Didn't know you were coming in today."

"I come in every Friday afternoon." Scarlett kept her eyes on her recipe and baking supplies.

"Yeah," he said, smacking his lips. Scarlett hated the sound. One of her mom's ex-boyfriends used to make the same sound while he was thinking. "I wasn't sure Carole was still renting this place out to you. I tell her all the time what a mess you make of it. Isn't worth it to us to have you hanging around just so she can have some cookies."

Scarlett leveled her gaze at him as she beat the eggs. "Carole called before. She was looking for you."

"And what did you tell her?" Don asked. He prowled towards her, his dark eyes never blinking as they glared straight into hers.

Scarlett had to look away to measure the brown sugar, but tried to keep her voice firm and strong. "I told her I hadn't seen you. Because I hadn't."

"That's a girl," Don said, close enough to pat her butt. "Well now, part of your contract for using the pool house, Scarlett, is that you're not in our way. Isn't it?"

He picked up an unwrapped cookie and popped it into his mouth.

"I'm almost done. I'll start loading the car now." Scarlett tried to move past him, but he grabbed her wrist and pulled hard until her body slammed against his.

"There's another way to apologize," he murmured, grabbing her breast and squeezing hard. Men like Don seemed to think every breast was made just for him to touch. Scarlett knew just what to do: stay impassive. Don reacted just as she'd suspected, pushing her away with a look of disgust at the sound of the door squeaking open again.

The young woman must have been barely twenty. She stood in the doorway, her bikini bottom barely covering her private areas, like one of those influencers on social media. Her skin was smooth and tan, without a stretch mark or ounce of fat visible, and there was a mile gap between her thighs.

"Who's this?" she asked, narrowing her eyes at Scarlett.

"No one," Don said, pulling the woman into his arms. She giggled, kissing him loudly on the mouth. Scarlett kept her gaze down, wrapping cookies in plastic as quickly as she could.

"Good," the woman said. "'Cause I don't do threesomes with fat girls. Geez, have enough carbs here? Is all this your snack?"

Scarlett ignored her laughter, hoping the two of them would leave the house so she could clean up and leave. But it was clearly her very unlucky day. Don pulled the woman into the small bedroom instead of leaving. Within minutes, the pool house was filled with noises—noises no one made unless they were filming a professional video.

Maybe the woman did that for a living. Scarlett smirked at the silent putdown, trying to breathe to calm her shaking hands. She started the mixer, watching the dough come together and using the sound to drown out what was happening in the bedroom. Unfortunately, she miscalculated, turning off the mixer just as the young woman screamed out her final pleasure.

Scarlett rolled her eyes. Then came Don's yell. Scarlett thought she might vomit.

Quickly, she placed the gooey dough onto parchment paper in a long strip and rolled it up tightly. It would need an hour in the fridge, but instead of leaving the cookies already on the pan, she could leave instructions for Carole. She wouldn't like it, but she had no intention of hanging around in case Carole showed up.

With the straight metal edge of a spatula, she scraped the extra flour from the counter into a trash bag, then generously sprayed everything down with vinegar cleaner as sounds from the bedroom started again. She moved faster, circling the kitchen putting away her things, testing the scones for their temperature and grabbing the baked sourdoughs from the oven.

Then she started throwing the rest of her ingredients into two large plastic tubs. Snapping each container shut, Scarlett stacked them into towers of two. Usually she carried one at a time, but today she took the chance to grab more. Back and forth she hurried, sweat first beading and then pooling at her waistband.

When she tiptoed in for the last time to pack the sourdough, the young woman was standing stark naked in the kitchen, gulping down a large glass of water. Her nipples stood at attention, and her ass and thighs were shiny and hairless.

"You gonna clean this up?" she demanded, sighing as she finished her water. Probably the only nourishment she'd had that day.

Scarlett looked around. The kitchen was clean except for the pan prepped for Carole, the log of cookie dough, and her cooling boules. She bit back a retort and answered as simply as possible. "Yes."

She carefully placed her sourdough boules into the last boxes. When she stood up, the woman poked her in the breast through her sweaty T-shirt.

"You're not my type at all, though I guess you got nice tits. You want to join us?"

"No," Scarlett snorted.

The woman's eyes narrowed. "Prude," she said, before snapping a selfie next to Scarlett.

"What the hell are you doing?" Scarlett snapped, trying to swipe at the phone. The woman held it above her head, out of reach. Scarlett inhaled slowly. "Whatever. Keep the damn photo. I'm outta here."

She deadlifted the stacked boxes in silence and waddled out the door. With the last two containers slipped into place on the truck, she took a deep breath and headed towards the main house with Carole's order for a weekend of open houses.

Two minutes later, she pulled onto the interstate able to breathe again, praying Don would find another place to have his affair by next Friday.

….Continue reading Scarlett's story in *Bended Love.*

Bended Love

Chapter 1

At the ding of the kitchen timer, Scarlett pulled the oven door open and whisked out her second-to-last batch of scones. Pretending she was on a reality cooking show, she hurried to place the last batch inside the scorching oven, then ran to set the timer again. Imagining that someone like Gordon Ramsey was ready to pounce on any little thing she did wrong helped to keep her entertained as she prepped for the farmer's market.

The initial burned-alive feeling from the oven heat disappeared, leaving her to the most satisfying, or the most disappointing, part of her job: evaluating the product. This time it was satisfying. Another fifty seconds was exactly what the scones had needed. Baking was such a precise art that even such a short time could make a huge difference, depending on the day's humidity. Scarlett congratulated herself with a sip of flavored tonic water.

Having baked for six months in this kitchen, a pool house her only private customer let her use, Scarlett was beginning to perfect her system. Once the scones were in, she usually kneaded the sourdough once more before letting it rest. When the last batch of scones were done, she would up the oven temperature to heat the pizza stones, then quickly dump the sourdough on the hot stones, swipe them with a clean razor to allow them to blossom in the oven, and slip them in to bake. Then she cleaned the kitchen.

Through the kitchen window the pool's cool, sparkling water taunted her. It was only June, but Kentucky heat was already bearing down on them. And though the pool house had air conditioning, the electrical bill was the one thing Scarlett had to pay for in order to use the space, so she rarely turned it on lower than seventy-eight. Carole Barten, the property owner and the top realtor in the county, had given her permission to use the pool anytime, but Scarlett got the feeling she hadn't really meant it. After all, jumping into the pool while she was technically renting the space to create her business would look odd, to say the least. She and Carole weren't friends; they conducted business together, so Scarlett wanted to look professional. And splashing around during working hours was anything but.

Another timer beeped, reminding her she didn't have time to daydream about the pool. There was a farmer's market in the morning, and she had already been paid for the four dozen cookies Carole had ordered. Trying to keep up with her checklist, Scarlett grabbed the bread dough that had doubled in size and dumped it onto the counter. Just as she sprinkled the counter with flour to knead it one last time, her phone rang. Had it been anyone other than Carole, she wouldn't have answered.

"Scarlett, doll, how're you doing? Baking the cookies for me? That's wonderful." Carole spoke in the cadence Scarlett expected from east-coasters. When they'd first met, Scarlett assumed she had studied at Harvard or Brown. Carole had actually never been to college, but she'd been married to a man for two years from the Boston area. "Do remember I need a sheet of perfectly round cookies to place into the oven. Don't forget, like you did last weekend. I want the house I'm showing to smell like I'm baking. If there's no smell I might as well buy them from the store."

Scarlett pulled each sourdough boule across the smooth counter one last time before letting them rest. She glanced at her watch. "I have everything here for you and ready." It wasn't ready, though. She had forgotten to leave six cookies raw from Carole's order. Again. This was the third week in a row, so she'd have to make up a new batch before leaving.

"No broken cookies, right? I don't want any broken ones like last week."

The cookies had broken because Carole had dropped the box. Even admitted as much.

"There won't be any broken ones. I've made them very sturdy."

"Alright. Please leave them at the house on the counter. The cleaners should leave the sliding door open for you," Carole said.

"Okay." Scarlett left the boules and went to check her supplies, crossing her fingers she had brought enough vanilla, sugar, and chocolate chips. "I'll leave them there. Is there anything you need?"

"One more thing."

Scarlett bit back an expletive. In all her planning, she had forgotten to make up the brownie batter. Now she didn't have enough chocolate chips to make the brownies and leave Carole her raw cookie dough. She'd have to bake the brownies at home in her small apartment. With the crappy oven that sometimes over-heated.

"Have you seen Don around? My husband?"

The question made Scarlett pause. It sounded friendly, but also out of place.

"He hasn't come around the pool house," she said cautiously. "I haven't been up to the house yet. When I go up there, I can ask him to call you. If I see him."

"No, don't worry," Carole said quickly.

"Okay."

Carole started speaking to someone else, hanging up on Scarlett without bothering to say goodbye.

"You're the one who called me," Scarlett muttered. She dumped two cups of flour into a bowl she had recently washed and reached for the baking soda as a giant splash sounded in the pool outside.

Scarlett froze. Carole didn't have children, and she couldn't imagine her letting local kids use her property out of the kindness of her heart. The local smalltown kids had started daring each other to break into properties where the owners worked all day and never used the pool. Scarlett had heard about it on the radio news as she drove her nephew, Ben, to school. He was just finishing sixth grade, but even he knew all about it. It was becoming the thing to do when they got bored, apparently.

Fear froze her in place. Most likely they'd be teenagers. Perhaps bigger than her five feet five inches. She wondered if they would run scared at the sight of her or if they would confront her. Maybe she should ignore it, since this wasn't her place. But they might try to enter the pool house. And she needed to leave here in less than two hours.

Slowly, she moved around the small table to peek out through the window.

In the pool, a woman was wrapped around a rather hairy-shouldered man who was definitely not a high-schooler. Scarlett peered closer, trying to stay hidden behind the curtain. The man's hands pulled at the strings of the woman's bikini until the woman shrieked and laughed. She threw herself backwards into the water, her giant, perfectly round breasts exposed.

And also exposing Carole's husband. His salt-and-pepper hair, usually perfectly combed, was dripping water droplets and in full disarray. Once the woman came out of the water, Don yanked the dangling pieces of her bikini off, before gripping her breasts in his hands and kissing her hard on the mouth.

Scarlett couldn't believe her bad luck. This was not something she wanted to get involved in. Carole didn't seem like the type who would appreciate another woman knowing her husband was cheating. And there was no way to sneak past the lusty couple without being noticed. Plus, ever since she had refused Don's suggestion of exchanging the electrical bill for a romp each week, he had made it a point to complain about Scarlett's use of the pool house to Carole loud enough for Scarlett to hear. And if Carole wasn't around to complain to, Don would stand with his arms crossed and glare at her until she looked away.

Everything about this was awkward.

Suddenly Don's eyes moved towards the pool house, as though he could feel her watching. Scarlett stepped further into the shadows, but Don was already wrapping a towel around his waist and marching towards the pool house. He sauntered in as she started beating the butter and sugar.

"Hey there, Scarlett," he drawled. "Didn't know you were coming in today."

"I come in every Friday afternoon." Scarlett kept her eyes on her recipe and baking supplies.

"Yeah," he said, smacking his lips. Scarlett hated the sound. One of her mom's ex-boyfriends used to make the same sound while he was thinking. "I wasn't sure Carole was still renting this place out to you. I tell her all the time what a mess you make of it. Isn't worth it to us to have you hanging around just so she can have some cookies."

Scarlett leveled her gaze at him as she beat the eggs. "Carole called before. She was looking for you."

"And what did you tell her?" Don asked. He prowled towards her, his dark eyes never blinking as they glared straight into hers.

Scarlett had to look away to measure the brown sugar, but tried to keep her voice firm and strong. "I told her I hadn't seen you. Because I hadn't."

"That's a girl," Don said, close enough to pat her butt. "Well now, part of your contract for using the pool house, Scarlett, is that you're not in our way. Isn't it?"

He picked up an unwrapped cookie and popped it into his mouth.

"I'm almost done. I'll start loading the car now." Scarlett tried to move past him, but he grabbed her wrist and pulled hard until her body slammed against his.

"There's another way to apologize," he murmured, grabbing her breast and squeezing hard. Men like Don seemed to think every breast was made just for him to touch. Scarlett knew just what to do: stay impassive. Don reacted just as she'd suspected, pushing her away with a look of disgust at the sound of the door squeaking open again.

The young woman must have been barely twenty. She stood in the doorway, her bikini bottom barely covering her private areas, like one of those influencers on social media. Her skin was smooth and tan, without a stretch mark or ounce of fat visible, and there was a mile gap between her thighs.

"Who's this?" she asked, narrowing her eyes at Scarlett.

"No one," Don said, pulling the woman into his arms. She giggled, kissing him loudly on the mouth. Scarlett kept her gaze down, wrapping cookies in plastic as quickly as she could.

"Good," the woman said. "'Cause I don't do threesomes with fat girls. Geez, have enough carbs here? Is all this your snack?"

Scarlett ignored her laughter, hoping the two of them would leave the house so she could clean up and leave. But it was clearly her very unlucky day. Don pulled the woman into the small bedroom instead of leaving. Within minutes, the pool house was filled with noises—noises no one made unless they were filming a professional video.

Maybe the woman did that for a living. Scarlett smirked at the silent putdown, trying to breathe to calm her shaking hands. She started the mixer, watching the dough come together and using the sound to drown out what was happening in the bedroom. Unfortunately, she miscalculated, turning off the mixer just as the young woman screamed out her final pleasure.

Scarlett rolled her eyes. Then came Don's yell. Scarlett thought she might vomit.

Quickly, she placed the gooey dough onto parchment paper in a long strip and rolled it up tightly. It would need an hour in the fridge, but instead of leaving the cookies already on the pan, she could leave instructions for Carole. She wouldn't like it, but she had no intention of hanging around in case Carole showed up.

With the straight metal edge of a spatula, she scraped the extra flour from the counter into a trash bag, then generously sprayed everything down with vinegar cleaner as sounds from the bedroom started again. She moved faster, circling the kitchen putting away her things, testing the scones for their temperature and grabbing the baked sourdoughs from the oven.

Then she started throwing the rest of her ingredients into two large plastic tubs. Snapping each container shut, Scarlett stacked them into towers of two. Usually she carried one at a time, but today she took the chance to grab more. Back and forth she hurried, sweat first beading and then pooling at her waistband.

When she tiptoed in for the last time to pack the sourdough, the young woman was standing stark naked in the kitchen, gulping down a large glass of water. Her nipples stood at attention, and her ass and thighs were shiny and hairless.

"You gonna clean this up?" she demanded, sighing as she finished her water. Probably the only nourishment she'd had that day.

Scarlett looked around. The kitchen was clean except for the pan prepped for Carole, the log of cookie dough, and her cooling boules. She bit back a retort and answered as simply as possible. "Yes."

She carefully placed her sourdough boules into the last boxes. When she stood up, the woman poked her in the breast through her sweaty T-shirt.

"You're not my type at all, though I guess you got nice tits. You want to join us?"

"No," Scarlett snorted.

The woman's eyes narrowed. "Prude," she said, before snapping a selfie next to Scarlett.

"What the hell are you doing?" Scarlett snapped, trying to swipe at the phone. The woman held it above her head, out of reach. Scarlett inhaled slowly. "Whatever. Keep the damn photo. I'm outta here."

She deadlifted the stacked boxes in silence and waddled out the door. With the last two containers slipped into place on the truck, she took a deep breath and headed towards the main house with Carole's order for a weekend of open houses.

Two minutes later, she pulled onto the interstate able to breathe again, praying Don would find another place to have his affair by next Friday.

….Continue reading Scarlett's story in *Bended Love.*

About the author

Kat is a novelist and short story writer. She writes everyday and can't seem to stick to a genre, having dabbled in historical fiction, contemporary family drama and romance, as well as speculative fiction. Kat is the creator of the Pencils&Lipstick podcast, a podcast for writers with author interviews, craft talk and insight into the publishing world. She is also an accredited Author Accelerator fiction book coach. In between conducting interviews for her podcast and writing, you can find Kat traveling the world, reading, or volunteering with her church—always with a cup of cold brew close by.

You can find out more about Kat:

On her website https://katcaldwell.com

On Instagram @author_katcaldwell

On Facebook @katcaldwellauthor

On TikTok at @katcaldwell.author.

Find her short stories by subscribing to her mailing list at https:/katcaldwell.com/readers